The Last Fox

–A Soldier of Men–

The Last Fox

A Novel of the 100th/442nd RCT

Robert H. Kono

Abe Publishing
Eugene, Oregon

Printed in the United States of America

ISBN: 0-9713050-0-5

Library of Congress Control Number: 2001118259

For information or orders, contact:

Abe Publishing
P.O. Box 5226
Eugene, OR 97405
Toll Free: 800-535-5038; Fax: 541-485-3893
abepublishing@hotmail.com

Cover design by Kenge Kobayashi

Dedication

This novel is dedicated to my beloved
wife, Carol, and my sons, David and
Kevin, whose support and encouragement
made this inspired endeavor possible.

Acknowledgements

For their assistance, my gratitude goes to the
following veterans of the 100th/442nd
Regimental Combat Team.
Their accounts of actual combat conditions
are unforgettable
and reveal the life of the foot soldier.

Frank Hatanaka, Hqs. Company
Kenny Namba, L Company
Seige Nishioka, G Company
George Ishida, L Company (deceased)
Shig Hinatsu, Cannon Company
Arthur Iwasaki, I Company
Tom Yoshikai, B Company

This novel is a work of fiction.
Though the campaigns the 100th/442nd
Regimental Combat Team
fought are actual, the battles are
dramatized for novelistic purposes.

The characters depicted in the novel
are purely fictional.
No resemblance to living persons is intended.

"Forever bound to Duty,
Fighting for a great and noble Cause,
Though beset by unseemly Doubt,
The light of heights ascended
Glows in the eternal vistas of Honor."

–Author

Chapter One

Fred Murano hadn't always been afraid. As a soldier, he had fought for freedom to prove his loyalty–more for his own sake than anything else. He was forever trying to prove something to his own satisfaction. It wasn't as if he suspected his loyalty. His country did. All the odds were thrown at him, but he had volunteered to fight in the great, bloody war against the Nazis and survived to return with a chest full of medals and a shattered arm that terminated in a withered claw hanging below his coat sleeve.

But now the fear grew. It wasn't like the heart-pounding, needle-sharp fear that hit him whenever he went on the line. He was old. The fear was like a vague, insidious shadow reaching for him with horrible, experienced claws. He had watched his best friend, Mike Kojima, die of cancer, wasting away slowly and dying an agonizing death. Fred was with him till the very end when his once robust friend was reduced to a skeleton whose very bones seemed cracked with pain. He had just buried Mike that morning at Hillcrest Cemetery.

Fred Murano led the men to the upper floor of the Haishan Chinese Restaurant in downtown Portland, Oregon. It was nearing dusk. The reddish-orange flames of the dying sun reflected off the windows of the surrounding buildings that stood like garish, naked sentinels against the western flank of Mt. Hood in the distance bathed in deep pink. The bouncing light turned a blood-red as it merged with the vermillion of the walls of the large room and sliced dully through the shadows. Filtering through the venetian blinds, it lay a pattern of bloody stripes across the furniture.

The men, who had come from different parts of the country, took their places at the round table bathed in the barred, crimson strips of light and eased themselves into their chairs. In their seventies they were the last survivors of I Company, 3rd Battalion, 100th/442nd Regimental Combat Team, the all-Nisei fighting unit– the most decorated in World War II.

"Mike made it all the way to 1999," Fred mused sadly. "Almost to the millennium, all the way from the Vosges Mountains and getting shot up..." He was going to miss his friend terribly.

"I was sure we were all going to get it in the Vosges," Herb Sakata, a small man who was hunched over, said. He wore a pair of steel-rimmed glasses over which he peered like an acerbic columnist.

"Gawd! How the hell we ever survive that one?" Chik Tokuhara with the silver mane said.

The other men shook their heads as though struck with incredulity even after fifty-five years. Fred knew the men would much rather talk about surviving the Big One, as they referred to it, than about what faced them as old men, like metastasized cancer and the lingering, wasting death that had awaited Mike Kojima. With the passing of each year, Fred didn't know when his number would be up, just like he never knew if the next bullet had his name on it whenever he hit the line. Fear had been ever-present on the battlefield, but now at the age of seventy-seven it was like a dull ache, a resignation that turned into resentment with

Mike's passing. Death was the final insult, and it clawed its way into his consciousness as a reminder that his freedom was not perfect. The only time–and it was only for a brief moment–that freedom was perfect was when he heard the war was over.

"Fear is like a sickness," Fred observed.

"Yeah, it hit me when I saw my first dead Nisei. On our way to Monte Cassino. Laid out by the side of the road with the Jerries," Herb said, adjusting his glasses. "Until then I thought it was going to be like basic training, like an adventure we'd prepared for. No way."

"That's when I knew what gut-shot meant," Chik said. "'Never get it in the face or in the guts', they said."

"I just had to get a close look at the dead Jerry," Herb began. "My first look at the enemy."

"Yeah," Chik said. "And the smell of torn-up feces."

"Hey!" one of the other men shouted. "You're going to spoil my appetite."

"Shit," Chik said. "What do you think whiskey's for?"

"To wash the sins of man away," Fred said enigmatically.

"You got that right, Fred," Chik said. "It does what it's supposed to do. Cleans the brain, soothes the belly."

Chik Tokuhara ran his hand over his thick, silver hair, although it was already coiffed to stay in place, and looked around for the waiter.

"We need some drinks here," he said to no one in particular.

"More poison added to the system?" Herb said.

"Shit, yeah, and it's more than just a bottle of beer," Chik bragged.

"You're saying it's like killing a fifth as in the old days," Herb chided.

"Absolutely."

"At your age, Chik?" Fred said. "Come on, now."

"All right, all right. You know it's just old man's talk," Chik admitted and waved a disgusted hand. "It's more like three shots max. On weekends. Got to watch my goddamn triglycerides."

A young waitress dressed in a form-fitting gold and red Chinese dress approached the men sitting around the round table.

"What will you have to drink, gentlemen?" she asked.

"Been waiting for you, honey," Chik said and eyed her appreciatively. "A double bourbon on the rocks for me."

The rest of the men ordered beer, a Henry's for Fred and a Tsing Tao for Herb. The waitress smiled and said she'd be right back.

"All eyes and no action," Herb taunted Chik.

"Got to keep the interest up."

"That's all you can get up," Herb said and drew laughter from the men.

"Don't knock it," Chik said testily. "It's like saying you don't enjoy a good, juicy steak, medium rare, now and then."

"Not often enough," one of the other men said.

"You're still free to dream," Fred said.

"Is that all you do?" Chik shot the remark at Fred. It was a cruel shot.

"I manage to do just fine," Fred said and fell silent. He didn't feel like discussing his survival as a widower.

I manage to do just fine: Fred was just repeating what Mike used to say, even when he was the sickest. Doing just fine, he'd say. He'd answer with that twisted smile. He fought till the very end. He never did give up. Just before he slipped into a coma–he must have felt it coming on hard–he gripped Fred's hand in the

4

final moments and said: "Go For Broke."

A general gloom of silence fell over the group. Mike Kojima had been one of the originals of the 100th/442nd, and his death, though expected, came as a blow. It was a somber occasion. Each funeral over the years took its toll and cast a dull sobriety over the remaining men. The resplendent colors and fragrance of the floral arrangement seemed a mockery of death. The only colors that had meant anything were the Stars and Stripes, the regimental flag with its "Go For Broke" emblem and the numerous fluttering guidons.

That morning the droning voice of the pastor, reading from the Psalms, and the all-too-familiar routine of the ceremony had burst a logjam of memories–especially this time–that crashed through their minds like a crazily tumbling torrent of long-forgotten thoughts and feelings. Too many things had happened during their days as soldiers to be sorted out so easily. They hadn't been able to get together often; now jagged snippets of recollections begged to be dredged up.

"Remember 'Huli'?" Fred said to break the wall of the stymied words.

"Who can forget?" Chik said, forcing himself to brighten up. "Hisao 'Huli' Tsubota who was always overturning cars when he got drunk."

"He gave the 442nd a bad name in Hattiesburg," Herb said.

"Naw," Chik said. "He got us a lot of respect in basic training and on the line."

"He didn't have to get wild and turn over cars," Herb insisted.

"When he got drunk, he got mad. That's all. No harm done," Chik said.

"The biggest man in the outfit and always breaking up fights between the kotonks and buddhaheads," Fred said. "Everybody liked and respected him. Why, when sober, he was as docile and humble as a grandmother at her son's wake."

"He might have been docile and humble, but on the battlefield, he was a tiger," Chik said. "One of us gets hit, and he'd run through that solid wall of bullets, pick us up like a sack of rice and runs back, hollering 'Medic! Medic!'"

"And he was fast for a big man," Fred said.

"Yeah, you're right, I guess," Herb agreed. "'Huli' was one you'd want right by you on the line. Probably had to let off steam at Camp Shelby what with all that hard training, chickenshit details and being investigated all the time. To see if we were loyal or not. All the while trying to be the best damn outfit in the U.S. Army. If I had a temper like his, I'd probably wreck the car."

Because of his predilection for overturning cars when drunk, Hisao Tsubota, Fred recalled, was called "Bad Boy Huli" behind his back, until, with his five eleven, 195 pound hulk, he began to break up fights between the boys from Hawaii and the mainland who didn't get along together at first. He became known as an easy-going peacemaker, and then he was referred to as "Big Boy Huli" or plain "Huli." He claimed to have Samoan blood in him which was highly unlikely, Fred knew, because both his parents had come from Kumamoto Prefecture in Japan. A peacemaker during the day while training, he turned into a terror in the bars at Hattiesburg at night. Nobody wanted to see him get riled up.

The men fell silent as though a door had slammed shut on the inner mechanism that made lighthearted banter possible, even desirable, especially in the circumstances under which they were struggling to treat the occasion like any other get-together–which it was not. Death was a catalyst of memories.

6

"Now Chikao 'Chip' Shioura was one to believe anything you told him when it came to food," Fred said to keep the chatter alive.

"I remember why he was called 'Chip', too," Herb said, following suit.

"Because he used to stuff his mouth so full his cheeks puffed out and—" Chik began.

"...and he looked like a chipmunk," Herb said. "And he ate as if each meal was his last."

"He was the fastest eater of anyone, bar none, in the company," Chik said.

"He used to say that once the fighting started, there wouldn't be time to eat," Fred recalled for everyone's benefit.

"And who wanted to eat that K ration crap?" Chik said.

"'Chip' was the only one who would eat everything, even the cheese," Herb said.

"That was a mean trick you played on him in basic training, Chik, when you told him the white meat he was eating was snake," Fred said, chuckling lightly, as he sparked the men's memories of the snakes abounding in Mississippi. It was the first time the Hawaiians saw snakes, and they were both fascinated and fearful of them.

"And he didn't know whether to swallow or spit," Herb said and laughed.

"And that time between barrages," Chik laughed apoplectically, "what they called Spam to make it sound good...that cold, greasy, pressed chunky pork. He had his mouth full of it, cheeks bulging out."

Herb threw his head back, unable to contain himself, his eyes swiveling at the ceiling, his mouth wide with laughter. It was exactly the kind of reminiscence they needed to break the chill of death, Fred thought.

"You told him it was ground-up horse cock meant for POWs," Herb said.

"Yeah," Chik said and grabbed his head in mock agony. "And he believed it, it was so bad. And he got that look on his face. I can still see it. He turned green. I never saw a man turn so green. I thought he was going to throw up."

"He just sat there, his cheeks bulging," Herb said.

"Like it was a life or death decision," Chik said, growing misty eyed. "And then he swallowed the whole mouthful in one big gulp."

The men all laughed heartily at the recollection of someone they considered the "baby" of the company.

"Ah, yes," Fred said. "Chikao 'Chip' Shioura. One hell of a fighter." What he didn't mention was the report he had to make out as to how he died in the Vosges Mountains. "And then there was Joe 'Siesta' Hakamada."

"'Siesta' Hakamada," Herb said musingly. "Sleepy-eyed 'Siesta'."

"He needed his beauty sleep, he'd say," Chik said.

"Every spare minute he had, he'd sleep, whether it was during bivouac, a break in field exercises, in the barracks or front line foxhole. He could sleep anywhere, anytime," Herb recounted.

"It got to be such a habit he got noticed by the CO," Chik said. "There's something wrong with you, isn't there, he was asked. No sir, he said. You're depressed by your folks being in the concentration camps, aren't you, the CO asked. No sir, he said. Then what is it, the commanding officer asked. Just conserving energy, he said. And he meant it. He always finished first in the forced twenty-five mile marches. And I'll bet all that sleep made him see better in the dark. Remember the patrols in the forest?"

"I remember them well," Fred said. "Too well. 'Siesta' was a good man."

The door slammed on the conversation again. A heavy silence fell over them. Fred wanted to keep the chatter going. Old men—old soldiers—had no business getting serious about anything. Not at their age. The business of living and dying took up all their strength. But Fred knew that, though toughened by combat, they remained vulnerable. Their youth was gone and along with it went their fallen comrades...down into the repository of painful memories. The concern of what lay around the corner was on everyone's mind, certainly all the more as each year passed. Fred counted his lucky stars that he hadn't been struck down by some illness, but he was rapidly running out of stars as the others were, and he knew the odds were against him and getting slimmer. He hated the idea of rounding a corner one day and hitting a cold, hard dead end. As long as it came quickly, he thought, like a bullet to the head, not a lingering death in which one rotted from the inside out. Poor Mike, he thought. A massive heart attack would have been better.

To break the lull in the conversation, Fred said: "Wally Sawada says hello to everybody. Says he's sorry he couldn't make the funeral and reunion."

"That back of his still bothering him, huh?" Herb said.

"He's lucky to still be alive," Chik said, "hit by a mortar that way. Lucky it was a dud."

"You can thank the Nazi slave laborers for sabotaging that one," Fred said.

"He was wounded but no blood," Herb said. "The only one

with a bloodless wound. It just broke his back."

All of the men had been wounded, some multiple times, but they did not talk about their injuries, just as Fred did not mention how he wound up with a withered claw for a right hand. When he was hit, the impact didn't sink in; he lay on the ground, his arm and hand shattered, bullets in his chest and legs, with a sense of disbelief.

"Stan Nakagome couldn't make it, either," Fred continued. "Alzheimer's getting worse. Still knew who I was, though. When he asked who was coming to the funeral, he said he remembered who you all were. Said he was sorry he couldn't make it to say his final goodbye to Mike."

"We're a dying breed, men," Chik said and turned to look around. "Where in the hell are those drinks?"

A dying breed indeed, Fred thought. Mike Kojima, shortstop of the Portland "Samurais" with Fred as the pitcher, had been his right-hand man in the squad. Fred and Mike and two others who had volunteered together formed an effective fighting team.

The cute waitress came back with the trayful of drinks and handed them around. When she slid Chik's double bourbon in front of him, Fred thought he was going to grab her, but he merely called her "sweetheart" and thanked her and instructed her to come around again in five minutes, because he would be needing a refill.

"With Mike gone, Fred is the last *kitsune*," Herb announced. "There were four. Now there's only one. The Four Foxes of I Company. They all volunteered from the same concentration camp, Minidoka, trained at Camp Shelby, got drunk together in Hattiesburg and fought in the same squad to become legends. Fred Murano and Mike Kojima from Portland, Sam Hatayama and Jimmy Hikida from Hood River." He recited the names as in a litany.

Chik Tokuhara got to his feet unsteadily. Fred knew he wasn't drunk. It was his hip wound received in the Vosges Mountains where I Company was reduced to eight men. Chik raised his glass in tribute. The men all eased their chairs back and stood up, clutching their drinks.

"Here's to 'The Last Fox,' Sgt. Fred Murano," Chiks intoned. "He brought us through a lot of tough spots."

"*Salut*," the men said in unison and tipped their glasses.

"May The Last Fox outlive us all," Herb said.

Fred waved his clawed hand deprecatingly. He raised his own glass to the men. He wasn't one to make speeches but felt compelled to say something.

"Here's to the remnants of I Company," he toasted. "May its glory remain undiminished." He wanted to say more, much more, but a persistent kind of reserve overtook him, and he found the words catch in his throat.

"Fred Murano is a complex man," Herb said. "He is a man of few words, but he is a man of action. The less said, the more gets done. Through his actions. Did he not organize the Youth for Equal Rights, and did he not finance them through his own business?" The small man took a swallow of his drink. "On the line, you always knew what he was thinking," he continued. "How best to get the job done and get us out of it alive. When he was in the rest area, lying flat on his back, he seemed to be dreaming all the time, starry eyed, but you knew he was thinking about the next battle."

"You should of got a field commission, Fred," one of the men said.

"He didn't want to become an officer," Chik said. "The Last

Fox lived for the dogface. Besides, he would have had to take orders from a bunch of assholes, like that General Bunting, and who needed that? Would've cut into his improvisational tactics outwitting the Jerries so bad it made them dizzy keeping up with him."

"We were trained not to think..." one of the other men said.

"...and there's nothing more dangerous than a thinking soldier," Herb said.

"Try harder, you guys, but you can't get me fatheaded," Fred said. "Remember it took all of us to cover for each other. So here's to Mike Kojima, who represents the 'Go For Broke' spirit. He just wouldn't give up, not even in the end."

"To Mike Kojima," Chik said. "One of the original foxes. May his spirit live on." He drained his glass and looked around for the waitress.

"And here's to a damn fine outfit, the 442nd Regimental Combat Team," Fred said, tearing up with his voice cracking.

The waiter took Chik's order, including the others who wanted a refill. When he returned with another round of drinks, he wrote down what Fred, rubbing his eyes dry, read from the menu. He ordered a six course dinner and chose the dishes with care to show that he knew as a connoisseur what to combine in the way of a memorable meal.

Silence fell over the men like a crimson sheet bleached white by the final dying of the sun. Dusk had fallen in a matter of minutes, and the feeble glow of lights barely cut through the settling shadows. The waiter turned a knob. The room jumped into brightness, and everything was highlighted by the array of Chinese colors: red, gold and black. Fred's blood raced through his veins ferociously, pumped by the initial onslaught of alcohol on his tired, old body and by memories of too much violence.

Chapter Two

The harbor at Naples was devastated. The war-ravaged scene brought home to the replacements of the 442nd Regimental Combat Team the enormous destructive power of war. Shattered hulls of ships stuck out of the water like broken steel fists with only the thumbs protruding. The piers were demolished and crumpled and the warehouses torn and collapsed. The cranes were like so much twisted wire tilting at crazy angles. Over all the scene hung the odor of scorched destruction, the most powerful of which was burned creosote and oil.

Zigzagging across the Atlantic to avoid the U-boat wolf packs, the journey from Newport News, Virginia had lasted for twenty-eight days which were filled with boredom broken only by shooting craps, playing cards and the strumming of ukeleles. The Liberty ships were crammed to the seams with men and equipment, and when the men went topside to stretch their legs on the deck, they had to make sure they stayed upwind from a soldier vomiting his meal over the railing. The sighting of Gibraltar signified relief. The waters of the Mediterranean Sea were calm and belied the violence of war, the remnants of which crowded the shoreline in the form of gutted cities.

The men were bivouacked outside the bombed city of Naples. Near the mess tent collected emaciated urchins in rags who begged for food and chocolates. The mess sergeant arranged two garbage cans for the disposal of food: one for pure scraps and the other for partially consumed meals. Most of the men left something on their plates to fill the garbage cans with food which, on signal to the lines of starving boys and girls, would be distributed to eager hands. The men felt guilty with the children eyeing their every movement as they ate. Some held their hands over their mouths to conceal their chewing. The diminutive GI's sometimes gave up their cigarettes that came with the K rations, though precious as gold, to the children so they could use them to barter for other necessities.

The foursome set up their pup tents next to each other, Fred Murano and Mike Kojima in one and Jimmy Hikida and Sam Hatayama in the other. They had argued long and hard before coming to a common decision and volunteering at the same time from the concentration camp at Minidoka; they trained together at Camp Shelby as a unit and fortunately wound up in the same squad. Before the evacuation from the West Coast, they played baseball against each other with Fred and Mike being on the "Samurais" from Portland and Jimmy and Sam on the "Nippon" from Hood River, Oregon. They were initially incarcerated after the evacuation order in horse stalls at the Portland stockyards. While the three others and their families were shipped to Minidoka, Fred Murano, the first son of a shopkeeper and a student at the University of Oregon, and his family were sent to Tule Lake near the border between Oregon and California.

The Murano family was split by the loyalty questionnaire which was required to be signed by everyone seventeen and older. The main questions having to do with loyalty were Questions 27 and 28 which asked if one were willing to serve in the Armed Forces of the United States on combat duty wherever ordered and

14

if one swore unqualified allegiance to the United States of America and would faithfully defend the United States from any or all attacks by foreign or domestic forces while forswearing any form of allegiance or obedience to the Japanese emperor or any other foreign government, power or organization.

Shoji, Fred's father, who had wanted to become a naturalized American citizen but could not because of the existing laws had no choice but to answer No-No to both questions as did Fred's mother, Shizue. The younger children, Margaret, sixteen, and Arthur, ten, being underaged had no alternative except to join their father and mother while Rhonda, nineteen, and Fred, twenty-one, answered Yes-Yes to the questionnaire which created an uproar in the family. Having lost his business and assets and outraged and incensed at being treated like an enemy alien in their adopted home, Shoji was ready and willing to be repatriated to Japan. Fred and Rhonda were not, and in spite of Shoji's protests agreed to leave Tule Lake for Minidoka where Fred met up with his friends. The Yes-Yes "loyals" were shipped out of the camp and distributed among the ten other camps located in the deserts and hinterlands of the United States in order to make room for the No-No "disloyals" in what was called a segregationist camp at Tule Lake.

Now, with the cold winds sweeping the bivouac area and with Mike snoring loudly beside him, sleeping off the effects of a bottle of vino, Fred stretched out on his back under the pup tent and played the light of the flashlight on the last letters he had received from his sisters before leaving Camp Shelby. His sister, Margaret, wrote of his father's adamant attitude–he wouldn't even mention Fred's or Rhonda's name–and the activities of the infuriated pro-Japanese Hoshidan which was trying to coerce the inmates of the camp to renounce their American citizenship. By far the more disturbing, however, was Rhonda's claim that she was being given the cold shoulder by other internees, because it became known that their parents were among the No-No's at Tule Lake, and the question of loyalty, or 100 percent Americanism, was very much at issue in the camp. Even the block manager looked askance at her, and she said she was lucky to be able to get a job as a librarian which paid $13.50 a month so that she could prove how loyal she was by purchasing war bonds with whatever pittance was left over from buying necessities.

Fred ran his hand over the cold steel of the M1 rifle that he had cleaned earlier. He wondered about his capacity to fight a war with the single-mindedness required of a foot soldier on the line. He had his doubts, not about his courage to fight and get the job done, but about his leadership. Could he lead the others effectively when he was so encumbered? His family was always on his mind, especially Arthur who was growing up not knowing whether to love or hate his country, and Rhonda who was all alone in hostile territory. But he had to keep his mind on his job, the days, perhaps years ahead.

The four of them got passes to go into Naples, a city in ruins. They were followed by a horde of street urchins begging for something to eat or trade with some of the boys pimping for their sisters or mothers: "...nice body, big tits, small pussy." The foursome led by Fred stepped along the streets spotted by mounds of animal and human offal and looked for a cafe that was more or less intact among the rubble of the buildings that seemed to teeter precariously, rock balanced on rock with hollow windows and doorways lending themselves to the pile of weakened debris. They got rid of the children dressed in rags by scattering a handful of lira in the air.

They found a bombed-out shell of a building with the lower floor intact and a sheet covering the doorway where there was once a wooden door that had long since been reduced to firewood. Soon it would be getting even colder and the occupants would probably begin to wish they had a door to keep the weather out, but at the moment winter was held at bay, and the candle on one of the tables visible through the cracked glass showed that the establishment was open for business. They weren't sure if the place was off-limits or not, but since there were no MP's in sight, they were lured inside with the promise of wine. The proprietor greeted them in a profuse manner. They took a table away from any casual view from the outside and ordered several bottles of wine. The owner brought the bottles over with a plate of bread and cheese.

"You still have food like this?" Fred asked.

"Si. Not for lira but for cigarettes. You have cigarettes?"

"Yeah, we have cigarettes. How many for everything?"

"Maybe three packs. Is that too much?"

"Naw, three packs is just fine. Throw in another bottle of wine, and I'll add a pack," Fred said and turned toward the others. "All right, cough them up. The man obviously has a family."

They handed over the cigarettes, and Fred placed the packs in the owner's hand. He thanked them over and over again...he could now buy other staples on the black market. With a wave of his hand, Fred indicated that it was nothing, that the owner was welcome, and the men opened the bottles and drank from them directly, not trusting the dirty glasses placed in front of them.

"Cigarettes like gold, huh?" Jimmy Hikida said. "I don't smoke so I guess you can say I got a gold mine."

"Hey," Mike Kojima said. "This cheese is 100% better than K rations."

"Man, anything is better than K ration cheese," Sam Hatayama said. "No shit. Pigs wouldn't even eat that stuff."

The Last Fox

"I like it," Jimmy said.

"You like anything," Fred said and rapped him on the head affectionately. Jimmy was the youngest, and Fred considered him his ward.

They consumed the cheese and bread hungrily and washed them down with large gulps of wine. There were no other GI's in the place, only a local sleeping it off at a table in the corner. The stubby candles flickered and sent ribbons of smoke curling upwards. The wavering licks of flame bounced off the dim, cracked mirror against the wall like so many fireflies.

Led by Sgt. Murano the men filed out of the cafe and stepped out into the rubble-strewn street and began walking under the sagging, overcast sky that was bleeding a fine drizzle. They were still in their summer khakis and felt the chill through their clothes. The supplies were slow to catch up with them. Sometimes the clothes fit, sometimes they didn't. The average height of the entire combat team was five-four, and of the four of them Jimmy was the shortest and had to wear the sleeves of his jacket rolled up and his socks folded back over themselves. They stepped gingerly through the refuse in the street and examined the destruction surrounding them with awe. The Fifth Army under Mark Clark had done a thorough job of driving the Germans out and now were in pursuit as the enemy shrank into its dug-in defenses north of Naples.

They walked through the once bustling city. Very few buildings remained intact. The city wore the broken shroud of decay everywhere. Old men and women who could not fight but survived only to help the young to survive clawed through the remains of what had been their homes in spite of the rain. Makeshift lean-tos were anchored precariously to tilting walls of masonry. The smoke of the innumerable fires, weighted by the wetness of the weather, hugged the ground. Hunched and

18

immobile, the people sat around them as though extruded by the devastation.

As they were walking along the littered road, something shiny caught Fred's eye. He stopped and bent over to pick it up to examine it. He was amazed at his discovery. It was an Indian head penny that had been carefully polished, a relic of what seemed to symbolize the ancient past of America. He claimed it as his lucky penny and stuck it in his pocket. It had made the trip all the way from the States only to be found in a faraway, war-torn country. Must have belonged to some GI, he thought. He hoped it would see him through the war and carry him back home. Alive. They walked on.

They stopped in front of a broken hulk of a building. Huddled in the doorway was a young, dark-haired girl of about eighteen with comely features. She was obviously seeking protection from the rain and hunkered down with her arms about her shivering. Though her clothes were in rags, her beauty shone through the wreckage like a rare flower in the desert. Immediately upon seeing her Jimmy stood entranced, then took off his jacket without hesitation, climbed the few steps to the doorway and offered his coat to her, motioning her to take it. He also produced a bar of chocolate from his pocket.

The girl looked at him, her large eyes full of fright, and shook her head.

"Fred, you speak some Italian," Jimmy said. "Tell her I want her to have them."

Fred Murano, who had the prescience to purchase a dictionary in Hattiesburg, figuring from the news reports that the 442nd would be sent to Italy where the 100th Battalion was already fighting, told the girl the coat and candy were gifts.

She just shook her head vigorously and began to cry.

"I am not that kind of girl," she said in perfect English.

"You speak American," Jimmy said dumbfounded, then collected himself. "No, no. I don't want anything in return. I wouldn't take advantage of you. I want you to have these." He turned to the others. "Come on, guys. You got something left, haven't you?"

They came up with another pack of cigarettes and a few candy bars.

"Here, take these," Jimmy said. "For you and your family."

He took her hands and placed the items in them. She looked at Jimmy with tears in her eyes; her attitude softened.

"Thank you, thank you," she said. "But you must keep your jacket. The MP's will give us trouble if they found us with a GI uniform."

"What is your name?" Jimmy asked.

"Liza Bonachelli."

"Liza. That's a pretty name. My name's Jimmy. Jimmy Hikida."

Liza deposited the articles on her lap and wiped the tears from her eyes.

"Jimmy, thank you for all the good things."

"I've got more. I've got loads of cigarettes. You see, I don't smoke, and I just save them. When can I meet you again?"

"You want to see me again?"

"Yes. That is, if you want to. I hope you want to. I want to help you."

Liza hesitated a moment and studied Jimmy's youthful features. He was looking at her with wide eyes. The sincerity of his desire was reflected in his hopeful smile.

"We could meet here."

"When? Tomorrow? The same time?"

"Yes. That would be fine."

Jimmy and the men bade her goodbye and began walking back to the bivouac area through the rain that fell in earnest. Their uniforms were soaked, and the chill turned to freezing cold. They walked briskly on.

Sam elbowed Mike in the ribs and laughed and nodded toward their short friend.

"How come he doesn't let us call him 'Jimmy' like she does?"

"Hey!" protested Jimmy.

"Because he doesn't love *us*," Mike said and winked. "It's reserved for special people."

"Aren't we special people?" Sam bantered. "We've been together a long time."

"But we can't bring out the mother in a woman like he can," Mike rejoined.

"I don't need any woman to mother me," Jimmy said heatedly. "So why don't you two losers lay off."

"Well said, Jimmy," Fred said. "You got a real mother worrying her mind away all the time in camp, and I know your father is saying a prayer or two for you, too."

"How about yours, Fred? Do they think much about you, you being split up like you are and them getting ready to go to Japan?" Sam asked abruptly. Fred thought he knew why Sam had to get the poison out of his system. He didn't lash back.

"That's uncalled for," Mike said in Fred's defense.

"Nothing to get upset over." Fred said placidly. "Sam's just trying to sound nasty. He's really a softy."

"A softy?" Sam retorted. "You calling me a goddamn softy?"

"That's what you are, Sam," Fred said. "We know you. You can't prove otherwise."

"Oh, yeah, El Capitan of the Samurais. You just wait and see.

Nobody calls me a 'softy'."

"Don't forget your career as a choir boy," chided Mike.

"You want to go for it?" Sam said, nudged Mike roughly with his shoulder and waved his fist in his face. "That was the shit I had to put up with growing up."

"That's enough, Pvt. Hatayama," Fred said harshly. "Save it, you'll need it."

"Yeah, don't push your luck, Hatayama," Mike said. "Or you'll get a fat Purple Heart in the mouth."

"Hah, hah," Sam laughed harshly. "I got to hand it to you, Mike. You got a way with words. But that's all it is. It's all mouth, nothing but mouth. You shoot it off all the time."

"Sure, sure," Mike said, "and yours got hair-trigger ever since we landed in Naples."

"You'd think you two would save it for the Jerries," Fred said. "Word has it that we're moving up to relieve the 100th."

"How soon?" Jimmy asked concerned.

"As soon as the supplies catch up, I suppose," Fred said. "It's the usual hurry-up-and-wait situation."

When they reached their bivouac, the rain had stopped, but they were wet and cold. They lined up at the mess tent, guiltily ate their heated-over K rations and scraped the remnants of the food into the garbage can for the awaiting, hungry children who always gathered around at meal time. Then they retired to their tents and shucked off their wet clothes. It was going to be uncomfortable putting them on damp in the morning, but that was in the morning, and now they curled in their blankets that stayed dry.

The artillery barrages rumbled in the distance like muffled thunder, and they knew they would soon be sent into battle. They could not imagine what it would be like in a shooting war; they could only hope that they would do what they were trained to do when faced with flying bullets. Soon after breakfast the next day they got their orders. They were to be ready to move out by 1400 hours to advance on the formidable Gustav Line and join the beleaguered 100th Battalion, which had been so badly mauled crossing the Volturno River and penetrating the winter defenses in the mountains north of Naples that they earned the sobriquet: The Purple Heart Battalion. The Hawaiian Nisei paved the way.

Jimmy stuffed his pockets with his horde of cigarettes before they left and grabbed Fred to take along with him to see Liza. They met her at the designated spot but had to hurry so as not to miss their outfit moving out. She insisted they visit her family, and they walked quickly among the gutted buildings to a lean-to inhabited by her mother and father and three other children, all much younger than she. She introduced Jimmy as Pvt. Jimmy Hikida, their benefactor, and Jimmy emptied the contents of his pockets on a rickety bed.

"For food, clothing, firewood. Anything you need," he said and looked fondly at the beautiful young girl. "I'll bring you some more when I get back."

They thanked him profusely and invited both of them to partake of a cup of "caffe" made from redried grounds of coffee salvaged from the garbage cans and sold on the blackmarket. They said they were finally able to get some the previous day. But both men had to refuse.

"We're in a hurry," Fred said in Italian. "We're moving out."

"I hope I will see you again, Jimmy," Liza said.

"Don't worry, you will. By the way, where did you learn your English?"

"My aunt from Brooklyn—"

"I'm from Oregon..."

"Oregon? I never heard—"

23

"Never mind. Goodbye, Liza. I'll be seeing you."

The two men stepped out of the lean-to and hurried back to their camp. When they returned, they found that their packs had already been readied by Mike and Sam and all they had to do was to throw their duffle bags on the 2-1/2 ton truck and join the rest of the men lined up ready to march. There were no extra trucks to take all of them to the front, so packed was the destroyed harbor that the unloading of vehicles, equipment and supplies was almost down to a standstill. But reports of savage fighting filtered back, and there was no time to lose. The men would have to make do with what they could carry. At precisely 1400 hours they moved out in formation. They would arrive at the outer edges of Benevento by dusk to await further transportation and join their battle-tested brothers of the 100th Battalion.

Sgt. Fred Murano marched at the head of his squad and passed the word along: "Don't turn your back on the Jerries." It was drummed into them during basic training and became a battle cry second only to "Go For Broke." It was tacitly acknowledged that it would even be better to be shot in the face–every soldier's nightmare–than to be shot in the back and thought to be running from the battle instead of into it.

Chapter Three

As they trudged under the sagging, black clouds, it began to rain again and soon they were soaked to the skin. Their boots made sucking sounds in the mud like so many tentacles popping loose from the ground. The large drops of rain pelted their helmets, and the water ran down their necks. The vigor of the march kept them from becoming chilled. There was hardly any wind, but when it blew in gusts, it was as though the thunder of the artillery in the distance stirred a synchronized cadence matching the rhythm of barrages, the thrusting cannonades whipping the air. They could see the pall of smoke hanging over the mountains in the distant horizon, and they were marching directly toward it. Fear clamped its icy hand on their necks, making them feel limp, and their bladders were loosened. It was their first time on the line as untried, untested troops. How would they perform? They kept up the fast pace, fixing their eyes on the figure of the man ahead, and tried to limit their thinking to the task at hand.

The trucks returned to pick up several other platoons to take them to Alife, the jump-off point, and the closer they got to the town, the more apparent the ferocity of the carnage became. They saw their first fallen comrade, a Japanese American of the 100th Battalion, his blackened body twisted in the agony of death, and the war suddenly became real. The training at Camp Shelby and the mock maneuvers were seen as a stage play, something they had endured in the distant past. As earnest as their training had been, it could in no way prepare them for the horror they felt when they saw the shattered bodies of their brothers mingled with the fallen enemy and the burning hulks of half tracks with the bent barrels of self-propelled guns tilted toward the ground in stunned defeat. A redoubtable Panzer 88 stood smoldering with its tracks blown off and its turret twisted askew as though it had been hit by a swarm of shells. A Sherman tank lay on its side with its gun turret torn away, obviously a brave victim of a duel with the Panzer before its demise. The trails of smoke were whisked away by the wind. The Germans had moved beyond the town and were apparently going to make a strong stand in the mountains.

"I *knew* they were going to throw us into a goddamn meat grinder," Sam Hatayama said.

"Can it," hissed Fred Murano, swallowing his own fears. "Don't let the others hear you."

"Why didn't they send in the 132nd Regiment, the white guys?" Sam growled under his breath. "They're doing nothing but resting."

"It's because the Colonel has faith in us," Fred said resolutely. "It's up to us to get the job done. He's bound and determined to make us the 'can do' outfit, and we're not going to disappoint him."

"I volunteered to fight, not get sacrificed." Sam breathed his resentment on Fred's neck as they marched in the muck.

"Sacrifices have to be made," Fred said. "That's what it's all about...it's not only for the folks in the camps. A vicious enemy is waiting for us."

"And that enemy is pure prejudice."

"Not only prejudice, Sam. It's the entire concept of freedom."
Fred wondered if he wasn't saying that more for his benefit than
Sam's.

"As guaranteed by barbed wire fences and gun towers."
Sam's whispered retort was like a shot. "Is that what you're trying
to say?"

"You've got to look beyond things like that. The concentration camps happened...they shouldn't have. Look beyond the
fences and fight for the guarantees that make us a free people, all
of us, not just some of us. That's what America stands for...you've
got to believe that in your bones to fight this war." Fred knew he
was preaching to himself as his boots sucked mud with each step.

"I volunteered so I could get out of the stinking camps. You
think I'm trying to be loyal? I just want to kill Jerries. They're the
next best thing to killing—"

"That's a hell of a way to look at things." Fred stopped him
before he said what he would regret. "We're here to get a job
done the best way we can...prove that America was wrong to
doubt us, show we're tops when it comes to fighting."

"Think that's going to make any difference?" A statement,
rather than a question, of restrained bitterness.

"You have to believe that it will."

"Shit, man," Sam said and fell back. "I'm just going to kill
Jerries and let the rest of the world go to hell."

Mike Kojima approached them. "What are you guys
whispering about? Anything I should know about?"

"Just talking about this picnic we're on," Sam said.

"It's going to be a turkey shoot," Mike said, forced
enthusiasm in his voice. "We got the best riflemen of the company
in our squad."

"Always the optimist," Sam chided cruelly. "Keep wearin' your rose-colored glasses."

"Better an optimist than a pessimist," Mike said lightly. "Pessimists are dime a dozen. War cranks them out like Carter's Liver Pills. Hell, we're a rare breed. The optimists will save the world."

"And you're the first ones to get knocked off, *bakatare*. Me, I intend to survive this war."

"You sure turned into a rotten sorehead, Sam."

"And the more cheerful you are the worse things get," Sam predicted.

"It gets to you, doesn't it?" Mike said.

"All stargazers get to me," Sam announced forcefully but there was dread in his voice. "I'll know you'll be smiling when you get yours."

"Lay off Mike," Fred said, knowing how the poison of incarceration was working in Sam. "He's cheerful because he has to be. Otherwise, he gets too serious for his own good."

In the middle of the night, the two platoons reached the forward elements of the 100th dug in around the designated periphery, and Sgt. Murano and his squad dug their slit trenches just behind them. They lined the bottom of the trenches with branches to keep themselves off the water that collected on the bottom. Exhausted from the long march, they slept cradling their rifles after a quick, cold meal of K rations. They went easy on the water, since they knew a canteen would have to last them a whole day or more. The lieutenant told them to be ready to attack at dawn. They had little time to sleep.

At first light the artillery barrage commenced and after thirty minutes it lifted, and a dead silence fell over the landscape. The mountains ahead loomed large and ominous. A deathtrap. As though fear were an added weight, the men slowly rose out of their holes, bayonets fixed, and moved through the screen of smoke. Their feet were leaden and a paralysis set in. It turned them numb with doubt that they would acquit themselves well in their first fire fight, but their training took over, and they followed one another, crouched over by instinct, ready for all hell to break loose. The silence was eerie, laden with death.

They crept forward out of the edges of an olive grove to confront a plain flooded by the Germans who built concrete embankments to divert the Rapido River and cleared the plain of all covering to give them an open field of fire with unlimited visibility. Thick stumps of trees protruding from the three-foot deep water obstructed the movement of tanks.

When the 442nd to which the 100th Battalion was attached by now because of its decimated ranks entered the mined quagmire and made their presence evident by the tripped explosions, the Germans unleashed their fury. Interlocked machine gun fire and artillery barrages opened up instantaneously and the dreaded nebelwerfers–the "Screaming Meemies", fired from six-barreled rocket launchers–shrieked like bloodthirsty demons as they exploded among them.

The men, slogging their way through waist-high water, were cut down. Man after man dropped after being hit or tripping a mine. The cold, churning water turned a bright red. The pre-dawn artillery barrage laid down on the mountainous terrain ahead hadn't made a dent in the enemy's capability to unleash havoc. The spitting machine guns were murderous. The men carrying ladders were targeted and fell one after another only to be replaced by others as the 442nd pushed ahead toward the high embankment topped by mined barbed wire barriers. It was an impossible situation, but the men pushed forward.

Fred hunched involuntarily to make a smaller target of himself as the bullets zipped around him and whipped up sprays of water. His first impression under fire was one of incredulity. He was actually being shot at; there were men like him with guns who were trying to kill him–and he had caused them no harm. In his mind, all the scenarios he had run through while in training–training for war–could not compare to the chaotic havoc of watery explosions and small arms and machine gun bursts that ripped into the ranks of the men who fell dead or wounded. The whistling and screaming of the nebelwerfers, the rapid fire of the 88's and the deadly sputtering of the heavy machine guns, the explosions of tripped mines all lent a hellish atmosphere to the scene marked by the combined smell of gunpowder and fresh blood. Cries for the medic rose from the throats of men thrashing in the water. Other bodies lay still, immobile as if in rest. Fred felt a heavy thud on his head, a hammer blow of a bullet that ricocheted off his helmet. He crouched lower and hunched smaller, fear weakening his belly and legs, but he forced himself to press on toward the embankment and look around for the men in his squad.

Belying the sudden loss of confidence he felt as he waded through the water toward the dike, still fifty yards ahead of him, he waved his hand with vigor and repeatedly yelled: "Let's go, let's go, keep moving!" He felt the sting of an angry wasp. A bullet had nicked his ear, and he felt the warm blood dribble down his cold neck. His legs were frozen, but he kept pumping them in his effort to trot through the water. He put his hand to his ear and fingered the torn lobe. Too close for comfort, he thought. An inch or so and he would have caught it in the face.

"Sarge!"

It was Jimmy. Fred whipped around in alarm.

"I'm hit!"

"Where?"

"In the arm and in the leg...I think." Jimmy wore a look of incredulity.

"Can you still walk?"

"Yeah, I think so."

"Move back so the medics can find you, but keep firing at the machine gun nest closest to the dike. We've got to keep the pressure on them."

"All right, I'll try my best....are we going to get out of this one alive? I never thought—"

"Don't worry, you're due for a nice, warm bed. Now get going and keep firing," Fred said, keeping his voice steady.

Fred turned his attention to the embankment. One thing at a time, he told himself. He rallied the men on. The lanky, tall lieutenant from Wisconsin was just a few feet ahead of him. He was firing his Thompson at the hill from his hip. Fred doubted he was even looking at any target. Fred paused to trigger off a few rounds at the nearest machine gun raking the troops who were hoisting up the ladders. The soft, deep mud sucked at his feet.

There was a thud of a bullet striking home, and the lieutenant let out a sigh and fell backwards, still clutching the Thompson submachine gun.

Fred screamed: "Medic! Medic! Medic!"

He retrieved the submachine gun from the officer and removed the extra clips from his belt after shouldering his own rifle. He looked at the lieutenant. He knew he was dead. Rushing forward he picked up a ladder from a fallen soldier and slogged his way to the wall. The bullets were zapping into the concrete and leaving deep pockmarks. He anchored the ladder in place and looked around and found Mike and Sam right behind him.

"Follow me," he said.

Those ahead of him had already thrown themselves at the mines and cleared a path through the barbed wire and the top of the dike. The three men who were followed up the ladder by six others of the same squad dashed to the foot of the hill and hugged the dirt as machine gun fire plowed the ground around them, pinning them down.

"What now, Sarge?" one of the men asked.

"I don't know. Let me think." Survive to fight, fight to survive. Even that desperate reminder was lost in the din of battle. His training turned into instinct. "We have to knock out that nest under those rocks there." His words were punctuated by his spasmodic panting.

He pointed to a rock outcropping under which the Jerries had dug an emplacement. It had the men pinned down and a clear field of fire to rake at will the embankment the men were still trying to scale. It was suicide to tackle it head on.

"Anybody see Jimmy make it back?" Fred asked, voicing the nagging concern while trying to focus his thoughts.

"Last I saw, he was backing into the olive grove still firing his M1," Mike said.

"Thank God!" Fred said, sighing. "I think he'll be all right."

"Want me to draw fire while one of us crawls up to put the gun out of commission?" Mike asked.

Always the first to volunteer, as usual, always too eager, thought Fred of his childhood friend. "You don't stand a chance," Fred cautioned, thinking hard. "The sniper will nail you the moment you sit up."

"We can't just lie here," Sam said, his voice on edge. "We're pinned down so bad we're eating dirt! Can't move to dig in!"

"I know that...we've got to do something fast," Fred said. "There's no time to dig in, and this is not the place. We've got to take the pressure off the men coming over the wall...now."

"But how?" Sam shouted above the noise of battle.

Fred raised his head to view the machine gun. Amidst the chatter of small arms fire and the spitting burst of the machine guns came the distinctive crack of a long-barreled sniper rifle. The bullet kicked dirt in Fred's face. He had to decide quick. It was instinct over mind.

"Screw up their aim," he said, more to himself than anyone in particular. "Make them keep shooting."

"What?" Mike said, ready to move into action.

"Mike, you crawl to the left thirty yards, and you, Sam, crawl thirty yards to the right and pop up and down, taking turns shooting at them. Aim for the mouth of the dugout, but it doesn't make any difference if you hit anything. The idea is to get them to keep swinging their barrels and use up ammo. At one point there's going to be a pause. That's when I'll nail them, crawling up the center. The rest of you men give me cover and keep the pressure on them."

Fred waited until Mike and Sam were in position. Then he raised his hand to set the plan into action. First Mike rose and fired while the machine gun trained its sights on him and released a spurt that harmlessly plowed dirt as Mike instantly sank to the ground and Sam popped up, causing the gun to recklessly swing in his direction with the same result. The two timed their pop-ups to make the Jerries hesitate in confusion. A lot dirt kicked up, and a lot of ammunition wasted. Fred slowly inched his way up the middle with the men concentrating their firepower on the mouth of the dugout with such accuracy that the Germans didn't have time to aim. When he could move no closer, he waited while gripping the Thompson, hugging the ground tightly.

There was a pause, the exact moment he had been waiting for. He rose to his feet, firing the submachine gun and raced up to the rocky emplacement to lob a grenade into the opening. The machine pistol and machine gun were silenced instantly, and he ran up to the nest to finish off the sniper who was wounded and still trying to manipulate his rifle. He entered the hole and grabbed the scoped rifle and a bandolier of ammo from the dead German and waved his men on to the next machine gun emplacement higher up, after handing the sniper rifle to one of the men.

"Force them to keep their heads down," he ordered as the Nisei soldier took up the prone position, squinted through the scope and began to fire. The squad moved into position.

"Dance!" Fred barked at Mike and Sam.

They spread fifty, sixty yards apart and pranced up and down, drawing fire from the next emplacement up the hill and causing the Jerries to expend their ammo. The men's smooth coordinated efforts produced results similar to the first. Fred slithered up the slope, watching the barrel of the machine gun swing wildly from one target to the other while sparing the men climbing up the ladders and over the embankment. More men managed to gain a foothold at the bottom of the mountain and take on the other machine guns. They moved through the interlocking fire unfalteringly and never took a backward step. The mortar rounds landing among them took their toll, but by far the more dangerous and deadly were the M-42 heavy machine guns.

Fred flattened himself behind a rock. He was still too far to accurately throw a grenade and triggered off a burst from his grease gun to draw fire toward himself while Mike and Sam inched up on either flank as they presented themselves at random. The Jerries shot at anything that moved, so Fred turned around and yelled at the two men to dance as they had done and watched with fearful satisfaction the barrel of the German gun oscillate left to right and back again without having time to aim properly. One of the squad members had clawed his way up to Fred's position and started to fire his M1, but Fred told him to wait. The German gun continued to erupt methodically in six-round bursts that tore up the ground around Mike and Sam, but neither man was hit and no one else in the squad was, either. So far the team held intact. Then came the inevitable pause.

"Now," Fred said and slapped the helmet of the man beside him. They both rose and rushed the emplacement and threw grenades into the opening and lay flat on the ground to escape the concussion.

Through the smoke and dust, they sprayed bullets into the orifice and raced up the hill only to be stopped by another machine gun. The mountain they had to scale was infested with them, and each yard they advanced was measured by the dead and wounded. But Fred's squad was spared. He was close enough to take on the nest himself, but he turned to the man with the sniper rifle and yelled "Sniper!" and while the rifleman threw off the aim of the Germans and drew fire at the same time, Fred dashed up the flank and rammed a grenade home as he threw himself on the ground. The explosion blew several Germans out of the hole, propelling the heavy machine gun into the air, and Fred rolled over, got up and sprayed bullets into the hole to make sure no one would come out alive.

His legs were tiring on the steep slope, and he moved as in a dream, dashing from rock to rock, covering for his men as they made their way up and leaping out into the open to locate the next machine gun. The ripping spurts sizzled through the air and richoceted off the rocks, whining down an errant path in the air, while Fred crawled like a lizard up the incline after signaling to Mike and Sam. He waited. The Jerries commanded the high ground and were literally firing down their throats. There had to be a pause. And then it came. The ten-second pause. Which proved how rattled the Jerries were. That was all he needed. He rose and ran to the outcropping that had the deadly snout poking at them, firing as he ran and reaching for a grenade.

There was none. He had used them all up. In desperation he fired into the pit and saw the frightened faces of the Jerries as they scrambled about in confusion.

"Grenade!" Fred yelled.

Like the shortstop that he was, Mike flipped him a grenade underhanded, and Fred yanked the pin out and dropped it into the hole and rolled to one side. The concussion hurled the bodies of the Germans into the air. Shaking with exhaustion and the fear that was catching up with him, Fred pumped several rounds into the inert bodies of the already dead soldiers and raced to the next rock with bullets whizzing all about him. Their objective was to neutralize the mountain, and that meant scaling it above the timberline. Hours of fighting lay ahead. Fred didn't have time to think of the impossibility. He could only hope his legs would hold out.

In taking the high ground, both Herb Sakata and Chik Tokuhara were wounded. Fred lost several men in his squad but with Mike and Sam and the man with the sniper rifle, he managed to take all the machine gun nests in their way and made it to the snow line where the fortifications were sparsely spaced. They were still dressed in their summer uniforms and shivered in the cold as they dug in, scraping the snow away and shoving the blades of their shovels vainly into the frozen ground. Instead of trying to dig a slit trench, they merely piled rocks in a circle and curled inside of them.

Fred was exhausted. His throat was parched, and he withdrew his canteen of water only to discover it empty. A bullet hole had pierced it neatly. He drank the few drops left in the canteen and brushed the dirt off the stomped on snow as well as he could and ate a handful, spitting out the mud coating his tongue. They shrank in their holes like frightened rabbits as the Screaming Meemies landed among them. But the barrage was sporadic, and it appeared that the Germans were withdrawing to the other end of the mountain. Fred didn't have time to think of what lay ahead. The battle cry of the Red Bull Division, the 34th, to which they were finally attached was: Attack! Attack! Attack! And that was precisely what he intended to do. In the back of his mind, however, was the insistent maxim: Fight to survive, and survive to fight.

Supplies were slow in reaching them. The mules could make it up the trail only so far, and the food, water and ammo had to be brought up the last three miles of the slope on the backs of the men who were constantly picked off by sniper fire and tumbled down the mountainside in a twisted heap. Here and there over the ground they had covered came the cries of the wounded for the medics. Fred could hear their faint voices. He could also hear the cries of the dying: Mama, Mama, Mama.

When the K and C rations were finally passed around, the men tore off the wax covering and built a small fire to warm their hands and ate their food cold. Fred got an extra canteen from one of the bearers and drank just enough water to slake his initial thirst. He reloaded the clips with .45 caliber ammo. Although the Thompson submachine gun was accurate only up to seventy-five yards, it was the best firearm they had to counteract the machine pistols the Germans used to great advantage.

As dusk settled over the landscape, the battlefield turned quiet. The silence was broken now and then, like an unpredictable burning block of cedar, with the popping crackle of small arms fire and the smooth burping of the machine guns. The sporadic sounds stuttered in the cold mountain air. Overhead the star-studded black velvet of the night winked desperately through the closing cloud covering until the darkness became so thick with fog that a bayonet would remain stuck in it. It began to snow, soft, powdery stuff. Fred licked it off his lips and hands and hugged himself as he curled up in his trench, trying to catch a few winks of sleep.

"Hey, Fred, you asleep?" Mike called hoarsely.

"Naw, who can sleep in this cold?" Fred shivered and drew his knees in closer to his chest. "You better try to get some, though. It's going to be another rough one tomorrow."

"Can you smell me?"

"Yeah. I can smell you." It was their first baptism under fire. Fred knew they had acquitted themselves well.

"I shit in my pants."

"I know, Mike," Fred said. "Don't concern yourself. I pissed in mine." He lied. But he wanted to make his friend feel better. He felt like a kid again, looking after Mike. What he wouldn't admit was how fear nearly paralyzed his legs. The war hadn't become real yet.

"I can smell you clear over here," Sam said and gave vent to a nervous cackle. "Imagine trying to run with a shitload between your legs."

"At least he's not going to have to take a crap in his helmet, Sam," Fred said.

"I'll jus' dig a hole in the trench and—"

"Dig a hole in the frozen ground? You'll just wind up lying in shit, since you're so full of it," Mike said irately.

"Quiet. Try to get some rest," Fred said.

He wiggled around on the hard ground to massage some warmth into his body. He clenched his teeth tightly to keep them from chattering and shook from the cold. It was going to be a long, miserable night, one of many he knew were to come. The snow continued to fall. Dawn seemed eons away. But he didn't look forward to it. They had the rest of the mountaintop to take, and the Jerries would surely be ready for them. So far they had been lucky. With the ground more open than the foothills, perhaps they stood a better chance of maneuvering around and outflanking them. One advantage they had was that they were flexible; the Germans were trapped in holes, and Fred tried to think of ways to work it to their advantage. Lacking artillery support since they were so close in, they were going to wind up having to dig the Jerries out by hand.

His ear began to throb. It was the only part of him that still seemed alive. He rubbed some snow on the torn lobe and broke open a packet of sulfa that he sprinkled on the wound. It was cold enough that the pain wasn't unbearable. It couldn't even compare to what some of the men were going through that very instant, torn and bleeding. He had seen so many cut down and fall in the flooded plain and foothills. He tried to blink away the vision of his fallen comrades, men he had trained with and lasted only a few minutes, a few seconds, into their first skirmish. A sharp pang of sorrow welled in his throat and brought tears to his eyes. They were all like brothers. Training together, enduring the endemic suspicions–the security checks and censorship–getting drunk together in Hattiesburg. He was bound and determined to bring his squad and platoon inherited by him through it, if it was at all within his power.

At first light the men began to stir and like a frozen fist uncoiled their stiff bodies and unconsciously straightened up. Exactly what the German sniper was waiting for. With each shot a man fell mortally wounded. Everyone fell flat back into their holes. The nightmares were not fleeting fantasies; they were for real. For a moment they had forgotten they were in a war.

Somewhere to their right, the other platoons of I Company opened fire, and the men, on Fred's orders, began to belly along on the rocky surface of the terrain toward a machine gun that opened up and broke the dawn with the sounds of war. No breakfast–as unpalatable as it was–no slaking of thirst, no relieving oneself.

Splinters of rock and gravel rapped their helmets like so many hammers as they buried their faces in the ground. After each spurt of machine gun fire, the men got to their feet and rushed forward. Some were torn to pieces with a well-placed spurt and died instantly. The BAR man, the first one to be targeted because he carried an automatic weapon, was in the lead but was pinned down and tried to roll to his left and right to change positions. His all-essential weapon was useless. Another machine gun provided interlocking fire, and the men were pinned down under a murderous curtain of fire.

"Sniper," Fred yelled to the man with captured sniper rifle, "keep that second nest busy and tie them down." He rolled over and called out to Sam and Mike. "Spread out and dance!"

He then motioned to two other men to flank the emplacement while he crawled like a frantic crocodile to get within range. The stream of M1 fire behind him tore chunks of rock from the opening. Fred hoped the Jerries were frantically shielding their eyes from the fragmented debris. Seemingly trained to fire automatically at anything that popped up as a target, the machine gun chattered at random until the inevitable pause. Fred rose to his feet and lobbed one grenade, ducked and followed it with another and charged up the slope hollering "Banzai" and firing his Thompson. The bloodcurdling scream—an ancestral cry of vengeance—galvanized the other men to fix bayonets and follow suit.

"Banzai! Banzai! Banzai!" they cried out and stormed the emplacements.

The BAR man was freed up and began splattering the dug-in Germans with a stream of jacketed bullets. He and his assistant raced along with the rest of the men, and their advance was so swift and their cries so unnerving that the Jerries rose out of their holes as though by telepathic empathy hollering "Kamerad" amidst the furor and stood with their arms held high. They looked at the short Nisei men, fright and astonishment etched into their features.

"Japanisch?" they asked, their eyes wild with confusion.

"Nein, nein," Fred said and broke out into a smile in spite of himself. They must have thought Japan had surrendered and was fighting for America. "Amerikanisch, Amerikanisch."

"Amerikanisch?" an officer said, stepping forward.

"That's right," Fred said, his Thompson pointed at his belly.

Sam stepped up to him and pulled himself up to his full height which was no more than five-six. He flexed his arm and shook his fist in the officer's face. "Made in the good, ol' U.S. of A., Kamerad," he proclaimed.

"But you look like Japanese," the German officer said in English.

"And looks are deceiving," Mike said and stood in front of him, his feet set wide apart and arms akimbo. He stood no taller than the German's chest, but he struck a pose of a conqueror.

The officer screwed up his nose and regarded Mike for a minute. Then he broke out into a sly smile. He dared not laugh with the submachine gun pointed at him.

"And you fight for America? A country that put your people into concentration camps?" he said with as much contempt as was safe.

"That's a big misunderstanding we intend to clear up," Fred said. "We're freedom-loving Americans." He turned toward the men who had gathered around. "Right, men?"

"Damn right," one of the men said. "Say hello to a new breed of Yankee Doodle Dandies."

Fred picked three men from the second squad to herd the prisoners together and to take them to battalion headquarters. There were eighty in all. First the men relieved the Jerries of their overcoats which they eagerly shrugged into. The coats draped around them like tents. They bore a strange, foreign odor. But they dragged around in them in the powdery snow as they began digging in–or, as it turned out, scraping the snow off the rocks and piling them up. Their objective had been achieved, and they set about securing their sector. Collecting prisoners had been exciting at first, but the novelty soon wore off, and they were just plain dogfaces again. Sounds of fighting were still coming from their right flank where the rest of the company was clearing off the mountaintop.

The mountain, Hill 1140, was one of the anchors of the Gustav Line that stretched across the Italian Peninsula. They had to take it before they could attack Monte Cassino which lay before them as part of another mountain sitting in the middle of the Liri Valley dotted with clustered hamlets and ribbons of roads running its length. The monastery on top of the mountain set it apart from the surrounding mountainous landscape of mounded humps and jagged peaks. It was transformed into a fortress by the German Tenth Army and commanded all the access routes north to Rome. The Germans spared nothing in fortifying the Gustav Line, and Monte Cassino was the linchpin of the next line of defense, a deadly network of a massive collection of armaments and ordnance.

Fred expected a concerted counterattack, but the rest of the 3rd Battalion to the east was absorbing most of the fighting that remained, and he and his men sat in their trenches and caught up with eating a belated breakfast. Eat when you can as fast as you can. Some curled up in their huge overcoats and slept on the frozen ground.

Toward the end of the third day, a 2nd lieutenant appeared on the mountaintop with a contingent from the battalion that was held in reserve.

"Sergeant," he said to Fred, "where is the officer in charge?"

"Dead, sir," Fred said, noting that the young blond officer had a faint fuzz covering his cheeks and chin. Strictly against regulations but maybe the youth was trying to prove something. "He was killed crossing the flooded plain."

"I'll take over from here," the green lieutenant said

importantly. "You and your men report back to the rear."

"Yes, sir."

"And I'll take that tommy gun."

"No can do, sir," Fred said, gripping the submachine gun possessively. "It's part of my arsenal."

"You still have your M1 there."

"I was hanging on to it in case we had to mount a bayonet charge."

"A bayonet charge, eh? I heard you fellas hollering 'Banzai'," the lieutenant said, scratching his neck. "You sounded like a horde of Japanese."

"I guess it's the samurai in us, sir," Fred said and grinned. "Just comes natural."

"I see. But you're aware of the difference, aren't you?" The officer seemed to want to make a point of the obvious.

"Yes, sir, and proud of it," Fred said without showing that he was somewhat insulted. "As Japanese Americans you might say we have a little twist, and we try to work it to our advantage."

"Like what?"

"Like shooting the works," Fred said. "If and when we need to."

"Go for broke?"

"Yes, sir." Fred smiled.

"Carry on, soldier." The officer returned Fred's salute.

Fred gathered his men together. It didn't take them long to collect their equipment when they heard they were ordered to the rear. The descent was much easier; they slipped and slid down the side of the mountain, past the dead Germans and their own fallen who hadn't been picked up yet. The first thing Fred anticipated was a hot meal. Nothing sounded better at the moment unless it was a hot shower. He slid past the troops making their way up to the position they had just evacuated. He couldn't believe they had become a real part of the war. He reached into his pocket and fingered his lucky penny. He let out a heavy sigh.

Chapter Four

Fred's anticipation bore fruit. As soon as they arrived in the rest area in Alife, they were given a hot meal of stewed chicken, mashed potatoes with gravy and canned peas and all the coffee they could drink. Mike remarked on how few of them there were left. Fred said nothing. The vision of the killed and wounded on the hillside and mountain was still too fresh in his mind. The medics and litter bearers were roaming all over the battlefield.

"You brought us through, Fred," Mike said and patted him on the shoulder. "If it weren't for you the platoon would have been wiped out."

"It pays to know what the Jerries are using against you," Fred said modestly.

"How about them 88's?"

"They're the best artillery piece in the war. An anti-aircraft, anti-tank and anti-personnel gun all in one."

"And accurate! Gawd!" Mike said in awe. "No wonder the Jerries are cocky."

"And you have to know where the kinks are."

"An 88? How are you going to—"

"Not an 88," Fred noted. "That, you stay out of the way. I was thinking of the MG-42 and 34."

"Is it true they can use our own M1's against us?"

"In a way, true enough. Our ammo fits their Mausers but not the other way around. They designed it that way."

"Clever sonuvabitches."

"We just got to learn to improvise."

"Throw more lead at them."

"Something like that."

On top of the hot meal, the army brought in the mobile hot shower units and told the men to discard their mud-encrusted and torn summer uniforms in exchange for new winter uniforms. They had three minutes per man in the showers: one, to rinse; one, to lather; one, to wash and rinse. They shucked off their dirty uniforms and stood shivering in line, yelling "Hurry up, hurry up. Get the lead out." A hot meal and a hot shower. The feeling of luxury was such that Fred had never felt before, not even after the long, sweaty train ride to the concentration camp in Minidoka and the first shower they were able to take as soon as they settled in the barracks. When he climbed into the fresh set of clothes, he felt like a new man. Not all the men were lucky enough to find clothes that fit, but he was of average height, five-eight, and found a set that fit perfectly.

The hot water felt good, but it stung his torn ear, so he decided to have it sewn up at the aid station. No sense getting an infection and get sent behind the lines, away from his outfit and the fighting, he thought.

"That was a close one," the doctor said. "Another Purple Heart for your incredible unit."

"I don't want a Purple Heart for something like a nick in the ear, Doc," Fred said. "I slipped and fell on the rocks."

"So you say, soldier."

"That's the way it happened, so help me." He couldn't add "God"...so help me, God. Why was that he wondered? Probably because he witnessed the carnage of war and saw so many good men die...his men.

"If you say so," the doctor said. "Now hold still. This is going to smart a bit."

Fred clenched his teeth and stared straight ahead at a point on the grey wall that had a hole blown open by an 88.

"There," the doctor said, putting the finishing touches to the bandage. "My first case of plastic surgery this afternoon. You're lucky."

Fred rubbed the penny between his fingers. "I know," he said.

He left the aid station and was looking for his friends when Mike caught up with him and pat him on the shoulder.

"You got yourself a Purple Heart," he said.

"Naw," Fred said. "I slipped on the damn slope and fell."

"Sure."

"You sure smell different. Like sweet lilacs."

"One of the guys had a bottle of perfume to send home. But he used it on himself. And me, after the shower."

"Smelling like that, Mike, you could lure all the Jerries out of their holes," Fred said and punched his friend in the shoulder.

"No joke. But smelling like I did, I could have stunned them, and then you guys could have picked them off one by one. How's that for improvisation?" Mike laughed, although the joke was at his own expense, and he knew it.

"You been hit in the head or something, Mike?" Fred laughed with him.

"No joke. Not even a scratch. Can you beat that? And they threw everything they had at us. It's probably because I had 'un' (luck) on me. You know, the 'un' of 'unko' (shit)."

"And there's probably more from where that came from," Fred said, knowing his buddy had been scared witless. "*Now* you can joke."

"Now I can. But I never knew the first time could be so bad. I could barely raise my rifle, I was so weak."

"Yeah, I know," Fred said, recalling his near-paralysis.

"Oh, by the way, the CO wants to see you."

"What for?"

"I don't know, but he looked serious."

Fred walked through town, dodging the jeeps and 2-1/2 ton trucks, and found his way to battalion headquarters, the building that once housed the mayor's office. He knew the orderly. They exchanged greetings.

"Major Haskins is expecting you, has been for hours."

Fred knocked on the door to the inner office and entered to face a tall man with rugged features who was puffing on a cigar.

"Sgt. Fred Murano reporting as requested, sir." He didn't know if the CO's scowl was for real or just a mark of a professional soldier who was out to make an impression as the new replacement for Maj. Sanders.

"So you're Sgt. Murano," the major said, flicking the ashes off his cigar. "I don't know whether to give you a medal or court martial you."

"Sir?" Fred said startled. The wounded Maj. Sanders would never have been as brusque. The new CO must be trying to make sure the men knew the difference between the two.

"I heard about your taking over the platoon when Lt. Weatherby was killed," Maj. Haskins said, punching his cigar at Fred, "and I heard about your clearing the left flank of the machine gun nests. But I also heard of your recklessly exposing your men to enemy fire. They were jumping up and down all over the place. What was the big idea? Are you trying to get everybody killed or just corner the market on medals?"

The major seemed to be a straight-shooter, and Fred decided to take a chance and be forthright with him.

"Well, sir, the Jerries had us pinned down and were ripping us up," Fred said, nervously reaching up to finger his bandaged ear but stopped short. "We had to keep moving, but in so doing I wanted them to use up their ammunition indiscriminately and shoot at targets they couldn't possibly hit. So I developed what I call the 'Brahms Hop'."

"The Brahms..."

"...Hop."

"What in the hell is the 'Brahms Hop'?"

"Well, sir, it's to widely disperse the targets at least forty-five degrees apart to force the Jerries to fire at the men who keep popping up and down. Apparently, the Jerries have a shooting gallery mentality, and they'll shoot at anything that moves. I was just providing them with targets they couldn't hit, because they had to keep swinging the heavy barrels of the MG-42's to and fro without having time to aim. They kept squeezing off six-round bursts at random just like they were trained to do."

"And that's what kept you men pinned down, wasn't it?"

"Not exactly, sir," Fred explained. "I headed in a direct line up the middle with the other men giving me cover to wait for the pause."

"What pause?"

"It's the critical pause that occurs when they use up their 250-round belt from the belt box and have to change barrels to keep them from overheating. It takes them anywhere from six to ten seconds, depending how rattled they become. That's when I rush up and put them out of commission with a couple of grenades."

"How many in your platoon were lost to the machine guns?"

"Just three. The mortars and Screaming Meemies produced

most of the casualties."

"Incredible," the officer intoned in admiration without changing his expression. "Who told you about the MG-42's?"

"I learned about them from an ordnance manual in heavy weapons training at Camp Shelby, sir."

"I suppose if it works, it works," the major said, taking a puff of his cigar. "But what made you abandon your tactics if they were so successful and go on a suicidal Banzai bayonet charge in terrain like that where you could barely crawl?"

"We had to keep moving, sir. The men were bunching up together, and we were being pinned down, and it was getting more and more dangerous. They were rolling their grenades down our backs. The situation was intolerable."

"Didn't you think of falling back and digging in on the foothill below?"

"No, sir, that would have been unthinkable," Fred said, stiffening as if his spine were a steel flat spring. "We would have had to show our backs to the Jerries."

"Well, I'll be damned!" The CO pursed his lips and blew a steady stream of smoke into the room. "Sergeant, did you know yours is probably the first bayonet charge ever mounted against the Germans?"

"No, sir."

"They're not used to that kind of treatment."

"I'm glad we took our objective, sir," Fred said casually but was nevertheless extremely pleased. For himself and his men.

"Yes...well, er...your platoon sustained the least number of casualties and took the greatest number of prisoners. Now I can see why. You leave me in a quandary, sergeant. Next time try to go by the book, will you? I know you'll probably disregard that."

"I'll keep it in mind, sir," Fred promised and added: "My men always come first."

"By the way, sergeant. Why Brahms? He was a German. Is there something I'm missing in the irony?"

"No, sir," Fred said and allowed a slight smile to brighten his features. "Brahms is my favorite composer." He did not mention how listening to Brahms had always been life-giving. The music never failed to send his soul soaring.

The CO looked at Fred as though he were befuddled. He waved his cigar, ready to say something further but wordlessly stuck it back in his mouth.

"That is all, sergeant."

"Thank you, sir," Fred said and saluted smartly, did an about-face and marched out of the room.

"Got your tail chewed off?" the orderly asked.

"I wouldn't call it that," Fred said cryptically.

"The old man has been issuing orders all day long to get ready for the push against Monte Cassino."

"I don't want to hear about it."

"You will sooner or later."

"I'm sure I will."

"I'll need your report."

"Lt. Weatherby died instantly in the flooded plain at the Rapido River."

"I'll need more than that to complete the I Company report."

"Later," Fred said, his stomach churning. The nervous grumbling of his innards turned into hunger now that the debriefing had ended. He stuck his hand into his pocket and rubbed the penny between his fingers as he stepped out of the building.

Fred joined Mike who had been waiting outside during Fred's meeting with the CO. As the two of them were walking toward the outskirts of town, Sam Hatayama came running up to them.

"Been looking all over for you," he said, out of breath. "Where you guys headed for?"

"Someplace dry and warm to bed down for the night which is going to turn nasty, certainly not a night to spend in a freezing tent," Fred said.

"Like a soft bed with a goose down mattress," Sam said.

"And kick the farmer and wife out of their room?" Fred said. "No, nothing like that, just something simple like a dry barn."

"A barn?" Sam said. "Shit, we liberated the town. We should be able to get a room and the full royal treatment."

"You forget," Mike said, "this town doesn't belong to us. We're just passing through."

"That's correct," Fred said. "We're guests, and we had better act like guests. The people didn't ask for the war."

"Hell, help yourself to what you can get is what I say," Sam said, his bellicose attitude still intact. Killing Jerries seemed to be his cup of tea.

"It's not going to work that way while you're with me," Fred said.

They approached a farmhouse that was more or less intact, except for several blasted out windows. Fred knocked on the battered door. It was answered by a short and stocky farmer. His wife peered apprehensively at the men over her husband's shoulder.

"We have nothing," the farmer said. "The Germans left us nothing."

"Don't worry," Fred said. "We'll pay for everything in lira and cigarettes. All we want is a warm place to sleep the night, and I don't want to take your bedroom away from you. Your barn would be fine, just for the night."

Fred placed a stack of bills and a pack of cigarettes in the farmer's hand. "Enough?" The farmer nodded.

"How much more for a bottle of wine and a candle?" Fred asked.

The farmer held up one finger. Fred turned toward Sam and said: "Fork over a pack."

"That's pretty steep. The goddamn geezer is making money off of us," Sam said as he reluctantly fished the cigarettes from his shirt pocket.

"They've got to live, too," Fred said and took the pack from him and handed it to the man. He went into the house and returned with a bottle that was almost full and a stubby candle. Fred thanked him, and the three men made for the barn which was empty, devoid of the usual farm animals that must have abounded in it at one time: chickens, pigs, cattle. There wasn't even a stray dog or cat roaming in town. The men dropped their gear on the hard-packed ground. They lunged into the pile of hay and lay spreadeagle on it. The first thing they did was to remove their boots and massage their feet.

"Now for a nice, warm fire," Sam said.

"Make it a small one or you'll burn the place down," Fred said.

"Not to worry. I didn't go camping as a kid for nothing. All I got to do is clear a space in the center of the dirt floor," Sam said, setting about the task.

"What're are you going use for firewood?" Fred asked.

"I'll bust up some of these chicken coops."

"No, you're not. Mike, go find some outside, debris, bits and pieces of anything that will burn. We're not going to destroy the man's barn."

"He's just a goddamn Mussolini-lover—"

"I said we're guests in the man's house, Sam. This is part of his house, and we pay as we go. Those are the rules."

"Sometimes, you get on a man's nerves, Fred," his wiry friend from Hood River said, annoyed.

"And sometimes you can be a pain, buddy," Fred shot back. "Now keep the fire small, because all we need to do is to heat our rations."

"Betcha they're eating better in the farmhouse."

"I doubt it."

Mike came back with an armload of kindling, and Sam proceeded to build a small fire which lit the dim interior of the barn with flickering licks of light. As they ate their canned rations of meat and passed the bottle of wine around, they sank into a melancholy of silence. They had all received mail from back home. Instead of tearing open the letters in ecstasy as some of the others did who did not have families behind barbed wire fences, they opened theirs in private and read the contents circumspectly. The three of them had known each other since they were boys, and they shared their thoughts freely–which was rare among those with interned families. They were usually very private people. Mike and Sam sat around the fire to read their mail, while Fred placed the stub of the lit candle on a shelf and stood and read his.

"Says here my sister is engaged to get married to a draft resister," Mike said incredulously. "Now they're going into the camps to draft the boys while they're still imprisoned. They're not about to let them sit out the war and warm their duffs. And some of them are organizing to resist the draft like they're doing in a big way in the camp at Heart Mountain, Wyoming."

"I don't blame them," Fred said. "Not in the least bit."

"*We* volunteered, didn't we?" Sam said and spat into the fire.

"Volunteering and being drafted against your will under the circumstances are two different things," Fred said evenly.

"But where's their fightin' spirit?" Sam said. "Patriotism doesn't change."

"Neither does the voice of conscience," Fred argued. "You still have to listen to what's right in your heart according to your beliefs." Fred felt like launching into a lecture, much like the kind he listened to studiously in the classroom–a long time ago, it seemed.

"Some marriage," Mike broke in. "She's going to be stuck in the mud and dust of Minidoka, and he's going to rot in Leavenworth if they organize like the boys in Wyoming, both behind fences and gun towers. What a joke, eh?"

"Funny, funny, funny!" Sam sneered.

"Funny, hah-hah, no," Mike retorted. "Funny, queer, yeah. The government is queer in the head."

"It's the grossest kind of irony," Fred said.

"Yeah, you're right for a change," Sam said pointedly. "But what about this one? My mother writes this...my sister is going out with a yogore, a bum who is a member of a gang of teenage punks. They go to the mess hall together, hang out together and smoke and everything and roam around the camp getting into fights."

"No irony there," Mike claimed. "Everybody's gone queer in the head with nothing to do but get into trouble."

"For once, Mike, *you're* right. Out of a whole camp of nice boys, she has to pick a yogore. As her big brother, I'm going to write to her to break up with him. The whole thing is nothing but a mistake."

"He could also turn out to be a decent man and citizen, given half a chance," Fred said. "We were all teenagers not too long ago."

"Playing ball, going on family picnics, feasting on New Year's *gotchiso*," Mike said, scooping a last bit of meat out of the tin with the spoon. "And before the evacuation, we all—"

"Don't even talk about it, Mike," Sam snarled.

"You're like a hair-trigger mouse trap, touchy about *everything* ever since we landed in Italy," Mike said. "What happened to that cheerful, good-natured, easygoing guy we played ball with, whose idea of a cuss word was 'Bless it'? It was 'Bless it' this and 'Bless it' that when you botched a grounder or struck out."

"Can it, goddamn it!" Sam said. "That was then, before the war and roundup, and now is now. Everything has changed."

"You mean," Mike laughed cruelly, "I can't even joke about your talking yourself into being seduced by that babe in camp, the one who—"

"Save it, Mike," Fred said. "And you can quit acting tough. I was downwind of you, remember?"

"Yeah, yeah," Mike said soberly and finished the remnants of his meal and as though to castigate himself added: "Like I said, if smell could kill, I could have won the war singlehanded." He turned pensive for a moment, then looked up at Fred standing at the shelf. "Anyway, Fred, what's up at Tule Lake? Your Papa change his mind about going back to Japan and taking Arthur and Margaret with him?"

"Not a chance," Fred sighed. "He's bitter about everything. How's this one for the books? There was a riot in the camp with tanks, armed troops and tear gas and the whole bit. Seems a trigger-happy guard gunned down one of the truck drivers when he was leaving the camp to pick up supplies. He was a new guard and words were exchanged before he would open the gate. And he just shot the guy. Can you beat that?" Fred paused with a catch in his throat and snapped the letter in the air angrily. "Margie says the atmosphere in the camp was volatile to begin with. Rumors were flying around that the camp authorities were selling their meat destined for the mess halls on the black market. The pro-Japanese leaders being crammed in the stockade and being tortured, and the shooting was the last straw. The driver lay on the ground and bled to death while the guard waved everybody away. He was hauled off by some other guards who personally knew the driver. What a place to grow up in! Poor Margie and Arthur!"

"Sounds like Tule Lake turned into a hellhole," Mike said.

"It has," Fred agreed and continued. "The worst part is Arthur going to Japanese school to learn how to be a good little Japanese, instead of an American. He's caught in an impossible situation. Poor kid. He's probably more confused than a lost pup."

"It's hard on the youngsters," Mike said. "At least we're old enough to exercise our own grey matter."

"The young ones are going to come out with a stinkin' persecution complex," Sam predicted. "At least we have a chance to work that kind of shit out of our system by killing Jerries."

"Killing? All in the name of proving our loyalty?" queried Mike caustically. "You're in love with your M1."

"Something like that. Kill as many of the sonuvabitches as you can to get the damn war over and done with."

"As far as I'm concerned, it's got nothing to do with proving you're loyal," Fred said. "I already know I'm loyal. They've doubted us, but I don't doubt myself. I'm a free man fighting for freedom, for our folks and all of us."

"Us Nisei?" Mike said. "You think we're free men?"

"Of course," Fred said. "We're born free...just haven't had a chance to act like it."

"You still an ever-lovin' idealist, Fred?" Sam asked, snickering.

The Lost Fox

"Yeah, you might say that. You got to be in order to stay sane."

"You got it turned around, Fred," Sam said. "You got to be a filthy cynic, and the filthier the better."

"Never!" Fred said and snapped the letter angrily again. "You have to be a *tempered* idealist to see what's happening to the world."

"You're training to be a preacher, aren't you, Fred?" Sam asked archly.

"Might have to become one after this is over," Fred said, ignoring Sam's acrimony which he thought he understood. "Who knows? But I had planned to teach college before I was yanked out of school."

"You see what kind of dreamer Fred is?" Mike said. "I mean it. His dreams keep us alive. No kidding. Here we can get jobs only in the fields, warehouses and produce, and he thinks about becoming a college professor."

"You got to dream and dream big," Fred said with conviction. "The bigger the better."

"They'll just shoot you down!" Sam said knowingly. "Life is a nightmare. The war is a nightmare, racism is a nightmare, and you better get ready for a shitload."

"Whatever," Fred said and turned toward the candle. He was going to say, a dreamer in their position had to be tough at the same time to achieve that fine balancing act between being an idealist and a realist, but he thought better of it–it would be too much like preaching to which he was given–and Mike and Sam already knew all there was to having to be tough. He opened the second letter he had received. It was from his sister, Rhonda, in Minidoka.

As he was reading her letter in which she wrote about her

59

loneliness in camp, the harsh winter–the warm clothes she had ordered from Sears had not arrived yet–and the unpalatable diet and communal living, Fred traveled back in time to the days of the mass evacuation. He was a junior at the University of Oregon in Eugene and was shocked to find notices posted that alerted the Japanese population to the fact that they were to be incarcerated. They were given a week's notice to dispose of their homes and businesses and belongings and pack only what they could carry. He could still see the gigantic mountain of tagged baggage, bearing the numbers that they wore around their necks. Impersonal numbers that took the place of names which the whites found unpronounceable, numbers that did not reflect the reality of real human beings being herded into camps against their will. There was generally no show of resistance, only a docile kind of ac-quiescence, since the older community leaders were hastily rounded up by the FBI after the bombing of Pearl Harbor, and the Japanese American Citizens League, led by a 21-year old spokes-man of the Japanese, urged submissive cooperation with the government. The rest of the populace was left without a voice. There was no means of resistance. What few guns they had for self-defense were confiscated along with swords, cameras and radios. Fred himself could not see himself shooting another American. Nevertheless, they were guarded by soldiers with fixed bayonets and by machine guns directed straight at them in the concentration camps.

He remembered the stench of the horse stalls at the first assembly center built at the Portland stockyards. A slab of asphalt was layered over the straw and manure covered stalls which were whitewashed and equipped with a naked light bulb and a couple of beds. They were given ticks that smelled like mold to fill with straw for their mattresses. Their first meal in the huge mess hall was chunked tripe stewed in milk. The latrines weren't completed yet, so the men had to dig enormous trenches for the outhouses. Named *Camp Adventure* to rival their northern neighbor's *Camp Harmony*, it was their first introduction to what the authorities called "protective custody."

Fred was angry but sobered by the enormity of his dislocation and could only feel impotent. Helpless, without even the verve to shake his fist at the sky. Most of the evacuees were American citizens, but they were lumped together with the enemy because they looked like the enemy. They were no better than stereotyped animals with comic book features: Hirohito buck teeth and slant eyes. Japs, the designated scapegoats of the land. Fred felt the paralysis of the mind and soul along with the rest of the people. He had been studying world history and literature, but he could not conjure up any words of solace to comfort himself in his moment of crisis. The word that branded itself into his consciousness was BETRAYAL, and he couldn't even begin to comprehend the totality of the fundamental treachery that had been perpetrated against him and his kind without reason, without due process, only with the closed, blind fist of racist rancor. He felt small and battered–and yet unyielding.

Rhonda wrote that she worked at every job she could find which included joining a contingent of laborers who worked in the sugar beets fields and sent money to Arthur and Margaret in Tule Lake while spending the rest on war bonds. She still felt like an outsider, and the few people she did know from before the war treated her with disdain because of their father's pro-Japanese sympathies. She did not sleep well. The noises in the adjacent rooms kept her awake. Even the crying of the baby in the room at the end of the barrack could be heard through the walls. The food was terrible, but she didn't want to complain, because she was sure he was having a harder time of it on the battlefields of Italy. But she couldn't help crying out against the inequity of being singled out as scapegoats. They were even accused of hoarding food, sugar in particular, and a search party made up of armed security guards combed each barrack in each block looking for something that the general public on the outside sorely lacked and the internees were supposed to have, the rumor being that they were pampered.

As he read his sister's letter, Fred could not help but feel the same confused anger rising in his belly. He tried to tamp it down and remind himself why he had volunteered. It wasn't only for the virtues of democracy, but it was something more, something deep within him that had to be proved. The entire backdrop of the concentration camps and incarceration only served to fuel an intense desire to find within himself the freedom to be. If he were fighting for any one thing, it was precisely the kind of freedom that guaranteed his prerogative to explore his own potential as an individual, not as a sociological entity that had to bow down to the dictates of society or to any stereotypical model. In a sense he was challenging and pitting himself against the odds to start on a journey of *becoming* by taking the first step toward fighting the battle of virtual survival. In the battlefields of Europe, confronted by the Nazi menace. Fight to survive and survive to fight, he told himself, as though the reminder were an essential part of a battle plan. He was fighting for everything America represented–the dreams and hopes of an unlimited promise.

But beyond that lay a vast, nebulous wilderness of uncharted terrain and the desolation of a lonely exploration that would take him into the unknown. What he was facing was none other than the completion of himself. The first great barrier was the war, a war he had volunteered to fight, a war which he *had* to volunteer to fight, if ever he was to know manhood.

He took out a pencil and paper and began writing a letter to Rhonda. He told of the fighting and the conditions they had to face, but he tried to sound lighthearted as though he were in high spirits–belied by his perpetual dry mouth (he recalled the hammering shock of the first bullet slamming against his helmet) and slight tremor of the hands. His confidence was high; everything was going to be fine. Rhonda was sensitive enough to read between the lines and discern the true horror of the war. Fred only wished he could soften the blow of the letters she would receive from the front, from the only member of the family she had grown to trust.

Reminded of their responsibilities, he instructed Rhonda to uphold her end as the older sister by writing to young Arthur and Margaret and rallying them on, and he in turn wrote another letter to his young brother and sister to write to Rhonda to cheer her up. Even from the battlefield, he felt he had to try to hold the family together. He didn't mention his parents' projected return to Japan–the land of their enemy. He knew his father to be a stubborn man and his writing him a letter in his primitive Japanese would not dissuade him from repatriating. His main concern was the safety of the family in a land that was increasingly subjected to daily bombing raids, as was written up in *Stars & Stripes*.

As morning dawned, the men nestled deeply in the dry, warm straw stirred awake and rose up to slip on their boots. They built another small fire to heat up their canned ham and eggs and chewed meditatively, wondering what the orders were to be. They knew they weren't going to spend much time in the rest area with the fight for Monte Cassino mounting each day; they were determined to make the most of the amenities provided by the lull in fighting.

Shouldering their rifles, they were making their way toward the bivouac area when they decided to stop in at the USO club and chat with the Doughnut Dollies and have a cup of java. The scent of the woman who served him coffee and handed him a doughnut stirred Fred, and he almost blushed at his own reaction. He conversed smoothly enough with the blonde, but his heart was racing as if he were going into battle. Her freshly pressed uniform made her stand out among the drably clad soldiers who crowded into the building. It managed to remain intact in spite of the shelling.

Still munching a handful of doughnuts, they stepped along the rows of tents and slid into the ones they had set up for themselves but left unused. They took off their boots to air their feet and lay on the blankets, wondering what turn the war was going to take next. They didn't have to wait long.

Maj. Haskins bellowed at the rows of tents set up in the clearing at the edge of town.

"I Company! Get ready to move out in an hour. Off your asses and move. We've got a war to win."

"He's no Maj. Sanders, is he?" Mike said, lying beside Fred.

"Certainly not the father figure Maj. Sanders was, that's for sure," Fred said. "That was one of his shortcomings, they said. He cared too much for his troops and took too many chances and almost got himself killed."

"The best kind of officer," Sam said tiredly, as they readied their packs, "is the kind that thinks his men are walking pieces of meat armed with rifles. That way nobody gives a shit."

"You saying we're expendable and disposable, Sam?" Mike asked with ringing indignation.

"Haven't said it aloud yet."

"That's a helluva attitude," Fred said. "A good officer always has to be ready to commit, regardless of his personal feelings."

"Could always work the other way around," Sam said, pursuing his point. "Good officer or not, he's gonna have to feed Japs to the Jerries."

"Are you saying 'yellow gristle' for the sausage grinder," Mike said sarcastically to add to Sam's brutal analogy.

"Exactly."

"Come on, now, Sam," Mike enjoined. "We're here to do a job. Get rid of your damn sour attitude."

"That's why they need us noncoms," Fred said to change the subject. "To play wet nurse to both the green horns and fresh officers."

"And at the rate we're being chewed up, you got your work cut out for you, mother," Sam said.

Fred nodded wordlessly. Let Sam get it out of his system. He could only try to exude the kind of confidence he really didn't feel, but it was his job as the platoon sergeant. Bolster the morale of the men, keep them in a fighting mood, regardless of his own reservations about himself. He had supreme confidence in them, having trained together and knowing them and how they thought and felt. An undying sense of brotherhood was the blood-life of the esprit de corps instilled in them. There were buddhaheads from Hawaii and kotonks from the mainland. Though they didn't get along together well in the beginning, as time went on during basic training in Camp Shelby, they were forged into a unified combat team whose spirit had been amply exemplified already by the sacrifices of the 100th Battalion, which, ripped up by the Germans till it could no longer function, earned more Purple Hearts than any other group of men.

Chapter Five

The men of I Company climbed into the string of awaiting trucks, thankful now of the winter clothing since the freezing cold had turned bitter, and bounced along the road that would take them to the outskirts of the town of Cassino, partially liberated for a while by the 100th Battalion. But it was retaken by the desperate Germans. From there they were to march to the line where fierce fighting had already begun with Allied casualties mounting by the minute, so entrenched were the Germans on Monte Cassino where the Benedictine monastery was transformed into a fortress that they could annihilate anything that moved in the plains of the winding Rapido River and in the open spaces and roads of Liri Valley. Tanks, self-propelled guns, artillery, including the deadly 88's, nebelwerfers, MG-42's, MG-34's, mines, mortars, a division of crack veteran German troops armed with machine pistols, grenades and flame throwers turned the mountain into a juggernaut of Teutonic defiance.

The clouds soared over the mountains in convoluted, tortured explosions of manifold shapes, and the blue sky hid its vast expanse except in patches that escaped the cruising clouds. The peaceful sky and mountaintops forced one to guide his vision toward the lower regions where the cannonade of artillery fire rumbled and rolled through the valley as thunder split the air ahead of the men.

Every farmhouse they passed had somehow been a casualty of war, bitterly sought and fought for by both sides. Farm animals hastily and partially carved for their meat lay stiffly in the fields. The wounded and dead had already been evacuated, and the burned and twisted hulks of the machines of war were pushed off to the sides. The road had been cleared of mines, and the troops sped on toward their destination, the outskirts of the town of Cassino which lay sprawled at the foot of Monte Cassino. It was designated simply as Hill 165. According to what Jim had heard, he renamed it "Butcher Hill."

The men alighted from the trucks at the edge of Cassino and were immediately subjected to a bombardment of artillery fire. They hugged the walls of isolated farmhouses while their ranks were formed and at the command dashed out into the open and crossed a field to join the assault on Hill 165 only to be slowed down by another flooded plain, a result of diverting the Rapido River flowing by the town.

The area had been swept of mines and the going was easier than the previous confrontation, but Fred couldn't help noticing the red tinge of blood in the muddy water. Many of the attacking 34th Division which included the 100th Battalion had fallen in the water, cut down by the machine guns and mortars. The company had to slog its way to the foot of the mountain where Fred could spot his comrades in a firefight with the crack SS division. The enemy was well concealed. He could only see the American troops attacking and falling on the slopes. Most of the destruction was concentrated on them, but as Fred and his company approached the line, they too came under fire and took casualties. The men trotted clumsily through the water, which was in some places waist deep, and then crouched down in the vacated slit trenches as the Screaming Meemies began to descend on them. The horrendous rocket-launched projectiles screeched like insane banshees out to terrify and decimate. Fred's platoon commander, a replacement, 2nd Lt. John Partridge, waved them on to a skirmish line facing a formidable redoubt while the rest of the platoons spread out to cover their flanks. The terrain was rocky, and the redoubt stuck out like a promontory commanding the higher ground with a 180 degree field of vision. The ground ahead of them was littered with the dead and wounded. Their own artillery created a protective smoke screen as they advanced to within a few hundred yards of the nest of machine guns, but the dense sheet of fire stopped them cold.

Lt. Partridge called in the coordinates and within minutes the incoming shells started to scream overhead to pound the rocky ledge. The shelling lasted for a quarter of an hour but it seemed longer to Fred. The ground beneath him shook. Nothing could survive such a barrage, Fred thought, and when the firing lifted, the lieutenant waved the men on: "Take 'em."

They got up and started to run across the open ground which still had a few grape vines growing out of it but were stymied by a stream of burping bursts of machine gun fire. They hit the ground. They were too close for artillery support again, and Fred knew they would have to dig the Jerries out by force—or by luck. He turned to look for Mike and Sam.

"Sir," Fred said to the officer, "if you can get the BAR to occupy the second machine gun, I think I can take the one on the end."

"Go ahead, sergeant."

"Sam, Mike," Fred yelled and pointed to the machine gun. "The hop."

The two men crawled left and right while Fred inched his way up the middle. "Now," he yelled. The two men acted like pop-up targets at a carnival. Fred slithered up, keeping his eye on the barrel, while the BAR man and the second machine gun were dueling it out on his left. The flanking platoon, sensing what was going on, gave him support from his right. Fred hugged the ground and crawled from rock to rock like a snake to within thirty yards of the entrenched gun. A German spotted him and stood up in the opening to kill him with his machine pistol, but Fred shot him first with a burst from his grease gun. Without waiting for the pause, Fred rose up and threw a grenade into the nest and silenced the gun. Before he could rise up again, the men on his right, the 3rd platoon, who had been crawling up with him, rushed into the cavity left by the grenade and proceeded to infiltrate the network of trenches that linked the nests. They managed to clean out each nest in succession and secured the ledge that guarded the entrance to the road up the mountain.

The 3rd platoon took over the trenches and remained in them through the night while the rest of the company dug in, expecting a counterattack at any moment. The entrenchment was vital to the overall security of the mountain, and it was unlikely that the Germans would let it go without attempting to retake it. The flares lit up the other parts of the battlefield where a line had been established and the fight raged on, but in their sector no flares burst overhead to light the ground, possibly because it was open, and the Germans feared their own machine guns they had left behind when they fled would be turned on them. Instead there were probing night patrols to determine the company's whereabouts and their readiness, and it resulted in sporadic firefights. The company sent their own patrols out to locate the enemy's defenses, and even took a prisoner who told them of tanks and minefields ahead. He was escorted to battalion headquarters. The men spent a sleepless night, holding their weapons ready as the Germans probed their lines.

Fred took a squad with him to investigate the left flank skirting the road, crawling noiselessly in the dark and trying to avoid setting off any mines. His heavy winter clothes had not dried completely since crossing the cold, flooded plain, and the night air filtered through the dampness to chill his whole body. He could never get warm enough in action so far; he was afraid that even if it were in the middle of summer he would still feel the cold chill of fear and the dryness of mouth, his tongue like a piece of rough cardboard. The six-man squad glided smoothly over the ground, feeling with numb fingers for trip wires and other signs of mines ahead of them. It took them an hour to cover a 100 yards when they stopped cold. The voices of the Germans could be heard penetrating the frigid night.

Fred squinted hard in the darkness and crawled closer. He could see the barrel of a machine gun pointed toward where they were entrenched. He and his men reconnoitered in a lateral line toward their right and heard more voices, more numerous and concentrated this time. He was convinced he had hit the next redoubt which the enemy had built up and would try to hold. The enemy defenses were staggered 100-200 yards from their own position.

As they were crawling back, they encountered a German patrol returning to its lines and flattened themselves against the ground. They held their breath. The night was dark, so dark Fred could hardly see his hand in front of him. The cloud covering worked to their advantage, and the patrol passed them without becoming aware of their presence just a few feet away. Fred and his men were under orders to avoid a firefight, if at all possible, and to get back in one piece, since there were no men to spare, and report their findings.

They began slithering back to their position. When within reach they were challenged: "Geronimo."

"Apache," Fred said hoarsely.

"Come on in," came the voice. "But be quiet."

Fred reported back to the lieutenant who relayed the information to the command post. The 3rd Battalion of which I Company was a part was to join the remnants of the 34th Division and 100th Battalion which had been on the line for a week to mount an all-out assault on the mountain that had defied previous Allied efforts to go through it rather than around it, which was inconceivable because of the German command of the heights covering Liri Valley. So far Allied casualties amounted to 30,000 dead or wounded, and the SS Panzer Division still held fast. The debate whether or not to bomb the historically important monastery raged back and forth in the upper echelons of the general staff and in Washington and London while the ranks of the men on the slopes were decimated.

Fred and his squad turned in for the night but remained only half asleep, since the sporadic gunfire up and down the line kept them awake and on the alert. They had to be fresh in the morning, however, and tried to get as much sleep as they could. Fred doubted whether they could easily take the next line of fortifications. The moans of the wounded left behind them filtered through the darkness. They haunted Fred; the sounds came from his brothers. The comforting voices of the medics still at work in the dark could be heard interlaced between cries for help. Fred felt they would have their hands full again the next day. So far he had come through with only a torn ear, but would he be so lucky in the morrow?

As the dark of the night was gradually overtaken by the grey dawn, the men began to stir. Though the fighting in the other sectors had raged on all night under the light of flares, the men on either side of the field seemed reluctant to confront one another when they could see each other for only brief moments at a time. The men of I Company expected a counterattack at any moment, and it came at first light just as they had anticipated. The Germans attacked in force. The shrieking nebelwerfers, mortars and machine guns accompanied the attack. They approached the captured entrenchment dangerously close, but the men of the 3rd platoon had mastered the sights of the MG-42 and began cutting the attacking Germans down with their abandoned guns and sent them scurrying back to their fortifications. The 1st and 2nd platoons rose up in pursuit but were pinned down and had to dig in. The German attacked again, desperate to regain their original position, but the men of 442nd held. The medics rushed from one fallen soldier to another under intense fire. Some fell to sniper fire, and the rage grew within the men. Many wanted to mount an attack of their own but were restrained. The snipers continued to take their toll as the men tried to find shelter and clawed their way into the ground.

Fred wished he had a sniper rifle of their own, an M1-D with a superior Lyman scope, so he could pick the eyes out of the Jerries, but they had to make do with the iron peep sights of the Garand M1, the standard issue. Now he had abandoned even the M1 in favor of the tommy gun for close-in combat. But he lay pinned down with the rest of his men and could only feebly exchange fire with the machine guns, jumping up every so often to fire at the closest one just to harass them. The feared MG-42's raked the field with interlocking fire so that the men could not move from their hastily dug slit trenches. They spent the day exchanging fire with the Jerries, but there was hardly any point to it. The men of the 442nd had to take the fortifications in order to advance to the next line of emplacements, and the mountain was covered with nests and bunkers. How they were to proceed against such meticulously prepared defenses was beyond understanding; all they knew was that they had to keep moving forward.

Word was sent up and down the line that they were to attack at 2200 hours after night had settled in. They were to crawl noiselessly across the field and take out the bunkers and nests with grenades–the hard way, with fixed bayonets. At the given moment, the three platoons moved silently into the night with the 1st platoon taking the road that flanked the German position. Fred's own platoon moved up the middle with the 3rd, leaving behind a team of machine gunners, occupying their right flank. They crouched as though they were beasts of burden under the cold sky and made their way slowly toward what appeared to be certain death. If they could only get close enough to take out the first few nests, Fred thought, they would stand a chance of routing the others. Their orders were to proceed to straighten out the skirmish line with the other companies that had advanced a 100 yards into the German position elsewhere on the mountain.

Someone on the road tripped a mine, a Bouncing Betty, that jumped up waist-high into the air and exploded with a din and a flash and spread shrapnel like a deadly orange blossom. That was what the Germans were waiting for–some sign of activity. Flares streaked into the sky and bloomed with an eerie light that illuminated the field and men. Machine gun and small arms fire opened up; the captured machine guns behind the men responded as the men raced across what seemed a vast open expanse, every inch of which was covered by gunfire. When they were about to close in on the emplacements, they entered a mine field, and the explosions threw men and debris into the air. The machine gun fire was an interlocked curtain of carnage. Men fell clutching their bodies at odd angles or were simply hammered down, and they cried out, "Medic! Medic!," while some lay slumped and did not utter a sound.

A German tank rumbled into action and fired at the 1st platoon at point-blank range, its machine gun chattering death and ripping up the road and embankment the men tried to climb only to be met by a hail of bullets from above. More flares sailed into the sky, and the brightly lit battlefield erupted into violence with the tank spouting the orange-red flame of massive firepower. The men of the three platoons could not get close enough to use the grenades effectively. The man with the bazooka was killed and his weapon rendered useless by a direct hit from the tank. The ranks wavered for an instant, then pushed forward. The Germans resisted fiercely, and the men of the 442nd fell one after another, vulnerable shields of flesh that were torn and ripped.

At last a command rang out: "Fall back! Fall back!"

The men stepped backwards, never turning their backs, and kept firing their weapons. They moved back to their original position and slid into any slit trench they could find. The wounded were crying out in pain, and the medics began to dash about in the sudden darkness. Night covered the battlefield like a thick poultice. A strange silence washed over the dead and dying; it was broken only by sudden shrieks, much like the scream of terror when the unexpected happens in dense darkness. Where there were gunfire and explosions ripping the air in the blossoming light of black and white shadows only moments before, now there was cold silence, an unnerving dead stillness, punctuated by cries for help and the moaning of the mortally wounded.

Fred's breath came in ragged gasps that wracked his body. He wasn't out of breath; his belly was tight with fear. How he came out of that firefight without even a scratch was miraculous. He drew in the air in large gulps. As he fingered his lucky penny, rubbing it between his fingers, he felt himself relax and the cramp in his stomach disappear. He called out to Mike and Sam in the darkness. They were on either side of him. They, too, were all right. Nothing short of a miracle, thought Fred. He wondered what orders Lt. Partridge had next. The blackness of the night was as dense as a thickly painted backdrop. It was as if someone had taken a brush and swept it across the landscape and sky. Fred squirmed in his hole to stay warm.

The lines held by the 34th Division had buckled in places, but the 100th Battalion and the 442nd Regimental Combat Team held their ground. The casualties were numerous, and the medics and litter bearers wandered about among the squads hustling up ammo, water and food. Every so often a German gun would open up to harass the men, but the fighting for the night tapered off into a sporadic exchange of gunfire.

The bastion of Monte Cassino, the monastery fortress, remained intact. Several hundred civilians who had worked as laborers in building up the fortifications remained hidden within. No decision had been reached as to when or if the monastery would be bombed. It was considered a world treasure housing priceless works of art that the Germans, however, had already removed for safekeeping elsewhere. The Germans were committed to holding Monte Cassino at all costs. It represented the last stronghold in the Cassino Line–north of the now broken Gustav Line–that halted the Allied advance to Rome through the Liri Valley.

Fred dozed fitfully in the chill that robbed him of any warmth provided by the winter coat, and as dawn broke as grey as he was wretched, he stretched his stiff body and wondered what was in store for them that day. As if to answer his question, the German guns raked the field of fire with short bursts at first light to dissuade the troops from even thinking about mounting another attack. Fred crawled out of his hole and scrambled to the trenches where the lieutenant was concealed along with the radioman.

"What's the plan, Lieutenant," Fred asked after sliding into the trench. The officer was studying a map.

"I don't know yet, Sergeant," came the reply. "But we can't try what we did yesterday or we'll lose the whole outfit, and artillery support is concentrated on the eastern slope below the monastery, and they can't cover for us right now. I'll let you know as soon as I establish contact with battalion headquarters."

"Right," Fred said and rushed back to his hole. He knew he had a few minutes before any orders were issued, so he took advantage of the lull by digging out his rations from his pack.

"What's the story?" Mike called.

"Wait and see," Fred said, his mouth full. He tried frantically to work up enough saliva to swallow the dry crackers.

"Wait and see," Sam repeated sarcastically, "while the Jerry snipers pick us off one by one."

"Just don't stick your dumb head up," Mike said.

"Yeah, yeah," Sam said. "He sees a head and it turns into a melon in his scope, ripe, red and ready to burst. The sharpshooter is going to have a field day."

As if to test his theory, Sam peered over the edge of his hole at the German position to scan the field for a few seconds. He pulled his head back like a turtle shrinking into its shell just before a bullet kicked up dirt where his head had been and was followed by the report of a high powered rifle.

"That lousy, goddamn Jerry was ready for me," Sam said, hunkering down.

"Better get something to eat," Fred said, chewing quickly as if under orders.

Fred finished the rest of his meal. He tossed out the plastic-like cheese that tasted like a rubber shoe and ate the rest of the crackers, washing the mouthful down with a small swallow of water from his canteen. The lull didn't last long. As he was defecating in his helmet, sounds of a firefight erupted on their left flank, and the tank proceeded to creak and rumble down the road. A contingent of infantry followed it. Without help the 1st platoon would be wiped out. Fred emptied the helmet outside his hole, wiped the inside off with a piece of tissue and crammed it back on his head. He gathered a squad, and the men ran hunched over toward the sounds of the fray. He picked up a bazooka, reasoning that the one the 1st platoon had was nonfunctional or they would have knocked out the tank as soon as it rounded the bend in the road, and he had Sam collect several rockets. On cue the MG-42's opened up and followed them across the field, tearing up the ground around them.

In a matter of seconds, Fred and his men reached the road and crossed it in several leaps and wound up in a ditch with the remnants of the 1st platoon. The tank's guns had them plastered to the ground. Fred asked the sergeant who had taken over where his bazooka man was, and he was told he had caught it full flush.

Fred rose up and took aim with the bazooka. Sam loaded it and tapped him on the helmet. Ready to fire. The Panzer had been approaching their position inexorably, but upon spying the bazooka leveled at it put itself into reverse and was backing away when Fred pressed the trigger. The rocket knocked off the track and the tank was stopped, but it kept spitting deadly fire at them.

"Gimme that thing," a noncom said angrily and grabbed the bazooka.

He ran out into the open with the men firing futilely at the fist of metal behind which the infantrymen hid. He crawled to within twenty-five yards of the tank. A tense moment followed when he was wounded and rolled over stunned. With agonizing slowness, he retrieved the bazooka and let loose at the soft underbelly. The tank exploded into flames, and the Germans who survived the blast hastily tried to exit from the hatch but were cut down by rifle fire and lay draped over the burning pyre. The Nisei men emerged from the ditch and raced up the road, past the tank, chasing the fleeing Germans in a flanking move around the bend in the road but were stopped by a bunker flashing withering fire. They withdrew behind the shoulder of the road and waited. In the meantime, Fred and his squad dashed back to their original position, and Fred dropped the bazooka into the hands of the owner on his way to sliding into his hole as the machine guns followed their progress. As luck would have it, no one was hit. When they slid into their trenches and had taken cover, the firing stopped and again a heavy silence that was vigilant with death hung over the battlefield.

Overhead two P-51 Mustangs were dueling with a duo of German ME-190's in a move to prevent each other from reaching the battlefield of Monte Cassino where they could do great damage with their bombs and strafing. They turned, twisted and wheeled in beautiful arcs to fight for an advantage. Fred had to marvel at their agile freedom of movement. The infantryman was tied to the ground, in the dirt, often on his belly, always clawing at the earth to make himself a smaller target, but the fighters' task was to defy gravity while performing amazing acrobatics in the air. The aerial show lasted for about twenty minutes without any damage to either side, but in the end the Messerschmitts hightailed it with the P-51's in hot pursuit.

With the churlish droning of the fighters gone, the only sounds were the muffled explosions of an artillery barrage below the monastery to their right. Otherwise, their sector was quiet. Fred felt guilty that he wasn't in the thick of it. He knew the 100th Battalion made up of the Hawaiian Nisei were catching the brunt of the action. As the "Purple Heart Battalion," they had survived all the Germans had to offer from Naples to the Volturno River crossing to Monte Cassino until more replacements arrived. Fred wondered what the lieutenant was thinking. All he had heard after they returned from dispatching the tank was his uncharacteristically loud voice cutting through the silence: "Then, goddamn it, at least give me a smoke screen."

Word was passed along the ranks that the attack was to commence at 1400 hours under cover of smoke. At least that much was promised. The men waited. Some spent their time cleaning their rifles. Others curled up in their holes and caught up on some sleep, blowing their breath into the air. A mild breeze laden with a drizzle had arisen and carried the smells of war on their flank across the field. The weather was harsh and frigid, and the men clasped their rifles to their bodies lest the rain freeze the bolts in place. Fred put the grease gun between his legs and waited, staring up at the lowering clouds.

Just before the jump-off point, the shelling began, and plumes of smoke rose into the air. The shelling stopped just as suddenly as it had begun, and the platoon leaders led the way into the dense curtain of smoke as the German machine guns started to burp. The men ran doubled over. Some straightened up with a cry and were thrown backwards as if kicked by a mule and lay still. The smoke screen did not last long because of the wind and drizzle and was sucked away by the weather, leaving the men exposed and rushing toward the blazing guns. They were cut down right and left, but this time there was no turning back nor was there an opportunity for fancy tricks. They had to take the German position the hard way, the only way—with fixed bayonets. The men hit the ground at a run and crawled frantically to get within throwing range for their grenades.

The 1st platoon had already breached the German line of defense on the left flank, and Fred's platoon, the 2nd, and the 3rd platoon squirmed quickly over the rough terrain. Some of the men, riled with impatience and fear, rose up and raced toward the Germans with grenade in hand only to be shot and blown up by their own grenade. As they approached closer, German potato mashers sailed out of the pits and exploded among them. Now it was just as dangerous to be cautious as it was to be brave, and the men rose to their feet and raced across the open space, yelling, "Banzai, Banzai!" The nearest to approach were picked off by snipers, but the men kept moving forward without faltering.

Dodging left and right, Fred ran ahead with his tommy gun blazing. He could see the faces of the Jerries and their grim, determined expressions, and leveled his gun at them to force them to duck. A soldier with a machine pistol rose from the pit to challenge him, but before he could raise his weapon Fred sprayed him with a blast from his gun and switching hands threw a grenade into the emplacement. The concussion threw the Jerries out of the pit, and Fred killed a soldier who was merely stunned and was reaching for a grenade. Jumping into the pit, he then trained the MG-42 on the right flank to take the pressure off the 3rd platoon which had a greater distance to cover and engaged the machine gun which he knocked out with a few short bursts. He swung the gun to his left and caused the crew to rise up and flee. He cut them down one after another as they fled toward a concrete bunker about 200 yards up the slope. In the confusion of the firefight, the 1st platoon overextended itself and advanced within range of the bunker's guns. They withdrew to the new skirmish line, dragging a wounded white officer with them.

Mike and Sam jumped into the pit with Fred. Their bayonets were bloody. They flopped down and sank to the bottom of the large hole, as exhausted as Fred was, their breath coming in great gasps.

"Us screaming, 'Banzai', must scare the shit out of the Jerries," Sam said, breathing heavily. "I had a hard time catching up with them. Seems the bigger they are, the slower they run."

"I hate to get them in the back," Mike said, wiping his bayonet clean with an olive-drab handkerchief.

"What choice do you have?" Sam said. "You, the optimist, want to let them live to shoot you someday?"

"I just don't like the idea," Mike said, slumping to the bottom of the hole.

"It's no worse than doing it when they're staring right at you, like terrified animals," Fred said.

"Man, oh, man," Mike said, looking over the rim of the hole at their original position. "How'd we make it in one piece? Look at all our guys lying out there."

"Sheer luck," Fred said, becoming increasingly superstitious. He had the penny pinched in between his fingers.

"Never knew I could run so fast," Sam said. "I must have covered the last 100 yards in ten seconds flat, and that includes time to pig-stick a couple of Jerries."

"Now you're exaggerating," Mike said. "You never did that before, either. Now you're a common blowhard, choir boy."

"Yeah?" Sam said belligerently. "Then you tell me why I've been trained to use this damn 50-pound M1?"

"Look at what we're up against, fellas," Fred said, nodding toward the concrete bunker higher up. It looked impregnable. "Maybe if we can take that we can take the road, too, although they must have it covered right up ahead."

"And hide behind what?" Sam said. "Our tanks can't make it across the flooded plain. They're like sitting ducks for the 88's."

"We do it the best way," Fred said. Which meant shot up comrades...he hoped he could come up with some way to reduce casualties. Any way he could and still take the objective. He was obsessed with keeping casualties low.

That evening they repulsed attack after counterattack. The entire field erupted into violence. When the Germans approached their positions too closely, the 442nd rose out of their holes and countered with bayonets fixed, scattering the attackers with their screams of "Banzai," but they were prevented from advancing any distance by the heavy machine gun in the bunker and retired to their newly held ground. Both sides sent out patrols at night to feel out each other's strength and intent and engaged in a running skirmish with the Germans fleeing behind the protection of the concrete edifice.

For two days the battle for the open ground raged with both sides engaged in skirmishes that resulted in heavy losses. Lt. Partridge was wounded and hastily carried off the field. That put Fred in charge of what was left of the platoon. The wounded lay moaning. They dared not move lest they attract a viciously vigilant sniper and his bullet. In some instances they would lie dead still, as in the flooded plains, for days before they were rescued and evacuated to the field hospital. The Germans had the habit of picking off the medics as well, in spite of which the medics performed miracles under fire. There was an unspoken bond between the men of the 100th Battalion and the 442nd : whenever you needed help there was always another buddhahead or kotonk right alongside of you ready to help out whatever the situation, be it on the battlefield or a barroom brawl. The mainland kotonks and the Hawaiian buddhaheads were brothers on a mission.

On the third day the 1st platoon lay siege to the bunker that commanded a view of both the road and the field and after driving off the German infantry trying to defend the position took the bunker frontally with grenades and suffered great losses. With their flank secured, the 2nd and 3rd platoons proceeded to take on the formidable bunker that lay ahead of them. Screaming Meemies, exploding in clusters and spreading a deadly spray of shrapnel, 77's and 88's and the big guns as well as Bouncing Betties hampered their progress, and the men hugged the ground and pulled themselves forward inch by inch. Their losses mounted. When the German barrage lifted, they had to beat off the Germans in hand-to-hand combat. With the 3rd platoon engaged with the Germans, Fred urged the 2nd platoon forward.

The "Brahms Hop" saved the day. Following Mike and Sam's example, the men of the 2nd platoon spread apart and jumped up and down and made targets of themselves while Fred forced himself to half crawl and half run in a flanking move toward the spitting machine gun. He waited for the inevitable pause while playing dead thirty yards from the bunker. When the pause came he rose to his feet and ran up to the opening and rammed two grenades in quick succession into the bunker. The force of the explosions blew a helmet with half a skull intact out the opening. Fred stood at the aperture and sprayed the interior of the bunker with his Thompson submachine gun. It was over. The Germans positioned near the bunker took flight for their next defensive position.

But the three platoons were slashed to the bone. They could not pursue the enemy, not without reinforcements, not without supplies. They did not have enough men left to withstand a determined counterattack. They had gone on the line undermanned, the

Allied command having withdrawn seven divisions from the Italian theater of campaign for the cross channel operation called Overlord. But in spite of their thin lines, they fought fiercely and elements of the 34th Division and the 100th Battalion even reached the walls of the monastery only to be driven back. The debate whether or not to bomb the historic monastery turned into a fortress still raged on. With the promise of taking the monastery within such close reach and with the toll of men and materiel so high, it seemed inconceivable that the Allies would merely withdraw to absorb their losses without taking their objective.

For the next several days the men of the 442nd , which had not been brought up to full strength even before the battle for Monte Cassino, managed to beat off the Germans and hold their position, with ammo, food and water running out. The wet weather added to their misery. Their soaked winter clothing locked in the cold. Nothing stayed dry. Their feet swelled in their boots. They lay in the abandoned holes, ignoring the strange smell the Germans left behind, and hugged themselves and curled and uncurled their toes to try to work some warmth into their bodies and swollen feet.

After a few more days of desperately clinging to their costly piece of land, the men looked into the sky with disbelief: the rain had stopped, and the wind was driving the clouds apart, ripping and tearing at them as though they were a nefarious veil that had blotted out the sky and the warm, life-giving sun. They wanted to cheer as the sun broke through. They drank in the warmth lustfully. Even within the range of death, they felt like playful children.

Fred took off his sodden overcoat and spread it out flat on the ground to dry. His feet were painful, but he still worked his toes. With grim satisfaction he watched steam rise from his clothing as both body heat and the sun merged to drive the moisture from the wool. Hunger–forgotten during the heat of battle–attacked his collapsed, shrunken belly, and thirst scratched his dry throat. Running his hand over his stubble, he washed his face in the rays of the sun. Fatigue burned his eyes; each blink felt raw. Nearly out of ammo, he knew the situation was desperate. But for the moment–even for a short moment–the war did not exist. The sun had come out in all of its glory, and he felt it was meant for him and him only, to revel in and wash his soul clean.

It sounded as though tens of thousands of bees were buzzing among the banks of clouds that fringed the hills and mountains of Liri Valley. The sun shone warm and seemed to stir the valley into activity as German reinforcements from the eastern sector of the Cassino Line wended their way along the roads amidst explosions coming from Allied shelling. But the activity stirring in the air seemed even more ominous. The droning sounded angrier as the moments passed. Soon the first wave of B-17 Flying Fortresses cut through the billowing cumulus clouds. They knifed through them as a blade would through whipped cream and headed straight for Monte Cassino. In minutes they cruised overhead and began unloading their bombs on the abbey. The ground shook and trembled as the cheers that rose from the throats of the men of 34th were drowned out by the thunderous explosions. The men of the 100th and 442nd were more subdued. They just watched in awe as wave after wave of B-17's dropped their load on the mountaintop and threw up massive chunks of the once magnificent architecture, flinging the debris into the air like a collection of toy building blocks. The sound of destruction was deafening, and the men had to cover their ears lest their eardrums burst.

The sky was black with B-17's. The bombing continued throughout the day and was extended to the next day as soon as it was light. The decision had obviously been made to blast the monastery into oblivion, and after each pass the once massive and magnificent monastery was flattened until the men thought that nothing could possibly remain alive within its confines. The tonnage of bombs dropped was enough to reduce a small mountain to a rubble of hammered rocks. When the droning of the last phalanx of bombers faded away, the ancient and well-built landmark was pounded to pieces, more like a crushed skeleton of a building than a juggernaut of a fortress the Germans had transformed it into. The men felt that Monte Cassino, simply designated at Hill 165, was now theirs. They were confident that nothing could survive such total destruction. "Butcher Hill" had turned into a nightmarish reality for Fred.

As thinned out as their undermanned 442nd ranks had become, they were given the order to take the demolished abbey, and they rose up in a body and charged the remnants of the German positions which they took with ease as the enemy withdrew into the rubble of the fortress to make a stand. The men closed in, confident of victory. But they were wrong. Suddenly they were sucked into a deathtrap. The Germans had dug in deep and from underground bunkers rolled out the Panzers and the big guns as well as the 77's and 88's and from behind the protective rubble blazed the machine guns. Incredibly, the fortress was as formidable had it remained intact, perhaps even more so because every block of rubble concealed machine guns and machine pistols that spit out a deadly stream of fire. The Germans put up a fierce resistance.

The men of the 100th Battalion and the 442nd were stopped cold. They could not advance a hair, not with their depleted ranks and supplies. The elite SS division still held their ground. The 100th Battalion which had seen continuous action was pared down to a mere eighteen men still standing while the 442nd could muster only a few squads out of the original number of companies.

The Last Fox

Had they gone into the battle at full strength, they might have taken Monte Cassino but with seven divisions siphoned off for the Normandy landing, the Allies were taking a calculated chance in attacking the monastery. The 34th Division, the Red Bull Division, had almost done it alone. But it would take five fresh divisions of French, New Zealanders, Poles and an assemblage of other units three more months to quell Hill 165. In the meantime, the 34th including the 100th and 442nd had no choice but to withdraw.

Fred was exhausted. He could barely walk. His floppy overcoat had bullet holes in it. With the men who made it safely down the mountain, a barrage of shelling following them, he waded through the mucky, flooded plain where so many of them had been killed and boarded trucks for the rear. For a while at least the fighting was over for them. They were due for a rest. Fred was too tired to think. He could only vaguely recollect how often the "Brahms Hop" worked and how often it was impossible to employ it and they were forced to unleash five or six grenades at a time to confuse the Jerries with Fred flanking the machine gun nest and forcing the last one down their throats. It was another one of his tricks. The other was to have the men scurry up both sides to keep the barrel swinging to give one or the other flank a chance to drop a grenade in their laps. Otherwise they did it the old fashioned way. They rooted the Jerries out with disciplined rifle fire and fixed bayonets.

Fred and his men were trucked to San Giorgio not far from Naples for rest and reorganization. Fresh replacements from Camp Shelby had arrived, and the 100th Battalion which had been cut to ribbons was brought up to strength again and then absorbed formally into the 442nd Regimental Combat Team, but because of their conspicuous valor, they retained their designation as the 100th, the Purple Heart Battalion.

The hot food and showers were an indescribable joy. Fred was amazed at how quickly they could recover from the rigors of the battlefield. A few days away from the spitting bullets and the memories of the nightmare subsided. He even found the time to write letters back home. Mail call produced letters that Fred found difficult to read and comprehend. Conditions in the concentration camps back home were deteriorating.

The first chance they had Fred, Mike and Sam hitched a ride to Naples to visit Jimmy Hikida as well as Herb Sakata and Chik Tokuhara in the hospital. The city remained a bombed wasteland. Military traffic was dense as jeeps, ambulances and 2-1/2 ton trucks dodged each other along the streets packed with begging children and strolling GI's. The field hospital was housed in a former hotel that escaped the main brunt of destruction which leveled the rest of the city, and its relatively unscarred state attested to the haphazard, almost insidious capriciousness of war.

Chapter Six

"Hey," Jimmy yelled from his bed as the three men strode into his ward, "you're sure a sight for sore eyes!"

The three foxes stood by his bed.

"How you doing, Jimmy?" Fred asked. "They treating you right?"

"They sure are. Hot food, warm, soft bed. Can't beat it."

"You look too happy to be stuck in bed all this time," Sam said and winked. "Been seeing Liza, haven't you?"

"How'd you guess?"

"We didn't farm and play together without me knowing something about you," said Sam warmly. The fatigue of battle seemed to leach the lust for killing out of him, thought Fred.

"You're not going to rat on me, are you?" Jimmy asked.

"Hell, no. Course not," Sam said. "What you do with a woman of yours is no business of mine."

"How in the world do you manage it with all those MP's wandering around the place?" Mike asked.

"I got my ways," Jimmy said wisely. "You'd be surprised how easy it is to blend in with all the Nisei boys roaming around. Looks like they transferred all of Camp Shelby here."

"And how is Liza and her family, Jimmy?" Fred asked. "Still looking after them?"

"You bet. The Bonachelli family reminds me of my own."

"Except you're in LOVE, my boy," chided Sam. "Remember a soldier will fall in love with any skirt, especially if—"

"Don't you wish you had someone of your own, Sam?" Fred said quickly to keep his friend from saying something he'd regret. He knew how the poison worked. Volatile and flammable.

"I was just kiddin'," Sam said. "More power to you, buddy."

"Liza Bonachelli. What a name, huh?" Jimmy said. "Sounds like music. And she has the face of an angel."

"You really are smitten," Mike said. "Don't tell me we're going to be hearing wedding bells soon? Just imagine you—"

"As soon as I get out of the army, I'm taking her back to Oregon," Jimmy beamed.

"You think they'll let you back!" Sam barked suddenly. "They chased us out, and they'll keep us out! Goddamn racists!"

Precisely what Fred was afraid of...Sam's bile was still boiling.

"You've got to believe what we're doing to prove ourselves is going to make a difference, Sam, a vast difference," Fred said calmly. "You've got to believe that." He wasn't at all sure that he was right. He had no assurances. He could only hope. Survive to fight, and fight to survive.

"There you go again, Sarge," Sam said, lowering his voice contritely. "I still say you should have become a chaplain."

"He couldn't sit still long enough," Mike said and nudged Fred's shoulder with his fist. "He's made for combat duty. Had to take over the platoon twice already when the *haole* (white) officers caught it. If it weren't for him, we wouldn't be here."

"Some meat grinder, huh?" Jimmy said in a subdued voice.

"You wouldn't believe it," Mike murmured.

"I should of been there with you guys."

"You were, remember?" Mike said. "And the first to catch it. We're happy you're on the mend...you know, well enough to get out."

"I feel guilty, sneaking out at night, what with the other guys...no legs, no arms, shot in the face. I leave partly to get away from the moaning and crying. My wounds are minor by comparison. It gets bad at night. I can't sleep."

"They should put the badly wounded separate," Fred said.

"They tried to, but the wards are full, and they ran out of beds," Jimmy said. "They keep bringing them in day and night all shot up, and here I am hopping around."

"Don't come down on yourself because you weren't hurt worse, Jimmy," Fred said.

"Just a flesh wound in the leg and a chunk of bone out of the elbow."

"Then you'll be back with us in no time at all," Fred said, thinking of them as a foursome again.

"They promised me as much. I keep pestering them," Jimmy said pensively. He looked at each of them in turn. Fred knew he was thinking of the squad. Then Jimmy broke out in a broad smile. "Say, you guys wouldn't have any extra cigarettes, would you? For the Bonachelli family."

Fred emptied his pockets as did Mike and Sam theirs without hesitation.

"That ought to be enough to get them through the month, the black market is booming. Thanks, fellas. Thanks a million. Liza might even be able to get a new sweater for herself."

"Tell her hello from us," Fred said.

"Will do."

"We got to hunt down a couple of other guys here," Fred said. "See you."

"I'll be back with you in no time at all," called Jimmy as the three foxes walked out of the ward.

The rooms they searched through were filled with mutilated bodies. Many of the wounded were dying and were softly moaning to themselves, a hopeful prayer to a God who must have been in hiding. Interspersed among the white soldiers were the Nisei of the segregated unit and many of them lay crippled and swathed in bloody bandages with their purplish feet, too tender for the weight of the sheets, hanging out. The entire hospital smelled antiseptic. The nurses in starched uniforms briskly went about their business. They found Herb and Chik on an upper floor. They were sitting up playing cards on a make-shift table set in between their beds. When the three men made their presence known, they all exchanged handshakes heartily.

"How in the world did you make it back in one piece?" Herb said.

"Lady luck," Fred said, lightly brushing the pocket that held the Indian head penny that he kept burnished.

"Has to be a relative of the cute, blond nurse in this ward," Chik said.

"They must have put you through the wringer," Herb said, "because most of the guys in here are off Monte Cassino. They just keep pouring in. It's unbelievable."

"I caught mine in the butt," Chik said. "Took a chunk out, but the blond said it would keep me from becoming too cheeky. Cheeky Chik, she calls me. I guess it's because I give her a lot of lip, especially at bathing time."

"He still thinks he's a lady's man," Herb said. "Carryover from Camp Shelby days."

"Even when I'm flat on my back," Chik said. "I take what I go after."

"Still full of shit as usual," Sam said. "You should of been with us on Monte Cassino. You'd change your tune in a hurry."

"You guys aren't alone," Herb said. "I'm getting out of here as soon as I can by hook or crook."

"So am I," Chik said. "Can't keep me out of it."

"What about the cute blond?" Sam asked. "Are you going to leave her behind?"

"I'll probably be back here to pick up where I left off," Chik said, ignoring Sam, "with the other side of my ass blown off."

"No joke, man," Mike said. "You're lucky to be alive."

"I know, I know," Chik said. "I'm just sounding off, because I'm on the mend."

"That blond partial to you?" Sam asked with a broad grin, still egging Chik on.

"You might say that."

Sam managed a laugh. It was not a harsh laugh. "There's no cure for you, Chik," he said.

Sam's trying, Fred thought. He's trying. But what he had in his guts was not easy to live with.

"I don't need a cure for such a *proclivity*."

"A pro- what?" Sam frowned as though he had been insulted. Obviously, "proclivity" wasn't part of his vocabulary.

"He means that's the way he's made," Fred said, fearing an explosion, and put his hand on Sam's shoulder.

"That's why the nurse calls him Cheeky Chik," Mike said.

"You will have to get the other half of your ass blown off," Sam said testily, "to make yourself *proportionate*. How's that for a pro- word?"

"We'd better go," Fred said and grabbed Sam's arm. "See you guys on the line."

"Can't wait to get back," the wounded men said.

The Last Fox

The three men walked out of the hospital and into the crowded streets of the city. Hordes of children were everywhere. The three weren't overlooked. When the children surrounded them, they passed out chocolate bars and fled around the corner into a cafe where a few Nisei GI's were sitting and drinking wine. They introduced themselves and joined them. It turned out they were from L Company which had also seen action on Hill 165. Fred ordered a bottle for himself and Sam but Mike wanted one all to himself, so he ordered separately. They were drinking and talking about the presence of what could only be replacements for the 442nd in the city when there was a loud outburst from a group of white soldiers sitting in the corner of the room.

"What the fuck are the goddamn Japs doing here? They're stinking up the place."

There was a moment of stunned silence. Then the Nisei rose to their feet in a body, hot, red anger etched into their features. They stood no higher than the chests of their antagonists who were obviously aching for a drunken brawl. Chairs were overturned as everyone got to their feet. Judging from the empty bottles, the whites had been drinking heavily. Fred had noticed them eyeing the Nisei all the while, gesturing toward them with a cock of their heads and thumbs. They approached each other slowly, deliberately, their arms tensed like compressed coils.

"Hey, you, *bakatare*," Sam shouted angrily. "Nobody calls us Japs and gets away with it, you understand! We've had a bellyful of it!"

"Please," the owner called out, "no fight in here. No fight, please."

Fred put out his hand and held Sam's cocked fist down. He then walked slowly over to the group and confronted the tallest haole. He was a sergeant with an ugly scar down his cheek.

94

"Us noncoms are fighting this war," Fred said, "and we're the ones who are going to win it. We shouldn't be fighting each other. Save it for the Jerries."

"You Japs just clear out of here," the tall, white GI said. "You fuckers don't belong with us. Go find a place of your own."

"You must be a fresh replacement," Fred said.

"That's right."

"Aching for a fight?" Fred said, trying to remain cool.

"You got it."

"Then you better get ready to be surprised."

The tall GI sneered at him.

Fred felt bitter rage burn its way up his belly. Where was it all going to end? The urge to launch into the coarse vernacular like an outraged stevedore was overwhelming. So was his restraint as an urbane college boy who loved Brahms. Racism, the disease of the blind...Bigotry, the bastard offspring of the misbegotten...Stupidity, the hatemonger's pap. It only made him angrier. He had to choke down the stevedore, force himself to obliterate the connection between the letters he got from home and the nitwits he now faced in some godforsaken bar in a bombed-out city. He had the MP's to think about and the reputation of the 442nd. They were so sensitive about their unacknowledged status that they even shied away from the whores to keep from being accused of catching VD and producing a "self-inflicted" wound.

"Listen," Fred said coolly, "I should warn you that I have a black belt in the martial arts. Jujitsu, judo, kung-fu and karate. My hands are deadly weapons. I promise to tear your throat out with two fingers and feed the bloody leftover pieces to you." He scowled menacingly, hoping to avoid an all-out confrontation.

The white sergeant paled visibly. But he was no slouch. He started to breathe heavily and cocked his fists.

"Oh, yeah? And I'm the personal trainer of Joe Louis, the Brown Bomber," he said with a snarl that was halfway between a smile and a grimace.

He let loose with a swing. Fred deftly blocked it. He grabbed the noncom's arm and threw him over his back with a *seoinage*, slamming him hard against the floor and knocking the breath out of him. Fred quickly twisted the collar of the man's jacket around his throat and locked his fist against his neck. He kept tightening his hold. The white noncom tore desperately at Fred's strong hands.

"A little jerk and I can snap your miserable, worthless neck," Fred panted ferociously. "It's a judo trick only Japs know. Now apologize. That goes for your men, too."

The man struggled on the floor, clutching Fred's arm locked behind his head. His breathing turned ragged and his face red, then purplish with the veins popping out on his forehead.

"All right," the man gasped. "I'm sorry I called you a Jap. Men, apologize."

Although they outnumbered the Nisei, the men apologized, amazement written all over their features as they regarded their helpless leader held down by a smaller man. Fred released his hold suddenly, raising his hands as though to signify the demons were banished, and the white sergeant rolled over on his side and moaned, feeling the side of his neck gingerly. His men helped the sergeant to his feet.

"You're going to be one sorry sonuvabitch, if we ever meet up again," he said as he and his men cleared out of the cafe. Fred knew it was a quickly-mouthed, face-saving remark, a cheap parting shot from a man who had just asked to be killed. But he wrung his hands as though they were soaked with something deadly.

The Last Fox

Fred upended a chair and resumed his place at the table, taking a long swallow of wine. He had never experienced such anger before and could only feel dismayed that he was ready to break the white man's neck out of sheer, cold fury, something he didn't even feel when confronting the Germans. With the bullets spitting around him, he felt fear, a kind of fear that made him want to empty his bladder, but when he held the man down with the word "Jap" ringing in his ears and with his arms tensing and his fist tightening against his neck, he could only feel rage. And he was afraid that if he ever heard the word spat at him again, he would indeed kill someone. Dismay turned to fear, fear of himself. He wasn't sure what he was capable of. Surely not murder. If not murder and mayhem, then what? What if the provocation were great enough? But that would not be like him. He was too collected, under control. Which made his momentary loss of control even more fearful. He had to remind himself that even as a trained killer the enemy was not the bigot–certainly not a sotted bigot in a bar–but the Nazis and fascists. He was a soldier, not a brawler.

"I've heard of judo and jujitsu," one of the men at the table said with admiration, "but I've never heard of kung-fu or karate. You got a black belt in all of them?"

"Just something I read in a book," Fred said, studying his hands in a detached fashion, as if they were someone else's instruments of destruction. "I just took some judo lessons along with kendo."

"They say that's why we're so good with the bayonet," one of the other men said.

"How's that," Fred asked absently, studying the contents of the bottle.

"Because of the *otsuki* thrust of the kendo sword."

"Could be," Fred said. "We trained long enough and hard enough to be the best."

"No way should we have to put up with that kind of racist shit," Sam said. "Not here in Italy when we're straight off the line. Shit, I just might kill one of the sonuvabitches just for having lip."

"Save it for the Jerries, Sam," Mike said, shaking his head

"I will, you better believe I will," Sam promised. "Didn't I tell you killing Jerries is the next best thing to—"

As if to allay his own suspicions about himself, Fred broke in and said: "There's no glory in killing. None. There's been too much already."

"Hell, what did we train for?" Sam shot back venomously. "We're nothing but killing machines."

"It'll be a sad day when that's all we are," Fred said. Again, he felt like a hypocrite. He could still feel his fist and arm around the GI's neck, tensed and ready to give it the fatal twist. "Drink up. It's about time we headed back."

Fred and Sam quickly took another sip from the bottle while Mike quaffed his as though it were his last bottle that would have to last him for a long time to come. The men talked about the "Red Bull" division to which they were attached and marveled at the fact that they had almost accomplished alone what a corps had failed previously to do...the breaking of the Cassino Line. For many it had been their first baptism under fire, and they had acquitted themselves well. They took pride in the fact. Nobody saw anybody show his back to the Germans.

They hitched a ride back to San Giorgio in a supply truck later that night. In spite of Fred's impatience, they hit another crude bar where Mike would have liberated a bottle of whiskey had it not been for Fred's insistence that they pay for everything as far as they had any lira left on them. By the time they left the bar, Mike was gloriously drunk and was singing "Sentimental Journey" over and over again. Sam staggered close behind him: he threw his arm around Mike's shoulder, lurching and dragging Mike with him, embalmed with alcohol, and bawled out the song, mixing words like "I wanna go home but not to no concentration camp..."

Fred was sober and stayed sober, although he had drunk his fair share. He hated to lose control, and he hated himself more for his inhibition. He would have liked to let his hair down, let it all hang out and turn into a slovenly drunk without a care in the world. But he was too disciplined. Too disciplined for your own good, he told himself. If he became too rigid, he would crack. Then what good would he be? To his country? To his outfit? To his family? A Section Eight in a world already gone insane?

When they returned to their bivouac area, they were surprised to see Herb and Chik occupying their tent. They had gotten rid of their bandages and were in full uniform.

"Go find yourself another tent," they said.

"You'll be reported AWOL," Fred said, ever mindful of the reputation of the 442nd.

"Reverse AWOL," Chik said. "We're reporting back to duty. What they going to do? Court martial us for doing our duty?"

"Latrine rumor has it that something big is up," Herb said. "Ever hear of Operation Shingle?"

"Nope," Fred confessed. "Never heard anybody mention it."

"That's because it's secret," Herb said. "It's an end run that's supposed to break the back of the Cassino Line. That's all I know. But I want to be in on it, both of us do, right Chik?"

"Damn right," Chik said. "Wouldn't miss it for anything. Got to get even for Monte Cassino. The Four-Four-Two is going to make mincemeat out of *them*. The goddamn Jerries are going to pay through the nose."

The Last Fox

"And you two just made up your minds to go AWOL," Fred said, ever the stickler for regulations.

"Don't sweat it, Sarge," Chik said. "The Army needs the manpower, and no way are they going to send us back. We're as fit as a fiddle."

"Scrounge up a couple of M1's," Fred said.

"We already have," Herb said.

"You're in my squad," Fred said. "I'll fix the roster."

"Wouldn't have it any other way," Chik said. "Home sweet home."

"Welcome back," Fred said and smiled, now reconciled to having them rejoin him. It was good to have familiar faces surrounding him. He had lost too many good friends already.

Many of the Hawaiians of the 100th Battalion who had added zest to their lives with their easygoing ways were either dead or wounded. The buddhaheads and kotonks had often traded blows in the early days at Camp Shelby until the buddhaheads witnessed firsthand the conditions of the concentration camps from which the kotonks had volunteered to serve in the army. It was almost incomprehensible to the Hawaiians that the mainlanders could find the courage to enlist when they and their families were confined and guarded behind barbed wire fences. A new kind of camaraderie and affection grew between the two factions and as basic training progressed the common bond was solidified and an extraordinary esprit de corps was born.

The days turned into weeks, and the ranks of the 442nd Regimental Combat Team swelled with fresh replacements from the States. Reorganization and training took up most of their time. But they still had spare moments to play ball and respond to mail. The hot meals were a great change from the K and C rations they had to subsist on while on the line, and they had movies to watch

100

and the Doughnut Dollies of the USO to chat with whenever they felt lonely.

While life hummed with its own kind of efficiency, as in the calm before the storm, Fred could not shake the feeling of impending disaster arising in the concentration camps at Tule Lake and Minidoka. At Tule Lake Margie wrote that food was becoming scarce at the mess halls and that rumors of the administration indulging in black market activities were rampant, and the pro-Japanese thugs were stepping up their campaign to intimidate people into renouncing their American citizenship. Little Arthur was running wild with a pro-Japanese school crowd and often argued with Margie that if they were Americans, why were they imprisoned in a camp? He always sided with his father, Shoji, while their mother, Shizue, remained sympathetic with Margie and couldn't bring herself to write off Rhonda and Fred for having gone their own way. Fred's younger sister was worried that they would soon be going to Japan and never see the family together again. She didn't want to go to Japan. America was her country, but she was a minor and had no voice in her own destiny. Fred couldn't fathom why the conditions in the camp were so bad. The stockade was full of the leaders of Hoshidan arrested at night and hauled away. It wasn't the America he envisioned.

Perhaps he needed to drape a lustrous veil over the ugly face of racism to preserve his own sanity, in spite of or because of being a victim of racism. Perhaps his love for his country needed to remain unblemished for him to carry out his duties as a soldier and called forth an unbridled form of patriotism. Anything less than pure love of country and freedom would have left him a wavering, ambivalent cripple. As it was he was in the grip of an unyielding kind of idealistic innocence that was unbecoming a man but necessary for his own survival. He had to believe. Maybe he was better suited to be a chaplain whose mind and soul were hidden in the nether reaches of an improbable heaven, but he took great pride in being a soldier and deemed it a great honor to put his life on the line to fight for a belief that had been betrayed but was worth dying for. He thought he saw the totality of America, and he had faith in that totality.

If he was puzzled by the events at Tule Lake, he was fearful of what was happening to his sister at Minidoka. In her letters Rhonda seemed distant and lonely. She had few friends, only acquaintances, but they never spoke much about what was on their minds, what was really going on in their hearts. They all tried to survive the harsh conditions of the camp and the inhospitable climate as well as they could. She wrote poems about the wind and the dust that swept across the desolate landscape and the barbed wire fences that served to remind her of the loneliness of both the incarcerated world and the outside world. She was lonely because she was a Jap. One look at her and anybody could tell she was a Jap worthy only of being locked up or ostracized by the world at large. She could not escape her features. The features shared with the enemy. The features that "proved" she was the enemy. But her soul was American, irrevocably, hopelessly, everlastingly. There was nothing she could do about that, either. She was born American. She was not a Japanese, in spite of their father's insistence that America, having taken everything away from them–their home, their property, their dignity–had nothing to offer them. She was torn. She wrote about tearing down walls and fences so that people could see the light within and know that she had the courage to look for goodness beyond the gun towers: a leap into the unknown, she said. She had no idea where she would land. In the midst of profane hostility or indifference? Or in the saving waters of love and acceptance? Or was there a no-man's land of blind and bland anonymity? After all, don't we all look alike, she wrote.

Fred folded the letters and put them back into his shirt pocket. He was worried. He wrote to Margie, including a note to Arthur, to use all her wiles to keep their father from taking them back to Japan, and he wrote in primitive Japanese a letter to his father, begging him to understand why he had to pronounce his loyalty as an American and volunteer to fight in Europe. If principles were involved rather than just feelings, then his father should understand Fred's position, especially as the first son of the family who had to take responsibility for his own life as an American and not blindly follow his father's will as a Japanese boy might have. Having been in college before the war, he had already learned to think for himself, and all he wanted was his father's blessings and understanding that he had done the right thing.

To his sister Rhonda he wrote that the war would soon be over–though he had his doubts–and he would return, and they could start over again, if not in Oregon or on the West Coast, then somewhere else in the United States. Do not despair, he wrote, for her fight to survive was just as lonely as his and perhaps even more fearsome, since she was all alone. At least he had his brothers-in-arms, and they had developed a bond by which they all were compelled to look after one another–just like true brothers. He felt mere words to console his sister were inadequate; of all the family members, he felt closest to Rhonda, the second oldest and closer to his age.

But he could only see the desolate expanse of land with the snow-streaked mountains in the distance that was Minidoka Relocation Center, and he didn't have any words of wisdom to impart when he also saw at the same time the earth torn by explosions and the blazing guns of the Jerries ripping through the ranks of the men. What words could convey the pain he experienced when confronted with the reality of the life and death of the body on the battlefield and of the soul in the concentration camps? He heard words like "irony." Irony was not the word. The tragedy of complicity in the Great Betrayal was more to the point. The tragedy of racial hatred translated into the dehumanization of the invisible people.

The well-regulated regimen of training and exercise was shattered late one week. Everybody scrambled. All of a sudden the wait-and-see routine turned into a hurry-up-get-moving mobilization. The 442nd Regimental Combat Team was ordered to Naples to take part in Operation Shingle. A long line of trucks carted the troops to the cluttered port to board LST's for Anzio, a beach just north of the Cassino Line. The end run was set into motion.

Chapter Seven

Sgt. Murano thought they were going to spearhead the movement, but as it turned out the beachhead had already been secured through stealth and surprise. The Allies had originally assumed they would run into stiff opposition and sent in two divisions from the VI Corps, including battalions of infantry, British troops, Special Forces and Darby's Rangers. But complete surprise had been achieved. The Germans were literally caught with their pants down.

As the Allies were busy consolidating the beachhead and cautiously establishing a perimeter several miles inland on the flat, marshy coastal plain, the Germans were quick to react when they realized the Allies were not going to make a dash for Rome. They tried to push the combined U.S. and British forces back into the sea, after siphoning off several divisions from the Cassino Line which is what General Mark Clark of the Fifth Army wanted in order to crack the stubborn German defenses which resisted for months all offensive efforts. With the reinforcements and units drawn from northern Italy and southern France, Field Marshal Albert Kesselring augmented the Nazi forces and engaged in a fierce fight to reclaim Anzio. Each side pitted about a 100,000 men against each other with the Allies having a slight edge.

In one of the initial engagements, Darby's Rangers who were

trained as assault troops to strike deep within enemy territory were infiltrating the enemy's positions along the shrub-covered drainage ditches that crisscrossed the Pontine Marsh like a grid, when they were ambushed and then methodically sectioned and quartered in a horrendous firefight that chopped them to pieces with machine gun fire and mortar barrages. The three Ranger battalions were reduced to a battered pulp. Only six men returned to friendly lines. In a single day and night the Rangers, toughened professionals, were rendered ineffectual.

Into this deadly fray entered the 442nd RCT and the 100th Battalion. The 442nd occupied the center opposite the settlement of Aprilia, dubbed the Factory because of the symmetrical, blockhouse-type of the stone buildings, while the 100th was positioned on their right flank with the Special Service Forces along the Mussolini Canal, the largest of the canals at 240 feet wide, with the British on their left.

Fred had theorized that they would be sent to take the Alban Hills from which the Germans could observe every move on the coastal range and beachhead itself. From the heights, they called down an artillery cannonade more to harass than to decimate the crews working like ants to unload shipload after shipload of materiel. The port was too shallow for the Liberty Ships and the supplies had to be transferred to LST's and LCI's to make the run to the beach. The operations weren't unopposed. Burned and gutted hulks of ships attested to that fact. The Germans dispatched JU-88 and HE-111 bombers to destroy the supply dumps accumulated on the beach, and ME-109's and FW-190's made regular appearances to disrupt activity that gradually found its way underground in bunkers and theaters that could hold up to 200 men at a time. A new weapon made its appearance at Anzio: the glider bomb fitted with wings and rocket-assisted and radio-controlled from the plane. It weighed about 2,500 pounds, was nineteen inches in diameter and capable of piercing armor. It was an effective weapon against the ships. Railroad mounted guns, monster 280-mm cannons situated miles away, called either the "Anzio Express" or "Anzio Annie" delivered their thundering projectiles with the acoustical drama of a wayward freight train on the densely crowded beaches. Death dropped out of the sky everywhere, on the beaches and the line; there was no rear or forward action. And the fire power was all directed from the Alban Hills, an eroded crater of an old volcano.

Fred quailed at the thought of having to take the hills, but it was the logical objective, especially if the beachhead were to be preserved and the march on Rome were to proceed. But that would mean splitting up their forces, and the powers that be were more inclined to sustain the losses due to the bombardment and go underground than to sacrifice the lives of so many men and possibly lose the chance to tie up with the forces that were trying to break through the Cassino Line and march up Liri Valley on Highway 6, the escape route of the German Tenth Army defending the Line. They wanted to be in a position to close in on the retreating army and annihilate it before it could join Kesselring's Fourteenth Army in the north.

Instead of advancing to and attacking the Alban Hills, Fred's outfit was assigned the task of taking the Factory, which had already been captured and recaptured several times. This time, in their overall attempt to confine the Allies to a small area around the beachhead, the Germans had heavily fortified the town, laced wire around it and mined the fields. Unlike the British sector which was hidden by what was called the Padiglione Woods, a dense stand of scrub, and their right flank protected from unwanted incursions by the deep Mussolini Canal, the ground that lay before Fred and his men was relatively flat and undulant. The only real cover were the wide ditches, but they were filled with waist-deep water and mined. Wading through the water was not as bad as it sounded. It was no longer winter. In fact the spring weather was balmy and humid. Which made the smoke screen and the oily carbonized residue all the more unpleasant; it clung to everything, including the rations the men ate, and clogged the pores of the skin.

Lt. Oliver Morris, a replacement for the wounded Partridge, was an affable southern boy who didn't know what to make of the small Nisei. He himself stood over six foot tall and towered among them. But Fred took him under his wing and informed him of the background of the 442nd and the 100th Battalion and obliquely hinted that they were hardened veterans of the Cassino campaign who would not let him down. Fred wasn't one for bragging, but he shared the general confidence of the other men that they were capable of taking any objective to which they were assigned. Fred spoke in a calm, self-assured voice that seemed to settle the nerves of the new 2nd lieutenant who was younger than he.

Headquarters wanted the Factory retaken. They also wanted prisoners. The impossible was always extracted from them, Fred thought. But he never really questioned the orders of the higher-ups, only how to carry them out the best way possible. The lot fell to I Company with K Company in reserve. Fred made sure Mike, Sam and Jimmy, who went AWOL from the hospital in Naples just in time to join them, were close to him. Their playing ball together before the evacuation and in the camp at Minidoka gave him confidence in the caliber of their teamwork.

At daybreak, soon after they arrived and had dug in, Fred and his men moved out into the ditches with Lt. Morris in the lead. They moved slowly as they approached the Factory. A squad in front of the lieutenant felt for trip wires with arms thrust into the water and cut through the coils of barbed wire. Their progress was painfully slow. It took them three hours to move 250 yards and another two hours to move into position which was well within the defensive perimeter of the enemy. Nerves were taut, and though they made every effort to be as quiet as possible, they couldn't conceal the collective movement of an entire company from the sharp ears that surely were awaiting their appearance. The problem was that the counterattack was expected, and the Germans had had ample time to shore up their defenses. At a particular point, the platoon leader called for a halt and checked his watch. He was synchronizing his movement with the timing of another contingent filtering into the German position via a second ditch on the other flank.

To Fred the minutes seemed like hours. He had to compose himself and release the nervous tension by breathing deeply, but the breathing exercises that came natural did not relieve the fear that lived in the pit of his stomach. He had been lucky so far. The bullet with his name on it would never be produced, he felt, not with his lucky penny tucked deeply in his pants pocket. He looked around, his chilled legs quivering. His friends were right behind him.

The time had come. At the given signal the men climbed through the shrubs lining the embankment and rose to rush for a predesignated cover, a small knoll that resembled an insignificant bump in the otherwise flat plain. The first man to rise to his feet was drilled neatly through the head by an alert sniper. The men dashed across the dirt road into a mine field and amidst the explosions of the mines and mortar barrage that swooshed down on them, kicking up pockets of dirt, slid and rolled behind the knoll while the platoon on their left attracted the fire from the block-shaped buildings. In a few minutes Fred and his men were ordered to charge the stone building on the right. As soon as they appeared over the knoll the machine guns opened up and their numbers were almost cut in half in the first few seconds of the attack. Fred, Mike, Sam and Jimmy kept running as fast as they could. Chik, Herb and the others were close behind. Fred had told Jimmy what the "Brahms Hop" was all about and that he was to take the left flank and Fred the right while Mike and Sam kept the machine gun occupied. When they heard the last spitting burp and then the pause, they were to rush to the window and eliminate the gun with grenades.

Within a given distance they all hit the ground in a body, and Sam and Mike crawled apart and began their measured dancing duel with the machine gun while Jimmy and Fred bellied their way on the ground in front of the window. The other men were caught in a firefight with riflemen ensconced in the upper floors of the building. Then there came the inevitable pause. Fred and Jimmy rose to their feet, rushed to the opening and dropped two grenades into the laps of the Jerries and without wasting a moment ran around to the entrance to eliminate another nest with grenades. A large explosion threw them to the ground. A Nisei with a bazooka scored a direct hit on a tank that had rumbled into the center of town. Kneeling alone in the middle of the road, he looked like a figure frozen in time as he reloaded and deliberately took aim at a self-propelled gun.

With the ground floor neutralized, the men poured into the building and one by one cautiously climbed the stairs. Fred reminded them of the need to take as many prisoners as possible. The only word that he could think of in the heat of the battle, only remotely related to the word "surrender" was "Ubergabe." He yelled the word at the top of his lungs. The men followed suit and screamed "Ubergabe" while ascending the steps. It must have been close, for it produced the desired effect when combined with cries of "Banzai." Nearly twenty Jerries evacuated the floors and descended the stairs and sat huddled on the ground floor with their arms about their heads, staring in amazement at their captors.

The lone soldier with the bazooka lay wounded in the street, and the medic dragged him into Fred's building and began administering first aid. A stretcher bearer followed close by. Fred grabbed hold of two stout Jerries and through gestures instructed them to carry the wounded soldier back. They nodded their understanding and seemed eager to comply. For them the war was over.

I Company had swarmed all over Aprilia or the Factory. Fred left two men to guard the prisoners and protect the medic and took the rest of the squad to join Lt. Morris in eliminating the riflemen and snipers in the upper floors. They managed to occupy another square building and flush out more prisoners. The rest of the Germans fled toward Cisterna, a large town that was a railroad junction. In the wake of the advance came K Company to occupy the town and prevent it from being retaken. I Company retired with half of its force either killed or wounded, but it returned with about sixty German prisoners who could provide vital information about the German's positions and troop strength, vital because the Allies had to know where to concentrate their strength for the long-awaited breakout from the beachhead and march to Rome. General Mark Clark was eager for his army, the Fifth Army, to have the honor of entering the Eternal City first, for in his estimation it had paid the price and earned the right. Also, he wanted to time it so that his entrance into Rome would take place before Overlord, the cross-channel landing at Normandy, and be covered by the world press so as to impress Washington and London that the Italian campaign was not a secondary operation.

The Last Fox

I Company withdrew to the rear which was actually still the front, since German patrols were constantly probing their lines for weak spots, and dug in. They lined their foxholes with any kind of insulating material they could lay their hands on: layered newspapers, slats of wood, discarded winter overcoats. Because they were trapped in a marshy plain, the water seeped into the holes to make dampness an ever-present matter of discomfort. For protection from the machine pistol fire of the marauding Germans and their mortar attacks, they stacked sandbags around the holes.

In between attacks it was the usual wait-and-see routine. The war between the defenders and attackers hit a stalemate. Fred and his men spent the time cleaning their weapons, playing cards and writing letters. Fred found it difficult to vary what he wrote. He would not complain about the conditions on the front, the high casualty rate of the 442nd and the nature of the assignments handed to them. Instead he felt it necessary to rally Arthur, Margie and Rhonda on and try to bring cheer into their lives by telling them how well and fit he was. The men and officers got along well, he wrote, although sometimes they had little chance of getting to know them due to the intense fighting.

In the idle moments when there was nothing else to do, he would listen to the occasional roar of the incoming shells from the Anzio Express, the crackling of anti-personnel bombs dropped by German pilots nicknamed "Popcorn Pete" and the drone of the lone German reconnaissance plane which appeared punctually every night and was dubbed "Photo Joe."

Fred had to give Lt. Morris credit for trying to get to know the men he was leading. As a southerner he was inquisitive about everything the Nisei said, did and ate. In his friendly and open way, he commiserated with the men for having to fight the hated Nazis while their parents, brothers and sisters and sweethearts were rotting away in prison camps, as he put it. "Cain't see no justice in that," he'd say. "And the bastards in the guv'mint should be hogtied."

Once he came around with his mess kit piled high with rice.

"You boys got sumpthin' agin spuds?" he asked. "How kin you keep eatin' this blah stuff day in and day out? Us officers and gentlemen are gittin' mighty tired of it. Heard you traded all the potatoes you kin git for a bunch of this stuff, and now we're stuck with it."

"It's the diet of our choice," Fred said, reiterating what he had already explained.

"You guys got any apple sauce, pudding or sugar I kin put on it? Trade you a couple of chocolate bars for it."

"That's no way to eat rice," Sam said, chewing a mouthful hungrily. "You got to eat it straight and mix it with 'okazu'."

"Oka- what?"

"Okazu. Whatever meat or fish you have on hand. It goes pretty good with Spam," Sam said, "if the Spam is warmed up first."

"Maybe that's the only way you kin down Spam," the lieutenant said. "Didn't know ground-up horse cock got that greasy."

"It's still meat," Jimmy insisted. "And a little *shoyu* wouldn't hurt, either."

"Shoyu?"

"Soy sauce," Fred said.

"Never heard of it."

"We put it on practically everything, especially raw fish."

"You eat fish raw?"

"Indeed, we do and we love it," Fred said.

"What kind of fish?"

"You name it. Bluefin tuna, yellowtail, mackerel."

"I'd just as soon swallow a snake whole than eat a catfish raw. Imagine what an ugly critter like that would taste uncooked." The young officer shuddered.

"We don't eat fresh water fish raw. Only from the sea. Fish from rivers and lakes don't taste right."

"Eating oysters raw, yeah, but—"

"Practically everything from the ocean can be eaten raw. Clams, mussels, sea urchins, abalone, sea cucumbers, squid..."

"Hold it right there, Sgt. Murano," Lt. Morris said, holding his hands over his mouth and stomach in mock despair. "You're goin' to spoil my appetite."

"Here," Fred said, passing him a couple of items, "you can have my pudding and sugar to put on your rice. But you should really learn to eat it our way."

"Whoa. Rice is a cereal, isn't it," the lieutenant said, brightening as he took the packets. "It deserves to be treated like any other kind of cereal." He tossed a candy bar back to Fred and opened the pudding and sugar which he commenced to pour all over the mound of rice. He scooped up a mouthful and smacked his lips. "Now, that's that way it should taste."

The Nisei winced and rolled their eyes.

"Now, you going to spoil *our* appetites, Lt. Morris," Sam said.

"You people sure have some strange eating habits," the young officer said. "But I guess it's no stranger than our liking fresh, raw hamburger just ground with minced onions, salt and pepper."

"You mean a mess of raw beef?" Sam said and made like he was going to gag.

"That's right. Nothing like it. It's just like having a juicy steak done rare."

"That almost sounds barbaric to us," said Fred, digging into a tin from his K rations and scooping up a mouthful of rice.

"No more so than gnawing on raw fish," the tall southerner said, happily digging into the doctored cereal.

"We catch it, fillet it, skin it and cut it into thin strips," Fred said, watching for the effects of his description of making *sashimi*.

"While it's still alive?" the lieutenant said and raised his eyebrows.

"That's the only way. Get it while it's still flopping and the freshest," Fred said and smiled.

The lieutenant got up from a squatting position and kicked out his long legs to flex them.

"Well, I'll leave you to dream about your kind of feast while I catch forty and dream about Mom's southern fried chicken with all the fixings and topped off with a huge slice of apple pie. Now, doesn't that sound tempting?"

"We'll leave you to dream about your victuals in paradise," Fred said, still smiling, "and keep raw fish off the menu."

"And I'll keep my beef corralled," the tall white man said and smiled back.

A crack of a rifle followed the spurting up of dirt around the lieutenant's feet. The young Caucasian cursed and stamped his feet.

"Goddamn kraut. Always pestering us around mealtime." The whites referred to the Germans as krauts, Boche, huns and sometimes Jerries whereas the Nisei almost always called the enemy, Jerries.

The lieutenant picked up a rifle and emptied a clip at what appeared to be a distant dugout. He then slid down the bank of the ditch to rinse his mess kit off in the muddy water and climbed back up again. He stretched his lanky form in full view of the Nazis. The Nisei expected a shot to ring out, but none did. The officer eased into his slit trench with the admonition that he not be awakened unless the matter were important.

During the next few days the lines were beefed up. According to what the prisoners said, the German divisions were poised for an all-out strike against the Allies to push them into the sea. The German high command surmised that the Allies were making ready to break out of the beachhead and head for Valmontone which protected Highway 6, the Tenth Army's escape route, or for Campoleone which blocked Highway 7, a straight shot to Rome past Albano. Even Hitler's elite demonstration unit—the Berlin-Spandau Lehr Regiment—a crack infantry outfit used to train assault troops was added to the Nazi effort. The push was orchestrated to occur simultaneously along the entire front. For both sides it was a do-or-die proposition.

The guns roared their mutual defiance. The shelling ground up the coastal landscape, the ditches and trees and bodies. Stopped by the drainage canals, the Mark IV tanks that rumbled down the few available roads advanced dangerously close to breaking through the lines but were halted by the shelling which was concentrated on the lead tank so as to stymy the entire column. The German infantry had better success in storming the Allied positions and nearly pushed the front lines back in alignment with the rear echelon, but the lines held at the last moment and counterattack after counterattack beat back the Germans with enormous losses suffered on both sides. The fallen soldiers were littered all over the plain.

The Allies beat back the Germans with everything they had which in the ultimate sense meant the bone, tissue and sinew of the individual soldier in hand-to-hand combat.

Fred fought off the onrush of machine pistol bearing Jerries with blasts of his own tommy gun until it became too hot to handle, and in the confusion of battle found himself with only a knife in hand when he ran out of ammo, slashing and thrusting. He used judo tricks to throw the Jerries to the ground and slashed their throats and broke their necks. When he slit their throats, the screams of terror were mixed with a loud gurgling sound, and when he slammed the knife into their chests, the yanking out of the blade was accompanied with a hiss of air from the deflated and punctured lungs. The pitched battle left him shaking with fear and desperation. But there was no stopping for breath or for hiding and taking time out in the bottom of a hole. There were no rules except to fight to survive.

The Germans finally broke and ran, and the Allies' attack in Fred's sector carried them all the way to the outskirts of Cisterna, the vital junction. The main force of Germans retreated inland to take up a defensive position that blocked both the approach to Campoleone on Highway 7 which led to Rome and to Valmontone which sat astride Highway 6, the all-important escape route for the German Tenth Army out of Liri Valley. Fred's company finally dug in outside Cisterna and welcomed the break in the fighting while both sides toted up their losses and estimated the dubious successes of the future.

The only wound Fred sustained was when his hand slipped on the blood-slick grip of the knife and slit his hand. He was covered with blood, his own and the enemy's, and he was aghast. He dusted the cut with sulfa powder and bandaged it as well as he could with one hand. He would be damned, he told himself, if he was going back to battalion aid to get it taken care of. For all he knew they might find the deep cut a pretext to take him off the line–which, in one sense, he wanted more than anything else. All the while he fought the impulse to "chicken out." He could not leave the company, not while he was still standing. He had his duty to the others. It was like a silent vow they had made to look after each other. But he was on the verge of admitting that he had had his fill of fighting. More than enough. Not yet, he told himself. He had a long ways to go yet before the war was over.

In his newly dug foxhole and alone with his thoughts, he couldn't help but think of his fallen comrades. War was like an overwhelming demand that commanded all his energy. Every firefight demanded of him not concern for life or death, although the fear in his guts screamed for the pre-eminence of life, but for wit and stamina, for the tactics of staying alive and killing Jerries. He was astounded, even frightened, by the violence that made his arms and body rigid as an instrument of death, a killing machine, half-maddened with fear and, at the same time, saved by the taught skills of warfare, of killing without being killed oneself. It became an instinct. Be swift, be wise, be bold, be strong, strike first, think before and after, learn, don't let fear paralyze the mind or body. Expect the unexpected; be ready for anything. Above all, don't hesitate. Move, move, move.

He was stunned by the loss of his friends in the company. Immobilized. He felt guilty each time he survived a bloody skirmish–and yet secretly glad. He mourned the eclipse of lives cut too short too soon and was consumed with pain at the thought of the agony of the wounded whose bodies were so shattered that they would never be whole again. A single bullet hole in a non-vital region seemed a blessing: an excursion away from the screaming bombardment, a soft hospital bed, warm food, sweet smelling nurses. A period of time when the fear in one's belly eased away like some lost demon. A vacation to reclaim sanity. But Fred knew that even while convalescing in a hospital his brothers-in-arms would be thinking of their own on the battlefield and returning to jump into the middle of the war again. The thought of the dead being lost and gone forever weighed on him like a dense cloud of things that came to a final end. There would be no more laughter, no more hula dances or songs sung to the strumming of the ukelele, no more hot showers to wash away the sordid grime of war, no more delight of eating superbly prepared food, no more azure skies, sunlit trees or the scent of flowers, no more favorite ballads or stirring symphonies. They were dead. Casualties of war. Man's insanity turned into a policy that moved the machine of destruction by word and deed around the world.

Squirming in his hole like some feral animal, his thoughts loosened by the blessed lull in the fighting and his senses ever alert, Fred castigated himself for being overly sensitive. About having to kill, even though he was a soldier. No one could tell just by looking at him. No one knew how weak his legs would become when in battle. He always maintained a cool and tough exterior. His tortured sentiments, his confusion of conflicting feelings–of fear, guilt, anger, relief, anticipation–never found expression. The reality of the battlefield remained tightly bottled. He wanted his men to see him as keen-witted, dedicated and tough. He needed to win and keep their trust, precisely because, once in combat, he was cast on his own resources and wanted to communicate his confidence–to lead his men. It was a desperate need, because the trust he had in himself was as a tentative individual. When it came to taking responsibility for the lives of the men in his squad and platoon, he was always assailed by serious doubts. He could lead, but the way ahead was fraught with the unknown dangers of death, and at times he could not help but question his judgment. Fortunately or not, in battle there was very rarely time for such questioning. On the line, he was instinctively an infantryman.

He slept a troubled sleep. The Jerries would unleash a random artillery barrage intermittently. If a round landed too close, he would be jarred awake, then nodded and dozed. He had no idea what the next move would be. The mechanics of war were decided at the top, and Washington, the Commander-in-Chief, the Chairman of the Joint Chiefs of Staff, the generals and their aides, the strategists and planners were about as far removed from the ordinary foot soldier as the planets and the stars. He could wonder, doubt, curse, weep in frustration but it would be in vain. The bone-deadening wait-and-see tussle and repose put him in a trance. The marvel of an order was that it set into motion, as though by a push of a button, an armada of men, equipment and materiel in the pursuit of war and its perpetuation marked by a series of objectives, whether they were intelligible or not.

His more immediate concerns included his family in the concentration camps. What was to become of them? He needed to survive. They would need him after the war. Just as his country needed him now. In the name of the supreme sacrifice–for the cause he loved so well, freedom and peace. A multiplicity of wars was being fought within a war and like racial prejudice and the fight against it, the raging conflict had to do with love and hate. Could it be as simple as that? Love and hate. Indeed it was. Racial hatred made the concentration camps possible. The roundup, evacuation, cities of tarpaper barracks surrounded by barbed wire fences and presided over by machine guns in watch towers were an end result of a thinly-disguised brand of snarling hatred sugar-coated by government propaganda. Shorn of the mask of civility, the policy of racism bared its teeth.

Disgusted by the memory, Fred could not kill the recollection of the newsreel in which the government portrayed itself as a loyal master that was giving the inmates of the camps a chance to make the deserts bloom again, the same kind of chance they had before the war to farm land largely unwanted by the whites. Betrayed and yet committed to the cause of freedom, Fred was called upon to choose between love and hate. In his innocence, to preserve his idealism, Fred chose love. The love of freedom and mankind. Under the circumstances, it seemed a giant leap. But it really wasn't. It was *too* easy to hate. In the very beginning, he had to fight to make the right choice. Nothing was more precious to him than his birthright. No one, nothing could deny him what he treasured. Only he could by his choice. And because of his choice no power was capable of taking his birthright away from him, neither the Nazis nor even his own government and country. Whether he realized it or not, beyond perceiving it dimly on the peripheries of awareness, he was in for a lifelong fight.

Chapter Eight

Fred became attached to his foxhole. Except for the times when he was on patrol to probe the enemy's defenses around Cisterna, he lived in it and during the interlude managed to make it as comfortable as possible by lining the bottom with old copies of *Stars & Stripes*. He imagined himself to be a mole, secure in the knowledge that he had his own hole that he could call home and the rank as a noncom to kick out any presumptuous denizen of the battlefield who coveted its comforts. Being well into May, it was getting warmer by the day, but he had dug the hole deep enough to stay cool even with the sun beaming directly down on him. The slight moisture of the dug out sides, kept constant by the occasional drizzle, gave relief from the heat, and the hole, barring a direct hit, was quite safe. He indeed felt like a mole or gopher at home.

He was reconciled to his fate as a foot soldier. He emerged only when ordered. Since he was within range of the snipers, he did his business when nature called in his helmet and dumped the smelly contents in a spot designated for refuse and trash from his K and C rations.

The hurry up-and-wait routine continued, and he knew that with each passing day the Jerries were fortifying their positions all the more intensely and that the slaughter would begin anew as they raged back and forth in sheer defiance of probabilities.

The day came when the higher-ups at long last made up their minds. It came in the form of sixty light bombers flying overhead to drop hundreds of tons of bombs on the fortified town of Cisterna. Fred watched in fascination as the explosions from the saturation bombing raised a pall of smoke and dust over the town that slowly settled like a shredded veil to reveal what the passage of destruction from the air had wrought: flattened buildings, rubble, debris, a wasteland of abodes where people once ate and slept. He knew that now Cisterna, as block after block of broken chunks of masonry, was transformed into a deadly rattrap with machine guns and rifles hidden behind the tumble of debris. To break any form of organized resistance, hundreds of big guns around the periphery of the beachhead bellowed their fury and rained shells upon every square yard of the already destroyed settlement. The scene reminded Fred of Monte Cassino. It also reminded him of their failure to break through the Cassino Line which, as far he knew, still held and continued to frustrate Allied attempts to breach it even after months of a massive offensive.

As soon as the barrage lifted, Fred found himself in the forefront of an attack to take the town. He jumped out of his foxhole to lead his men into the mountains of rubble. Resistance was fierce. The Jerries crawled out of the basements of the buildings and manned their guns, making a swift takeover of Cisterna impossible. Their orders to hold the town at all costs were just as firm as the orders for the 442nd and the 34th Division to take the town at all costs, for Cisterna was the key to both the attempt to cut off the retreat of the German Tenth Army on Highway 6 and to advance on Rome along Highway 7 in the direction of Campoleone which lay west of the Alban Hills.

The Jerries tenaciously held on to their positions. The tattered remains of the seasoned 362nd Division did not yield. It was fighting a rearguard action as were the four other Nazi divisions along the nearby river, the Albano road and the Mussolini Canal to stay the VI Corps onslaught to break out of the beachhead. Fred and his men had to dash from cover to cover and assault each position frontally with rifle and automatic fire to dislodge the Jerries, working methodically from one end of the town to the other. In some instances they worked in teams of four, outflanking the dugouts and rushing the machine gun nests with fixed bayonets when they ran out of ammo. The close-in fighting always sliced into Fred's nerves, for he could see the expressions on the faces of the enemy–expressions of sheer terror–an instant before he cut loose with a burst from his Thompson. When his clips were empty, he picked up the enemy's machine pistol and continued the attack. The battle raged for three days and three nights ceaselessly before Cisterna fell into Allied hands. The major junction had been secured, again at great cost.

Fred learned from Lt. Morris that the all-out push from the beachhead was made to coincide with the Allies' breakthrough in the Cassino Line and their rush up the contested Liri Valley along Highway 6 in hot pursuit of Kesselring's Tenth Army. For reasons of his own, General Mark Clark split up the VI Corps and sent the 3rd Division, First Special Service Force and part of the 1st Armored Division northeast to cut off the retreat of the Tenth Army at Valmontone and rerouted the rest of the forces, including the 34th Division and the 442nd Regimental Combat Team plus the 100th Battalion, to the northwest to attack up Highway 7 in order to reach Rome. The decision resulted in weakening the VI Corps' chances to crush the Tenth Army, and because the British Eighth Army, held up by the Adolph Hitler Line north of the now broken Cassino Line, was tardy, Kesselring's Tenth Army was able to filter through the Allied defenses and join up with the Fourteenth Army in the north of the Italian boot.

The northbound units of the VI Corps, proceeding to Campoleone along Highway 7, ran headlong into three well-supplied, largely intact veteran divisions, including the 3rd Panzer Grenadier Division, that were prepared to defend the Caesar Line south of Rome to close off Allied access to northern Italy. Operation Strangle, designed to cut the enemy's lines of communication from southern France and northern Italy, manifested itself in a grand display of 50,000 sorties flown over bridges, viaducts and arterials and 26,000 tons of bombs dropped on trucks, tanks and equipment for six weeks as a preliminary to the push. Captured prisoners spoke of the roadside being a wrecking yard of demolished transports and vehicles of all types. But the mountainous terrain limited the effects of the all-out attempt to prevent fresh divisions from coming to the aid of Kesselring. The Caesar Line, stretching from the Tiber River west of Rome, skirting south of Albano and the Alban Hills and anchored in the mountains east of Valmontone, was an elongated, strategic perimeter of defense meant to stop the Allies from capturing Rome, the prized possession of the Third Reich and the pivotal objective of the Allied campaign in Italy. General Mark Clark was in an understandable rush to take Rome, because Operation Anvil, the invasion of southern France, was scheduled to take place immediately, and both Anvil and Overlord were drawing off supplies, materiel and reserves from the Fifth Army that he still desperately needed, not only to seize Rome but also to bring the Nazi's to their knees on the entire Italian peninsula as he had the fascists. Time was of the essence.

But the divisions of the VI Corps ran into a ferocious, dug-in wall of determined resistance. Directed from observation posts in the prominent Alban Hills, the firepower of the 88's, 77's, Screaming Meemies and big guns was concentrated with great accuracy on the attackers. The shells tore up the ground in giant clutches, uprooted trees and blew men apart, throwing their bodies into the air like torn dolls. Machine guns, mortars and the hail of fire from MP 739's and the Schmeissers, the submachine gun of the German infantryman's choice, reduced the Allied advance to a desperate crawl measured in inches and feet. The multi-purpose artillery piece–the 88's–were tank killers, and before long scores of Shermans were reduced to burning scrap metal. The sniper's target of choice were the men equipped with the Browning Automatic Rifles, and the men, accompanied by an ammo bearer, would dash forward a short distance, hit the ground to escape the concentrated fire and rise up again at the opportune moment. They ran in a zigzag pattern to get into position to engage in a duel with the MG-42's and MG-34's.

Fred and his men pressed doggedly on. He followed closely behind Lt. Morris who was cursing loudly. Fred knew from his pale features that he was scared to death, but he also knew that the lieutenant would be damned if he would show it. Fred himself felt the weakness in the pit of his stomach, and his breath came in short gasps, the stricture of fear in his throat keeping him from breathing deeply. But he fixed a grim expression on his face as though the thin line his lips made were sculpted in stone instead of bare flesh. He stumbled forward, his legs weak but still miraculously able to carry his weight, and glared through the chaos of exploding shells, smoke and shards of rock. Someone ahead had his bowels ripped open, for the smell of feces permeated the air. He tried not to notice. His legs moved of their own accord, running hard but hardly fast enough, for he seemed to float as if in a dream through the smoke, an invisible cloud himself, one that the enemy could not see and hit. He was like empty air, and he took the field in slow, bounding leaps, high into the air and above the withering riptide of bullets.

He could see the dugouts now with the barrels of the machine guns oscillating and spitting death. The enemy's defenses were formidable. Reinforced bunkers and nests, gun emplacements, self-propelled guns, Tiger tanks pirouetting cumbersomely to maneuver into position all received a vicious pounding by the guns of the VI Corps, and the battlefield became one vast arena of hammering concussions from the trained explosions that sought out for destruction anything that could cause destruction. He was entering a zone of mutually assured annihilation. Soon, if he survived, he would be staring into the faces, into the terror-struck eyes of the Jerries as he blasted them into oblivion, a burden of the war rendered lifeless by his finger frozen on the throbbing trigger, without fully realizing the intensity of the scream that raged silently in his own throat.

Lt. Morris, waving what seemed like a toy version of the .45 ACP, so puny and feeble was it against the thunderous explosions around them, motioned them to take cover in a ditch. They were pinned down. Involuntarily, they ducked their heads as the bullets raked the dirt shoulder. They hugged the muddy embankment as though desperately enamored of protection.

"We need a BAR here!" the lieutenant hollered. He stretched his neck to look around him. No one with the heavy automatic weapon was nearby.

The bullets sizzled through the air right overhead. Fred knew the Jerries had the sights of the machine guns set to hit anything a few inches off the ground. A head stuck above the lip of the ditch would be blasted off instantly. They could no more attack in force than singly without being shot as soon as they emerged.

"Goddamn it!" Lt. Morris said, spitting mud out of his mouth. "We can't just sit here and do nothing. We've got to take out that nest on the right."

"Might be able to," Fred shouted above the noise of battle.

"Got any ideas, Sgt. Murano?"

"I'll need three other men."

"Pick 'em."

Fred tapped Jimmy, Mike and Sam on their helmets and gave them their instructions. He nodded to the lieutenant.

"Move all the way over to the left, sir, and concentrate everything on the nest while we four exit on the right."

The lieutenant gave the order, and the men spread out down the ditch. At his command they brought their rifles to bear on the target. Fred and the others dashed to the end of their side and leaped over the edge and ran as fast as they could over the level ground before they had to flatten themselves when the MG-42 swung in their direction. The machine gun bursts tore up the ground around their heads, and they rolled to the left and right to change positions, got up and charged toward the nest when the fire was again directed toward the bulk of the riflemen firing from the ditch. Fred and his team inched their way on their bellies with Sam and Mike taking turns exposing themselves, triggering off a few rounds and falling to the ground before the swinging barrel of the machine gun could fix its sights on either of them. The sheer volume of the riflemen's firepower concentrated on the site was enough to make up for the lack of a BAR, and the team was able to make good enough progress for Jimmy to launch a rifle grenade. It fell short. But the concussion was enough to throw the Jerries into panic, and when several of them rose out of the pit to flee, Fred gunned them down with disciplined bursts from his weapon, and he marveled at the fact that he was able to hit them at all, such was the distance and confusion and the tommy gun's characteristic to climb when fired rapidly. Rising fully to his feet, he jumped and slid the last few yards as if he were heading for home and threw a grenade into the pit just as the gunner was bringing the machine gun to bear on them. Even before the rocks and dirt settled, Fred was on his feet, spraying the dugout with .45 slugs that ripped into the bodies of both the dead and wounded. Only one survived. He was shot up badly. Fred squinted at him with narrowed eyes, his legs quivering with the exertion of the battle. He didn't know whether to trigger off another burst or not and hesitated.

"Kamerad," the German said weakly, held out his hands and tried to smile.

"The war's over for you, buddy," Fred said more to himself than to the young German. He didn't trust him and kept his gun trained on him, expecting him to leap up suddenly and start firing at him. He kicked the machine pistol lying at his side out of reach and continued to regard the soldier suspiciously. Fred felt that if he let his guard down, he would find a knife in his belly. The German youth kept holding out his hands, both to stay Fred's wrath and in supplication.

"Wasser, bitte." The German made a drinking motion.

Just then Mike, Jimmy and Sam jumped into the pit. They were unhurt. They ducked their heads, for the bullets were thudding around them, and looked wildly about, their bayoneted rifles held ready for a counterattack. When it didn't come, Sam began throwing the bodies of the dead Germans out of the hole.

"Shit," he said, pointing to the soldier by Fred's side, "that one's still alive."

Fred was frisking the soldier for grenades and other concealed weapons. He drew a sleek dagger out of its sheath and tossed it aside.

"Kill the sonuvabitch," Sam said and made ready to skewer the German youth.

"No, don't" Fred said and deflected Sam's rifle with a wave of his hand. "He's not part of the war anymore."

"He's still a goddamn Jerry. The bastard must have killed dozens of us."

Mike pulled Sam back. "Looks like he wants a drink of water," he said.

Fred unhitched his canteen, unscrewed the cap and passed the water to the youth, pressing the mouth of the container to his lips. For some odd reason, he reminded Fred of a popular classmate in high school back in Portland, Oregon.

"Danke," the blond youth said weakly. "Danke."

"You're wasting precious water on a goddamn German," Sam said, almost beside himself with hatred. "He doesn't deserve to be treated decently. The sonuvabitches are always shooting our medics. They don't go by the rules. Let him die."

"Back off, Sam," Fred said as he began undoing the buttons of the soldier's tunic.

Mike lit a cigarette and passed it to the youth who took it eagerly and drew on it, letting out a stream of smoke and coughing and wincing with pain.

"Danke," he repeated with tears in his eyes.

Fred spread his shirt apart and exposed multiple wounds. He shook his head at the sight of torn flesh caused by his own weapon and reached into his pack for a packet of sulfa powder. He sprinkled it liberally on the gaping wounds that only a tommy gun could produce. The youth was going to die. But Fred used up the packet anyway as though in atonement.

"What a waste," Sam said. "What if you need the sulfa

yourself? Or maybe one of us might."

Fred said nothing. Closing the tunic, he drew a heavy muslin bag from the bottom of the pit and used it as a pillow, lifting and cradling the soldier's head on it. He looked at Fred with gratitude in his eyes and smiled. Almost as a friend. He must have known that he had only minutes to live, and those few, final minutes were to be spent with a fellow soldier–an enemy–who had shown him kindness. Fred felt he knew what the youth was thinking, that they had engaged in mortal combat by accident. At the moment, it was totally irrelevant who started the war. The lonely final minutes of life on the battlefield made no sense. It was not a grand death. The womb of the universe was not going to open up for one lone soldier as he lay dying. Too many had passed on before him, too many were to follow. It was like the hand of malevolence striking him down, an indifferent, capricious hand full of thunder and fury and death. Only the touch of a mother could have made any difference.

Fred wiped the blood off his hands on his pants and reached for the abandoned sniper rifle and handed it to Jimmy along with a belt full of cartridges.

"Scope the next dugout and take out as many Jerries as you can." Dirty, nasty business, Fred thought.

"You're a wonder, Fred," Sam said sarcastically. "You try to save an enemy who's going to die anyway, and then you turn right around and order them killed. You a hypocrite or something?"

Fred stared hard at Sam, but it was with a kind of understanding that kept him from retorting or even becoming angry. Playing ball together before the war was a long ways in the past...eons ago when a bobbled infield grounder prompted Sam's favorite cuss word: Bless it! He couldn't even say "Damn" without blushing, not even "kuso" (shit), so strict was his church-going family at home. But the hard training at Camp Shelby and arriving in Italy had changed him as it had no one else. Fred knew why. It was the poison. And Sam was always as scared as he was. Maybe more so.

"Hah! What did I tell you?" Sam crowed. "The bastard's dead already. All that for nothing."

He picked up the gleaming knife Fred had discarded and proceeded to undo its sheath from the dead youth's belt. Fred felt the soldier's pulse, then closed his eye lids. He felt inexplicably sad as though it was indeed his white classmate who had just died.

"What's gotten into you, Sam?" Mike asked.

"Nothing that killing more Jerries won't fix. A souvenir. That's what this is," Sam said as he stuffed his booty into his pack. "Too bad it isn't a Luger. I could've made money off of it. The guys would pay plenty for one of them. Too bad. Maybe next time."

"You're getting to like it too much. A bad sign, my friend," Mike said.

"I didn't make this damn world, but I have to live in it. And nobody said I have to be polite about it."

"You going into butchering when the war's over, Sam?" Mike insinuated.

"Watch your mouth."

"Easy you two," Fred said and then rapped Jimmy on the helmet to commence firing.

After scoping the gently rising ground at the foot of the hills, Jimmy began to pump round after round into the nearest enemy position, squinting through the long rifle scope. The responding fire thudded into the stacked sandbags. The Germans soon determined where the sniping was coming from.

The captured sniper rifle barked, and Jimmy grunted: "Got

him. Right in the throat. Man, this thing's accurate. He had his scope on me, too. Just a second longer, and he would have gotten me." The rifle barked and jumped again. "That makes five."

With the last shot, the Germans left their post and fled up the slope in disarray.

"Look at the Jerries run," Jimmy whooped. He followed the fleeing figures through the scope and knocked two more Germans down as if they were ten pins. They soon disappeared behind a rolling knoll.

Mortar rounds began to fall around them and soon had their position bracketed. Fred leaped out of the pit.

"Come on, let's get out of here," he called to the others.

They sprang out and made for the just vacated position. Fred grabbed Jimmy to tell him to bring along the sniper rifle and remaining ammo, but Jimmy raced on, saying he had his own M1 to haul, and Fred spun around, dashed back and retrieved the heavy rifle and ammunition belt. When he reached the cleared dugout, he found it occupied by Lt. Morris. He crowded in beside him and the other men anyway.

"Better find a hole of your own, sergeant," the lanky lieutenant said. "This one is taken for the night."

"You don't mind if I borrow it for a moment, do you?" Fred asked, strapping the rifle sling around his arm.

"There's plenty of real estate around here. Dig yourself a slit trench like all good soldiers were trained to do."

"I like my comfort," Fred said as he aimed the sniper rifle at one of the numerous bunkers dotting the Caesar Line. He could see the sniper assigned to the position clearly through the scope, and cranked a round into the chamber. The action was butter-smooth, and he knew the trigger pull would be crisp. Just a touch, he reminded himself, as he fixed the reticle on the target. The range was about a 100 yards. The machine gun, occupied with firing on troops advancing on their flank, hadn't swung in their direction yet. Fred squeezed the trigger gently and watched the German soldier throw his hands up to his face and topple. He chambered another round and took aim at an infantryman firing a Schmeisser at the men of L Company who were being chewed up. He fired and watched the soldier crumble and quickly reloaded and began to methodically pick off whomever he could scope. The rifle was a marvel to shoot, and the picture of the target through the scope was crisp and clear. He couldn't help thinking that had they been similarly equipped with their own .30 caliber M1-D with the Lyman scope they would have made better and systematic progress in eliminating the opposition.

The Jerries didn't break and run this time. The MG-42 spat bursts of death all over the field. Fred wanted to cry out to the men of L Company to wait for the pause when the gunner and assistant had to change barrels and thread another belt of ammo through the action and then rush their position. The assault troops were brought to a crawl, pinned down and helpless. Their own machine gun chattered at a slow rate of fire; it was no match for the MG-42.

Fred took aim at the machine gunner himself. He could clearly see half a head, the cheekbone and jaw. He steadied the rifle and triggered a shot. He missed, but the shot must have been close, because the German ducked and looked wildly around. He spotted Fred–he could see the German swing the barrel of the machine gun toward him–and Fred planted the cross hairs right on his left eye that was narrowed with intensity. Fred fired before he could get off a burst and blew his face off. With the gun silenced, the men of L Company got up off the ground, yelling "Banzai," and rushed the bunker to end the stutter of the burp guns with grenades.

"That was some fine shootin'," Lt. Morris said with a cigarette pincered between his fingers. His other hand was holding a pair of binoculars. "Jus' like an ol' fashion turkey shoot back home. But what are you goin' to do about your comfortable hotel accommodations for the night? Looks like L Company pre-empted your spot."

"Turn into a mole again," Fred said, thinking of the long days spent on the Anzio beachhead.

"Might as well," Lt. Morris drawled, "because we're goin' to have to hold this position, for a while at least. Two battalions from the 135th Regiment got the shit kicked out of them by the krauts at Lanuvio...on the way to Campoleone...and they're sending in the 'One Puka Puka Battalion' to clear the bottleneck."

"You can depend on the 100th to get the job done."

"But that's only one battalion. They should send in three, not just one."

"The 100th has a lot of 442nd replacements, and they're fresh and eager and have a good combination of Hawaiian Nisei and recruits. They'll break through."

"I sure do hope so," the lieutenant said, "'cause I'd hate to give up all the real estate we took. That would really piss me off."

The cost was too high, thought Fred and repeated the thought with each stroke and bite of the shovel into the dirt. Even one dead Nisei made it too high. But they had come to fight. And fight. For themselves and their families.

Thoughts of them languishing back home were like lonely ghosts. They were fighting for them and their future...and Mankind's. Certainly, a great cause. And great causes never failed to stir Fred's idealistic mind–just as Brahms' symphonies stirred his soul. He desperately held on to the last vestiges of his

135

sullied innocence. He was only 23 and wanted to remain 23.

The fight against fascism and Nazism welded the Allies in a historic crusade with its heartbeat pulsing in common accord...all the way down to the foot soldier on the ground where the killing was a dirty and desperate affair. On the ground, in holes and dugouts one looked into the eyes of the enemy, both reflecting each other's terror and rage as one grappled and fought. One smelled the other and knew they came from different countries.

Only with death came the accidental realization of brother-hood that was marked by a shared agony of pain, regret and longing. For home, for peace, for one's mother and her gentle touch. For a final glimpse at the marvelous stars on a dark night before darkness descended, and there were no more governments and regimes and crusades of war, not even the ability to pray or seek the unknown. Was God the universe and the universe God? Did one disappear into the oblivion of all universes as an insignificant speck of consciousness, the progenitor of a spark of life in some form somewhere? Or was decay the final answer? A soldier's resting place should be noble. But wars were not noble. Only bloody. A soldier's bones were as common as anybody else's.

But there had to be a difference. "For he died so that his people–*his people*–shall be free." A soldier was honor-bound. That had to be the difference. Fighting and dying for one's country to prove one's loyalty did not make sense to a sentient American. Loyalty was a given. To demand that a man give his life for his country while questioning his loyalty was an inconceivable, obtuse insult. Love of country. It was featureless, and yet some people would define it according to a person's ancestry: some Americans love their country more than others by virtue of race. Ridiculous. And sad.

Accomplishing what two battalions could not, One Puka Puka–the 100th Battalion–succeeded after a thirty-six hour firefight in breaking through the bottleneck and advancing further into the Caesar Line. But time was running out, and General Mark Clark wanted the VI Corps to push harder. Bitter fighting broke out around all the strongholds along the Caesar Line, yet the veteran German troops held fast. Some ruse, feint or ploy had to be devised. Breaking through by sheer force seemed improbable. The German line of defense was impregnable. The patrols probed the line for weak spots. They found none. Though exhausted the 100th was still making progress on Highway 7, but the battalion needed a flanking move to take the pressure off of it. What was decided on was a night infiltration of the German defenses on the western slopes of the Alban Hills. A break in the line at that point would force the Germans to withdraw and assume a rearguard action to keep from being cut off from one another. I Company was included among those chosen for the night attack.

The night was moonless. Good because they could not be seen, but bad because it meant hand-to-hand combat. And the fighting had been going on for days; the troops were near the point of dropping. Lt. Morris led the way, his .45 drawn and pointed into the darkness. As far as Fred was concerned, nothing was more useless than a .45 ACP pistol in combat conditions. The clip held only seven rounds, and in the heat of battle no one could hit anything beyond twenty-five yards–a miracle, if he did. The effective combat range for the ubiquitous pistol carried by officers was seven to ten yards. Perhaps that night it would be effective and come into its own as a known man-stopper, since it was so dark that you had to bump into a man before you saw him. They advanced deep into the darkness.

They took care of the unsuspecting sentries first. They were guarding a ridge that overlooked a draw from which Lt. Morris,

Fred and his men emerged undetected. Loud German voices converged in the darkness. The sound of laughter rang out. The men slowly crept closer, the Nisei with their bayonets fixed. Fred almost stumbled into a pit before he realized it was one of the machine gun emplacements.

He immediately sprayed the occupants with submachine gun fire. There were cries of surprise and fright and the sounds of fighting breaking out in the night elsewhere. Someone grabbed him around the legs, and he practically had to shoot his own feet to get the Jerry to loosen his hold. Another Jerry grabbed him around the neck, and Fred threw him over his back, drew his knife and stuck it into his chest. Groping for his tommy gun at his feet, he fired at the dark, faint figures who in their terror must have realized they were under full attack and were fleeing as barely visible shadows into the night. He ran after them on the uneven ground, almost stumbling and falling, but kept advancing with the others in a body toward another tier of emplacements that fired at them blindly with muzzle flashes giving away their positions and attracting a response from the attacking troops. Small arms fire and orange-red flashes added to the rage of the fighting that rose in the throats of the men clashing. As though from a black swamp, grunts, moans and cries merged with the general pandemonium which was made all the more frightful, because nothing could be seen. Fred grappled with a figure that rushed at him out of nowhere. His breath was foul as if he subsisted on a diet of rotten meat. They tussled in a death struggle. The Jerry had a knife, and when he paused to aim a thrust, Fred instinctively stepped aside, grabbed his arm and threw him to the ground hard. He brought his own knife down on him several times, each time accompanied by a gasp and grunt from the soldier that matched Fred's own exertions, and then the Jerry was silent.

Fred got jerkedly to his feet, picked up the tommy gun and ran forward. Move, move, keep moving. Instinct took over. He passed a dugout where men were grappling and swearing, but he dare not fire for fear of hitting one of his own. So he raced on and shot at figures that were obviously German, since their form in the darkness suggested wild flight, and saw–rather perceived–several fall for they suddenly disappeared in the blackness as if they had dropped into a deep hole that was to be their grave. He kept running in pursuit until his lungs were about to burst. Then he stopped and fell to his knees and sobbed with exhaustion. But he kept firing in the direction he saw the shadows flee. He knew they had broken through. He knew the Caesar Line was finally breached. But he maintained his position, the submachine gun held ready and breathed in great gasps of air.

He had been kneeling on the ground when footsteps approached him and a body tripped and fell over him.

"Goddamn it," Lt. Morris cursed and picked himself up. "Is that you, Murano?"

"Yes, sir, it's me."

The lieutenant was panting, too, as were the men who began to collect around them.

"The war isn't over yet," the young officer said and helped Fred to his feet. "Where'd the bastards head for?"

"They disappeared toward the rear. I lost sight of them."

"Cain't see a damn thing anyway, but it looks like we broke the line in two places. The 100th got the Boche hightailing it for Rome on Highway 7."

"We have to close the gap, join forces and take Albano."

"I doubt the Boche would even leave a rearguard," the lieutenant said. "It's only fifteen miles to the city from there, and they're probably making a beeline for it. Nope, we're really on our way to Rome now."

"What do we do? Pursue them?"

"Dig in and hold this position, tho' I doubt they'll be back. They're on the run for sure."

"Dig in!" Fred shouted to the men around him. He wasn't quite convinced that the Jerries wouldn't try to push them back come morning.

Soon the sound of shovels biting into the dirt made a crunching sound as the men dug slit trenches right where they stood. It was still several hours before dawn, but the order had been given just in case the Jerries decided to return to patch the Caesar Line. Lookouts were posted, and the men, exhausted from days of fighting, stretched in their holes to catch a few winks of sleep. Fred followed suit and weary to the bone stretched out in the shallow trench and let sleep overtake him in waves of relief Alert to the sounds of his own snoring, he awakened himself several times. The sound was startling in the silence. It was as if someone had shouted in his ear.

The morning came in stages of grey and before the sun topped the Alban Hills the troops had already gathered their gear for their march down the slope to join the rest of the Corps along the highway. No Germans were in sight. The pits and dugouts they passed were filled with abandoned equipment and supplies and evidenced the haste with which they had fled. They marched in an orderly fashion to take their place in the rear of a long line of tanks, tank destroyers, trucks, engineers. The entire column was on its way to Rome.

They entered the town of Albano cautiously, but it was empty both of Germans and civilians. There was no point in defending it, since the Caesar Line had been crushed, and the only logical course of action was for the Germans to save themselves and regroup either in Rome or in the northern terrain.

The forward echelons, including motorized infantry, rushed on to confront the remnants of the German Divisions and secure the bridges in Rome, preparatory to General Mark Clark's entry into the city. The 100th Battalion and the 442nd RCT marched smartly the fifteen miles from Albano to the outskirts of the Eternal City with mounting eagerness, but they were stopped and ordered to sit by the road and let the white units precede them to lead the way.

Fred was outraged that they could not share the honor of being among the ranks to enter the city with the general and crushed by a sense of personal defeat. Hadn't they proved themselves yet? What was it going to take? They had marched hard to make the triumphant entry into the city that was the coveted prize of the Italian campaign. Now after days of continuous fighting since late May, they were forced to sit out the grand parade and line the road outside the city in stunned dismay. Battle-weary and dejected, Fred found it difficult to stomach the affront.

Sitting beside Fred, Sam sat with his rifle across his lap and with his eyes blazing with fury managed to stretch a grin over his features and wave at the smiling GI's cheerfully.

"Hey," he yelled, waving his hand back and forth. *"Bakatare! Bakatare!* (Fools)"

It was June 4, 1944, and General Mark Clark at the head of his Fifth Army proudly assumed control of Rome. The Germans had retreated to the north and left the city intact, blowing up the bridges that led into and out of the city while leaving everything else untouched. Rome was only an hour's drive away from Anzio, but it took the Allies four months of preparation and vicious fighting to make the trip. The Fifth Army entered the city to the hysterical cheers of throngs of Italians lining the streets and leaning out of the windows of the buildings. Rome had finally been liberated. And the Nazis were on the run. But the Fifth Army did not remain idle; it moved into position along the Tiber River and made ready to march north into the mountainous terrain where the Germans were building their final line of defense: the Gothic Line.

Chapter Nine

The next day under the mediterranean sky of early June–a warm day that foreshadowed a hot summer–the segregated Nisei unit boarded trucks and joined the entry into the Eternal City. The trucks got lost and meandered around the intricate grid work of the city, passing numerous fountains and such streets as Via Pannonia, Via Del Cerchi, Via Arenula and crossing the Tiber River, running north to south, twice. The detour was fortuitous, for cheering crowds greeted them everywhere. The people gathered at the windows and doorways of the old buildings made of tuff–a volcanic rock–brick, stucco and concrete among the remnants of the ancient ruins of Rome. They waved and shouted their gratitude, and the men of the 100th/442nd couldn't help but feel triumphant, as though they carried with them the soul of the legions of liberators and conquerors that pulsated in the hearts of the populace throughout history.

Fred could hardly contain his excitement as he rocked with the hard movement of the truck. He could see some of the landmarks of the city: the circular colonnades of a temple that looked like a wedding cake–he had forgotten the name of it–the dome of the Church of St. Agnese and St. Peter's Basilica. To the east beyond the plain of Rome which was reclaimed swampland rose Mt. Terminillo. He wished he had the time to climb one of

The Last Fox

the prominent hills interspersed throughout the city to see what he could recall from his student days when he had studied with fervor the seat of western civilization. Just being in the midst of such antiquity stirred his soul. Rome embodied the spirit of all that came before and after it. It endured invasions and wars and absorbed the influence of the Greeks, Spanish, French and Germans as well as the upheavals sparked by family feuds and the appetite of barbarians. The papal authority was forever shifting, but the people of Rome remained Romans and like the Chinese possessed the resilience to swallow the outsiders and digest their foreignness while maintaining their own unique identity which seemed to grow out of the volcanic ash that formed the land and out of the rolling hills and the crops so carefully cultivated, in spite of the passing of popes and emperors.

Rome was declared an open city and spared the devastation of massive destruction in what Fred could only see as one of the rare civilities of warfare. The Germans, upon evacuation, had not destroyed the bridges crossing the Tiber River which coursed like an artery through the city. Nor did they destroy important buildings. Fred was grateful, not so much for the Teutonic character of sentimentalizing historical ties and treasuring art but for the symbolic value Rome represented in the life of the civilized world being so alive that no nation would dare extinguish it. If he was fighting for anything it was precisely the principles that grew out of the western tradition that espoused and honored the freedom of the individual. He believed in what he had been taught, that the paramount importance of his singular conscience was accepted by both the secular and ecclesiastic authorities steeped in antiquity and anchored in history. He was in the part of the world that gave man deities and laws, philosophy and religion, art and culture that defined man what he was to be unto himself. He was born into a civilization that found its roots not in society's control over the individual but the individual's responsibility to himself in the name of a higher order of things, and he was part–a small part, to be sure–of a great, sweeping movement to fight and destroy the very core of what would desecrate and annihilate the conscience of man to make choices for himself. It was a great war of herculean proportions, a war that aimed the lance at the very center of what corrupted the heart of freedom.

Fred wanted to stop the truck. He wanted to stop the war, at least for a short while, so that he could stroll through the city, down Via Cavour to see the famous Colosseum where 50,000 spectators could witness at a time magnificent events on a six-acre expanse that could even be flooded for a demonstration of naval warfare; so that he could walk across the Tiber River to visit the Vatican and marvel at St. Peter's Basilica, so that he could tour the Pantheon and dream that he had shucked off his filthy clothes and soaked in one of the ancient baths to allow the hot, warm and cold water leach out the foulness from his mind, heart and soul. After the bath he would laze around in the attached club house, lecture hall or library or work out in one of the gymnasiums or take in as much of the statuaries, reliefs and paintings as he could in the city with a special eye out for the works of the Renaissance artists. Thinking about art and culture was a necessary antidote to war. He was numb with fatigue, but he could still think and feel. Though colored with perpetual fear, his will to find the fine balance between war and the love of humanity was unwavering. Traveling through Rome gave him a surge of renewed hope, although his immediate concern was for creature comforts which would have taken over his mind were it not for the palpable sense of breathing in the soul of a tacitly understood and accepted appreciation of his own origins as a man born in the land of freedom. He dimly perceived, beyond the brutal realm of everyday reality–kill or be killed–that he was fighting for his own freedom as an individual and that of his family.

Why he didn't think of God in more intimate terms was a mystery to him, although he attended the services offered by the chaplain. He wasn't particularly religious, but he felt he was swept up as a fragment of a human being by the often baffling and haphazard torrent of history that stretched back to the beginning of time, ever since man raised his hand against another, and he felt both lost and secure in the knowledge that he was but a part of mankind that either God looked after or didn't. It didn't seem that he had much say in the matter. The concept of God's possible indifference toward him made him both self-reliant–and lonely.

As he bounced roughly on the uneven surface of the road, wanting to stop even more when he recognized some of the ruins from the books he had read, he caught glimpses of the Forum and the Piazza Navona and the Arch of Septimius Severus, erected to commemorate the emperor's victory over the Parthians. He was inspired by the sight of the arch. To the Romans the arch was a symbol of victory, triumph, and in some personal way he felt it was dedicated to him and his survivability as a soldier. Just catching sight of it heartened him, and he rubbed his hand against his pocket that held his lucky penny...a thoroughly appropriate gesture, given his sense of relief and awe. If only he had time, he would have explored Rome in its entirety and its outskirts, the catacombs, as well...to experience the fleeting illusion of immortality. But the convoy of trucks raced along, one following closely behind the other, as they pursued the Germans, the enemy, who had once been as integral a part of Rome as the Caesars were along a route Napoleon Bonaparte and his armies took to annex Rome to the French Empire.

The Last Fox

When they left Rome, Fred felt as though he were leaving an unreal world behind him, real only for a brief moment and replaced by a grosser kind of reality, and headed for an unknown future and an ultimate kind of threat. It was almost like leaving the University of Oregon mid-term to comply with the egregious evacuation order that threw their lives into chaos and uncertainty. Civilization was transformed into a fantasy, the future into a battle with a form of death. But for the moment the deep blue sky joining the hilly countryside with its vineyards and olive groves promised nothing but peace. Dense stands of beech, umbrella pine and chestnut trees packed the hills, and the wind-swept grassy fields were riotous with the color of red poppies and sunflower yellow. The farmers were out in the fields again. The passage of the machines of war and the shooting and explosions signified that the terror of the storm had passed, and life was obligated to resume its normalcy. Otherwise, so it seemed, the universe would be in danger of being tilted and the axis of the earth thrown off balance. Farms without farmers seemed an improbable perversion. When the convoy stopped, the men were determined to act as soldiers did: they quickly stormed an orchard and filled their blouses with peaches.

The 100th Battalion had veered off in the fields of maize and headed for Civitavecchia, the trading port that served Rome. The port had been heavily bombed and had to be secured. That day the sky was so blue that Fred thought nothing bad could possibly fall out of it. The hand of destruction could perhaps be stayed for days, even weeks, if the Jerries had decided to head for the Apennine range of mountains to the north and join forces there. For some odd reason, Fred wished he were part of the 100th occupying Civitavecchia so that he could have the chance to visit the Sant'Agostino Church and gaze upon the image of the Virgin

Mary said to have shed miraculous, bloody tears. Somehow it was important to him. In the midst of war and the clashing of forces beyond his control. He was not religious, but his heart ached, and the legend was so awesome that he wanted to be near what might have been considered God's holiness.

The trucks carried them directly into the hills north of Rome, and they alighted to begin training to fight on steep terrain as if they hadn't already been exposed to mountain warfare on Monte Cassino. But they brushed up on marksmanship, went on long marches up the slopes covered with scrubby trees and occupied the heights made up of rocky, barren soil. The observation from the top, shorn of obstruction, afforded them an unlimited view of the surroundings, the dips of the valleys and red tile roofs of the hamlets that looked so peaceful amid the colorful fields dominated by the green of the olive groves and grape vines. The war could all but be forgotten. And Fred had to catch himself lest he question why he was where he was, aching in every part of his body from the arduous training.

Word reached them that the 36th Division had pushed far ahead into the German lines, and the 34th Division was to relieve it and join the 100th Battalion driving up the coast from Civitavecchia to engage the enemy in the series of small towns leading up to the Cecina River. The 442nd was rushed into battle. The blue of the sky, and the green of the mountains were no longer of any significance. They became irrelevant and represented an ill-afforded serenity that presided over the treacherous, all-too-real battlefield, at once tumultuous and chaotic–and silent once the enemy had been killed and beaten and the dead were strewn about in anonymity.

With the 100th held in reserve, the 442nd swung into action. It was already late June, and the summer sun caused the men to sweat through their fatigues as they marched into position. It was inconceivable, thought Fred, that the lush hills sheltering the innocuous homes of the farmers could be bristling with death under the serene, cloud-puffed skies overlooking the landscape they were entering. What scene–rolling hills and cultivated fields–could be filled with treachery lurking behind every curve in the road they were traveling? The respite from fighting that they enjoyed had a way of loosening the gripping realization of why they were fighting so far away from home, so far away from one's loved ones, so far away from the perfidious symbols of betrayal that kept following them as shadows of dark reminders.

The reasons all merged in Fred's mind...stultifyingly huge ones that made each step he took as a foot soldier heading into battle seem senseless. Their passage through the splendor of the Eternal City was somehow tied into the preservation of western civilization and the very life of their beliefs that had been trashed with the incarceration. Fred had to remind himself why he had volunteered from the camp at Minidoka, why he had trained so hard at Camp Shelby while putting up with the chickenshit details of policing the grounds, pulling latrine and KP duty and tolerating the monthly security checks, and why he needed to lay his life on the line to prove not only that he was just as good an American as his next door white neighbor but also that he loved his country with an unequivocal lust that belonged to a man born into freedom. No one, not even his government, and nothing, not even the tyranny of war, could diminish his insistence on the prerogatives of his birthright.

Heavy weapons fire greeted them as they approached the small town of Suvereto. The 2nd and 3rd Battalions split up to flank the German position, but they were pinned down by the well-prepared defenders. With Teutonic precision–and predictability–the Germans were going to make sure that every Allied advance would require the maximum expenditure of men and materiel in order to gain a few hundred yards, a few miles before their main lines of defense could be challenged. It was a strategy that seemed to be frozen into stone. What Fred couldn't understand was why the Jerries would sacrifice so much in the way of men and equipment in what were forms of pocket resistance when all the tactic amounted to was a delaying action that whittled down their vital resources which were not easily replenished. Perhaps the Hitlerian mentality of rigidly moving bodies of great military forces, whether advancing or retreating, in epic and historic proportions was founded, after all, on a kind of superstition, a mystical faith in the infallibility of an unrelieved sense of superiority. The Fuehrer could do no wrong, whether in victory or defeat. There would always be another chance to enact a policy of dominance, regardless of the expenditure.

Despite heavy machine gun fire and the thick carpet of artillery and mortar rounds, the 3rd Battalion of which Fred's platoon was a part sent out patrols to ascertain the German layout and discovered a gap in their defenses which they relayed to headquarters. The 100th was immediately brought on the line and penetrated the weak spot, and the momentum of their thrust carried them to the next town of Belvedere where they took the high ground and were able to observe German artillery and infantry movements of the highly effective SS motorized battalion upon which they called the accurate firepower of their own 522nd Field Artillery Battalion.

With the Germans in disarray, the combined push of the 100th and 442nd, which controlled the road linking the chain of towns south of the Cecina River, made rapid progress until they encountered stiff resistance at a town called Sasseta. The fighting there was just as vicious as it had been anywhere, but they dismantled the German military apparatus summarily and continued their advance.

Fatigued by days of continuous combat, Fred and his platoon led by Lt. Morris strayed in the darkness into a field of broken terrain and ran into a heavily defended roadblock. In the ensuing, short-lived firefight, the Jerries took flight–to Fred's amazement–presumably because they had been surprised and assumed they had been outflanked. When morning arrived, they were joined by the 100th Battalion which had been given the mission to remove the roadblock. But...fait accompli. The 3rd Battalion regrouped and joined the march north preceded by the 100th and 2nd Battalion which inexorably removed the lingering barriers that stood in their way. When Fred's battalion, the 3rd, caught up with the main body, it was shunted to the extreme right flank, to the northeast, to Monteverdi in anticipation of a counterattack while their dog-tired comrades passed into division reserve for a well-deserved rest.

In Monteverdi Fred and his friends, Mike, Sam and Jimmy, stumbled upon a hidden cache of barrels upon barrels of wine. Its location was never discovered by the Germans who failed to counterattack even after the 442nd waited nearly two days in town. Had they known about the thousands of gallons of wine, they very well might have, thought Fred. Relaxed and thoroughly delighted, the men tapped into one of the barrels.

"Hot dog!" Mike shouted. "My Mama's going to scold me now! I'm going to get drunk!"

"Shouldn't we tell the lieutenant?" Jimmy said.

"Later," Fred said, filling his canteen. He was eager to shed his burden of responsibilities.

"Shit. We could spend the rest of the war here," Sam said, drinking rapidly from his kidney-shaped pan, belching and gulping down another swallow.

Fred slumped down on the cool floor and took a long swallow of the wine, relishing its tangy bite and the way it drew saliva into his mouth. Now for a hunk of cheese and bread, he thought. Not the K ration cheese. If you threw it into a can of gasoline it would gum up the engine. That was one way to sabotage the Jerry's tanks. It had been such a long time since he had had any wine that by the time he finished half his canteen he felt the buzz of alcohol lighting up his skull like gold on fire.

"Hey," Mike said, "I wish we had some music. Wouldn't that be swell, though, to get drunk in the middle of a war to the strains of Glenn Miller?"

"Maybe you'd like me to sing to you," Sam said in a deep, faked baritone, battle fatigue thinning out his bitterness, at least for a moment.

"And spoil a good thing?" Mike retorted.

"You got no appreciation for true talent," Sam accused.

"I do," Mike said. "That's the problem."

"You can go to hell, Kojima," Sam said and waved his hand in disgust.

Jimmy wiped his mouth with his sleeve. "You know something, you guys. I never been drunk, not once in my life."

"Now's your chance," Sam said. "We can stay here for hours and drink. They won't miss us. We can tell them we had to find a place to take a shit. A long, healthy one."

"We really should tell the other guys," Jimmy said.

"And stir up a riot?" Sam said. "There'll be plenty of time later."

Soon Jimmy was lying on his side with his arm as a pillow, snoring. Fred and the others continued to drink as though imbibing the chance discovery had to last them the rest of the war.

They toasted everything they could think of. Mike toasted his mother over and over again. He also toasted the sun as hot as it was; it was better than the rain and the cold any day, he said. Sam toasted the big blast they witnessed when they saw a German tank explode. He toasted what he called the bloody war, women with big tits, and the next steak they were to have. Wagging his head drunkenly, Fred toasted everything from Nero and the Christians, General Mark Clark, the 442nd Regimental Combat Team, man's ability to wage war, the blue skies of Tuscany, ripe peaches and Italian wine, and the blessed accuracy of the 522nd Field Artillery Battalion and nimbleness of the Cannon Company. As an afterthought, he raised his cup wearily and toasted peace. Although he had had enough, he filled his canteen to the brim for Lt. Morris. Too bad it wasn't whiskey, he thought. Southern gentlemen dearly loved their whiskey. But vino was all he had, and it had to do.

After they had had their fill, they jostled Jimmy who mumbled something about dreaming he was with Liza Bonachelli and that they should not have awakened him as they dragged him to his feet. They shook themselves like guilty terriers and walked with stiff strides toward the secret entrance to show they were not drunk and exited the cellar to look for Lt. Morris to report their find so that the rest of the battalion could partake. The officers, of course, would make sure they all had their duly apportioned rations so as to mark the occasion with an unofficial celebration–just enough to be tempting without becoming debilitating.

Fred had little trouble tracking down the tall lieutenant. They were dug in in the middle of an olive grove, and the young officer was shaking the branches of one of the trees to retrieve the fruit. When Fred approached him, he had stuffed the olives into his pockets and was going to strap on the .45 pistol that he picked out of the slit trench. As Fred stood beside him, he unscrewed the cap of his canteen.

"Where the hell have you been?" the lanky white officer asked as he took the proffered canteen. He sniffed it, and his eyes widened. "Gawd Almighty! It's a miracle. You turned water into wine." He tilted the container to his lips and took a long swallow. "Where'd you get it?"

Fred told him about the stash of barrels in the cellar at the base of the nearby hill. He stood weaving slightly but kept his body rigid and ramrod straight.

"I thought the men would like to liberate—"

"Goddamn it, man! We just got our orders to move out to rejoin the regiment, and that means right now. We don't have time to enjoy that find of yours."

"Pity," was all Fred said and belched.

The lieutenant passed the canteen around to those closest to him. "Sgt. Murano produced a miracle, and it tastes just like wine," he said. "There are barrels of the stuff hidden away, but we won't be able to celebrate having the krauts on the run. Sorry, men."

The men moaned disappointingly as they slipped their packs on and passed the canteen around. The trucks were waiting, and they boarded them dejectedly. As the convoy rumbled along the dirt road, Fred had to hang on tightly lest he slide off his seat. He felt a little guilty for having had his fill unbeknownst to the other men, but the twinge of conscience didn't last long, and he rocked and bobbed and looked straight ahead to avoid the looks of the others. He and his friends weren't being selfish, he convinced himself; they were just being prudent. They hadn't wanted to start a stampede and get the whole battalion wiped out. The results would have been disastrous had the Jerries counterattacked. He didn't question how he would have performed himself. The temptation at the moment had been too great. Besides, if he could sleep while marching and still fight, being drunk would in no way hamper him in carrying out his duties as a soldier.

They were trucked to the town of Bibbona to join the rest of the 442nd and marched to an assembly area just south of the Cecina River. By that time–even before the forced march–Fred was stone cold sober and wished he were drunk again. Every time they went on the line, the fear that his number was up grew greater. So far he had been lucky. But there was such a thing as the law of averages. He countered that bleak view by secretly insisting that Lady Luck was on his side. She had bestowed upon him a rare charm found in the middle of a war-torn land. He rubbed it between his fingers. It was warm from the heat of his body.

The summer runoff was over, and the Cecina River was easily fordable. But the Germans were waiting for them. Resistance was fierce, though sporadic. For the first time in a long time Messerschmitts swooped out of the sky to strafe their positions, even as the Germans eased back to a more defensive position in the north, and captured prisoners spoke of orders to slow the Allied advance as much as possible in order for defenses around Pisa, the western anchor of the Arno River further north, to be completed. It was a disciplined withdrawal before the Allied onslaught to a prepared position which became apparent: a heavily fortified observation post. The 100th and 442nd ran head-on into the main line of resistance. Hill 140.

All approaches to the hill were blanketed by heavy small-arms and artillery fire, and the initial attack took the men of the 2nd Battalion as far as the southern base of the hill while Fred's battalion on the left flank was stymied by a ferocious artillery barrage that lasted for five hours. A kind of paralysis set in, although limited forays were made to try to improve his battalion's position. All along the 34th Division front, the Germans resisted with more determination than had been seen since Monte Cassino and Anzio, and the 100th and 442nd took the brunt.

As the 2nd Battalion attempted a night infiltration, successfully, on the eastern slope of the hill, the 3rd Battalion skirted the western portion of the German position which was honeycombed with caves. For five days the battle raged. Every foot of contested ground was purchased at a horrendous price. Neither side would yield. And the dead and wounded lay inert, for the Nisei learned that the slightest movement on the part of the wounded would only attract fatal gunfire.

Working as a team Fred and his men tangled with the enemy like driven tigers. Mike, Sam and Jimmy were with him at all times. The "Brahms Hop" was useless in the uneven terrain. They had to take out each dugout and cave with grenades and bayonets. It was like physically eliminating the enemy by tearing him apart limb to limb with both trepidation and daring. When one machine gun was silenced, another would open up on them with the trained and calculated six-round bursts they had come to know so well. Lt. Morris called for a mortar barrage to break up the counter-attacks as they worked their way up the western slopes, and the mortar platoon responded with over a thousand 81mm shells rained on the Jerries who scrambled to assume new defensive positions even as they were cut down by M1 fire grimly trained on anything that resembled an attack. The Cannon Company, located several hundred yards to the rear, laid down a creeping barrage that preceded the riflemen. Fred spotted a machine gun crew going into position and crawled into range and rose suddenly, fifteen yards away, and sprayed the Jerries with blasts from his tommy gun. He tried not to notice the terror in their eyes as they looked pleadingly into his.

The Germans did not submit. They rushed in platoon-strength clusters to stem the onset of the attack, but the companies of the 3rd Battalion were equally as persistent and broke up the desperate counterattacks with all the means at hand. Sam had gotten hold of a 60mm mortar tube and using his helmet as a baseplate fired round after round into the German ranks while Jimmy shuttled back and forth with ammunition. When an 88 located his position, blasting the dip on the hillside and half-burying him in dirt, he quickly abandoned the site, grabbed his rifle and ran to join Fred and the others in a cave. They spent successive nights in a series of caves that marked the hill like the pox.

A coastal town that also served as an observation post and wreaked hell on Fred's 3rd Battalion by directing artillery fire against them was pounded to pieces and taken over by elements of the 34th Division, thereby taking some of the pressure off and enabling the Nisei troops to advance more rapidly up Hill 140. The tenacity of the German defenders could only be compared to the desperation of a cornered grizzly, and each forward step demanded the tight fist of a tried and tested dedication. The Nisei kept advancing. "Keep moving, keep moving," was the catchword. And move they did until they had taken their objective and sent the remnants of the 36th SS Regiment scurrying down the northern slopes to take up positions on top of the hills surrounding the next town. With the eastern slope already taken by the 2nd Battalion, Hill 140 was now fully in Allied hands. So vicious was the fighting that Hill 140 was called "Little Cassino" by the chewed up GI's.

Beyond "Little Cassino" lay more small towns and hills that spelled bone-weary misery for the men of the 100th and 442nd.

They bowled their way through each one with dogged determination and smooth coordination until they were stopped at Luciana, a hilltop town that commanded the heights overlooking the port of Livorno. Livorno was vital as a line of communication for the Nazi war machine in northern Italy and was, therefore, heavily defended. It was the middle of July, and the men of the 100th Battalion and 442nd Regimental Combat Team were exhausted.

Fred was dazed with fatigue. The weariness ate into his body; his legs were like rubber and his arms dangled weakly by his sides, his hand tightened around the tommy gun like the involuntary clutch of death. It was the kind of tiredness that corroded the soul, the soul that had been somehow lightened just by passing through the city of Rome and the history it represented. For a short while, the experience of absorbing the grandeurs of civilization firsthand had broadened the vistas of the spirit and enabled him to hope that the world would soon come to its senses. He didn't yearn for peace as if it were an unattainable luxury. He had become too hard-headed, so much so that he dare not allow himself to wish for something that was so obviously beyond reach. Circumstances condemned such wishfulness. All he could manage was stunned stoicism. The horrors of war that imposed on the soldier the necessity of killing constantly for survival, for tactical objectives, for satisfying orders from on high demanded an aberrant mentality. He was forced to engage in the battle between life and death and, at the same time, detach the soul of being human from the enormity of the consequences of killing. The foot soldier did as he was told and if he began to question the sanity of what he was doing, he might just as well turn his weapon on himself, for he would be rendered useless as a tool to prosecute the wars determined by the vaunted leaders he served whether they were honorable men or not. The honor of the soldier lay in doing his duty though his faith lay in tatters. He had to wonder if it was the training–or the pride he had as a soldier.

As Fred Murano, he could not help but question the deeds for which he was responsible. He could not immunize himself against the sheer terror expressed in the eyes of his victims just before he sent them into an errant round in eternity. He was caught between two poles. One pole submitted itself to the tyranny of the conscience that demanded that questions be asked; the other depended on unquestioned obedience to orders. As a trained soldier thrown into battle, he became a desensitized instrument of killing, distinct from the enemy only by policy and the color of one's uniform. And the bone-weariness he felt turned his body into a recast blob of lead, heavy and lusterless, leaving a weak center in the pit of his bowels. Therein lay the limits. His body might be sacrificed but the core of his soul survived precariously in a special protective receptacle. Sometimes it remained sealed–sometimes not. But he kept himself intact by a singular focus: he knew what he was fighting for as Fred Murano, soldier and man.

The German defense of the strategic town of Luciana was comprised of a platoon of tanks, self-propelled guns, heavy machine guns, mortars and a plethora of automatic weapons. To add to the fortifications, the Germans had lain a mine field around the town to make any approach extremely hazardous. Although they were on the run, they clearly were going to make the taking of the town close to impossible without inflicting enormous casualties with a kind of suicidal readiness to be destroyed themselves. At dawn the Allied attack began.

Elements of the 442nd jumped off first to make an end run around the eastern flank to attack the town from the rear. They followed the line of a ridge, but when they emerged and tried to cross a gully, a withering concentration of machine gun and automatic weapons fire made any attempt to attack from the rear impossible. The entire company was pinned down, whereupon another company of the 442nd , backed up by bazookas, 81mm mortars and heavy weapons, made a decisive frontal attack through the mine fields with Fred's company held in reserve and after hours of a vicious give-and-take firefight blasted their way into the edges of the town by nightfall. No one slept, for the fight went on as patrols from both sides clashed in the darkness marked by the slashing flames of gunfire and the raw, staccato stutter of automatic weapons.

The next day Fred found himself in the middle of a maelstrom. The fury of the fighting was filled with the sizzling whine of bullets and the crashing explosions of mortar fire that seemed to come from everywhere, from the doorways, windows and behind buildings. On rubbery legs he ran. His mood was frantic, and he took little care in the selection of his targets. He engaged whatever he saw and lobbed grenades into broken windows and triggered bursts at anything that appeared in the upper balconies. He ran from building to building and became even more frantic when he ran out of ammunition and grenades. Until supplies arrived, delayed because of the mine fields, he had to make do with whatever weapon he could find among the dead Germans. The machine pistol or burp gun was ubiquitous, and he readily armed himself with them as he, Mike, Sam and Jimmy dashed from doorway to doorway, giving each other cover. In spite of the intensity of the fighting and the skillful coordination of the forward observer and the ever-responsive Cannon Company, they managed to hold only a quarter of the town and could move no further, such was the fierce resistance of the Jerries. Fred could not help but marvel at their tenacity and obstinacy. It was a lost cause they were fighting. But causes did not seem to matter much in the heat of battle. In the end it was soldier pitted against soldier, driven by the pitiless urge and need to survive.

There was a sudden break in the fighting. Tumbling into a vacated building with the others, Fred sank to the floor and almost sobbed with relief. Was there something wrong with his legs? He could hardly stand. He rubbed and massaged them. They were on the verge of refusing to perform for him. He slapped them as though to command them to return to life. It was as if the fear in his stomach filled with doubts and questions had found its way into his legs and would turn him into an untimely invalid. With his body propped up on crutches, a body that could no longer be contributed to the war effort, he would as useless as a scarecrow. Doubts and questions...he had no business entertaining human emotions. Feelings–except fear–were the poisonous bile that turned a soldier's life into a coward's hell. His mind told him that he had a duty to perform, but his legs were telling him otherwise, and he slapped them again as if to admonish them and then lapsed into gently kneading his thighs. He suddenly realized that he was brutalizing himself and would probably go on to taking reckless chances on the battlefield if he didn't keep himself in tow and use his wits.

To take Livorno, Luciana had to be captured. It could not be bypassed, and on the second day the Commanding General assigned Division and Corps artillery to the aid of the 3rd Battalion in the contested town. The big guns were moved into position. Soon they were all thundering. They rained destruction on the northern half of the town in what was called "The Serenade," time on target (later known as TOT). The town literally exploded. The booming explosions followed the screeching of the incoming shells fired with conspicuous air-splitting punctuation in the distance.

The ground underneath Fred trembled and shook with each explosion, one following so closely upon the heels of another that the barrage was a deafening, saturated sound of continuous concussion. The jeeps carrying the supplies made it through the mine fields, mortars and sniper fire, and Fred discarded the Schmeisser pistol and replenished his ammo with a plentiful supply of .45 slugs and as many grenades as he could carry. Fred waited for the barrage to end. The quaking of the ground was violent enough to shake plaster off the ceiling, and soon the men were coated with white powder and gave every appearance of being dipped in flour like oysters being prepared for the frying pan.

When the barrage lifted, the men cleared the leveled town house-to-house. The destruction reminded Fred of the town of Cisterna lying beyond the Anzio beachhead. That was a long time ago, centuries ago, it seemed, and long, agonizing days of fighting had followed. There was not one hill or town that the Germans gave up willingly north of Rome. There was no grand "drive" to push the Jerries up the peninsula. The only momentum created was the dogged elimination of the enemy from each hill and town as if one were scraping a new trail through the hilly terrain with a small shovel, a scoop at a time. Now at Luciana the men swept through the ruins to catch sight of the last remnants of the enemy bearing their numerous dead and wounded down the northern slopes.

Fred sat down to give his failing legs a rest. He had willed them to work for him. The last thing he wanted was for his body to betray him. From the heights of the occupied town, Fred could see the 100th march toward the port of Livorno which was even then under bombardment. Without Luciana, Livorno would fall into their hands like an overripe plum.

The respite was brief, for the 3rd Battalion was ordered to move forward to take the next town and deprive the Jerries of any breathing space. The 2nd Battalion was given similar orders, and together they proceeded north. Such was the plastering the Germans received at Luciana that the ordinarily disciplined rearguard was scattered and disorganized, and the 3rd Battalion, despite the hard push, took the last piece of high ground just before the Arno River. When the 2nd Battalion caught up, the two battalions established outposts near the Arno River along Highway 67 which was the main link between Livorno and Florence. The Cannon Company had a field day–a turkey shoot. They zeroed in on the highway and blasted the German convoys running the gauntlets of the cannonade.

As soon as they had secured their new positions, they were relieved by other elements of the 34th Division and ordered to move to the rear to a rest area near the Ligurian Coast. When the 100th Battalion finally joined the 442nd RCT after completing their duties of guarding Livorno, Fred thought they all had a chance for some real R&R to stretch out on the white sands of the beaches, swim and fish under the blue Tuscany skies and enjoy what amounted to a gourmand's delight for a soldier: hot meals. Never mind if they were warmed up C rations. They were served up hot, and the food tasted like a heaven-sent reward. But Fred's expectations were not to be. After a brief period of rest, they were ordered to undergo training in mountain warfare. Mountain warfare, thought Fred. That's all they had been doing–fighting in the mountains, the ridges, gullies and draws, slopes and inclines, clawing and digging and running. If anything they were the ones who had perfected it. Now they were to be put through the paces some more. There was no time away from the war. They were always reminded that they were combat troops. Fred understood the need to learn from the lessons coming out of the previous battles, the tactics and strategy of taking objectives, but the training... The running up a damn mountain and digging in: they had done that hundreds of times. Nevertheless, the Division Commander wanted them to be combat-ready and honed to a razor's edge–which meant only one thing. They were going to be used to spearhead another attack on a highly fortified enemy position. They had either done too good a job to deserve such a dubious distinction, or they were considered expendable. Whichever was the case didn't interest Fred much. He had volunteered to get a job done, no matter what it took. Let the General Staff plan its plans, mold its strategies, issue its commands. As the nerve ending, Fred's immediate concern was staying alive to fight and hope to God his legs would not give out.

If it was not one thing, it was another. In the middle of August, they were sent back into the line. What else? Did Fred expect that they would be pampered and coddled? He was proud of the way they had taken every objective. If they were considered an elite unit, they had the responsibility of upholding the highest military expectations. Personally, Fred didn't feel like an elite example of anything. He was just a dogface following orders, but he understood, at the same time, that the "Go For Broke" unit was bound and determined to prove itself.

With the help of the fearless *partigiano* (Italian partisan) who showed them the layout of mine fields and German troop strength in different sectors, the 100th Battalion swept past Pisa north of Livorno and advanced as far as the Serchio River while the 2nd and 3rd Battalions moved into position beyond the Arno River just west of Florence. Patrols on both sides probed each other's strength, and many bloody skirmishes resulted. Twenty-men patrols were not unusual, and the firefight that followed when the opposite sides met were fierce and frequent. Apparently, neither side wanted to divulge its intentions, whether one was to push forward and take over or the other was to push back and hold at the Arno River. The 442nd was issued orders to engage the enemy as often as possible in sizable force in order to create the illusion that a major thrust was in the making.

Whether by design or accident, the Germans decided at the end of August to withdraw its forces to what was to become their main line of defense: the Gothic Line in the Apennine Mountains. The Allies had reached the foothills of the formidable line, and Fred expected that his unit would spearhead the Fifth Army attack on the string of strongholds. Why else the grueling training in mountain fighting? But just as the attack was about to be launched, the totally unexpected happened. It was as if a giant hand had taken a cleaver and chopped all the neatly laid plans in half. The entire 442nd Regimental Combat Team, including the 100th Battalion, was called off the line and attached to the Seventh Army attacking up southern France in Operation Anvil also known as Operation Dragoon. With the loss of the 442nd RCT along with seven divisions, Mark Clark's Fifth Army, on the verge of breaking through the Gothic Line and poised to drive the Germans all the way back to the Balkans, came to a standstill.

The 442nd was trucked and shipped back to Naples. Their withdrawal and whereabouts were kept secret, for captured documents indicated that the unit was so effective as a fighting force that the Germans had to double their defenses whenever they confronted the Nisei. The major body of the Combat Team embarked on Liberty ships at Piombino, south of Livorno, and the rest of the contingent boarded trucks which passed in convoy through Rome. For a brief moment, Fred was once again able to view the Eternal City that inspired him just as much as it had the first time he entered it. He had carried that inspiration with him into battle, and now he was leaving with it, hoping that it would see him through the unknown which lay ahead. They arrived in Naples several days later in the middle of the night and bivouacked outside the city. It was the middle of September 1944.

Chapter Ten

The long rows of pup tents stretched out neatly like the jagged teeth of a saw, each point representing the crisp edge of tautly strung canvas. The sounds of sleep–snoring, the grinding of teeth, and the occasional groan that accompanied a nightmare–pervaded the darkness of the starlit night. The encampment was swelled by the arrival of nearly 700 replacements from Camp Shelby who had to be assimilated into the unit that had suffered severe losses in the hill- and town-hopping fight north of Rome. It would take ten days of intense training during which time the veterans would "adopt" the fresh recruits and teach them all they knew and had learned.

Armed with passes, Fred, Mike, Sam and Jimmy marched into Naples. The city was just as they had left it: in ruins. Children ran about begging for food and pimping for their mothers and sisters; old men sat in front of bombed out buildings with their hands held out; whores roamed the streets and beckoned. Amid the starving people, jeeps carrying officers dressed in sharply creased uniforms raced importantly along the roads.

The four men found the bar they had been to before deserted–much to their relief. They did not look forward to another run-in with the whites. As the others seated themselves at a table, Jimmy remained standing and stuck out his hand.

"For Liza and her family," he said.

The men dug into their pockets wordlessly and produced wads of money and cigarettes. Jimmy smiled broadly.

"I knew I could count on you guys."

"We'll wait for you here," Fred said.

"I won't be that long." Jimmy straightened his hat and exited hurriedly.

Fred had the barkeep bring them each a bottle of wine, and they paid the pale, underfed man in cigarettes. He smiled happily, displaying stained, yellowed teeth, and departed to maintain his post behind the bar.

Mike held up his bottle in a toast. "To peace," he said and took a long swallow.

"To our unbelievable survival," Fred said and followed suit.

"Ditto," Sam said. "Till all the Jerries are cold in their graves."

Even when Fred and Sam lowered their bottles, Mike was still pulling on his. He finally set it down, smacked his lips and drew the back of his hand across his mouth.

"I feel like tying one on," he said.

"I'm with you all the way," Sam snorted. Fred knew his bile still ran thick.

"To Axis Sally," Mike said and raised his bottle. "What would we do without her."

"To the bitch with the sultry voice," Sam bellowed. "Throw the meat to her, I say!"

"A church-going boy like you talking like *that*!" Mike accused and shook his head.

"Enough of your crap, Mike!" Sam retorted. "Church got nothin' to do with nothin'. Church doesn't—"

Mike put a hand over his mouth. "Before you say anything

you regret, Sammy, have a drink." He stuck the bottle in Sam's mouth and tilted it. Sam gagged.

"I ought to slug you," Sam hissed, stole the bottle from him and drank ferociously.

Mike waited, then retrieved his bottle. "Besides, what would we do for entertainment without dear ol' Axis Sally butchering the names of our beloved cities," he said.

"I'd show her what entertainment was all about," Sam seethed and belched. "I'd make sure she died of it!"

"Man, your mouth sure turned bad, Sam," Mike proclaimed.

"And you're nothing but mouth," Sam shot back.

Fred held his hand up to stop a fight and change the subject. "Her picking on the 442nd and our families is supposed to get us down and demoralize us," Fred said. "But I find it good for morale."

"It's good for a laugh, that's for sure," Mike said, unclenching his fist. He took out a cigarette, lit it and extended one to the owner of the bar who accepted it with an ingratiating smile.

"I wonder where in the hell they get those latest songs," Sam said, wagging his head drunkenly. "Sneak in while we're sleeping and steal them from us?"

"Why, haven't you heard?" Mike said archly. "They smuggle the records through Canada and use spies stationed in Great Britain to sneak them into Poland, stick them in the baggage of the Jerries retreating from the Russian front and rush them special delivery to Berlin. All for our entertainment."

"Her egging us on is just motivating us," Fred insisted.

Before long Mike ordered a second bottle and swallowed its contents greedily. He looked bleary-eyed at Fred, his head bobbing.

"Wonder what's up ahead," he slurred.

"Same-o, same-o. More of the same," Fred said with heavy weariness.

"But why take us off the line when we had the Jerries cornered in the Apennines?" Mike asked.

"Probably to take care of some other dirty work," Fred said.

"After which it's off to see gay Paree and live it up," Sam said, tilting his bottle.

"If we get that far," Fred said. "I hear there's heavy fighting in Rhone Valley."

"Anything would be better than the goddamn mountains in Italy," Sam said.

"We'll see," Fred said with resignation.

They spent several hours at the bar. Thoroughly in his cups, Mike was crooning "Sentimental Journey," his favorite song, in a loud voice that cracked every so often with emotion. Mike drank to get drunk, and when he was in his cups he became sentimental. The drunker Sam got the more fiercely he scowled–in silence. It was as though he were reliving the intense firefights they survived in between Rome and the foothills of the Apennine Mountains. The recollection brought a snarl to his lips. He drank some more. The conversation lapsed as they were drawn increasingly inward with each bottle of wine consumed.

The more he drank the more Fred wondered how they had emerged unscathed from the battles they fought. He shook his head loosely as he recalled the carnage. He felt he should stand up and proclaim for all to hear that he was among the appointed saviors of the U.S. Constitution and Bill of Rights, the American way of life, world freedom and western civilization and could not, therefore, be easily disposed of–the gods wouldn't allow it. Not until he had proved that he, Fred Murano, was every bit as loyal, trustworthy and reliable as John "White" Doe and was fighting not only to show that he could be trusted, in spite of his ancestry, but also that he loved his country just as much as any American from any walk of life. In fact, he thought drunkenly, the concentration camps were filled with the "Oriental" version of John Doe. His numb mind refused to probe the depths of the injustice, but the outrage, fueled by alcohol, simmered in the pit of his bowels, and he tried to transmute the corrosive feelings into something clean and pure–a cleansing wrath directed at the enemy. No bullet, grenade or mortar round would have the temerity to deprive him of such a singular drive that translated itself into sheer will power. The fury to survive.

He dropped his head against his chest, as if the will that had carried him up and down the slopes of the hills had suddenly evaporated. He kept his chin down, lost deeply in thought. The battles repeated themselves in his mind. Then he raised his head and tilted the bottle to his lips defiantly.

Before long Jimmy came bouncing back into the bar. He sat down, took his cap off and slapped it on the table. He ran his hand through his thick, black hair excitedly. The youngest of the four, he was still in his teens, although at nineteen he was already a hardened veteran. But the war hadn't reached him the way it had Fred and Sam. Fred could only envy Jimmy and his youthful and forgiving exuberance. He himself felt old, as old as the civilization that stood on the brink of ruin. Older. He could not forget that his people were imprisoned and guarded by real machine guns, the very same kind they used to kill Jerries.

"What gives?" he asked Jimmy. The golden buzz he had relished earlier had turned into a pounding headache. He gripped his head with one hand and gathered his forehead to a point.

"You know what, you guys?" Jimmy said.

"Whaaat?" Mike said, rubbing his bloodshot eyes.

"Yeah, what's up?" Sam said, arching his eyebrows sleepily. Alcohol had replaced bile.

"I'm getting married," Jimmy said and grinned widely. "Liza and me are getting married. I'm actually going to tie the knot. As soon as the war is over, I'm coming back to get her, and we'll get married and go back to the States."

"Back to Hood River?" Sam asked, awakening. "Back to the farm?"

"That's right."

"You and a white woman back in Hood River?" Sam couldn't seem to fathom the depths, only stunned by it. "The town will be up in arms."

"It would really set them on their ears, wouldn't it?" Jimmy said and smiled happily. "She's such a beautiful girl, too. Almost too good for me."

"You, an ugly Jap, and a beautiful white woman," Sam said in utter disbelief and quaffed a swallow of wine.

"Wait a minute...," Jimmy said defensively. "I'm not all that bad looking. I've got my good side."

"All right, same difference," Sam said. "A good-looking Jap and a swell-looking white dame."

"Don't call her a 'dame'," Jimmy said.

"You're still wet behind the ears, Jimmy. I'll bet she calls you 'Jimmy-boy'. Cute little Jimmy-boy," Sam said and sneered. "Shit, man, they'll tear you to pieces, the town will. Besides, how do you know somebody hasn't already gotten to her, Jimmy-boy?"

"Goddamn it, Sam!" Jimmy stood up and knocked his chair over. "You've been a friend, but you got no right to talk about her like that! She's not that kind of girl!"

Sam drunkenly studied Jimmy's features. Fred was about to intervene but thought better of it. Let the two old friends who grew up together in the same small town of Hood River work it out themselves, he thought.

"All right," Sam said and lowered his head. He nodded contritely. "She's a lady."

"You're damn right she is."

"...and I wish you both happiness. I really mean it, Jimmy."

"Same here," Fred and Mike said simultaneously and raised their bottles in a toast.

"May your progeny represent a new generation of peacemakers," Fred said, tilting the bottle to his lips to feed the gnawing juices coursing through his veins. "God knows it's too late for us."

"You feel like making a speech or something, Fred?" quizzed Mike.

"Not really."

"Then stop it. You're making me feel depressed."

"Yeah. Right. Sometimes, Mike, I think too much."

"Yeah, I know."

"Bottoms up," Fred said and drained his bottle.

The four men hitched a ride back to the bivouac area in a supply truck. Only Jimmy was wide awake and whistling; the other three were half-asleep, weaving and bobbing with each movement of the vehicle. When they reached the city of small tents, Mike and Sam marched stiffly to their assigned shelter and promptly dove in and fell sleep.

Fred let Jimmy lead him to the mess tent for a cup of strong, black coffee which he drank greedily. Everything that entered his gullet went down with the force of desperation, as though food, drink, water–whatever passed his lips–wcrc to be his last. It was a habit acquired during the heat of battle and the uncertain lulls between barrages and counterattacks. As the dark brew pooled in

173

his stomach, he began to feel a little better and chatted with Jimmy who proved eager to talk about his visit with Liza, describing how she delightedly interpreted every word he said to her family and embraced and kissed him full on the mouth, the first time a woman had ever done that to him.

"I'm in love with the most beautiful woman in the world," Jimmy kept repeating.

When the period of training for the replacements was over, the rows of tents were collapsed as though a gigantic exhalation had taken place, and the men of the 442nd RCT assembled at the staging area to be transported to the ships awaiting them in Naples harbor. Late arrivals included those who had gone to Pompeii on passes and made it back barely on time. Fred had visited Pompeii when they first landed in Naples and did not visit the ruins a second time, though they were of great interest to him. The unit was shuttled to the Navy transports in light assault boats and began its journey to southern France, the invasion of which had already included the 442nd's Anti-Tank Company in Operation Dragoon. The men disembarked at Marseille three days later.

After settling in a bivouac area ten miles outside the port city, the men were issued new weapons–rifles, bazookas, mortars–which they tested in whatever suitable ground they could find. Then they were introduced to the infamous Provence winds that swept the coastal region and bent the growth of the short trees near the marshlands. The wind blew down the sea of tents like flimsy rags before its continuous onslaught. The strands of ropes whipped about helplessly in feeble protest. And it began to rain, hard, lashing rain that slashed into the face and soaked clothing, bodies and equipment until the sodden men found themselves dragging around the extra burden of weight as though nature itself was bound and determined to add to the harshness of their training and prepare them for what lay ahead.

They heard they were urgently needed to break an impasse confronted by the Seventh Army that had driven 500 miles up the Rhone Valley in six weeks, rolling over everything in its path until it hit the brutal terrain and the fanatic determination of the Germans to defend the upper reaches of the long glacial stretch: the Vosges Mountains.

The trucks from the north gathered at the staging area to carry the men to the battlefield, but many had broken down on the mad-dash trip over the rough roads, and the 3rd Battalion, including Fred and his platoon, boarded World War I vintage boxcars called "40 & 8's"–40 hommes (men) et 8 chevaux (horses). Rolling stock was scarce, but the railroad still functioned. The men of the 3rd Battalion packed themselves into the box-like freight cars in an orderly fashion, resigned to the pervasive odor of horse manure which reminded Fred vividly of the Portland stockyards where they had been first incarcerated.

It continued to rain hard. The water dripping from the boxcars splashed across the opening. The land was awash with a dismal greyness. The azure Provence skies had disappeared. They lumbered past fields of wheat and almond trees and forested hills, a far cry from the scenes of Italy. What was familiar were the twisted, battered and scorched hulks of scores of tanks, trucks, SP guns–the remnants of the retreating German army–and the stiffened carcasses of dead horses strewn about the blasted landscape.

As they traveled up Rhone Valley that curved into north-eastern France, they passed Roman ruins and many small towns and cut through the city of Lyons without stopping, much to their regret. The hills became denser and turned into mountains. The rain kept falling. When the urge was upon them, the men urinated from the open door, adding to the driven rain streaking past them. They did not know how long the trip was to last, but the train was making all haste.

"What the hell do they expect us to do now?" complained Sam, shivering and his teeth chattering, although it was not all that cold.

"Do what the Seventh Army couldn't," Mike proclaimed, staring at him full in the face. He seemed to remember they had almost come to blows in Naples. "Do what we were trained to do."

"Win the war singlehanded, you mean," Sam said sarcastically.

"You got the idea," Mike said. "And it's not as if we're not good for it."

"Hah, hah!" Sam laughed. "Of all the bone-headed confidence of —"

"...of a Jap," Mike said, showing him a lot of teeth.

"That's right. Of a goddamn expendable. What else do you think we are?"

"You think they see us as expendable?" Mike asked. "Like the real estate we take?"

"Yeah. They see us as weeds. Weeds. Something that grows, not needing attention. They cut us down, and they grow some more."

"You got it backasswards...we're the best there is, that's why," Mike stated flat-out. He seemed to delight in getting on Sam's nerves ever since they almost had a go at each other.

"Sure, sure," Sam said bitterly. "Mr. Five-by-Five, they make him jive. Mr. Four-by-Four, they make him go full bore."

"Sounds like you're *begging* for pity, Sam," Mike said in a cutting tone of voice.

"Not pity. No goddamn pity for me. Just some recognition," Sam said and stared hard ahead of him, holding his arms tightly across his chest. "And a little respect. We earned it. We should've been among the first to enter Rome."

"All those unit citations and medals not enough for you?"

"Hunks of metal. Not nearly enough. I want them to kiss my yellow ass."

"Never happen," Mike said and again showed a grimace of teeth to aggravate Sam. "You have to learn to kiss theirs and like it." He said it casually and slowly to make it sink in.

"You're a born bakatare, Mike," accused Sam angrily. "And fools die fools. You would get on your knees to kiss ass. *You* would beg to get on your knees, just for a pat on the head. Not for me, goddamn it. Not after the camps and the folks rotting there. *Kesa mai asa* is no joke. It's not for me. It's for all 'Japs'."

"Your attitude stinks," Mike goaded. "And how do you propose to stick it to them?"

"By earning the Medal of Honor," snarled Sam. He was shivering uncontrollably.

"The Congressional Medal of Honor! You going to indulge in heroics just for the sake—"

"Yeah, that's right, Kojima," Sam said and sneered, tightening his arms around his chest. His whole body shook. "Then I'll shove it up their asses by turning it down."

"Hatayama, you are nuts!" Mike hollered, losing his cool. "They'll pin it on your stupid, dead body, and you won't know the damn difference. You'd be dead."

"I'm not going to die," Sam intoned. "Just that simple. I got this far without a scratch, didn't I? No Jerry can aim straight enough to hit me. Can't be done. I'll prove it to you."

"Man, now I do pity you," Mike whispered. "We've been

lucky, that's all. The next bullet just might have your name written all over it?"

"That bullet hasn't been made yet." Sam shifted his weight from side to side. "They'll always miss. They haven't even nicked me yet, not even a single scratch."

"Wishful thinking, man. You're bucking for a Section Eight." Mike shook his head. His expression turned somber.

"Shit, you're older than me," Sam retorted. "A goddamn city boy and the things you don't know. Why, you don't really know what war is yet!"

"Sure, I do, we all do," Mike said quietly. "We've been through it, the killing, the butchery—"

"Naw, naw. That's not what I mean."

"I can understand," Mike said. "You got keep a tight hold of yourself and—"

"Don't make fun of me, Kojima, goddamn it!" Sam shouted and stopped swaying.

"I'm not trying to, believe me," Mike said and quickly held up his hands defensively. "Listen, I want you to know something. I can hardly keep from pissing in my pants when a barrage starts up. No one knows if the next one isn't the one. It's the worse kind of feeling with the whole world blowing up around you, and you got nowhere to hide. Sure, I know what it's like. We all do. You think you're any different?"

"No, goddamn it! You just don't understand, that's all."

"Maybe you should talk to the chaplain."

"That's the last person in the world I want to talk to," Sam hissed. "I don't even want to come within—"

"He might have some sound advice for you."

"No, he doesn't and neither have you. Nobody does. Case closed.

"Maybe you should—"

"Can it, Mike," Fred said sharply. He had been following the conversation and watching Sam's features turn from one of feigned ferocity to outright, skin-taut fright. His shaking wouldn't stop. "It's going to be a long ride, and we need to set each other's minds at ease. God knows we'll need everything we can—"

"Don't use that word!" Sam shouted, his body now convulsed with shudders.

"It's only an expression," Fred said and gripped Sam's shoulder hard.

Sam sidled into the corner of the boxcar. He leaned against the wall and slid down to the floor where he squatted with his knees drawn up to his chest, making himself into a tight ball. He stared at the floor as though he were nailing errant thoughts into the rough planks, his concentrated frown like a hammer. He locked his arms around his knees and did not remove his eyes from the floor that seemed to hold all the terror of the war in one spot. He stared hard at it as if he were trying to smash something palpable by sheer will power.

Fred thought he understood what Sam was living through. But he tried to stop his own thinking processes by serenely studying the landscape fleeing past the boxcar. The stupendous wreckage of war was everywhere. He regarded it more with curiosity than horror. They were ratcheting their way up the Rhone Valley gashed deeply in places by the Rhone River that had its origins in the Swiss Alps, if Fred recalled his high school geography correctly. The train hauled them inexorably into one of the most historically rich and contested regions of France: Alsace-Lorraine, overrun by the Celts, Romans and Huns in ancient times and annexed to Germany in 1871 and returned to France in 1919 after the war to end all wars only to be taken over by Germany again in 1940.

Now the 442nd Regimental Combat Team was called upon to dismantle the defenses that had stymied the advance of the entire U.S. Seventh Army in terrain that was as strange and unfamiliar as it was brutal. As they drew toward the end of the week-long trip, the lush green of the valleys was dominated by pastures and vineyards, and the mountains were thick with evergreens and birch. The rain continued without letup as if the leaden skies followed them northward through France with the purpose of marching them sodden and cold and hungry to the very edges of the front lines.

With the damp greyness filtering in through the slats of the boxcar, Fred drew out the letters to read them a second time in the dim light. The turmoil of the battlefield was straightforward and simple compared to the convoluted events taking place at home. First, there was the letter from Margie. She was in the camp's makeshift hospital–with an "infectious" disease. As their father was making plans to return to Japan and catch the next exchange vessel back, Margaret faked an illness and admitted herself into the hospital and begged the doctor to diagnose her with something catching so she could hold up the family and wouldn't have to go to Japan. The sympathetic doctor cooperated. Margie had been fasting and lost a lot of weight and managed to look sickly enough to remain in the hospital and to convince Shoji that his plans were in vain, that he would have to wait for the next exchange vessel if it ever came. She ended her letter on a triumphant note that they would all soon be together as a family. The war couldn't last forever.

Rhonda's last letter was more troubling. She couldn't sleep, she complained. And the medicine they gave her at the infirmary didn't help. She was alone, more alone than she had ever felt. It was as though there was a blank hole where her mind should have been; she felt no one cared about her, that she was invisible like an unwanted ghost. Certainly, they did not know what she was going through all by herself. She said she was sorry to bother Fred with her problems, since he was sacrificing his life everyday for his country, their country, but she had no one else to talk to. She tried to talk to the block manager about her complicated feelings–feelings of being a Jap and betrayed and persecuted by the entire country–but he chased her away and said he had problems of his own and didn't want to hear anything about hers. She even dreamed of her white friends coming to her assistance and telling her she was like one of them and no harm would come to her. As if that were within the realm of possibilities. Fred had penciled a hasty note to reassure her as much as he could and encouraged her to write to him about anything that bothered her, although it was painful to read about her suffering, especially when he could not be beside her to help. Like Margie he could only hope the war would end soon and they could once again become a family. If only Shoji, his father, remained in America, he felt certain that he could convince him that their future lay in America, not in what would be a war-torn and ruined Japan.

As they drew closer to their destination, evidences of the intensity of the war as a great army slashed its way northward were seen in the blasted trees of the hills and the destroyed machines of destruction littering the floor of the notched valleys. What the 442nd RCT was wading into was nothing less than a grinding maelstrom, an occasion of a massive bloodletting. The train pulled to a stop south of the strategic town of Bruyeres, and the 3rd Battalion alighted and marched to the assembly area to join the rest of the outfit which had already arrived by truck. The rain was incessant. The men were soon soaked to the skin and shivered with the cold. The weather was a far cry from the warm Tuscany sun of Italy.

Upon arrival the 442nd was attached to the VI Corps, 36th "Texas" Division commanded by the ambitious and ruthless Lt. General Alvin Z. Bunting who lusted after the distinction of being the first general to break through the German defenses in the ominous Vosges Mountains and cross the Rhine River into Germany. The all-Nisei unit, the object of a tug-of-war in the higher staff, was his ticket to fame. Mark Clark's loss was the Seventh Army's gain.

Chapter Eleven

It was mid-October...still raining, and it was cold. The men of the 3rd Battalion were given a day's rest before they joined the main body of the 442nd RCT. Then they were marched two and a half miles to the line of departure. Lt. General Bunting, Division Commander, was eager to get them on the line. His own troops of the 36th Division were weary and ragged with fatigue after the rapid drive up the Rhone Valley, and he needed new blood. The Nisei were regarded as the best assault troops on the Western Front, and now they were under his command—the nerve endings of his whimsy.

Their immediate objectives were Hills A, B, C and D, so designated for the sake of simplicity, that ringed the town of Bruyeres, the vital road and railroad juncture which they had come to liberate in an attempt to open the way through the Vosges Mountains so that the Seventh Army could advance to St. Die, a major industrial, commercial and communications center, and beyond, to Strasbourg and eventually to the Rhine River.

They were told by Division G-2 that the hills were lightly held and the presence of Germans was practically nil. Which didn't make sense to Fred, since Bruyeres was heavily fortified and depended on its defense from the surrounding hills. If anything, the hills would have been turned into fortresses and deathtraps.

The Last Fox

Fred had a bad feeling about the setup, a premonition that had never accompanied him into battle before. His legs told him as much. They were weak with heavy doubt and fear, the ever-present weight on the bottom of his stomach. He couldn't face being incapacitated. He wanted to do his part; esprit de corps came first. Unlike the barren Italian countryside which lent itself to the effective range of the long-reaching M1, the broken terrain around Bruyeres and the Vosges Mountains was tommy gun country, and the forests and thick underbrush invited close and deadly encounters. But now they were poised to cross a wide, open field skirting the eastern sector of the town. Into the maws of death again.

It was October 15. Jump-off was at 0800 hours. Advancing into the open, they exposed themselves to hidden weapons. They had progressed about 300 yards when they entered a minefield, and the Germans opened up with everything they had from the surrounding hills, having zeroed in the area beforehand. Nebelwerfers, machine guns, 88's, mortars, self-propelled guns and tanks all blasted away. The men fell to the ground, clawing the dirt, and hoped that they fell on unmined ground. The enemy barrage stitched itself across the landscape, snaking this way and that, a yard at a time. The painful and frightened shouts of the wounded shrieked above the noises of the explosions. The men called in a barrage of their own from their cannoneers and the Field Artillery Battalion to blast a low-lying hill directly ahead of them where the enemy was dug in. When the friendly fire lifted and the 4.2 chemical mortars provided a smoke screen, the men ran the gauntlet and charged the hump of a hill that had to be overcome even before the attack on Hills A and B could begin and the town of Bruyeres liberated.

Fred raced through the driving rain that turned the tramped

184

soil into a muddy, alluvial swamp. With the incoming rush of the shells descending on them, the men slammed themselves on the ground and were showered with mud and shrapnel. The MG-42's and 34's ripped through their ranks. The Germans were well dug in. It was obvious from the ferocious bombardment that they had no intention of giving up ground to withdraw to the next defensive position as they had in Italy. Italy was a staying action; the Vosges Mountains bordered on their homeland. They would have to be rooted out every foot of the way, a give-no-quarter, ask-no-quarter battle. They advanced ruthlessly on the hillock, driving their bodies forward through the withering fire. They slipped and slid in the muck, some fortunately, because they fell below the line of fire. Others, less so. By the time they reached the Jerries' first line of defense in the woods, the men appeared to be figures soaked in a pit of muck, dripping mud-brown wax statues.

As soon as he spotted a dugout, Fred motioned Mike and Sam to flank it. Visibility was poor in the rain. The Nisei swarmed everywhere, and the machine guns responded accordingly. The "Brahms Hop" was no good. He had Jimmy give him covering fire while he dashed forward, firing his tommy gun, and making himself a target. Not too conspicuous. He hit the ground, crawled, stood up and ran, firing as he approached the dugout and gauged the time it would take Mike and Sam to eliminate the machine gun. His friends outflanked the gun while he engaged it frontally and maneuvered themselves behind it. With two grenades they destroyed the emplacement, and Fred and Jimmy ran as fast as they could to the next objective: another machine gun nest. It was indeed tommy gun country with the trees hiding both their advance and the camouflaged dugouts. A far cry from the battlefields of Italy, where one could pick off a target at several hundred yards with the exception of the breakout from the Anzio beachhead, when they went eyeball to eyeball with the Jerries who were just as fanatic but in the end took flight in a disciplined withdrawal. Such was not the case in the Vosges Mountains. They stayed and fought.

By the time the 442nd had overrun the hill, Hill 555, the first barrier to overtaking Hills A, B, C and D, Fred and his three friends had learned to change their tactics with each nest they demolished. With the absence of a BAR man to support them, they often had to improvise, since they were unable to rely on the firepower of the heavy automatic weapon which commanded respected and always attracted the enemy fire first. Fred and his team crawled and slithered, jumped up as pop-up targets at random while one of them, whoever was closest, would crawl within yards of a machine gun pit or outflank one to dispatch it with a well-placed grenade. There was no other choice. Grenades had to be used like explosive pickaxes. Each pit had to be scoured out, resulting in German corpses being thrown about. The rifle-launched grenades often landed short or right on top of the reinforced positions, doing little or no damage. A grenade had to be rammed literally between the teeth of the frenetic enemy–meaning, combat in close encounters. The four functioned as a team, each knowing the mind of the other, and executed a series of well-practiced double plays as in one of the games they had engaged in before Pearl Harbor, before the evacuation. Being able to read each other's mind in the feverish climate of all-out warfare helped. They knew what their next move should be whether it was outflanking the enemy and penetrating his rear or to charge his emplacement directly in a coordinated attack. Every so often they would all rise up to throw one grenade after another while one of them crawled to the very edge of the enemy's dugout to finish them off with a single fragmenting explosion.

The Last Fox

They were caked with mud and soaked to the skin. But they had taken the initial hillock after an all-day fight. They dug in and spent the night in what felt like a watery grave. They were so exhausted that they slept despite the wetness and chill...a fitful sleep where nightmares were anticipated but never appeared, where the closing of the eyes brought blankness, a black fatigue that was so familiar to them. It swept over the mind like a blanket of void, the crackling sounds of small arms fire registering dully on the peripheries of wakefulness.

Fred lay still as the cold rain pelted him, his mind a thousand miles away, his body in a warm, soft bed covered by a thick quilt. The hunger pangs subsided for a while after he had stuffed the dry contents of the K ration box into his mouth, feeling for the pieces of food in the dense darkness with muddy fingers and trying to work up enough saliva to swallow the dry crackers. He went easy on the water. Supplies would be difficult to bring up. Now he slept, or rather remained in a dazed trance, fearful of what first light would bring and yet not caring. Mortar rounds crashed through the trees and burst. The Jerries were doing everything to deny them rest, a tactic that reminded him of Italy.

At dawn the Germans counterattacked in force. They were supported by self-propelled guns and tanks. The 442nd called in an artillery barrage, and within minutes a whistling rush of incoming shells bracketed, then zeroed in on the advancing ranks of the enemy. Bodies crumbled. Torn and broken, they were thrown about like dolls. The earth exploded with thunderous force. The accurate fire from the big guns and pack howitzers exacted their toll and broke up the enemy attack. Although Allied tanks failed to break through the terrain to engage the enemy, a team of Nisei bazooka men knocked out the Mark IV tanks and routed the Germans. Then the riflemen of the 100th, 2nd and 3rd Battalions surged forward to try to take the four prominent hills.

But first they had to take the fortified farmhouses at the bases of Hills A and B before the hills could be attacked and the town of Bruyeres liberated. As the men propelled by the momentum of their push were crossing the valley to attack the fortified positions, they were stopped by a tremendous barrage directed from the hills and by another counterattack. The battle raged throughout the day as the Germans launched one attack after another until the Nisei pushed them back to the forward slopes of the hills and began to attack the sturdy farmhouses that remained impervious to the continuous shelling. The Germans and their machine guns had to be silenced. When the attack on the base fortifications was launched, a company from the 3rd battalion swung southward to attack Bruyeres from the north while Allied artillery pounded the hills in a TOT (time on target) serenade.

Fred's legs were like rubber, threatening to buckle at the knees. How could he depend on them? And yet he advanced with his friends, each covering for the other, from house-to-house, room-to-room, blasting everything that moved. A machine gun nest in the upper floor had to be eliminated. They leapt up the stairs but were stopped at the wooden door as a machine pistol riddled it with holes to ward them off. They plastered themselves against the wall, momentarily at a loss. One of them could risk opening the door while another filled the room with gunfire. But there would be casualties. Fred suddenly raised his hand to signal them to stay put. He heard a thumping on the wall. It was coming from within the room. He put his ear to the plaster surface of the wall and ran his hand around to feel for the exact spot of the vibration. Then he waited as his hand jumped with each pronounced thump. Several minutes passed. The patient pounding from within merged with the sounds of battle that erupted from the street below. The characteristic rapid belching of the unchallenged German machine gun made Fred wince as he pictured it tearing into the bodies of his Nisei comrades.

The rifle butt of the Mauser broke through the wall, sending pieces of plaster flying through Fred's hand. He grabbed the butt, yanked hard and as soon as he could finger the trigger, he angled a shot into the room. He heard a moan and the sound of a body thrown to the floor. A potato masher suddenly appeared through the hole, and Fred grabbed it out of the protruding hand and shoved it back into the room while simultaneously ramming the barrel of his tommy gun into the hole and raking the room. The explosion of the potato masher blew the door out, and the men rushed in to finish off any survivors of the blast. It was tacitly understood that they couldn't be hampered by taking any prisoners. They pumped a few rounds into the inert bodies and kicked them to make sure the Germans were dead. Young Jimmy pried the coveted German sniper rifle from death-frozen fingers and retrieved a belt holding the ammunition for the rifle.

"Now we go ged da buggahs, as Chip Shioura would say," Jimmy said, waving the rifle.

"Give me that thing," Fred said and took the heavy rifle from him. "And the ammo."

The four men clattered down the wooden steps and dashed out into the street. The firefight erupted all around them. They ran hunched to a spot where a squad from their company, crouching in a ditch by the shoulder of the road, was pinned down by a machine gun. The whole settlement of farmhouses bristled with them. The Germans were making sure the hills stayed in their hands.

Fred made the proper adjustment on the scope for the range and scanned the opening of the nest. The scope was bright enough for him to make out the shadowy figures supporting the machine gunner and his assistant. Even before he could take aim, a slug slapped into the dirt by his cheek. He spotted the sniper in the upper window. Another duel. Before the sniper could chamber another round, Fred aimed at his head and gently squeezed the crisp, two-stage trigger. The face snapped away from the window. Fred thought he had him. But the Jerry suddenly reappeared. He had a dent in his helmet, and Fred could see him aim directly at him. Suddenly, their positions were reversed, and Fred pictured the cross hairs planted right between his eyes. He felt the odd sensation of numbness between his brows, as if someone were stroking it lightly with the tip of his finger, and the hair on his neck stood up. He got what the Hawaiian Nisei called "chicken skin"and shook involuntarily as a shiver shot up his spine. He ducked and worked the bolt of the rifle at the same time. The sniper's shot flew over him, but it was close enough for him to hear the whistle of the bullet. Fred took careful aim and squeezed off another shot. The sniper flung up his arms and covered his face as he fell back, flinging his deadly rifle so violently that it appeared to be thrown out of the window at Fred personally.

Now Fred trained the scope on the lower window where the machine gun was placed and picked out his target. The machine gunner and his assistant were buried in the shadows and couldn't be made out clearly. He chose a figure in an adjacent window. With gentle pressure on the trigger, he fired and watched the green-clad German collapse. He picked off several other supporting riflemen until there was only the machine gunner and his assistant left. Fred handed the sniper rifle with the amazingly smooth Mauser action to Jimmy who was a better shot than either Mike or Sam.

"Rapid fire," he said. "You can't see the Jerries clearly, so aim for the machine gun if you have to."

As soon as Jimmy began to trigger round after round into the nest, Fred grabbed his tommy gun and told the rest of the men to hold their fire. He rose from the ditch and rushed across the road, firing as he ran. He cursed his legs but ran on. With one smooth movement, he lobbed a grenade into the opening of the nest and fell to the ground simultaneously to avoid the concussion. The machine gun, a bloody helmet, a piece of a jaw and debris blew out of the window. He waved the men across the road, and they raced to join him and began a flanking movement on another position.

It took them the whole day to clear out the farmhouses. They sent the prisoners and the wounded to the rear and dumped the German corpses into the street. Then they settled in the houses to get out of the rain which fell continuously as though the sky bled from a huge wound. Their own litter bearers arrived with the supplies. Included among the boxes of ammo and cans of water were cases of C rations, a welcome addition to the K rations. The C rations contained canned food which could be heated up, and the men eagerly set about making small fires in anticipation of consuming something warm. A small, comforting touch to an otherwise brutal day made worse by the cold and dampness. They ate hurriedly. There was no telling when the next counterattack would be launched. They expected a pause while the Jerries licked their wounds. Cutting across the valley separating the hills came the sounds of a fierce firefight still being waged by the 100th Battalion which was preparing to take Hill A.

To keep the pressure on the Germans, the 2nd Battalion clambered up the wet slopes of Hill B while elements of the 3rd Battalion which had taken the farmhouses consolidated their position at its base. No sooner had the 2nd Battalion broken through the German defenses on the lower slopes than a counterattack was launched against the farmhouses. Instead of fleeing up the hill the Germans tried to outflank the 2nd Battalion and attack it from the rear, but they had to reclaim the houses first or at least engage its occupants.

Fred and the men cursed, stamped out the fires and met the Jerries head on. They cut down what they thought was the advance guard with a controlled and sustained wall of fire from machine guns, rifles and automatic weapons only to learn that a larger German force had infiltrated the area behind them while they were engaged. The 3rd Battalion was bogged down and unable to cover the 2nd Battalion's rear, although they were ordered to do so immediately. What was left of the German contingent was scattered in the ditches across the road that Fred and his men had occupied earlier in the day, and now it was the Germans who had them pinned down in the houses with automatic weapons fire.

Lt. Morris devised a plan. It was as simple as it was dangerous. They occupied the last house in the row, and the plan was to take a squad and maneuver around the Germans and catch them in a crossfire. The lieutenant was armed with a tommy gun by now and said he would go first and that Fred was to follow with his. They and the men, including Mike, Sam and Jimmy, would cross the road, eliminate the Jerries directly opposite them and run down the line to catch them from behind with the hope that the men in the houses would charge the ditch frontally and kill those who remained.

The plan was so swiftly executed–time was of the essence– that the Germans were caught off guard. The tall, young officer and the men raced behind them, pausing only to aim and fire. As they broke up the German ranks, forcing them to turn and return fire, the rest of the 3rd Battalion rushed out of the houses to shoot point-blank at those who continued to resist. Toward the end of the fray, one German soldier who was playing dead rose up and fired a burst from his Schmeisser. Lt. Morris in the lead spun around, slapped his arm as though angry and cut the German down with a stream of slugs that stitched him from his crotch to his head, killing him instantly. The tommy gun climbed on the officer, since he was firing it with one hand, but they were only yards apart, and it was accurate enough.

The whole maneuver took only minutes. With their rifles pointed into the ditch, the men motioned the Jerries to come out, and the prisoners, discarding their weapons, rose up with their hands held high and lined the edge of the road. The men had them fashion litters out of doors and table tops to carry their wounded back to battalion headquarters.

Fred approached the lieutenant. "You're a candidate for a medal," he said in open admiration of the officer's audacity.

"Shiiit. Ah didn't join this outfit for no medal," Lt. Morris drawled. "Ah jus' wanted to be with the best."

"Need to go to battalion aid to get that taken care of?"

"Hell, no. Cain't see no use of doin' that." The young officer checked the ragged wound. "This is a band-aid job. Listen, sergeant, we've got to regroup, *tout de suite.*"

"Right."

Fred gathered the platoon together and with the other rifle companies, they made all haste to retrace the southern approach the 2nd Battalion had made up Hill B. The drizzle had turned to a downpour. It made Fred think of the rain forest country of the Pacific Northwest. As in the rain forests hung with moss, the clouds sagged heavily like sacs filled to the point of bursting. The soil could not contain the rain, and the trails that had been stamped through the forest up the southern slope turned into a swamp of pooling water. Each step the men took was like two steps backwards in the mud. They struggled forward, desperate to catch the Jerries before they could close in on their brothers-in-arms.

Before long they caught sight of the green uniforms filtering among the trees, and the forward echelon immediately opened fire. The rest of the men came abreast, formed a skirmish line and engaged in a touch-and-go firefight that kept moving up the hill until elements of the rear guard of the 2nd Battalion were forced to turn their attention to the more immediate threat behind them that would have made a rapid advance up the hill impossible. As luck would have it, they held their ground while the 3rd Battalion closed in on the Jerries, advancing and firing all the while, and caught them in another murderous crossfire. They annihilated the Germans.

Fred and the men hastened to add their strength to the attacking forces. The Germans must have anticipated the onslaught, for their barrage of mortars and 88's that produced the deadly tree-bursts was intensified and took its toll as the men were torn up by the flying shrapnel and splinters of trees that slit the air with the speed of bullets. There were also the dreaded Teller and Shuh mines–undetectable because they were made of wood–and the Bouncing Betties that shattered their bodies. Machine guns concealed in the heavy underbrush raked through their ranks. But they stubbornly pressed on, never turning their backs. A bullet wound in the back would have been intolerable–even treasonous.

On weak legs energized only by the heat of battle, Fred trudged on, each step slipping on the tramped floor of the forest as the lugged soles of hundreds of boots struggled for a hold on the slopes, and fired his tommy gun at anything in a green uniform. From one dugout to another they moved to root out the tenacious

The Last Fox

Jerries who yielded a foot, a yard of ground only in death, and the minutes amidst the crashing sounds of tree-bursts and the crackle of small arms fire seemed like hours and the hours like days, and yet Fred found himself still on his feet, moving forward with the body of men, some of whom crumbled and collapsed or were torn apart. There were no fancy tactics Fred and his friends, who followed closely behind him, could employ in the dense woods. This was not Italy where the enemy remained for the most part in sight. They were not fighting under the friendly Tuscany skies. It was wet in the woods; the underbrush was sodden. And it was cold and dark, even at midday.

A camouflaged trapdoor flung open a few feet in front of him. Two Jerries loomed out of the pit like grim specters, leering wide-eyed with terror and determination spread over their features. Fred instinctively triggered a couple of bursts from his automatic weapon at the terrible faces and blew their heads off before they could fire their machine pistols. In spite of the heavy dread that threatened to drag him down, Fred's senses were sharpened to a razor's edge, and he moved about like a tiger on the prowl. If he were to give in to his own personal doubts and fears, they would spread like a deadly virus among the platoon, and he'd just as soon have the lieutenant shoot him than let the men down. Their concern for each other was like that of brothers who shared an unspoken bond. He had to consciously stem an urge to stop and help a fallen comrade, though many of the men exposed them-selves to assist the wounded, because he knew the medics followed closely behind him. A phalanx with himself at the point, his tommy gun held ready as his friends formed a wedge, was the only viable formation. They moved cautiously through the dense woods, casting their eyes all about them to spot any suspicious movement. It was the only configuration he could think of in order to concentrate their firepower in any given direction without bunching up. He kept young Jimmy behind him.

The men of the 442nd pushed the Germans off the hill by nightfall. The enemy fled to Hill D located slightly to the east, and the men, to get away from the dreaded tree-bursts, emerged from the forest to dig their slit trenches in the valley facing the formidable hill to be taken. They would sleep in the wet fields molested by an occasional barrage of mortar fire coming from the hill. Where the Division Commander got his assessment that the hills were lightly held was a puzzle to everyone. In the meantime, the 100th Battalion had cleared Hill A of the enemy and was held in reserve.

The companies of the 2nd and 3rd Battalions were ordered the next morning to jump off as soon as the TOT bombardment of Hill D lifted. The rendition of The Serenade from the battalions of big guns, including those of the 442nd's crack Field Artillery Battalion, on the crown of the hill was impressive. The entire cap of the hill sprouted explosions until, after thirty minutes of a continuous barrage, the top was shorn of trees and was as bald as a friar's pate. The dome of the hill was shaven clean; not a single tree stood. The transformation of the forested hill to a naked mound of plowed up dirt attested to the concentrated firepower of thousands of shells saturating every square yard of ground.

The barrage had done its work. Several hours after jump-off the men took Hill D and by noon were lunching on C and K rations. They had to plow through enemy resistance on the lower slopes, but there were not as many enemy dead as they expected from the tremendous destruction of the bombardment. The Germans had presumably evacuated down the opposite slope as soon as the horrendous serenade began. After a brief respite the men slid down the muddy slopes, following paths where hundreds of troops preceded them, and gave chase to the next open valley which was cut across by a railroad embankment. The men advanced until they discovered the Germans dug in on the opposite side of the embankment–and until they found themselves in the middle of a minefield. They dug in gingerly and maintained a precarious position deep into enemy territory without protection on either flank.

Hill C, to the left and rear of them, remained in German hands and represented a threat to their flank. Though isolated the enemy gave no indication of evacuating the strategic position and put up a fierce fight when the 100th Battalion was brought out of reserve and ordered to take the hill. Which they did in short order. Many prisoners were taken.

The four strategic hills were now in Allied hands and cleared of the enemy which had commanded the heights around the town of Bruyeres. But not for long. The Germans succeeded in infiltrating the 442nd's lines and again seized Hill D and wreaked havoc in the rear echelons of the 2nd and 3rd Battalions which continued to confront the enemy dug in a 100 yards on the other side of the railroad embankment across a minefield.

In a concerted effort to regain lost ground, the Germans set into motion an attack along the road that linked Bruyeres with the next town, Belmont, in the form of an armored column backed by infantry and a concentrated artillery bombardment on the embankment positions of the 442nd. Elements of the 2nd and 3rd Battalions were diverted to retake Hill D while the remnants clambered over the railroad embankment to take on the Germans who were now backed up by tanks. The whole tenuously established front exploded.

Four P-47 Thunderbolts appeared out of the grey skies to dispatch the armored column with a series of direct hits. The accompanying German infantry hightailed it back to Belmont even as the mechanized unit was being demolished. On Hill D the fighting to take the hill again was agonizingly slow with progress measured a foot at a time till the troops were stopped by the interlocking fire of the efficient German machine guns. They remained pinned down for hours when the Germans made the mistake of violating the rules of war by gunning down a litter-bearing party carrying a wounded soldier. Those killed were clearly marked with the red cross of the medics. That mistake cost the Jerries the hill, for the enraged men rose up in a body without regard for their safety and charged into the massed ranks of the enemy and decimated them. No prisoners were taken, and the dead were scattered throughout the woods.

At the railroad embankment, the 2nd and 3rd Battalions charged across the railroad after a twenty minute artillery barrage laid on the enemy. But they made little progress because of being bombarded by the ear-splitting Screaming Meemies and caught in a minefield laced with a network of S-mines or Bouncing Betties that slashed the body ragged. They did manage to kill a German officer who was carrying information on the entire layout of the crisscrossing German defenses involving the strategic hills and the small towns north of Bruyeres: Belmont, La Broquaine, Biffontaine and La Houssiere. The information was rushed to regimental intelligence, then on to G-2. The result was a reshuffling of objectives and the formation of a task force which included forward observers for artillery missions, mine sweepers and radiomen.

Armed with the secret papers carried by the German officer, the task force succeeded in cracking German resistance through the hills and pulverized the enemy with accurate artillery fire. It paved the way for further penetration into the rugged terrain by elements of the 442nd held in reserve and relieved the pressure on the 2nd and 3rd Battalions pinned down near the railroad embankment. Though under intense fire and bombardment, some at point-blank range from the tanks, the two battalions managed to extricate themselves, and as the Germans gradually realized their position was becoming increasingly untenable, their rear now being challenged, they began to withdraw, and the companies of the two battalions that weren't drawn off made a sweep of the treacherous terrain ahead of them.

Though a brief respite in the weather had brought hope for a break in the thick clouds, the rain continued to fall mercilessly and lay a cold, sodden hand on the landscape and everything that crawled on it. Fred couldn't believe they were on the move again. Where were the white soldiers? The 141st Infantry. His legs could not hold out forever. So far they had not betrayed him. His feet began to swell from the cold and dampness, and he knew as an infantryman that he was in for trouble as he was in the battle for Monte Cassino. The trails worn through the woods headed in all directions; twice they ran into enemy patrols that were just as surprised to bump into them as they were themselves. Each time they beat them off by taking the offensive and yelling "Banzai," more from the fright rising in the belly from the sudden encounter than any kind of ferocity. At least, that was the way Fred felt as he dashed forward, slipping and sliding, where the underbrush had been stomped into the mud. He kept his finger locked on the trigger of his tommy gun at point-blank range. He was cold and wet and hungry. They were low on supplies and ammo. And yet they were told to keep advancing. He hoped they had not outrun their logistics. The lieutenant kept muttering under his breath: "Cain't understand what the goddamn rush is all about."

Fred kept his misery to himself. Nobody complained. They

were all equally as miserable and knew that griping would do no good. They had a job to do. Doing their duty was always uppermost in their minds. Fred kept checking Jimmy out. He thought of Jimmy as his younger brother. Playing ball against each other and volunteering from the same camp weren't the only reasons for his feeling an inexplicable closeness–and concern. He wanted to make sure Jimmy returned to Naples again so that he could join Liza. He had never really been in love himself. Or had he? What about the cute white co-ed named Colleen? An improbable time of hope and innocence.

As he stepped along the muddy path at a half-crouch, he blinked his eyes hard to banish the thought. He couldn't afford the luxury of a dream. The imperatives of the moment were stark and real, and he had to keep himself in line. He turned his thoughts to Sam. He was worried about him. Becoming overly concerned about the mental state of another soldier was not a good idea lest one discover a chink in one's own–and watch it crack open. Neither could he afford the luxury of introspection, though his physical condition screamed for attention. He just willed himself on.

But he could not overlook Sam's tendency to be reckless. He was as brave as any of them, often going out of his way to expose himself as if he were tempting fate. But then afterwards in his foxhole he would shake and shiver violently. When he caught Fred observing him, he'd curse the rain and the cold, but Fred perceived otherwise. The war and the constant fighting had a way of splaying the nerve endings of even the most stout-hearted and hardened veteran. Standing up to the cold and dampness and the physical torture was grueling enough, but the sight of a brother-in-arms lying dead, his life extinguished from his young body, was unbearable. Fred's persistent fear found a reflection in Sam's.

The Last Fox

They were both fighting a personal war on different fronts.

The sweep through the rough terrain and descent into the valleys and climb into the surrounding hills seemed to take weeks. In fact they had been in combat for six days continuously. The constant strain was like the weather; it was incessant, and there was no hint of a letup. Fred's feet were bothering him. He knew the other men were suffering, also. Some had full-blown cases of trenchfoot. Their clothing was never dry; they were soaked to the skin and slept in wet clothes in shallow trenches filled with water. Fred caught a few winks of sleep at a time. Only once were they held in reserve so that they could catch their breath and move away from the tree-bursts. Now they were mopping up pockets of resistance left in the wake of the rapid advance of the 100th Battalion which was forging ahead to the hills overlooking the hamlet of Biffontaine nestled in the crook of the valley north of Bruyeres.

The Division Commander, Lt. General Bunting, was like a man possessed. His catchword was: "Advance, advance, advance." His aides and advisors tried to take exception, and according to rumors emanating from headquarters, they counseled steadfast caution, but the general would not hear of it. He pushed the 442nd RCT to its limits. And when the 100th Battalion reached Biffontaine at an enormous cost of lives, he ordered the men to take the heavily fortified settlement of a few hundred souls, although it was of no particular strategic significance. But before the 100th could even budge a muscle, it had to fight for its survival as the Germans launched a series of three-pronged counterattacks against the defensive perimeter it had established with what troops remained standing. It had advanced so far so fast that the lines of communication were severed, and the armored train of tanks and jeeps carrying supplies, medicine, food and ammunition could not negotiate the wretched terrain, though they managed to beat off a determined German blockade due to the heroism of one wounded Nisei GI who machine gunned his way through the barrier from atop one of the tanks. The 100th was dangerously isolated. To attack Biffontaine in its condition would have been suicidal. It couldn't break the hold the enemy maintained against them. Also, the beleaguered battalion was running out of ammo.

Facing the moment of crisis, Fred and the men of I Company and elements of the 2nd Battalion, led through the forests by underground French patriots belonging to FFI (Freedom Fighters of the Interior), made all haste to break through to the 100th and establish a safe route for the supplies to be delivered and the wounded evacuated. They had to eliminate a contingent of Germans that had traveled down the road from Biffontaine on bicycles to cut off the 100th and attack it from the rear. The Germans were obviously using every means available to move the troops where they were needed, quickly. The fighting was brief but bloody, and Fred left many of his friends dead and wounded in the woods. Led by the French patriots without whom they would have been hopelessly lost, Fred and the men broke through to the 100th just in time. They were down to their last few rounds of ammunition, and their wounded needed immediate attention.

No sooner had Fred and the men of the 442nd established a line of communication and supply route than the word came from the Division Commander to take the hamlet of Biffontaine immediately. What for, thought Fred. There was no railroad, no strategic value to the settlement–except that it was a stronghold for the Germans. Fred could almost read the mind of the ambitious general: wherever the Boche lay hidden, root them out and kill them. The Vosges Mountains had to be breached. The factor of the cost did not seem to enter into the equation. Mixed with the coursing rain was to be the blood of American GI's–Nisei GI's. The red of their blood was the same as everybody else's. Fred wondered if that fact ever entered into the general's thinking. And yet Fred did not find himself becoming resentful. It was true that he was somewhat stymied by the reality that they were always given the tough jobs. He now knew why they were transferred from Italy to France. But the feeling was absorbed into the general stupefaction slathered over him like thick grease.

As soon as they regrouped and consolidated their positions, causing the Germans to withdraw in failure to penetrate their defenses, the 100th and the combined companies of the 2nd and 3rd Battalions streamed from the slopes of hills to take the hamlet of Biffontaine as ordered. The Germans were initially surprised and after a spirited fight were routed and took flight up the road to the next town north. La Houssiere. The victory was but an interlude. The enemy returned with a vengeance. This was not Italy where two or three days of fighting resulted in the enemy withdrawing to predesignated areas of defense. This was the Vosges Mountains where the enemy had his back to the wall, pressed against the last barrier to the homeland like desperate, vicious animals willing to sacrifice everything to protect the main lair.

The Germans returned with an armored column led by Panzers whose bulk took up most of the narrow road, whose firepower raked the houses the Nisei occupied, caving in roofs and crumbling walls with their 88's. The men sought temporary refuge in the cellars of the farmhouses and emerged when the cannonade stopped to engage the Jerries in hand-to-hand combat, fighting like tigers to hold on to each room and house. The Germans demanded their surrender in English and promised to treat them fairly as the Americans would not, and their answer was as direct as it was simple: "Go to hell!" A crack rifleman drilled the officer through the heart for his impertinence.

The pitched battle raged on. The tanks were firing at point blank range; some of the shells blew into the rooms, penetrated the walls and exited through the opposite side without exploding. Both sides were parrying, thrusting, lunging with fixed bayonets, and the blades that struck home brought forth loud grunts and shrieks. The noise of the fight merged as the crashing of the explosions, crackle of small arms fire, moans and curses became one undispelled series of sounds. A farmhouse detached from the rest of the houses became an aid station where the wounded were carried under fire, and the men fought off the attackers who tried to overrun them by manning each window and firing everything they had at the Germans, including rifle grenades which broke up wave after wave of attacks. The tide was turned when the lead tank was hit by a bazooka rocket and burst into flames. The rest of the tanks turned and retreated; they were followed by a demoralized infantry.

When the acrid smoke of the battle had cleared, Fred exhaled his breath as though he had been holding it ever since the counterattack began and slumped to the floor, still with his gun resting on the sill of the upper window and his gaze scanning the now empty landscape which was as heavy with rain as it was with the sudden silence. To his amazement he spotted a lone farmer toiling in the field to harvest his crop of cabbages. He had remained oblivious to the firefight as it erupted around him. His bent-over form suggested an earthbound defiance of death–and the stubborn serenity of a man who devoted his life to working the soil. Fred marveled at the force of life that the figure of the farmer represented.

The moans of the wounded lying all about him brought him back to the small pocket of reality that comprised his world of life and death. The mattress upon which a wounded soldier lay was blood-soaked. His bowels were torn open, and his intestines hung out like twisted pieces of bloody rope. Some of the wounded tried to dress their own injuries; most of them lay still already in shock. Fred rubbed his legs vigorously and crawled over to a man he did not know–a recent replacement–but who was still conscious and grabbing his side in pain. Wordlessly, Fred pulled up his shirt to expose an ugly wound in his lower abdomen, sprinkled sulfa powder on it and taped a compress in place. He could do no more. As he was dressing the wound, the soldier on the bed cried out loudly once–Mama!–and died.

When the medics came clambering up the stairs to take care of the wounded, Fred vacated the room and went downstairs to look for his friends. He could not find them. Concerned, he almost fell into panic and left the house. In the field nearby the farmer was still harvesting his cabbage, weathering the downpour as he had the war. The solitary figure symbolized all the defiance mankind could muster against the machines of mass destruction–against war itself. In spite of himself, Fred stood and stared at him, regarding him with wonder, and somehow drew strength from the very sight of the defiant figure working methodically, slicing each head of leafy cabbage at its base with a sharp knife.

The battle for Biffontaine had lasted for less than half a day, but the Germans had grouped and regrouped any number of times to retake the hamlet with the final result of withdrawing dispirited in the wake of the destruction of its tanks. And now the 141st and 143rd Infantry Regiments of the 36th Division arrived to relieve the Nisei troops who had taken the town and withstood the counterattacks.

When Lt. Morris regrouped the remnants of their platoon

outside one of the demolished farmhouses they had so desperately defended, Fred caught up with his friends, Mike, Sam and Jimmy. Much to Fred's relief–and surprise–they remained uninjured except for Mike's bloody hand. He had it swathed in gauze and seemed unconcerned.

"You see that Panzer blow up?" Sam said more as a statement than a question. "That was me. I nailed it good. The bazooka man got hit, and I picked up the bazooka and got the tank that got him. I could almost hear the goddamn Jerries frying in the flames." Sam laughed aloud.

He was gloating. But with only half his face. His mouth was held wide with a triumphant grin; his eyes lined with dark circles were haunted with terror. Fred said nothing. He wondered if he wore the same tormented expression.

After eight days of continuous fighting in the rain and mud, including sleepless, water-drenched nights, the men of the 442nd were finally relieved by the fresh regiment of white soldiers and were ordered to the rest area in Belmont. They were received by the local citizenry joyously as the liberators of their towns which had been occupied by the Germans for four years. The people gathered from the nearby towns to shake their hands and thank them and referred to them reverentially as the "Little Iron Men." Hardly any of them stood much taller than their average five-four. The bayoneted M1 almost matched their height.

The hot meals were a balm to both body and soul. The men were shuttled to the mobile shower units and washed off the grime, sweat and mud. A month's worth of dead skin was vigorously scrubbed off; boils and pimples that covered their bodies healed rapidly with the cleansing action of hot water and soap. And they were issued fresh, new clothing. The only hitch was that they were designed and made for WAC's: the quartermaster couldn't come up with clothing that fit the small men. They grumbled about the women's uniforms, turned their noses up at the effeminate undies, but gratefully accepted the raincoats, although it had mercifully stopped raining–as if heaven had decided to withhold its punishing hand. The item that was sorely needed but lacking were boots. The men, many of whom had developed trenchfoot, had no choice but to try to dry out their old ones as best they could and yank them back on.

They also received their back pay and mail. The rest area at Belmont was still within the range of enemy artillery which continued to harass them with occasional barrages, but Fred and the others couldn't be bothered by the sporadic rounds that whistled over and among them. To Fred it seemed that the Germans couldn't get it out of their heads that they had been beaten again and again by a bunch of Asian runts from America, who had been given a raw deal by their own country, and that the master race had been forced to turn tail and run. Fred derived a sense of perverse delight from what he perceived as their ire– expressed by the harassing barrage–while they stewed and licked their wounds. The hot food and warm clothing, the absence of being shot at and his cutting insight into the enemy's indignation lifted him out of the mire of the awful circumstances of war. He found himself luxuriating in the sounds of birds singing in the trees and the sight of butterflies flitting among the wild flowers that managed to survive the cold. The songs of the birds and the wind soughing through the trees were odd counterpoints to the whining of incoming shells. As he recalled there were no birds in Italy; he could not remember hearing even one songbird during the breaks in the fighting. He had heard they were netted by the thousands for food by the starving populace.

Except for the occasional shelling, Fred felt at peace with the passing of the throes of combat that melted away from the core of his bones as he stretched out in his pup tent. He opted for life out in the open, away from the buildings, filled to the bursting point, that were targeted by the spasmodic but crushing barrage. Even his legs felt better. It never ceased to amaze him what a hot meal could do for a front line soldier. He turned around in the tent and with his head toward the light, he opened the letter from Tule Lake first.

As usual it was written by Margie who still managed to remain in the hospital but was no longer in quarantine. She said that she was happy that she had kept the family together and prevented their father from repatriating to Japan, that she considered it her obligation to keep everybody in America. But the atmosphere of the camp was charged. All was not right. There were continuing rumors of the administration selling the meat destined for the mess halls on the black market. The mood of the internees was ugly. She mentioned again the trigger-happy guard shooting a truck driver, an inmate of the camp, at the gate and the ensuing riot that erupted like a festering carbuncle. Fred knew the story. Tanks rumbled into the camp, and armed troops in gas masks threw tear gas into the crowds and fired volleys over their heads. She heard and saw some of the aftermath from the hospital window. The leaders of the uprising were still being hunted down and arrested. They were thrown into the small stockade where they were tortured. Some died, and there were further riots when the families couldn't claim the bodies and hold funerals. The riots worked to widen the rift between the pro- and anti-Japanese factions; the camp was in a turmoil of divided sympathies. She wrote that none of the events or hard feelings, as she put it, would have come about if they had been allowed to remain free and work in the war industry to prove themselves. A childish way of looking at the corrosive realities of racism, thought Fred, but thoroughly understandable. As the eldest of the children, he felt acutely that he was needed at home. He wanted to cry out over the distance for Margie to hold out and continue her fight to keep the family intact–in America–although Shoji, disillusioned and hurt as he was, could see no future in the country where his children had been born.

He turned the second letter over curiously. It was obviously from Rhonda. The handwriting on the envelope was hers, but there was no return address. Which struck Fred immediately as strange. He opened the contents and read rapidly. He paused midway through the letter in disbelief.

"Oh, no!" he groaned He whipped the letter away from him and slammed his head hard. Rhonda couldn't take camp life any longer. She had suffered a breakdown. She refused to believe that she could possibly be regarded as the enemy. She wrote that she was an outstanding, loyal American, certainly not someone who deserved to be put into a concentration camp in one's own country...to be separated from one's family and remain alone and isolated. But the reality of the situation was as simple as it was brutal. The perfidy of the betrayal ran deep. It was symbolized by the ubiquitous barbed wire fence and armed watch towers. Total isolation. She could not live with the reality of being incarcerated simply because she looked like the enemy. She began to demand of the camp authorities to be let out, she wrote, because she was white–actually white. They just couldn't see it. A terrible mistake had been made. She kept insisting. She was born white, and it was only by accident that she looked the way she did. She was as American as the next person. In her desperation, she figured her insistence was her ticket to the outside world. Her world, and the world at large where she belonged. She wound up being transferred to the Salem State Hospital in Oregon, now a lone, solitary Jap, the enemy, among the insane of a different color.

Fred picked up the letter with trembling hands and read on. Tears collected in the corners of his eyes. Rhonda was his favorite sister, and he was not there for her. He needn't have volunteered. He could have stayed with her and looked after her, knowing how sensitive she was about the evacuation and the split in the family. He could have waited until the long arm of the government reached into the camp and drafted him as it had the new replacements. But, then, he might have wound up resisting the draft on principle as some young men had in Heart Mountain, Wyoming and sent to Leavenworth Penitentiary. It was a horror story to reach him secondhand by the draftees who reinforced the horrendously depleted ranks of the 442nd. And as a result he would have been separated from Rhonda anyway and denied his part in the war effort.

He hadn't volunteered because he wanted to prove his loyalty, he reasoned. The burden of proof was imposed upon him. He volunteered because he loved his country. Something greater was at stake. It was ineffable, like the awesome significance of one's birthright. Who could possibly describe what one's birthright really meant and get down to the soul of the matter? If he was fighting and pitting his all for something, it was precisely for the undefinable significance of one's felt identity. Felt and perceived. Reaching for what was denied but promised?

Rhonda's identity was gone. She no longer felt she was herself. The medication they put her on robbed her of any sense of self. She did not know who she was, she said. She was a stranger to herself. And she didn't want Fred to write to her, because he had no way of knowing what had happened to her and that she was no longer the Rhonda he had known. He would be trying to communicate with an unknown and unknowable person, possibly no longer human and only a humanoid in a trance, dazed out of her mind and existence. She was both within and without herself, roaming the ward just like the others but not really like them at all. She could see herself among the dead, and yet in some vital center she was fighting to live. She did not want to burden Fred with her troubles, since he had enough of his own. Do not write, she reiterated. He would never hear from her again. Stay well, she wrote at the end, and come back home alive so that he could visit her someday...if he wanted to.

Beside himself, Fred roughly batted the tears from his eyes. He was momentarily struck with confusion; all kinds of wild ideas stampeded through his mind. He could claim a Section Eight and plead for a transfer. He could insist that his family needed him back home, since they were in danger of disintegrating. He could put the war behind him by putting a slug through his leg. When he thought of Rhonda being all alone in an insane asylum, a lone Jap who was sick in mind and heart with no one to understand her torment, he wanted to cry aloud. The tears streamed down his face, but no sound issued from his throat. He could only swallow hard, twice, three times, and let the paroxysm pass. He wiped the tears from his eyes, folded the letter and replaced it in the envelope. He had no one to talk to. Nobody was supposed to break down in the concentration camps; they were expected to practice *gaman* or perseverance. Besides, talking about mental illness was taboo. It made everybody feel uncomfortable, especially since cases of combat fatigue began to crop up. He was resigned to holding the pain within himself.

Then, as he focused on the folds of the tent as though he were an oracle who could read the creases, he grew calmer. It was a steady calm, verging on being deadly and deliberate. He had his part to do. He would not let the others down, regardless of any personal burden. In every skirmish, he fought to live. He fought to survive so that he could continue to fight and someday get the job done. For some reason, he never thought about dying in battle. Perhaps it was precisely because he was always staring death in the face that he refused to think about his own demise, which may or may not have been important in the larger scheme of things. He could only think of fighting and continuing to fight. If not for democracy, then for freedom. If not for freedom, then for a dream. If not for a dream, then for the next foot of ground. Always advancing, marching, moving through the sounds of fury toward an unseen end.

Rhonda's dilemma and the immediacy of the war had him in a vice. He couldn't chicken out. That much was for certain, regardless of the circumstances. Or even because of them. The war was insane, the world was insane, the governments were insane. General Bunting was insane. In the crucible of insanity, perhaps the final standard of sanity was the foot soldier's ability to follow orders and carry them out, relying on his training and sharpened wits. An infantryman would have made a lousy philosopher, thought Fred, for all of reality and truth was consigned to the business end of a gun barrel–who kills whom first– whereas the philosopher had the luxury of dreaming big dreams that could either begin or end wars or do both at the same time. But curiously enough the foot soldier always ended up with the eye of the philosopher, the main difference being one of succinctness and a sense of horror.

The rain receded, and the clouds shrank back into the skies which grew lighter, then cleared to expose patches of blue which augured a welcomed warmth of the sun. The wind blew cold and whistled through the trees amid the songs of the birds. The promise of better weather was like a gift of nature. The soldier was a victim of whimsy, but if the weather was kind, the entire world seemed a gentler place to be, and the battles to be fought could better be faced as men and soldiers rather than beasts of burden subjected to all the hazards of the elements designed as punishment for the prosecutors of war.

That evening Fred watched a rare, fiery display of a sunset that turned the clouds red and spread its crimson rays through the splayed fingers of the forest over the bivouac area. The swatches of blue sky turned azure, then became darker still as the straight evergreens stretched heavenward like feathered shadows distinct in every detail set against the dying day. The red turned orange, then purple with remnants of bright slashes of color streaking across the sky as darkness descended. He experienced a rare moment of unadulterated peace. The skies were smiling on them. Night came and with it the cold. In spite of the shelling that came in two's and three's, he felt he could sleep the sleep of total fatigue, free of the nightmares of combat.

Chapter Twelve

"Advance, advance, advance!" It was like a demonic incantation issuing from the headquarters of the Division Commander.

Outstripping their supply line, the 1st Battalion of the 141st Infantry which had relieved the 442nd RCT at Biffontaine found itself isolated and cut off from friendly forces on a ridge line they had been following in the Vosges Mountains. Assured on the basis of just one report that there were no Germans about, they had responded to General Bunting's orders to penetrate deep into the mountains, the last barrier to the homeland of Germany itself, in order to pave the way for the capture of St. Die, the immediate and next major industrial, commercial and transportation center. Their advance was rapid and smooth–too smooth. When they became separated from the rest of the regiment, the Germans exploded into action. The enemy's interlaced network of defenses in the dense forest thundered alive with artillery, mortars and machine guns, effectively driving a wedge between the 1st Battalion and their supporting units, which for two days tried to close the gap and maintain solidarity to no avail. They could not make a dent in the entrenched defenses of the enemy who fought fanatically to hold their ground with the smell of a clean kill in their nostrils. The stranded men formed a defensive perimeter on a knoll, dug in and fought savagely for survival. They became known as the Lost Battalion.

The men of the 442nd were luxuriating in the relative peace and quiet of the rest area at Belmont, writing letters, playing cards, shooting the breeze. For a single day, at least, the sun broke through the clouds and drove the chill out of the air. The mess cooks outdid themselves trying to prepare the best meals for the combat troops, and the hot meals as well as the absence of rain rendered the verdant setting idyllic, although there was always the reminder of the enemy's ire. They made friends with the townspeople, who noted among themselves what gentlemen they were, and gave whatever sweets they had, including the K ration chocolate bars and candy received in the mail, to the children with whom they became close.

But on the second day of their reprieve, the clouds closed as though to shunt hope aside, and it turned cold and began to drizzle. Toward the end of the day, the men were shivering again. The men from Hawaii could not get used to the climate. Then the call came through for them to assemble on the double. A collective groan heaved itself up in protest: "Oh no, not again!" The entire 442nd RCT was given its marching orders after less than two days of rest. They were to embark on an emergency mission. Rescue the Lost Battalion.

Fred was aghast. Why them again? Why not the 143rd Infantry Regiment held in reserve? But General Bunting, who had been a desk-bound officer before taking over the division, was adamant. It was up to the 442nd to extricate his men from a seemingly hopeless situation. They were already low on supplies and ammunition, having traveled light, because they did not expect the opposition they confronted. They were now completely surrounded. Clearly Division Intelligence had erred.

The Last Fox

Fred trudged along the muddy road behind Lt. Morris, trying to match his strides. Behind them were his close friends and Herb Sakata, Chik Tokuhara and the new replacements that formed the platoon. It was a forced march with full field packs that seemed to weigh a ton after the first few miles. The Nisei always carried extra ammo, rations and water with them in case of an emergency. They marched under the cover of darkness and could barely make out the form of the soldier just ahead of them. The rain fell harder, and Fred thought that the heavens had shut their doors to keep from witnessing something terrible to happen. The pelting downpour had a mind of its own and fell on them to soften them up for more misery to come. Before long his feet were wet and cold. It was going to happen again. The cold and dampness and swollen feet.

Outside Biffontaine they found the ridge the 141st Infantry Regiment had taken to enter the rugged terrain of the Vosges Mountains, a barrier running a 100 miles long, and relieved the remnants of the 2nd and 3rd battalion of the regiment that failed to break through to their comrades. It was 0300 hours. They went immediately on the line. It was there that they entered a strange world of blackness so dark that it was dense, as dense as the forest, and they had to hold on to the pack of the person ahead of them, slipping and sliding on the slick, muddy trail, for they could not see their hands in front of their faces. The 442nd infiltrated the night abreast with the 2nd Battalion on the left and the 100th Battalion on the right. The 3rd Battalion which included I Company headed straight up the middle.

Fred entered an eerie world of darkness and silence. It was as though there were disembodied spirits lurking in the woods to warn him of the enormous, unseen danger that lay ahead. From the hips down his legs grew weaker, and he silently cursed them.

They moved as quietly as they could, but nothing could completely conceal the cracking of branches and the rustling of the wet undergrowth.

Several hundred yards into the mountains and still groping their way into the silent darkness, they ran into the first defensive emplacements. In the ink-black night, orange muzzle flashes accompanied the eruption of gunfire. The slashes of light were startling against the curtain of blackness. Were it not for the whizzing of the singing bullets, some finding their mark with a thud, and the flying pieces of bark that stung the face, the muzzle flashes would have been considered a beautiful contrast to the depths of darkness. The men fell to the ground instantly and returned fire, and for a while the dark forest was filled with hundreds of streaks of orange-red in a rattling concert of sight and sound.

Fred did not return fire. It would have been a waste of ammunition, and it was difficult to determine what the range was in the darkness. He hastily dug in where he first hit the ground. The soil had a spongy quality to it and gave off the distinct odor of decayed vegetation, but deeper down he struck the underlying layer of rock. All up and down the line came the sounds of shovels crunching into the ground as the men dug in. It would have been folly to proceed any further, against a concealed enemy one could not possibly see. Digging by feel, he labored quickly to scrape open the slit trench that would provide some protection, until he could see what they were up against at first light.

The rain fell even harder, and he was soaked through, wet and cold. The hole he had dug soon filled partially with water. He dug one end deeper than the other so the water could run into it and he could scoop it out with his helmet. But he found himself lying in a cold puddle formed seemingly by the water rising from the saturated ground, the thin, spongy top layer no longer capable of containing the downpour. His socks were damp, and he could feel his feet throbbing painfully in spite of the numbness. Nothing but trouble lay ahead of him as a foot soldier. They said they had only four miles to go to get to the Lost Battalion, but it was going to be more like ten in the treacherous terrain where the highest mountain rose to about 4,500 feet.

Fred could not reconcile General Bunting's irrational demand for the men of the 442nd to push ahead as fast as they could with their battered condition. They had had less than two days of rest during the continuous fighting that lasted for eight days. The demand was tantamount to pushing them beyond their limits, beyond all expectations, something he dare not impose on the white troops. But that was the way it was. Fred warned himself of resentment. By now he was something of a professional soldier, always trying to fight to survive without letting fear get the best of him, whether the orders from the top made any sense or not. The whole business amounted to nothing but insanity anyway.

At first light the action began. The enemy was strung out in camouflaged positions about a 100 yards ahead of them, and the forward observers of both the Cannon Company and the 522nd Field Artillery Battalion called in a fire mission. First came the smoke rounds that bracketed the positions, and they were followed by the order to fire for effect. With the roar of the incoming shells, the entire floor of the forest exploded. The ground shook; bodies were thrown about, and the lesser saplings snapped like toothpicks that added to the web of the undergrowth.

The enemy responded in kind instantaneously. The dreaded 88's and Screaming Meemies, howitzers and mortars opened up and rained on them in a predetermined pattern. Tree-bursts, the most diabolical conception of maiming and killing troops, descended on them in the form of myriad, red-hot shrapnel that tore up everything in its path, trees and flesh. Shattered, driven spikes of broken branches flew about wildly like spears flung by the spirits of the forest. As the men rose up to wade into the sheet of machine gun and automatic weapons fire, they were impaled and torn, and they dashed from tree to tree seeking protection and advanced inexorably. They couldn't see the enemy clearly. They fired at the muzzle flashes in the dim light that remained almost as dense as the night. They tripped and fell over the broken saplings, crawled under them, rose to their feet and rushed at the Germans. The men fell like wheat being mown. They got within fifty yards of the entrenched positions when they were pinned down by interlocking machine gun fire.

Slamming into the wet ground, Fred grimaced with pain. He thought he had been shot in the face. With amazement he asked himself how he could still be alive. He put his hand to the wound, then realized his cheek had been pierced by a jagged splinter of wood. He gritted his teeth as he worked it out gently and threw aside the bloody spike which he first examined with curiosity as though it were something disgusting.

He craned his neck around to watch the men of his platoon draw up the rear and hit the dirt. Mike, Sam and Jimmy stuck close to him. There were no tactics to devise; the thick woods left no room for improvisation. The Germans, dug in as they were, had all the tricks up their sleeves. Out of the corner of his eye he saw Herb Sakata fall. He wasn't just ducking the gunfire. He was hit. Fred jerked upright and ran over to him. As he knelt over the writhing figure, Chik Tokuhara dashed over to him to help but was cut down by a burst from a machine gun. He fell–buckled–face down, clutching his arm and thrashed about.

Herb had been shot in the stomach, a bad place to be hit. Fred opened his blood-soaked jacket and pulled up his shirt to expose the wound. It was a clean wound but obviously an extremely painful one. Must have pierced a nerve center, Fred thought.

"You've been hit, too," Herb said.

"Just a sliver." Fred had forgotten the pain.

"Damn," Herb said through clenched teeth, "this one is worse than the first one."

Fred didn't know where the bullet had migrated or how bad he was torn up inside, but he dressed the wound as best he could.

"You'll be all right," Fred said to reassure him, although he wasn't certain of what he was saying. "Chik's down, too."

"Damn," Herb repeated softly.

The small arms fire crackled, and the sounds filled the air like a kind of static that was alien to the woods. Pieces of bark were ripped off the trees as the bullets flew about, and the bits of wood were splintered as though by an unseen force. By the time Fred got to Chik, he had stopped thrashing about and was going into shock. Fred gently turned him over. His right arm and leg were bloodied and torn up, both revealing gaping wounds. The blood was washed in an ever widening patch of red by the downpour. The cold contributed to the shock. There was little Fred could do except to put a compress on the wounds.

"Medic! Medic!" Fred hollered above the noise of battle. His heart began to race madly. Seeing his friends wounded made him think of the impossibility of the mission.

Chik opened his eyes. "Your face is bloody, Fred," he said weakly.

"I didn't get shot. A splinter of wood...probably looks worse than it is."

"You should get it taken care of."

"Later." Fred's breath came in short gasps. He looked around for the medic.

Ducking under the hail of fire and holding his helmet in place, a medic arrived to begin administering aid to both men.

"Take good care of them," Fred said, his throat constricted.

"Will do," said the medic, working calmly.

Wiping the blood from his face with his hand, Fred ran back to his original position beside Lt. Morris and flattened himself against the ground.

"We're being cut to pieces," Fred said, tempering the alarm in his voice. "At this rate, there'll be nobody left."

"That's why we've got to move," the lieutenant said, "and we've got to move fast."

A crack of thunder boomed above them, and Fred looked around, momentarily confused, thinking that the Jerries had unleashed a new weapon at them; then the thunder cracked again and rolled into the mountains to join the sounds of fighting erupting not only in their sector but also on their flanks as well. The gods were adding their own fury to the battle.

"I've got an idea," Fred said.

"Shoot," said Lt. Morris.

"Have the BAR engage the machine gun on the left while the rest of us concentrate our fire on the one to the right, and then I'll try to take it out, and we'll circle around behind the others and make a break in the Jerries' line."

"Do it. We've got to move."

Fred crawled over to the BAR man and instructed him to direct his automatic fire on the machine gun interlocked with the right one as soon as he got the other men in position and to cover him as he attempted to knock it out. The BAR man and his assistant nodded and wiggled into the depths of the underbrush by a tall tree. Soaking wet Fred slithered like a water snake over to

Mike, Sam and Jimmy and the others of the platoon who were pinned down and told them of his plan and to follow him as soon as he took out the machine gun nest.

Fred gave the signal, and the BAR boomed and stuttered and fought it out with the machine gun that located the automatic weapon and fired upon it. As the men opened fire on the machine gun to the right, Fred leaped and ran ten yards, fifteen, twenty, closing the range and firing his tommy gun with one hand and holding a grenade ready in the other. He slid to the ground, rose quickly and threw the hand grenade. It was short a yard but close enough to cause the machine gun to stop burping for an instant. He took advantage of the concussion the gunners must have suffered and, paving his way with a stream of fire, leaped ahead and sprayed the interior of the dugout with his tommy gun and finished it off with a grenade. The machine gun was silenced, and he waved the men on.

The lieutenant rose with his tommy gun held ready, and the platoon, already reduced to a squad, raced through the breach and circled behind the other emplacements. Observing what was happening, the other platoons, similarly decimated, rose up with fixed bayonets and charged the MG-42's and 34's. They literally hoisted the Jerries out of their holes while Fred and his men, now led by the lanky lieutenant, fired on them from behind. They broke the line and took over the position. So tenacious were the Jerries that very few prisoners were taken in the first skirmish. The few who stood up with their hands raised, yelling "Kamerad, Kamerad," were trembling and cowered with fear.

Among them were slender teenagers who had not yet reached manhood and flaccid men in their sixties. The lieutenant detached Mike and another man to take the prisoners to the rear. Then the order came from the major leading the attack to dig in and prepare for a counterattack. Lt. Morris laid claim to a previously occupied dugout and dragged Fred down into it. The hole stank heavily with a foreign smell that Fred couldn't identify. They both settled into the hole warily and waited. Small arms fire continued to crackle throughout the forest.

Before night fell, Mike and the new replacement returned to the line. Mike jumped into the hole with Fred and the lieutenant. Sam and Jimmy joined them. Jimmy heaved the body of a dead German out of the hole and rummaged through the abandoned weapons.

"What, no sniper rifle?" he mumbled.

The rain continued to fall mercilessly. The drenched men shivered in the cold. Fred felt the water run down his legs as though he had urinated in his pants and filled his boots. It was not warm piss coursing down his legs but ice cold water. There was no letup in the weather. He tried to keep his extra pair of woolen socks dry by folding them in his armpits, but it was futile. He knew nothing would stay dry in such a downpour with them sitting in a hole filled with six inches of water.

"The Jerries thought we were going to take them back and shoot them," Mike reported. "Imagine their surprise when we gave them cigarettes and something to eat. The poor kid was so young he choked on the cigarette, but he smoked it just the same. The war is over for him and the old man."

"They must be scrapin' the bottom of the barrel in the Fatherland," the lieutenant observed.

"They were told to hold the Vosges Mountains to the last man," Mike reported. "Hitler's Edict. The Fuehrer himself has taken charge of the battle and wants the Lost Battalion wiped out. A feather in his hat, you know. Man, those Jerries were scared when we took them back."

"The villagers said these mountains have always been a fortress," Fred said. "No army in history has ever breached them. The FFI fighters themselves claim as much. The terrain is too rough, and the defenders have the upper hand."

"That's comfortin' to know," Lt. Morris said laconically.

"Then what the hell do they expect us to do!" Sam said angrily and shivered with his arms held around him.

"Be the first," Fred said. His heart was still racing, but his breathing was more controlled.

"Shit, it would take the whole Seventh Army to conquer the mountains," Sam shot back, obviously maddened by the idea. "What the hell is a single regiment supposed to do?"

"We haven't failed to take every assigned objective yet," Fred said sternly to try to instill fire into Sam's wracked body.

"You forget Monte Cassino," Sam said, shaking.

"The 100th was cut to pieces, weakened, and the Combat Team wasn't brought up to full strength yet."

"What about the 143rd and all the other battalions of white guys? Why just us?" asked Sam belligerently. "Answer that, Fred!"

Fred swallowed his doubts; he wasn't about to express them to the men. Yes, why, he thought. They were embarked on a suicide mission. But to voice his doubts would have reinforced their fears.

"Because we're the best there is," he said quietly. "And the best always get called on to handle the toughest jobs."

In spite of his feelings to the contrary, the ring of assurance in Fred's voice was genuine. He hoped he had allayed any suspicions the men might have had, and he knew they couldn't help but have plenty.

"Don't hand me that crap, Fred!" Sam hollered and shook.

"It's because we're expendable."

Fred gripped his shoulder and squeezed hard. "Keep it to yourself, Sam."

Sam stared into Fred's hard eyes for a long moment. "Yeah, sure, Fred. Sure," Sam said, duly admonished. "Anything you say."

The men waited, and darkness descended. The counterattack never came. The rain beat down on them and swept in broken sheets through the thick woods as the wind picked up. The medics and litter bearers were still kept busy as the night deepened. The major sent out a patrol which spent two hours crawling through the dripping underbrush. They set off a couple of booby traps that called forth bursts of machine gun fire from the upper slope. When they entered a minefield, they raced back, dodging the bullets, to report their findings. Lt. Morris was informed what to expect.

"The krauts want us to come and get them," he said. "They're just sittin' there waitin' for us. We're not going to disappoint them, are we?"

"Nope," Fred said, echoing the officer's laconic style.

As though his words were a signal, the German artillery opened up with every piece of projectile from 88's, Screaming Meemies and mortars thrown at them. The air around them split wide open with the shrieking of the nebelwerfers and the deadly tree-bursts that flashed and thundered with a reddish light. Shrapnel sizzled and fluttered through the air, slicing everything in its path, slashing uniforms and tearing open flesh and ricocheting off equipment and gun barrels. The smell of burnt powder stung the nostrils. The sudden thud of the silent mortar rounds hitting the ground beside them and exploding was frightful. They were immobilized.

The barrage continued for hours without letup; it seemed the enemy had a limitless supply of ammunition and was delighted to unleash it against them. The machine guns on the slope raked their position as if to assure them of the obvious fact that they were pinned down and frozen into position. They had no choice but to hold up against the barrage and the dreadful tree-bursts that spread death in all directions. The men stiffened themselves against the cold, wet ground in the slit trenches and prayed they would not be hit by the hundreds of mortars descending on them or by the jagged, flying shrapnel. Those who had the foresight to cover themselves with branches and mud fared better than the others who lay exposed, shivering with both the cold and fear. Most of them lay on their stomachs with their faces buried in the mud for protection; some had their backs cut open and their spinal column severed.

When it was light enough to see the next morning, the major launched an attack on the fortified slope with what was left of the 3rd Battalion. Many men were killed or wounded during the night's bombardment and lay in their shallow slit trenches either silent or moaning and calling out for the medic. The sounds of fighting erupted simultaneously on either flank where the 2nd and 100th Battalions were facing similar difficulties. Sounds of the rumbling of their own tanks that managed to negotiate the terrain and the subsequent gunfire were comforting. At least they had some armor to confront the German's Mark IV tanks and self-propelled guns. When they heard shouts of "Banzai" ringing above the explosions and small arms fire, they were heartened and took up the battle cry and advanced up the slope into the sheet of machine gun bullets.

The enemy dugouts were camouflaged and hard to detect in the dense forest. Sometimes the Germans would let them pass and then pop up to shoot them from behind. The Nisei had to have eyes and ears all about them. They kept on moving forward without stopping and used bayonets, grenades and captured Schmeissers to dig out the enemy.

As they were resolutely advancing, the trapdoor of a camouflaged position sprang open, and a young German shot Lt. Morris with his machine pistol at point-blank range. The tall lieutenant crumbled with a sigh, a surprised look on his face. Fred immediately sprayed the position with his tommy gun and killed the two Jerries. He then dragged the lieutenant out of the direct fire and into a dip in the ground.

He examined the lieutenant's wounds. They were bad. He ripped opened a packet of powder and tried to pry the young officer's hands away from the worst wound in his belly, but he kept pressing them into the shredded flesh as though to hold his bowels intact. The blood oozing from the other wounds mixed with the water of his rain-soaked uniform and for some odd reason reminded Fred of the cherry Koolaid he used to drink as a kid.

"Medic!" Fred screamed. His heart pounded furiously.

"Forget it," the officer said weakly. "Ah really bought the farm this time."

"Don't say that, lieutenant. You'll be all right as soon as a medic gets to you. Now, let me dress that wound."

"Ah'm not lettin' go. My guts will spill out, and you'll never git them back in."

"Let me sprinkle some of this sulfa on it." Fred was desperate; he looked around for the medic.

"Leave it be, sergeant. Ah'm finished."

"You'll be back Stateside in no time at all with the god-awful war behind you, sir."

"You're a good man and soldier, Sgt. Murano, but you're also a goddamn dreamer, an idealistic dreamer." The lieutenant sighed heavily and took a deep breath and held it as though reluctant to let it go. "You're in charge now. Do right by the men, sergeant."

"I will, sir. But hang on. Help is on its way."

With a strained voice and a gurgling in his throat, the young lieutenant smiled and said: "Ah guess ah'll never know what raw fish tastes like."

Just then nebelwerfers, screaming like hysterical women, flew at them and burst in the trees. Fred threw himself on the lieutenant to protect him. When the shrapnel spent themselves and fell to the ground, Fred got off the officer who had weathered all the battles with him since the Anzio breakout.

He was dead. Fred somberly closed his blank-staring eyes, gazing unseeingly into the grey dimness of the forest, and looked upon the young features of the officer, the war a million miles away for a moment. The rifles cracked and the machine guns sputtered as in a distant scene. A dream scene of tumultuous nightmares. Then he picked up his tommy gun and ran toward the gunfire to join the fray.

They charged up the gradual, sloping woods. Squad after squad, platoon after platoon, the companies whose ranks were being slashed pressed on against the enemy in an unrelenting effort to break through to the Lost Battalion. Each successive enemy position was taken with the body of a Nisei often draped over the barrel of the machine gun he had silenced. But the forward movement of the 442nd was unstoppable. They hit the Germans with grim determination, always moving, shooting from the hip, pausing to grenade an emplacement, dueling with a sniper or grenadier.

Individual acts of heroism abounded with a bazooka man taking out a tank to break up a counterattack, a soldier armed with a BAR blazing a path through the Jerries' defenses, a lone Nisei platoon leader inspiring his men by rushing through the withering fire to blast a machine gun nest out of existence. The men followed one another moving from tree to tree, dashing across a large mined and fortified clearing, rooting out the enemy at the point of a bayonet. The Jerries broke and ran. They fled into the mountains to their next defensive position, always well concealed and prepared, sometimes counterattacked but always beaten back with the tenacity of the riflemen and the accurate fire of the artillery battalion and the pack howitzers. Some of the prisoners taken proved to be from units brought in as fresh reinforcements to guard the Vosges Mountains. Hitler obviously viewed the situation as critical.

So was the rescue of the Lost Battalion. They were low on ammunition, food and medical supplies; the airdrops helped but little, since the parachuted bundles usually fell into enemy hands or rolled down the knoll out of reach.

Fred dug in. The darkness of night and fatigue stopped them. Miraculously, his friends were still standing. Fred had Jimmy dig in beside him while Mike and Sam dug their slit trenches close by; they all collected and cut branches to pile on top of themselves in anticipation of more barrages. They didn't have to wait long. The Jerries had their position zeroed in and fired round after round of tree-bursts. With the flanking action of the 2nd and 100th Battalions, Fred's outfit had been able to take the hill, but the Jerries were intent on inflicting the maximum punishment on the men for every piece of ground gained. Now they had to endure another night of bombardment–and tree-bursts. The Germans wreaked their fury and frustration on the Nisei. Neither side would give up. Too much was at stake. The reddish-orange flashes of the explosions high up in the trees were like nightmarish hallucinations against the blackness of the cold night.

Fred was stunned with fatigue. He knew the rest of the men fared no better. Death burst all around them and whistled and fluttered through the air. It was as though he were in a trance. Nothing was real–and yet all too real at the same time. His mind and body reeled from the recognition of reality, the sights and sounds and smells of war and death. The cries of the men who were hit. Medic! Mama! It was never Dad, Father or Papa; it was always Mama. Fred's mind took him back to when they were mere babies suckling at their mother's breasts, being cared for as their feverish brows were gently stroked, scolded and pampered, when they romped and played innocently as if there were no tomorrow or the moment at the time would last forever, and when their scrapes and bruises were always soothed by a caring hand. And now they were men whose innocence was lost forever in a surfeit of killing and dying, who were caught in the irrevocable clutches of commands that were to be accepted unquestioned, of the reality of dying young, never to see the faces of loved ones again or the sun and the deep blue of the sky or to smell the scent of flowers and beautiful women or to taste fine food and drink. The terror of being obliterated with eternal finality was complete.

Swept by the winds of warmongering, they were like the chaff of wheat being blown about by capriciousness. Their orders were to advance against the impossible. But still they were men bent on surviving the last counterattack, the last bullet fired at them until their duty was done. Such was their devotion to each other that dying was not a single issue of a soldier whose time was up but a welling of a collective agony that was shared by a common recognition that, fairly or unfairly, they were a select group of men who had a job to do, a job that required of them a vision transcending their own personal, immediate needs and embracing a country that had denied them their birthright but represented their chosen way of life.

As Fred clutched the dirt with each explosion of a tree-burst, with the cacophony of war falling all about him, the bone-weariness that conspired with the ultimate insanity failed to blunt the sharp awareness of why he was fighting the war. He was supposed to prove himself. A simple kind of *quid pro quo*: his life for acceptance into society. That was not enough; that was not what it was all about. The doubts society cast on him only spurred him on to value freedom the more. Had his country not challenged his fundamental rights, he might not have fought to show he was a *free* man willing to charge into the maw of death–for the only cause worthy of his life. And yet he fought for his survival like a caveman who knew nothing of ideals.

The downpour drained itself and became a dismal drizzle. It was cold, and the wind gusted through the trees with a heavy sigh that sounded like remorse. Heaven must have regretted giving man a soul of his own, thought Fred, for man's depraved predation made him no better than the ravenous animals of the jungle. Weakness and power made for the poorest of kin and the greatest of temptations. Power gathered unto itself the grandeur of all illusions–that of unassailable control–and weakness could only follow, obey and suffer the behavior of the downtrodden who dreamt dreams of another kind of illusion. But the reality of the moment howled with the immediacy of the soldier's universe: the dampness, swollen feet, cold, hunger, fatigue, fear, mutilation, death. When the guns fell silent, the entire mountain succumbed to the spell of muffled, black denseness given life only by the cries of the wounded.

The supply teams could no longer make the journey into the forest by jeep; cooks, clerks, engineers were tapped to act as pack mules to carry water, ammunition and medical supplies to the troops and as litter bearers to take the wounded to battalion aid. Some were handed rifles and attached to the depleted companies to make ready for the push in the morning. Patrols that clashed with the enemy in the night returned to report enemy positions and strength. Some squads that ventured into the darkness never made it back. The situation was critical. Low on supplies and ammunition, the Lost Battalion continued to fight for its very existence while the men of the 442nd kept pushing ahead to come to its rescue. What should have been measured in miles was measured in yards. Time was running out.

The morning was fogbound. The mist hung heavily over the treetops, and the light that filtered through was dim and lent an ethereal quality to the forest. Fred could see only so far, then his vision disappeared into a veil that enshrouded the woods; but he could see far enough to spot the enemy moving about carelessly as though they were ghosts floating in the fogbank, appearing and disappearing, a head, an arm and a shoulder, a part of the body.

They were figures in a play, marionettes manipulated by strings and wires, not human beings. They were toy soldiers acting on orders to aim their guns, load and pull the triggers. Toy soldiers trained by martinets to run, jump, shoot–and march. They had to march to commands, orders and soul-thumping music, thousands of feet stomping the earth and stirring up a collective cloud of dust. Shouldering heavy packs and rifles, all of a single mind that was welded together in a seamless unity, they snaked along the roads like giant centipedes in order to engage other toy soldiers by the hundreds of thousand, by the millions–tens of millions throughout history. They swept in raving hordes over deserts and cities, through jungles and plains, across oceans and over mountains. Ceaseless waves of madness that filled the earth with graves. And soon the toy soldiers would be killing each other in the Vosges Mountains. But the blood was real and the wounds horrible.

The fog rolled into the mountains like a moist, vaporous poultice that drew off the pain of the immediate discomfort of the battlefield only to leave behind the looming and ever-present specter of death. The gross reality of dying merged with the numbing fatigue, the cold and dampness, and dreams of good food and a warm bed. Nothing seemed real but everything was indeed real, and the near-paralysis of Fred's legs traveled through his body to take over his mind. His thoughts reached out to Rhonda. Would he recognize his sister were he to see her again? She said she was no longer herself. If he weren't so tired, he would have wept for her. The stultification of his mind was a blessing in disguise, for he didn't have to think beyond having to act as he was trained and hold on to the seeds of dedication that fed the faintly glimmering, vital center where his instincts were kept alive.

Gunfire rattled beyond the gullies and draws in the distance. The flanking battalions were already engaging the enemy in their sectors. Fred gathered his men to ready them for the supreme push to reach the Lost Battalion. They pissed in the barrels of their rifles to clear them of ice and listened impassively to him tell them not to take chances but to cover for each other as they moved forward and kept the pressure on the Jerries. He reminded them that it took only one man to wipe out a machine gun nest, but they had to make sure he got through. He reassured them that they would succeed no matter how dismal the prospects. Just then he sensed a presence behind him and turned.

The three stars, polished and burnished, shone in the dim light. It was General Bunting himself. Fred snapped to attention and saluted the Division Commander. He was accompanied by an aide, a colonel, who was casting a wary eye about him, obviously uncomfortable and eager to leave as soon as he could. The general was a stocky man with pasty features that suggested an abhorrence of the outdoors and that he was at the moment on the front lines only as an act of desperation. He didn't even bother to return the salute.

He rapped Fred's helmet. He wore a grim, drawn expression. "Soldier," he said in a high-pitched voice, "you've got to get your men moving. Push, push and keep pushing. My boys are up there dying by the droves, and they need help right away. It can't come too soon. Get moving. Fix bayonets and charge and keep charging until you reach them. You boys are known for your bayonet charges."

"You'd better get down, sir. The Jerries are just beyond that gully," Fred cautioned.

"They can't see anything in this fog," the general insisted.

"The trouble is, neither can we, sir."

"You've got to get moving. Fix bayonets and charge their positions. Put the fear of God in them, son. Keep on pushing until you've reached my men. They're depending on you boys."

A shot rang out from the edge of the gully. The general's aide crumbled like an empty gunny sack, a bullet hole drilled neatly between his eyes. The general's mouth dropped in astonishment and his features crumbled as he looked down at his dead aide. Fred knew that the fog was no deterrence for the bright lens of the sniper scope. The question was: Why the aide instead of the general whose three stars must have shown up like sparkling gems in the scope? The general was now ducking with his hand on his shiny helmet and retracting his neck into his coat like a scared turtle.

"Charge, you hear, soldier! Charge!" he said as he turned to scurry off.

With scorn rising in his belly, he watched the retreating form of the general and turned toward the men: "Orders are orders. Let's do it."

It was a suicide mission. But the men fastened their bayonets wordlessly and spread out in a skirmish line. The stand of trees was sparse, and there was little concealment. Fred knew from the reports that the Jerries were dug in along a rim of the gully lying several hundred yards ahead. The mist hung like a mournful presence above them. They must have looked like small ghosts emerging from the shroud of dimness with the wind whispering their thoughts among the trees. Some of the men stumbled and picked up their feet gingerly. Like Fred whose every step was painful, they suffered from trenchfoot. His feet were wet and cold; they had ballooned up so badly that he dared not take off his boots, even to change to a drier pair of socks that he kept in his armpits. The rain had soaked everything, and the frigid cold froze corpses overnight. The weather itself was demonized. The war was maddening enough to drive the gods to hate the arrogance of mankind. They cast upon the men the curse of the heavens. The wind gave voice to the sepulchral fog, sighing with remorse through branches that fanned the mist in alarm.

A hundred yards away and the enemy guns opened fire on them in unison across a narrow clearing. Instinctively, the men hit the ground and began crawling forward. Sparking muzzle flashes and tracer bullets crisscrossing the open ground and disappearing into the fog defined the enemy's line of defense. The hail of bullets sizzled through the underbrush, ricocheted off trees, tearing off chunks of bark, and dug up the loose, wet dirt around the men. Some found their mark. The thinned ranks of the platoons crawled to within fifty yards of the Jerries, and singly and in squad-size groups they rose and charged the enemy, yelling "Banzai." The call was taken up, and Fred and his men, without bothering to follow the prearranged pattern of engaging the enemy, ran as fast as their painful feet could propel them toward the spitting guns, shouting as loud as they could so they could be heard above the noise of the battle.

To their surprise, the Germans broke and ran. They leaped out of their dugouts, shouldered their machine guns and automatic weapons, and fled through the woods. Fred wanted to stop and assess the situation, for it was unusual for the Jerries to carry their weapons with them when they fled in panic. They would leave everything behind and run for their lives. But the momentum of the charge carried the men into the opposite woods in pursuit of the enemy who ran down a draw, crossed it and clambered up the slope of a rocky ridge. The men of the 442nd followed.

The draw was a deathtrap. When the men were collected at the bottom, the enemy artillery suddenly opened up and mortar rockets landed on them by the scores. The draw had been zeroed in and was now going to be turned into a slaughterhouse. Machine guns and automatic weapons trained their fire on them from above the ridge. The men clutched the ground as though to will themselves to sink into it. They were pinned down. They could not retreat back up the draw the way they had come. They had no choice but to move forward. They began to claw their way up the slope of the ridge. As in Italy, the Germans commanded the high ground and were shooting down their throats.

Chip Shioura raked the rim of the ridge with a BAR and attempted to climb the slope. He was blown up by a potato masher, and Huli Tsubota picked him up, slid down to the bottom of the draw, crying for a medic, and tried to climb the opposite incline when he was splattered by machine gun fire. He sank to the ground and lay still with the inert form of Chip over his shoulder. Siesta Hakamada almost made it to the top of the ridge when he was blasted in the face by a machine pistol. He tumbled head over heels down the slope and lay spreadeagle, faceless and dead. One of the men picked up his helmet and placed it over his featureless face. It was no sight any soldier wanted to see.

Fred, Jimmy, Sam and Mike were together, making their way up and firing at every movement that loomed above them. The German grenadiers lobbed grenade after grenade into the draw. The men below Fred and his friends were unfortunate; they caught the brunt of the potato mashers. The explosions merged with the artillery barrage that rained shells on them. Fred led the way with his tommy gun, blasting away at every figure that popped up wielding a Schmeisser. With Fred maintaining a steady stream of fire, they slowly climbed up the draw and were making headway. Then a burp gun sputtered above them. Fred killed the German with a fiery burst but not before he got Mike.

"I'm hit!" Mike yelled as he slid back down the hill head first.

Without a second thought, Fred immediately bounced down the slope and squatted beside his boyhood friend. In wrenching dismay he watched the blood spread from the wounds stitched across his upper body and involving both arms which were shattered. The German barrage was merciless; the explosions covered them with mud. The potato mashers landed all around them. Fred slapped his hand angrily at his arm when a fragment of a grenade sliced through his uniform. He dug into his pack and found he had run out of the medical packets; he reached into Mike's and began dressing his wounds as well as he could, especially the gaping wound in the arm that was spurting blood.

"God, it's cold," Mike said through clenched teeth. "I'm freezing."

"Just hold on, buddy," Fred said and spread a blanket that he had cut in half to save weight over his friend. "Help is on its way." He waved his hand at the figures hunched against the explosions and moving from body to body and cried out: "Medic!"

Fred wanted to move his friend to a safer spot, but there was none in the draw which was still filled with men, bayonets bared, waiting to climb up to the ridge. The going was too slow. They had to move faster or be slaughtered. But he wanted to stay by Mike.

"So this is what it feels like to die," Mike said, his eyes half closed and his body quivering. "I wish I had a bottle of vino. I always knew this day was coming."

"You're not going to die," Fred said frantically.

"We're all going to die in these godforsaken mountains," Mike mumbled sleepily. "It's been decreed."

"Nothing's been decreed," Fred said. "And stay awake! Don't go to sleep, Mike!" He looked about wildly and waved his hand.

When he saw the figure of a medic running toward him at a crouch, he picked up his tommy gun and patted Mike on his leg. He looked about him, frustration and anger mounting in his belly. The men were bunching up at the foot of the slope, unable to make any headway. They were caught in a trap. The situation looked hopeless. And the feeling of helplessness–*shikata ga nai* (it can't be helped)–was anathema to Fred. It reminded him too much of the mass evacuation, barbed wire fences, gun towers with machine guns. It reminded him of what happened to Rhonda and her predicament, her battle for her own mind and soul. It reminded him of General Bunting. A cold, maddened feeling swept over him. It was a feeling of dead sobriety.

"Go, go, go," he urged the men and shoved them up the

truncated hill. He clambered up the incline, his gun held high, and yelled: "Go For Broke!"

The cry, "Go For Broke," galvanized their ranks, and the men clawed their way up to the ridge and began pouring over the rim and engaged the Jerries in hand-to-hand combat, thrusting, slashing, shooting, using the tricks of judo and jujitsu they had learned in their boyhood to throw the enemy to the ground and skewer them. The ridge was packed with soldiers tussling and struggling with the resurgent cries and shrieks of battle. The Germans tried to push the Nisei off the ridge, but the men of the 442nd held their ground and forced them to retreat into the surrounding woods where the Germans established a defensive perimeter from which they launched counterattack after counterattack. In each clash the Nisei fought furiously and beat the Jerries off. But the fighting took its toll, and after hours of doing battle, the men sprawled out exhausted during a lull, and both sides retired to their positions to regain their strength for another assault.

Jimmy lay gasping for breath. His sternum had been blasted open by machine gun fire and his hands shattered as he tried to protect himself in vain. He still held the remnants of them over the wound in his chest. Fred bent over him, despair etched into his features. There was nothing anyone could do for him.

"Liza...all my back pay," Jimmy whispered into Fred's ear, "in my backpack...all the money I have...get it to her, please."

"I will, I promise," Fred said, the lump in his throat tightening. "Now don't talk."

"I got to talk...not much time left...tell her I love her. I'll always love her. Always."

"I will," Fred said, his eyes welling. A sudden heavy load of fatigue settled on his back.

Sam was kneeling by his fallen friend. "You're going to be

all right," he tearfully blurted. "You're going to be fine, Jimmy."

"Not this time," gasped the young man. "Tell my Mama...why...why I died. She didn't want me to...volunteer."

Then Jimmy closed his eyes, let out a raspy sigh and died. Fred was overwhelmed with grief. Why? Why Jimmy? He had everything to live for. Why, indeed. His mind refused to consider the question.

He could only look at the youth with a tremendous sense of sorrow and loss, a loss that encompassed all the hopes and dreams of his fallen comrades. So many hopes and so many dreams, all sacrificed to war. In an instant, the spark of life was extinguished. Death became a burden for the living and begged the question of why. The universal why.

Sam sobbed openly. He tried to frown the tears away, but they streamed down his dirt-streaked face.

"Shit, war is for fools and is started by fools," he cried.

In a few moments, Fred regained his composure. "Sheer insanity," he said with finality but was grief-stricken. And yet he was caught up in it and had to survive it. How a human being could subject himself to such unrelenting torture without giving up, on himself, on his fellow man, on the world at large, was beyond him. Perhaps the only answer lay in the affirmation of an ideal...and the constant renewal of dedication to honor and duty.

But the loftiness of one's convictions was no answer for the painful, swollen feet, the battle-weary fatigue and the frayed nerves compounded by the damp chill. Some of the men had pneumonia but managed to stay on their feet. Idealism may have stiffened their determination, but it was the promise of simple things like hot food, a shower and a warm bed that kept them going. Jimmy was beyond even such a promise now. Fred shook himself to remove the sadness that clutched his throat and constricted it. He doubted they would make it to the Lost Battalion.

They had to ready themselves for another counterattack surely to come. And it did. The Germans were desperate to eject the men from the coveted piece of ground and attacked in force. The men fought savagely, dueling the fire spitting from rifles and machine guns with all the weapons at their command, including captured Schmeissers, and with bayonets still fixed fired their M1's from the hip and chased the shot-up survivors back to their hiding places along the edge of the woods. Borne on the backs of the Nisei GI's who formed a pack train, the supplies arrived even while the fight was going on; they distributed the medical packets, C and K rations, water and ammunition, dashing from one slit trench to another and helping to evacuate the wounded and dead.

The fighting continued through the night. There was no respite. The weather challenged their endurance: the wind blew colder and carried with it sleet and snow. The men who were already chilled to the bone froze and their wet clothes stiffened with ice. They kept their hands around the action of the their weapons to keep them from freezing tight. The soldiers of both sides raged back and forth in the darkness only to break apart on the narrow ridge that soon turned into a slippery snow-laden piece of shoveled ground. When they were not engaged in close combat, the Nisei and Germans exchanged gunfire from their dug-in positions with the tracer bullets slashing a phosphorescent path over the battlefield. Flares lit the packed arena all during the night. There was to be no sleep even if it were possible. Shortly before daybreak, there was finally a break in the fighting as if the wounded and dying on both sides willed a cessation.

With an involuntary sigh of relief, Fred lay aside his gun and took a drink from his canteen, jostling the frozen slush, his hand shaking with fatigue. His throat was parched, his belly begging for food. Breaking open a box of K rations, he ate the contents slowly, patiently working up enough saliva to swallow. The ridge and the woods were ominously silent, a dreaded and yet welcomed change from the tumultuous cries emanating from the throats of desperate men. More was to come.

Out of the early morning gloom appeared the snow-whitened figures of a squad of GI's from the woods to the left of the ridge. They had tramped through the forest without trying to conceal their movement, so Fred and a dozen Nisei were on one knee hunched and ready to receive them. Fred was surprised at the sight of whites in American uniforms; he had received no report that relief was on its way. Though immediately suspicious, he wanted to believe that General Bunting had sent them some extra men to make the final push to save the Lost Battalion. They had lost too many already. He ordered the GI's to halt while he gave them the once over.

"Put your gun down, sergeant," said a tall youth not much older than Fred. "I'm Sgt. Sparks. Daniel Sparks." He carried his M1 casually in the crook of his arm.

"Which outfit are you from?" queried Fred.

"B Company, 143rd Infantry Regiment."

"Where are the rest of your men?"

"Hidden beyond the draw back yonder." The GI was about to take a step toward Fred.

"Hold it!" he said. "The password. What's the password? Washington...?"

"Washington? Are you trying to trip me up, sergeant? It's Boston..."

"Yeah..."

"...Red Sox."

The Last Fox

Disbelief swept over Fred. Could it possibly be that they had reinforcements now? He lowered his gun and stood up, disregarding the enemy in the woods. It was snowing too heavily for them to see anyway.

"Need any food, cigarettes, water?" the GI asked.

"Nope. We got our supplies earlier. Thanks, anyway."

"Sure," the GI said and commenced to load his rifle.

"Say," Fred said, his eyes narrowing, "where's your clip? Our ammo comes in a clip."

"I'm conserving ammunition. I retrieved these rounds off a dead kraut. S-2 said the prisoners told them that they were using our ammo in their Mausers when they ran out of their own. Our cartridges fit their rifles. They were designed that way, and the krauts are able to shoot us with our own ammunition. Can you beat that? That's why they never run out. The clever, goddamn bastards, those krauts."

Fred gripped his tommy gun. It was the way the GI said "clever," in addition to the impeccable grammar. He slowly brought the muzzle up. "Sorry about trying to fool you," Fred said. "That was yesterday's—"

"You mean, Washington Senators. I'm a baseball fan myself."

"No, you clever, goddamn bastard!" growled Fred. "It was 'make wa shinuru' (dead is dead). Drop your rifle and put your hands on your head."

The Nisei immediately surrounded the Jerries in American uniforms. They dropped their weapons in fright and raised their hands as Fred motioned the German who had called himself Sgt. Sparks to throw his M1 down. Instead the tall youth brought the rifle up at the hip and would have shot Fred if he hadn't triggered off a burst that sent the German flying backwards into the snow.

243

The Last Fox

The sound of gunfire brought forth a response from the woods up front, and the men hit the ground and spread themselves flat. It was a nervous, spasmodic response that quickly ended in a rattling echo in the mountains.

The German youth lay sprawled on his back and clutching his midriff with bloody hands. Trying to raise his head, he gestured with his fingers for Fred to come to him. He crawled over to the youth and looked at his wan features. The blood had already drained from his face.

"I have only a few minutes left," the young German soldier groaned. "This is what my university education amounts to, and I must tell you of my sadness. All the grand philosophy, literature and history courses I took, and all my learning and dreams are summed up by a handful of bullet holes in the belly here in the Vosges Mountains. If I had a few more hours to live I would write poetry about life and war. All life is war, and war is never far away. It will be so as long as we settle our differences with bullets and bayonets. My name is Hans Knecht. In my shirt pocket...a picture."

Fred reached inside his jacket and drew out a photograph of a plump, pleasant-looking woman who was smiling and carrying a spray of flowers.

"My mother," the soldier said and took the picture from Fred with a bloody hand. He gazed at the picture with tearful eyes. "If you are ever in Dusseldorf, tell her that I never believed in Hitler's lies and that I was, nevertheless, a good soldier. Please tell her that I died a brave death and that my last thoughts were of her. And you, too, must believe the insanity will soon be over."

The youth was beyond help. Fred knelt beside him for a moment longer and watched as he closed his eyes. He reminded Fred of the youth he had shot in the fight that followed their breakout from the Anzio beachhead with one main difference–the eyes. The youth in the dugout near the Alban Hills wore the look of a terrified animal; Hans Knecht, in his final battle, was cool, determined and duty-bound, a disciplined soldier to the end. What for, to what end, thought Fred. He died a soldier. Somehow that was not enough. Fred's mind reeled with the surfeit of violence and death that was continuous.

He tried to kill the questions but could not. His mind was still alive, a separate part of his nearly paralyzed body. *Ideals*, it cried as though seeking a firm footing that was lost. It sounded as if the German youth had died for what he had learned from philosophy, literature and history, and his learning amounted to nothing. Except as an empty protest in the form of death. Jimmy Hikida, the ignorant Nisei farm boy from Hood River, Oregon, and his death on the battlefield was no less meaningless. If it had any meaning at all, it came in the form of the mourning of the living for the dead. The noble cause that was the catalyst could not diminish the ugliness and horror of butchery on the battlefield. In the end, war made everyone its slave.

Driven by the wind the snow kept falling like the torn shreds of a shroud cast over the swaying trees. The temperature dropped to below freezing. Many of the wounded had died over the night and were frozen stiff. Impassively, the men readied themselves. They were ordered to keep pushing and make all haste. The remnants of the two companies on the ridge prepared to break through the lines of the German defense without delay.

They rushed the enemy's perimeter in force, yelling "Go For Broke!" And in their first assault they succeeded in smashing the German resistance and sent the enemy fleeing into the depths of the mountains. They followed and pushed on toward the upper slopes. When they were in the thick of the woods, the German artillery commenced to shell them and produced hundreds of tree-bursts that blossomed overhead with a deafening syncopation and sent red-hot shrapnel flying in all directions.

Fred thought it uncanny that the Jerries would know their exact location as they moved through the dense forest. Where there were no trees, there were eyes and ears in the open spaces blurred by the snow turned into sleet, and the Germans kept dropping their barrages not behind them or in front of them but right on top of them. They must have a way to calibrate their progress, thought Fred, and the tree-bursts followed them, matching their own pace. Mortar rounds rained on them, and from the floor of the forest rose a curtain of explosions that tore off branches and split open trees.

One man several yards to Fred's left was caught in between a tree-burst and a mortar explosion and was torn to pieces. His body parts were scattered. Skewered by a branch imbedded in the trunk of a nearby tree, his dangling arm swung in the wind that sighed through the trees, the clawed hand inviting the men to continue to move forward. And move forward they did–in lesser and lesser numbers as they fell. The shrapnel sizzled all around them. A piece sliced off the antenna of their radio, and Fred found himself cut off from the command post.

With the tree-bursts following them, they moved ahead several hundred yards when Fred felt the concussion of an explosion overhead and was instantly knocked down by what he could only imagine to be a vicious blow of a sledge hammer against his back. He had the breath knocked out of him, but he could feel no pain. Perhaps the shell had severed his spinal cord, he thought in alarm; he could feel nothing. But he could still feel the weakness in his legs and the throbbing pain of his swollen feet. He felt all around his back. Nothing. No blood and no pain. He guessed that his thick, aluminum mess kit had caught the full impact. So far his luck held out, and he unconsciously rubbed the pocket that held his lucky penny. But he rose to his feet shaken. He moved ahead once again cautiously, bent at the waist, wondering where the Jerries were dug in. It couldn't have been much further to the knoll where the Lost Battalion was isolated. How long had it been? A week? How long had the 442nd been fighting in the Vosges Mountains? Fred had lost track of time.

By the time they had traversed the length of a flat portion of the forest, the sleet had turned into a driven sheet of rain, and the men were soon soaked to the skin in near-freezing weather. They were high enough in the mountains for the clouds to sink their swollen bellies into the treetops and pour right above the men. Through the gloom of the forested mountain loomed a shape of a Mark IV. It was sitting and waiting for the Nisei as were the German infantry behind log barricades. The men entered a mine field. As the Shuh and Teller mines and Bouncing Betties gave away their presence and position, the Jerries opened fire. The Nisei did not stop. They kept on moving forward, urging each other to keep going. It was either move onward or be slaughtered where they stood.

A bazooka team got within range of the tank and fired their rocket but managed only to knock off its track and cripple it. Before they could reload, the tank's machine gun located them and killed them outright with stuttering vengeance. Sam raced over to them to retrieve the bazooka and crawled closer to the tank that was firing its cannon and machine gun into the advancing ranks of the men. He stood up, took aim and fired. He scored a direct hit and shouted with glee when the tank exploded and was reduced to a mangled heap. He reloaded and took out a machine gun emplacement. Out of rockets he unshouldered his M1 and marched toward the enemy, firing from the hip and crying: "Banzai!" The battle cry was transformed into "Go For Broke," and the men ran for the log barricades. Then Sam tripped a Bouncing Betty that blew him backwards and slammed him to the ground.

Fred caught his form flying through the air out of the corner his eye. He couldn't go immediately to his aid. He had begun a duel with a machine gun and kept firing to force the Jerries to duck their heads and to disorient them while he bellied his way closer to eliminate the dugout with a grenade. He sprayed the disabled occupants with several short bursts from his tommy gun, and then only after making sure they were dead, including the accompanying sniper, he dashed over to where Sam had fallen.

Fred knelt by his friend. He was horrified by the mutilation. Sam was nearly blown in half by the Bouncing Betty. His crotch was ripped apart, and his lower belly was torn open. The smell of feces penetrated the damp air. Sam looked at Fred with an expression that was akin to pleading. His face was contorted with pain and agony.

"Bless it, Fred, it hurts."

"Don't talk, Sam. The medic will be with you in a jiffy." Fred didn't know what else to say. The words froze on his lips with a sense of horror. He took his friend's hand in his. Sam gripped it tightly as though squeezing it hard could give him a few more minutes to live.

"I have to talk, Fred. I'm afraid nobody will ever understand me. Maybe you will," Sam rasped. His breathing was shallow. Suddenly, it was the old Sam of Fred's boyhood days. "I killed my fellow human being. Men like me. But I couldn't watch you guys volunteer and leave me behind. It was my war, too. That's not all of it. 'Thou shalt not kill'..."

"Hold on, Sam," Fred said panicking. He did not want to hear it. He could not let his own doubts as a soldier breach the last veiled, flimsy shreds of a belief. He squeezed Sam's hand hard. "I understand. I truly do."

"I killed and killed," gasped Sam. "I taught myself to like killing. Killing Jerries was a game. I thought only the good died young, that's what they all say, and I was..."

"I understand, Sam," Fred said with tearful fervor.

"I don't think you do. You see, I'm a coward."

"You're no coward, Sam. You're the bravest man there is, and I understood you from the very beginning. Believe me. I'm putting you in for a medal."

"No medal for me, Fred. Not me," Sam said, his grip on Fred's hand loosening. "Bless it, it's cold. I'm freezing..."

"Sam!" Fred shouted helplessly. "Remember the playoff for the Pacific Northwest championship? Before the war. Turn your thoughts to before the war."

Sam unlocked his eyes from Fred's intent gaze and focused them on the wet clouds hanging from the treetops. "Oh, Lord on high, forgive me, thy servant who has sinned. Look upon me with mercy, for I really didn't want to die."

"If I can understand you," Fred said with tears in his eyes, "I'm sure God can, too."

"Bless it..." Sam sighed. His hand fell away from Fred's grip and his eyes stared unseeing at the sagging sky that bled with indifference on the dying and the dead.

Wearily, Fred bowed his head, not in prayer but in profound sorrow which might have been a kind of prayer that was known only to soldiers. He had lost all his friends. He wondered about the wounded. Did they make it? Was Mike all right? With Sam Hatayama gone, the last of an effective team was gone. Fred felt naked, alone and unprotected. The Minidoka foursome was pared down to one: Sgt. Fred Murano. What could he do now that he was all by himself?

With the weight of weariness pulling his shoulders down, he straightened up, gripped the tommy gun and threw one last parting glance at Sam's inert figure. Then he rushed to join the sounds of battle that were coming from the slope of another hill confronting them. The barricades had been breached, and they had the Jerries on the run. Fred slipped and slid on the muddy, rain-soaked ground churned up by the troops stomping through the undergrowth. When he reached the gentler incline of the hill and caught up with his platoon or what was left of it, he joined the skirmish line and proceeded slowly and watched for any movement coming from behind the trees or the floor of the forest.

They approached a clearing in the densely wooded mountain and moved cautiously. Fred strained his eyes until they were watery. The rain became a misty drizzle; it was freezing cold. The heavy clouds allowed very little light through to illuminate the ethereal shadows surrounding them. As they advanced slowly, indistinct figures could be spotted straightening out of foxholes in the clearing. They held their fire; neither were they fired upon. Fred moved ahead. The closer he got the more clearly he could make out the figures. They were wearing American uniforms and jumping out of their foxholes as the men of the 442nd entered the bare knoll where they had been dug in. They had finally reached the Lost Battalion.

There were no shouts of joy or general jubilation. Just a spontaneous gripping of hands and a mute hug of comrades in arms. The bedraggled men, the besieged and rescuers alike, milled among each other happily and in utter disbelief that their ordeal was over for the moment.

"Boy, am I glad to see you," said one towering GI to Fred, grabbing his hand to shake it.

Fred was at a loss for words. The sense of the impossible being accomplished was overwhelming. So was his grief. His legs trembled with fatigue and a weakness that stayed.

"You need rations? A cigarette, maybe?" he asked the bewhiskered GI, popping out a smoke.

"Yeah, sure," the soldier said and lit up. He held the lighter up for Fred who tipped his cigarette to the wavering flame and drew in a lungful of smoke.

"How many men survived?" Fred asked, looking around the blasted clearing. The trees lining the edges of the forest were snapped in half by the barrages; some hung like shattered arms or legs at an oblique angle.

"There're a little over 200 of us left with about seventy-five dead and wounded. It was hell on earth. I never thought we'd live through it all."

"We'll evacuate the wounded right away," Fred said, looking around for his men.

"It's a miracle we survived, because the goddamn krauts threw everything they had at us, and we had to keep beating them back like they were a pack of hyenas. They made us think none of us dogfaces would make it out alive or ever see a friendly face again."

"Yeah, I know," Fred said. "The 2nd and 3rd Battalions of your regiment tried hard to break through to you, but they were too exhausted, I guess."

"Where's the rest of your men?"

"We're down to less than a squad."

"And you started out as a company?" the GI said astounded.

"I Company, 3rd Battalion."

"Goddamn! You 'Go For Broke' boys earned our eternal gratitude, that's for sure."

"Yeah, it was bloody all right," Fred said simply and closed his mind to the horror of losing his closest friends.

"My name's Bill Hansen. If you're ever in Kerrville, you have to look me up. That's not too far from San Antonio, Texas. We don't have much there, but we'll do the town right. You have got to promise me that much."

"I promise. I'm Fred Murano. Portland, Oregon. If you're ever in my neighborhood, you have to stop by, too. Bring your buddies with you. It'll be on me."

"Ditto. Goddamn but it's good to see your face," Bill Hansen said and slapped Fred on the shoulder.

Fred winced with pain. Hansen looked at his hand briefly and wiped it on his trousers.

"You've been wounded."

Fred looked surprised. He had forgotten about his shoulder; his throbbing cheek and feet occupied most of his attention. Now that he was standing still, the pain became all the more noticeable.

"Let me look at it," Hansen said and peeled the tear in the uniform back. "You got gashed good."

"I'll have it taken care of when we get back to the aid station."

"Yeah, you'd better. Doesn't look good."

"Thanks," Fred said. "Got to go and get my men together."

The two men parted, and Fred looked for the remnants of his company. The survivors were new replacements, and he didn't know the names of some of them. The men of other decimated companies of the 442nd began to emerge from the thick forest. They were greeted heartily by the Lost Battalion that still seemed too dazed to accept the reality that they had been saved. Soon the Nisei formed teams to evacuate the wounded GI's. The walking wounded shuffled into the woods that were now safe, and the rest of the GI's set about gathering their equipment in the rain to prepare to move to the rear.

Fred found a radio in working order and called the command post to report the contact made with the Lost Battalion and seek further orders. He envisioned a long rest, with all the "trimmings", in the rear area after four sleepless, wet and cold nights and constant combat. Dry clothes, a warm bed and hot food sounded like a heaven-sent temptation to give up fighting and soldiering altogether and to sleep, especially sleep, a deep sleep that was suffocating in its repose. He wanted to smother his body with a kind of pampering that not only relieved the pain and fatigue but also mended his raw, frayed nerves. He delivered his report and listened to the instructions–in disbelief. He had to ask the Battalion Commander to repeat the orders.

"General Bunting wants us to continue on through the mountains, occupy the foothills and open the road to St. Die..." Fred repeated in a hollow voice. He was stunned. "But, sir...my men...we're down to...yes, sir...the other companies, too. Yes, sir. With all haste. Will do. Over and out."

Fred's shoulders slumped with an unseen load. He still didn't believe that he had heard right. Advance and keep on advancing. Advance all the way to the floor of the opposite valley to open the way to St. Die and Strasbourg near the Rhine. He could see how the Seventh Army and Eisenhower's forces would meet at Strasbourg to cross into Germany. And now it was up to the 442nd Regimental Combat Team to spearhead the move. In their condition? Fred asked himself. They were impotent as a striking force. And yet they had created the momentum that sent the Jerries reeling into a defensive position, and they had to hit them again and again to keep them off balance without allowing them to become entrenched. The entire concept of using the 442nd for the push left Fred in a stupor.

Chapter Thirteen

As the GI's of the Lost Battalion withdrew to safety, the men of the 442nd slumped to the ground, sitting either in an exhausted heap or lying flat on their backs in the drizzle. They drank from their canteens and broke open their rations for a quick meal, since they did not know when they would have another lull to themselves. They checked their supplies which had been replenished but sorely depleted in the fighting and found that they still had adequate ammunition, which was next in importance to having enough water. Food, they could always put off if necessary, but they could not do without water.

In spite of their condition, Fred gathered his men together and relayed the orders he had received over the radio. A collective groan of disbelief rose from deep within their throats: "More?" Fred himself felt that something vital in him had been surgically removed so that he could not protest or shake the feeling of doubt and incomprehension. The foot soldier was like the tip of a bull whip manipulated by the higher command. When it was swung the dogface swung with it to lash out with rifle and bayonet at the enemy wherever he was. And he was continually swung and lashed by the whip itself to push ahead and advance. Till he dropped dead. Then a replacement would step over his dead body to take up the raging cry of combat as the fortunes of war swept the battlefield with dreaded unpredictability.

Fred and his men joined forces with the men from two other weakened companies of the 3rd Battalion. They dug a defensive perimeter encircling the knoll to prepare for a counterattack that never came, and the next day they filtered through the forest to the foothills while being subjected to a densely concentrated enemy barrage. Their own Cannon Company and Field Artillery Battalion responded with thousands of rounds poured on the German positions around the railroad tracks and houses lying at the bottom of the hills. The 3rd Battalion took on the Jerries at every turn and was assisted by a Tank Battalion that paved the way for further advances. Then they approached a roadblock that was the final barrier to the valley floor leading to St. Die. It was heavily defended and fortified.

Fred stumbled on as though in a state of shock. The heavy clouds hung over them like a pernicious presence and willfully drained its laden moisture on the land. Body heat alone could not drive the dampness from his clothing. The rain hounded him like a personal nemesis. He could barely walk, and his feet felt as if they would burst out of their skin. He suffered from the onset of pneumonia and was wracked with feverish chills that added to the pain of walking. Ever since the battle in the Vosges Mountains began, he was haunted by thoughts of Rhonda's isolation and predicament and by the split in the fabric of the family. While shivering alone in a slit trench, his mind was filled with his concern for his family and how he was to mend Rhonda's mind, if that were at all possible, and heal the split by convincing his father that America was for every one, including him, in spite of his despair.

As he doggedly pursued the Jerries, his single-minded, deliberate movements seemed to be guided by strings and wires manipulated by General Bunting himself, a possessed commander who was bent on extracting the last ounce of energy from him in his mad quest to breach the Vosges Mountains and race for the Rhine. Fred's exhaustion put him in a sheer, numbing trance that eventually emptied his mind of everything except the need to keep moving and fighting.

They confronted the last hurdle–the roadblock. The enemy was well entrenched. They kept attacking like a mongoose fighting a cobra, dodging and striking. With whatever strength they could muster, companies cut down to platoons and platoons reduced to squads, they engaged the enemy, and after several hours of fighting, the men of the 442nd broke through and cleared the way for the Seventh Army to proceed to St. Die.

When the remaining pockets of German resistance were eliminated, the men were finally relieved, at long last, by contingents of the 36th Division and ordered to a rest area in the rear. Hot food and showers, dry clothes and desperately needed rest awaited them. The fighting seemed to be over for them. Locked in a state of dazed incomprehension, Fred needed to believe it was.

After two days of recuperation, the Nisei were called out for a dress review in front of General Bunting. When they were assembled, their officers were rebuked by the general for not having all their men present. He was told tearfully by the handful of surviving officers that all were present and accounted for. The tattered remains of the 442nd stood stiffly and silently at attention. Some of the men could not control their trembling–or their tears. They had lost too many of their friends. By protocol the Division Commander perfunctorily fulfilled his duty by praising the men for their valiant effort to save the Lost Battalion and summarily dismissed them. But not before ordering the 2nd and 3rd Battalions on the line again to man established defensive positions.

The Last Fox

At the time of the dress review, Fred's company, I Company, was whittled down to eight men. Other companies were similarly undermanned, but none as drastically as I Company. In the month following their arrival in the Rhone Valley and the liberation of Bruyeres, the 442nd Regimental Combat Team was reduced by more than 2,000 men, almost half its original strength with 800 killed or wounded in the four-day battle waged in the Vosges Mountains to rescue the Lost Battalion–nearly four Nisei for every Texan saved. But the 442nd was not officially credited with crushing the Germans in the Vosges Mountains.

General Bunting was anointed with the coveted garland of being the first military commander in history to breach the formidable natural barrier between France and Germany. He was awarded his fourth star and invited to join SHAEF of the Allied Command. Nevertheless, word of the Lost Battalion and the exploits of the 442nd RCT spread throughout the Western Front, and letters written by front line GI's in *Stars & Stripes* extolled the fighting abilities of the Nisei and referred to them as the best combat troops in the European Theater of Operations.

Finally relieved of its duties by mid-November, 1944, after more than a month on the line, the 442nd was detached from the 36th Division and ordered south down the Rhone Valley, the way it had come, to Nice. The men were trucked in convoys from the wintry landscape of northeastern climes to the sunny skies of southern France. The duties they pulled were light. In their own inimitable fashion, they were to dub it the Champagne Campaign, although the fighting was to continue across the border between France and Italy.

Fred wound up in a field hospital in Epinal, south of the town of Bruyeres. His hacking cough wracked his body, and his swollen feet had turned purple. His wounds were stitched up. He lay in the warm hospital bed, drugged with the heavy drowsiness that comes with the surfeit of sleep. The trance-like state of numbness, a lobotomy of fatigue and disbelief, gradually eased into a return to normalcy. To his relief he learned that Mike Kojima had survived his wounds and was transferred to a general hospital. But he mourned the loss of his friends. Their youthful faces seared themselves into his mind in remembrance, and he couldn't stop the tears from flowing when he realized with a sense of wrenching finality that they were gone and he would never see them again.

After several weeks of convalescence, Fred was discharged from the hospital, largely due to his own insistence, and eagerly hitched a ride in a jeep to make the long journey to Nice to catch up with his outfit. Down from the mountainous regions he rode to the flat lands of the Rhone Valley on his way south. Even the sky changed as he left the mountains, the horrendous fighting and the foul wintry weather behind him as though the carnage attracted and isolated itself in the northern battlefields. The clouds billowed softly like a ready embrace to welcome the weary warrior to its bosom, and the sun shone warm to drench the land in bright, blood-warm light. For the first time in a long time, he felt fit and whole, the weeks away from constant combat working wonders for his body and psyche, and again, perhaps against his better judgment, he developed an enormous appetite for living without regard or concern for what lay in the future. The present was what counted.

Upon his arrival, he learned he was billeted in the Continental Hotel in Nice. The other hotels were occupied by noncoms, and there was no room left, since he had arrived so late, except at the hotel that was designated as the quarters for junior grade officers. He roomed with a second lieutenant: Lt. Taneo Ohashi. The Nisei lieutenant had earned a field commission in the fight to free the town of Bruyeres. The two became close friends. Although it was unusual for an officer to fraternize with a noncom, Lt. Ohashi appeared to relish Fred's company, pointing to the need to stay in touch with the concerns of the ordinary foot soldier and feeling uncomfortable in his own new role as an officer. Upon learning that Fred was a veteran of Monte Cassino, Anzio, the northern Rome campaign and the Vosges Mountains, he asked Fred for his advice on morale and tactics, and the two of them had long talks on subjects dealing with the war and the mutual pursuit of an education before the evacuation. Lt. Ohashi was in Indiana attending college when he was drafted–his family was in the Mid-West and was not subjected to the evacuation–and went to Camp Blanding, Florida for training. He was greatly interested in Fred's story of the concentration camps, especially his experiences in Tule Lake and Minidoka, and his reasons for volunteering. Fred, on his part, did not elaborate on family difficulties, nor did he mention Rhonda's problems that landed her in the Salem State Hospital.

"With your record, why don't you have your CO put you in for a field commission?" the lieutenant suggested. "You'd be a shoo-in. You probably could use the extra pay, and you'd like the privileges."

"No, thanks," Fred said emphatically. "No special treatment for me. Rather be with my men."

"I used to be like you, wanting to be with my men, but with our *haole* officer killed, somebody had to take his place."

"Yeah, I know. I had to take over our platoon when our officer, Lt. Oliver Morris, was killed. He was a good man and soldier. He took chances that no other haole officer I know did. Shared our food with us and even got to liking rice without sugar and pudding over it. He was about my age, tall and easygoing. I had promised to teach him to like our food and our ways, but it's too late now."

"Say, Fred," Lt. Ohashi said in almost a brotherly manner, "why don't you join us at a party we're throwing in the upstairs suite tonight. Nothing fancy. Just a bunch of us officers getting together to drink and play poker."

"But I'm just a sergeant," Fred said with a sudden feeling of being out of place.

"No sweat. You'll be my guest, and if anybody has any questions, I'll tell them you're my personal driver. OK?"

"Fine with me."

That evening after supper Fred and Lt. Ohashi showed up at the suite and joined a group of other officers. The party had already begun. A number of local girls dressed in colorful clothes mixed easily with the officers which included both white and Nisei men, and they were dancing to the tune of Stateside big band music. A small group of them were sitting at a table in the corner of the room playing cards. They were all white. Lt. Ohashi and Fred approached them.

The lieutenant introduced himself, then said: "This is my friend, Sgt. Fred Murano. Mind if we join in?"

"Hell, no. Come on and drag up a chair," said a burly officer chomping on a cigar.

Fred pulled up a chair and before he sat down at the table, he said with some discomfort: "Now, I know I'm not an officer but—"

"Don't bother your head about it, soldier," said another officer. "You're welcome to join us."

"Shit, if the bars bother you, sergeant," the first officer said, blowing cigar smoke into the air, "we'll all take off our jackets.

And we'll all be plain, ordinary, ornery everyday government issue infantry."

The men took off their jackets and hung them on the back of their chairs and resumed their seats. Fred followed suit.

"Now you're one of us," said the first officer. "Your money is always welcome here. Ante up."

With the record player blaring Harry James, the men began playing poker in earnest, drinking copiously from bottles of cognac passed around the table. Fred dug out all his back pay and lined up the chips in front of him. It was a long time since he sat in on a game of poker, and he was struck anew with the awareness that the war was for the moment far away, that his survival was miraculous indeed. He played judiciously and took a swallow from the bottle every time it was passed around. Soon a quiet glow warmed his entire body like the sun had found the empty spot in the center of his stomach, and he felt relaxed and loosened, more so than ever before since they first landed in Naples in what seemed centuries ago. He felt lucky that night and rubbed his pocket.

The game lasted until the early hours of the morning. The music had long since stopped and the women and other officers departed. The men agreed to take a break around three and roamed around the room, their ties loosened and shirt sleeves rolled up, nibbling hors d'oeuvres and bread and cheese and washing them down with wine. They found places to stretch out on sofas and easy chairs in the large room. The top ranking officer who was a captain took over the bedroom. Fred slouched in an overstuffed chair, his legs stiffly spread apart, and caught a few winks of sleep which washed over him in tides of relaxation.

After breakfast the next morning, the game resumed. The men took the same places and the clatter of chips being tossed into the growing pile in the middle of the table was all the sound that stirred in the silence of the large room. The men were intent on playing. Other than a few necessary remarks dealing with the game of poker, conversation was nil. The deadly serious business of gambling was as intent as any engagement on the battlefield. The game lasted the whole day, marked by the bright sunshine washing through the windows, and into the night with a short break for supper.

Fred had an ever-fattening wad of money stuffed into the pocket holding the penny. He figured he had about 3,000 dollars already, and he continued to blink back the fatigue and played as a predacious, wily fox measuring each move. He was prepared to play until he dropped or the men called it quits. The bottle still made its rounds as though to both quench and fuel the educated greed that went into playing poker. With a kind of intensity matched only by peering through the scope of a sniper rifle, Fred played each hand as if it were his last and intended to double his winnings by the time the game ended, an ambitious goal that Fred had to admit was unrealistic but was fueled by the high stakes heat of the moment.

Hotel service brought them more food and wine and cognac throughout the day and night, and the men played Cincinnati Liz, Shotgun and Whiskey Poker but by far the most persistent favorite was stud poker, and Fred won most of his money at Seven Card Stud. The playing was so feverish and avaricious that when a player was cleaned out he was not allowed to quit but rather forced to toss in his markers to keep the pot enriched. Hundreds of dollars were heaped into the middle of the table and exchanged hands with each deal. With unadulterated satisfaction, Fred raked in his winnings in a campaign as well laid as the greatest battles fought so far.

Well past midnight the second day the captain who hosted the game called it quits, the unhappy loser by about 2,000 dollars, most of which Fred possessed. Many of the other men won, then lost all their winnings in the marathon session, and Fred, while unable to double his earlier total, managed to come out the winner 5,000 dollars to the good. He paid the hotel tab himself and staggered off to his room with Lt. Ohashi for much needed sleep.

During the weeks in the hospital and his stay at Continental Hotel, he learned to put the war out of his mind and was reminded of it only by the puckered scar on his cheek, the soreness of his feet and reports filtering in about his regiment that was on the line in the Maritime Alps to confront the Germans across the Franco-Italian border. Also, the Nisei regiment's crack 522nd Field Artillery Battalion was detached and sent north to aid Eisenhower's forces crossing into Germany. Technically, Fred was in charge of guarding a supply depot, but he left the details in the hands of another noncom.

He continued to write letters back home, especially to Rhonda, but the replies were long in coming. He received one response from Margie; nothing had changed at Tule Lake. He heard nothing from Rhonda and did not know if his letters reached her or were delivered at all because of institutional regulations. If only he could see her and talk to her personally, he could have tried to bring her back to the world. But he had no idea when that would be or when he was going home.

One day he decided to borrow the lieutenant's jeep and travel to L'Escarene, north of Nice, where his old outfit, I Company, was stationed. Although most of the men were now fresh replacements whom he did not know, he longed for the companionship of the ordinary Nisei dogface, their banter and appetite for life after such a horrendous battle in the godforsaken Vosges Mountains. He drove the short distance under sunny skies, filled with a sense of freedom that defied understanding. Perhaps the mere fact that he was dry and warm and could expect to sleep in a warm bed and consume hot food–the simple basics of human existence–was enough to free him of the specter of the battlefield. The sun drove the dark reminder of grief from the sky and lay open the vast possibilities of the future which were contained in the moment, a moment of drinking in the promise of laughter and forgetting.

Upon arriving in L'Escarene after a short drive, he asked the townspeople where to find the Nisei. They smiled in recognition when they saw him and pointed toward the middle of the small town. He drove through the narrow streets and waved at his fellow men in arms as they strolled about, enjoying the break from the dictates of war. As he penetrated into the center of town, he found what he was looking for: the hangout he had heard about in Nice. "Yuraku," the sign painted in large red letters read. Members only. Courtesy of I Company, 442nd RCT. A Nisei guard armed with a captured burp gun stood at the door. Fred parked the jeep on a side street and sauntered over to the club.

"Mind if I go in?" he asked the guard.

"You no MP, you go in," was the no-nonsense buddhahead answer.

Fred entered the room. Liberated in its entirety, the makeshift bar sported a full display of wine, cognac and American whiskey behind a long counter. An added touch of atmosphere was lent to the naked bulbs by the red crepe paper lamps. Stubby red candles flickered upon each table. Several skimpily clad women, showing off their shapely bare legs, sat at the end of the counter. Others sat on the laps of the Nisei soldiers, laughing and drinking. They were trying to teach the Little Iron Men French and laughed delightedly at their awkwardness. A group of men were noisily shooting craps by the far wall of the room, while others smoked and played cards at a corner table. The game was obviously poker.

A noncom in shirt sleeves came up to Fred and said: "I'm Teddy 'The Stick' Koyama, Esquire. The maitre d'. Welcome to the best whorehouse in the French Riviera. What company you with?"

"I Company."

"One of the originals who fought in the Vosges?"

"That's right."

"Hotdamnit!" Koyama turned to the others in the room. "You know what we got here, men?" he called out loudly. "A hero of I Company from the Vosges Mountains!"

The men abruptly stopped what they were doing and stared at Fred with awe. Then as though on signal they all snapped off a salute.

Fred waved his hand deprecatingly at them. "Go back to what you were doing," he said.

The room returned to its chatter, rattling of dice and clicking of chips, although a few eyes remained fixed on Fred with admiration.

"For you, my kotonk, the drinks are on the house," Koyama said, slapping Fred on the back. "And pick any woman you want. They're special imports from Monte Carlo."

"Thanks," Fred said and sat at the bar. Kotonks, mainland Nisei, must certainly have an aura about them, thought Fred, that distinguished them from the men from Hawaii. The kotonks and buddhaheads were as different from each other as oil was from water, but what welded them together was their fighting spirit. An esprit de corps. There was not one of them who wouldn't give his all for the 442nd.

As he was sitting sipping his bourbon on the rocks, listening to the strains of a chanson whirled out of the record player, a young woman rose from one of the tables and sat by him. He smiled at her. Her scent was beguiling.

"My name is Monique," she said in a sensuous tone of voice.

"I'm Fred Murano."

"So you crushed the rotten Boche in the Vosges Mountains."

"I guess so."

"Nobody has ever beaten the enemy in the Vosges Mountains. Only the Little Iron Men. You are known throughout the Rhone Valley, maybe in all of France. I love all of you."

Monique grabbed Fred by the head and turned his face toward her. She planted a long kiss on his mouth, a stirring, probing kiss full of passion and tenderness.

"I heard what they did to your people in your own country," she said wistfully.

"A gross misunderstanding," Fred said cooly, in spite of the sudden surge of desire.

"Ah, but you must be a gentleman to state it in such a manner," she said and stroked the scar on his cheek lightly with her fingers.

"Would you like to join me in a drink?" Fred asked. He gazed upon her beauty. His eyes dropped to her full, red lips parted in a smile.

"Mais non, merci." Monique stroked his inner thigh and looked at him with intense longing. "But I want you to join me upstairs, mon cheri, *maintenant.*"

Monique's womanly fragrance inflamed him. The trace of her finger awakened a surge of passion. Everything about him yielded to the demands of the moment. He slid off the stool, and followed Monique up the stairs. They climbed up to a bedroom and entered a small room barely large enough to contain a double bed, dresser and full length mirror. The curtains on the window and the bedspread were a flesh-tone pink. The dark wood of the walls drew off the light covered with a pink shade that tried vainly to illuminate the corners of the room.

Monique began to undress slowly. Fred watched her motionless and transfixed. She unbuttoned her blouse, shrugged it off and reached around to undo her bra. She dropped it to the floor with an alluring gesture. Her breasts were full, upturned and her nipples were stiffened with passion. She approached him and grabbed his head to bend it to her breasts. Fred caught her pleased smile in the mirror as he kissed her breasts and eagerly took her hard nipples between his lips. Then she stepped back and slid out of her skirt and with a slow, suggestive movement worked her panties off her comely legs. She stood naked before him and struck a pose, her hands tousling her hair and her arms stretched up. She thwarted Fred's attempt to take her in his arms and began to undress him. Swiftly undoing his tie, dropping his jacket and bending over, he unlaced his boots and kicked them off. When he straightened up, she undressed him quickly. His stiffened manhood sprang alive when she pulled down his skivvies, and she lavished her attention on it. They stood naked confronting each other with undisguised desire in their eyes, and she guided him to the mirror and had him gaze at them together. Her alabaster body was exquisite, and he saw himself in the prime of manhood.

"I want to make the best love to you, my brave soldat," Monique said huskily.

They flung back the bed sheets and toppled on the mattress. Groping wildly they clasped themselves to each other with their mouths lustfully locked together. They rolled around on the bed, Fred on top of her one moment and she on top of him the next. He entered her moist firmness and violently grabbed her buttocks to force himself deeper into her. Twisting around to meld his body to hers, he crushed her soft breasts against his chest, and she entwined her legs around the small of his back to receive him. Then he turned gentle and with tender measured thrusts carried her along to heightened moans of pleasure–moans that forced him to prolong the ecstasy of his own moment. Her moans grew louder and were synchronized with his thrusting that increased in intensity. Her hips rose and undulated with each thrust, an eager, uplifted receiving. She lifted her hips as if to swallow his entirety, and he arched his back to find a deeper softness and firmness enveloping him. He cupped her firm, sweat-slicked breasts in his strong hands, and they held themselves locked tightly, motionless, suspended. Fred's body was rigid, his entire mind concentrated on the grasping, quivering hold Monique had on him. She suddenly let out a cry, an exhalation of ecstatic pleasure, and Fred rammed himself into her with the finality of a sun bursting. They arched their bodies, unwilling to let the moment pass, wanting only to prolong it without hope of its lasting but lusting for it to last forever. Then Fred collapsed on her, sweat-soaked, and Monique held him tightly to her and began whispering endearments in his ear in the soothing tones of her language. She nibbled on the lobe with affectionate afterplay.

"Mon Dieu!" she said. "You are a natural lover. How many women have you known?"

Fred looked down at her smooth cheeks and kissed her on her curving, red lips. "Not many," he said simply. A cold, tight fist had been loosened and detached. He felt whole again and now lay beside the woman who had brought him out of the war.

"But you must have had a lover, a girlfriend, a handsome man like you."

"No, not really." Fred recalled his student days and his

dalliance with a few coeds, especially the one called Colleen, but their making love did not match the desperation and need he had felt with Monique.

"I have a younger sister, Renee, who lives in L'Escarene. She would like you, and you would like her. This is where I come from, before I went to Monte Carlo. A man like you needs a steady woman, and I will introduce you to her. She is shy and would never dream of taking the chances I have taken. She is a good girl, and you two could become fond of each other."

"You are a good woman, Monique," Fred said. "A very warm and kind woman."

"Ah, it is good to hear a gentle man like you say that. But I am what I am, and I cannot help but love brave soldiers, the young men who are willing to die to fight the Boche."

"Your hatred of Germans must run deep," Fred said.

"Mais non. My love for the soldats fighting them runs high. They risk everything to drive the enemy from France. You Americans come so far to fight the enemy and free France. I can only love all of you with all my heart. It stirs my soul to see you marching and marching off to war, hundreds and thousands of brave men. And you die. Some of you come back hurt so bad. I want to cry."

As she continued to nibble on his ear, he ran his hand slowly over her smooth body. They lay in bed and pulled the blankets over them so as not to become chilled, although the room was heated by a small stove. An indolence swept over Fred; he stretched out languidly and fell asleep. The sleep was deep and settling, the kind of sleep that sank into the depths of his psyche where the warm glow brought back a renewed innocence. For the first time since he hit the battlefields of Italy and France, he slept the sleep of the dead. He was dead to the crashing thunder and din and cries of battle and the need to keep moving–into the finality of death. His senses were immersed in a calm sea, the bottom of which claimed the dregs of his wretched grief, sorrows and concerns. Now he was at ease and was cradled in the bosom of forgetfulness.

Monique introduced Fred to her younger sister, Renee. Renee Moreau. A beautiful name, Fred thought, for a beautiful girl of nineteen who resembled her sister but was more petite and had a doll-like face with large, sparkling, brown eyes and similar full lips. She was shy and virginal, but underneath the shyness lay the tentative and yet resolute reaching out of a woman. Fred was immediately taken with her. She had a way of casting her eyes down at her hands as if to hide her feelings, then suddenly look up at him brightly with a timorous smile playing about her lips. Although Fred was attracted to her, he felt protective–after all, he was four years older and a hardened veteran–and restrained. Least of all did he want to force himself on her.

"Do you speak...anglais?" Fred asked as they went out for a stroll.

"Oui. Je parle. I speak a leetle English." Her voice was sweet and soft.

"That's swell. What do you like to do most?"

"I read. All the books I can in English. Someday I would like to go to America."

"To do what? Study?"

"To live. But let us talk about you. The people of Bruyeres spread your story. What makes you Little Iron Men so brave?"

"We're not that special. We're here to get a job done."

"A job?"

"We're here to fight a war."

"I have an uncle in the Resistance. He is a very brave man.

The Last Fox

Tell me about America."

"Where I come from," Fred began, the landscape fleeting before his eyes, "there are many mountains and rivers, much farmland and fish and wild game. There are orchards and wheat fields. We live by a great river, the Columbia, where the salmon and sturgeon run. America is a vast country with mountains, rivers, plains and deserts. It is made up of many different kinds of people from all over the world. The Japanese are just one small part of them."

"You must be very strong."

"Why do you say that?"

"Because everybody I see who is like you is small. Not at all like the tall American soldiers. You have to be strong to beat the Boche."

Fred didn't want to think about the war, nor remember the weight of a full pack, the M1 or BAR which threatened to pull their arms out of their sockets after miles of marching. The foot soldier carried everything he needed and even cut his blanket in half to save weight. For the moment, all he wanted to think about was drinking in the warmth of the weak sunlight as he and Renee walked along the streets of the town. A slight wind had picked up and carried with it a harbinger of the winter chill that was soon to descend on them. Renee held a worn sweater torn at the elbows around her. He was walking her home after taking her to the canteen for coffee and doughnuts. The people had very little to eat, and Fred carried with him a ten-in-one package of food.

When they reached the small, modest cottage at the end of town, Renee invited him to stay for dinner. He wanted to decline, since he knew food was scarce but allowed himself to be persuaded out of courtesy, especially when Renee began pulling at his sleeve. He gave her the package at the door.

The Last Fox

Her parents were not elderly, but they had care-worn streaks of white in their brown hair. Monsieur Moreau was a thin man with angular features and wore his glasses low on his nose. His eyes were tired and he smiled as though unaccustomed to adjusting the fixed curvature of his lips. Madame Moreau had obviously been plumper at one time, since the clothes she wore hung on her loosely, waiting to be refilled. She smiled easily. Both wore threadbare jackets to keep warm in the unheated house. They spoke no English but with gestures and smiles motioned Fred to the dining table. Renee passed the package to her mother who exclaimed her delight in receiving the food and retired immediately into the kitchen. Monsiuer Moreau produced a bottle of wine and glasses, and Renee brought in a chunk of moldy cheese, a knife and a loaf of bread. They sat at the bare table eating and chatting about life in the town with Renee interpreting. Fred did not want to discuss the war and kept steering the conversation to what life was like before the war in France. His own thoughts kept wandering back to the days when he was busy as a university student, dreaming the dreams of innocence.

He made frequent trips to L'Escarene to see Renee and bring gifts of clothes and food. The Moreau family was delighted with the warm sweaters and jackets, and Madame Moreau would always have Fred stay for dinner while she cooked up something with the ten-in-one parcels he would bring. Neither did he forget to bring wine with him, and he and Monsieur Moreau would toast each other by name and drink to the end of the war. After several bottles of wine, Pierre Moreau would become rosy-cheeked like a young boy and seemed less rigid and smiled more often, a pleasant smile that lit up his eyes and gave Fred the impression that Renee got her bright expression from him rather than her mother. The more Fred visited them, the more friendly Monsieur Moreau be-

273

came, and he started to treat Fred like a son as did Madame Moreau who began to protest that Fred was too generous but seemed genuinely pleased to receive the gifts he brought.

At Christmas time, Fred outdid himself with the number of gifts. For Pierre there was a cardigan, a scarf and a carton of cigarettes; for Madame Moreau or Marie, a blouse, brooch and perfume, and for Renee, a pink sweater that went well with her rosy complexion, a pearl necklace and a gold bracelet that was once a young man's gift to his wife. Fred did not forget the food parcels, either. Besides the ten-in-one GI rations, he brought tins of meat and fruit. It was amazing how many doors a combination of cigarettes, food and money opened in Nice where everything was plentiful as long as one knew where to look. And his luck at poker continued to hold. Marie prepared a great feast for them, and Renee, in a high-fluted voice, led them in singing Christmas carols. She had a natural grace that enchanted Fred and softened his heart that had grown brittle with so much controlled violence. Watching her made him feel that he was recapturing something that was lost, something vital that used to nurture his belief in mankind as an innocent, young student. He was not much older than his student days, but like Hans Knecht who died at his hands in the Vosges Mountains, never to see his mother or homeland again, he felt old and dead inside, too often the victim of the world's madness.

After supper Fred invited Renee to join him in a visit to the local orphanage where the men of 442nd were throwing a Christmas party for the children. When they arrived, the place was in a bedlam of glee with the children, orphans of the war, sitting on the laps of the Little Iron Men and riding on their backs and eating the cookies, candy and cake the men had brought them. In their idle hours, when not fighting in the Maritime Alps, they had made toys for the children who happily towed wooden carts and trucks around the large room.

Fred's platoon was assigned to guarding a supply depot and was not involved in the fighting that proved sporadic in the steep mountains facing Italy; nevertheless, the men holding the cold heights complained of miserable conditions, minefields laid by infiltrating German troops, and the shortage of supplies that had to be hauled by intractable mules on slick mountain trails.

When the party was over, Fred took Renee home. At the door they embraced, and Renee, looking deeply into Fred's eyes, leaned into him voluptuously and regarded him with a wordless question. She was wearing the pearl necklace, the gold bracelet and had dabbed on some of the perfume he had given to Madame Moreau. Fred gazed at her for a long while, then kissed her lightly on the mouth. Renee looked disappointed when he broke the embrace and told her that he would stop by again soon. He told her he had to hurry and return to his billets in Nice for there were duties to take up. A handy excuse, just to make a break for it.

As he got into the jeep, he thought of stopping off at "Yuraku" to see Monique but thought better of it. If she found out that Fred and Renee were not making out, she would probably complicate matters by admonishing Renee for not getting on with him. Fred wanted to keep the status quo, to keep on seeing Renee and absorbing her fresh innocence and lavish his attention on her, a necessary balm. Without committing himself or breaking a silent vow, a vow that remained in his consciousness like an iceberg, mostly concealed but visible enough to remind him of the dangers involved for both of them. Monique and her passion was almost like a mothering, of Earth trying to heal itself. Of war, devastation and wanton death. A mothering that would take the dead and wounded and orphaned into the womb to give them life again. A passion that would inflame the spirit and urge a man to live–in the face of death. A mothering and a compassion that would shed tears of grief on the battle-torn earth to make it fertile once more. He would not want to wish that kind of torment on Renee, the fresh flower of Provence. He wanted her to remain untouched by the kind of grief that wrenched the soul.

He came to L'Escarene often to see Renee, each time bearing a gift or two. They went for long walks through the town or through the fields below and down to the river to watch its flow, ever-changing and peaceful in its predictable changeability. No one riffle or glide remained the same from second to second; in a blink of an eye it changed its pattern, and the change was constant. Change was the only constant, and the constant of changeability was in itself comforting, for the river would remain and the water would continue to flow as would–with luck–the blood in Fred's veins.

Toward the end of March, Fred received his orders: proceed to the staging area in Marseille. Destination: Top Secret. The day had finally come as he always knew it would. He made one last trip to L'Escarene to say goodbye to Renee and Pierre and Marie Moreau. He and Renee took a long walk down to the river banks. She took his hand and squeezed it warmly; he said nothing. The spring sun warmed the land again and turned the trees into a haze of fuzzy green. The sky was clear and blue but not yet the deep, summer blue. He wanted to make a farewell speech, something appropriate that had to do with war, life and circumstances. But the words would not come. They walked silently through the fields with Renee glancing up at him wonderingly every so often. But she too did not speak.

Renee had brought along a basket of cheese, bread and wine. They sat on a rock and opened the basket and ate and drank. Fred picked up a rock and heaved it as if it were a grenade as far as he could into the coursing water. He picked up another one and threw it to see if he could outdistance the first one. All the while he said nothing.

Renee got to her feet and lay a hand on his arm and said: "All you do is to throw rocks. Is there not something you want to say?"

"Yes, there is."

"I am a woman now. Just say it. Do you want me?"

"Renee...yes, I do. But—"

"You should have said so. There, the field there...the tall grass...no one will see us. Take me now, mon cheri. I have wanted you to," she said and threw her arms around his neck to kiss him and pressed herself against him hard.

"You don't understand, Renee. You are like a rare flower...to be touched with care and love...in the midst of a dirty war. I want to remember you as a rarity, as a breath of clean air. You see, I've been ordered back to the front."

"Then...you must go. But you will make me into a woman first. I want to remember you as my first man. Let us—"

"No, Renee. It can't be so," Fred said and undid her arms around him. He held her at arm's length and admired her figure. He was looking at her through the eyes of another man. "It mustn't be so. You do not belong to me, you belong to another man who will appear in your life in the future. You will fall in love with him and he with you. And you will have his children. You belong to the future, and so will your children. I am going away and dropping out of your life just as suddenly as I appeared in it. I will disappear forever and never see you again."

She bowed her head and burst into tears and cried: "Je t'aime. Je t'aime. Je t'aime."

Fred gathered her into his arms and held her until she stopped trembling and sobbing. His throat felt tight and his eyes welled. He could say nothing more.

When Renee had regained her composure, they put the food and drink back into the basket and made their way back to town through the tall grass and vineyards and past a long row of poplar trees that were green with the stirring of life. Back at the cottage, he said goodbye to the Moreaus. Pierre shook his hand vigorously and wiped his eyes, and Marie hugged him and kissed him on both cheeks. It was a simple goodbye, perhaps the same the world over when a soldier must leave for the front, bidding farewell to friends and loved ones. He turned once to wave at Renee framed by the doorway of the cottage. Sliding behind the wheel of the jeep, he looked straight ahead and drove back to Nice. The war clouds were again gathering on the horizon, and he was heading straight back into them, into darkness, doubt and fear and a weariness that never did leave him.

Chapter Fourteen

The men of the 442nd Regimental Combat Team streamed into the staging area at Marseille, stripped themselves of all identification, especially the unique shoulder patches that labeled them as belonging to the feared, renown unit, and boarded the LST's bound for Livorno, Italy. They themselves did not know for certain what their destination was. How Axis Sally knew where they were headed, when they themselves did not, was beyond speculation. Perhaps it was a lucky guess or perhaps the Germans had eyes and ears where General Mark Clark, who demanded their return to his command, did not suspect.

Upon arriving at Livorno, they were trucked to the assembly area at Pisa where they drew new equipment and were given their assignment: break the Gothic Line. For five months, during the 442nd's absence, the Allies had been pounding and hurling themselves against the impregnable German defenses dug in and reinforced by concrete bunkers and caves running east to west along the Apennine Mountains. The Germans did not yield an inch; the Allies could not advance a yard. The enemy held the high ground and could spot any movement in the valleys north of the Arno River and along the Ligurian Coast traversed by Highway 1. They could bring to bear at will on any cluster of movement to penetrate their lines, not only their string of 2,500 fortified machine gun nests, but also their long range guns, including their railroad guns salvaged from the Anzio debacle. The battle lines remained where the 442nd left them in September of the previous year and the stalemate continued well into March, 1945. General Mark Clark was desperate and after much haggling with the Joint Chiefs of Staff who were peppered by demands for the Nisei combat unit by other commands succeeded in persuading them that his need was greater.

After sighting in their new weapons and undergoing training maneuvers, the 442nd RCT swung into action. In battalion strength it was to flank and penetrate the western segment of the Gothic Line in a surprise move that would draw off enemy reserves around Bologna so that the Allies could punch through to the rich and fertile breadbasket of Italy, the Po Valley. General Clark had no doubts about the enemy's calculations once it learned that the 442nd was attacking its western anchor. The Germans would as usual double their defenses.

The Nisei marched north under the cover of darkness. Fred's company was headed for the mountain village of Azzano located high off the floor of the valleys below. Their movements were completely concealed. Once they arrived at the foothills, they had to make the eight mile hike up to Azzano during the night and remain hidden during the day. Their orders were to climb a saddle and scale Mt. Folgorito, a rugged 3,000 foot mountain which was but an extended part of a ribbed hump of mountains of similar height that the enemy had fortified for over nine months. The entire Gothic Line, made up of every conceivable weapon of destruction, was a murderous shield of death.

From his hiding place among the trees, Fred looked up at Mt. Folgorito. He couldn't even imagine a mountain goat attempting to climb its precipitous sides. As he studied the formidable fortress, a numbness that was all too familiar overtook his mind. Its deadness blocked out, even placated, the sharp stab of fear that accompanied him into battle. There was nothing to fear, he told himself. Hadn't he survived thus far? He wasn't as cocky or reckless as Sam had been...thinking that the bullet with his name on it hadn't been made yet. And yet he would prefer instant death to being maimed, shattered and transformed into a wasted invalid for the rest of his life. Peculiar, he thought in a detached fashion. The number his mind the weaker his legs. He tried to ignore the obvious. The Nisei had earned a reputation of being fearless. But perhaps it was because they concealed their fear so well and kept moving, forever moving forward, despite the odds, refusing to turn and run and be shot in the back.

As soon as it became dark, Fred and his company moved out. Lt. Ohashi, who had told Fred that he wanted him to be his platoon sergeant, led the way. Somehow the lieutenant arranged to have himself transferred to I Company. I Company was accompanied by L Company and together they climbed the saddle–soundlessly. They were to make no noise. Anything that clattered, such as mess kits, was discarded. They taped their dog tags to their chests. No one was to cry out even if they slipped and fell and were injured. No sounds. Their survival depended on it. Their achieving complete surprise depended on it. Fred trudged along behind the lieutenant, controlling his breathing which he wanted to take in great gulps. He breathed shallowly and exhaled noiselessly. The night was as black as India ink, moonless, and what starlight there was did not reach the mountain as though in trepidation.

They reached the base of Mt. Folgorito and began climbing with full packs. Fred looked up; all he could see was the looming, dark shadow of the mountain. The darkness was not the same as it was in the Vosges Mountains where dampness and the cold night congealed to form something that was frigidly palpable. Climbing Mt. Folgorito–almost straight up–was an exercise in animality. They pulled themselves up, grabbing hold of stunted shrubs, the leg of the man ahead, a gun butt rammed into the ground, and when they reached the upper portion of the mountain, they gripped the inner soles of their boots with their frantic toes, scrambling to get a better hold on the shifting shale which forced them to take two steps for every step up. Some men slipped, fell and hurled into empty space. They fell without uttering a sound and landed far below with a hollow grunt.

The night wore on, and still they climbed. Even starlight was denied them as clouds began to veil the sky as if to mask the mountains and separate heaven from earth. The field pack tugged at Fred's shoulder and threatened to throw him off balance, backwards into the dark void beneath him. He struggled with each step, clawing at the sharp rocks, his hands soon bloody and slick so that he had to wipe them on his sleeves before reaching for another handhold on the side of the mountain. No one uttered a sound. All he could hear was his own breathing. And shale grating on shale. Dawn would soon break, and still they had not reached the top. What would be waiting for them? Grim, determined, seasoned Jerries looking down upon them, ready to sluice them back down the mountain with a stream of fire?

At 0600 hours the first elements of the 3rd Battalion crested the ridge of the mountain. They fanned out across the rugged terrain that possibly concealed a machine gun behind every rock and expected a vicious response of gunfire, grenades and artillery. But none came. They had achieved complete surprise and caught the Germans asleep in their holes. They rooted the dazed Jerries out and advanced from one gun emplacement to another.

The Last Fox

But by the time Fred and his platoon led by Lt. Ohashi tumbled over the lip of the ridge, hell itself had erupted as the slumbering Jerries awoke and gave combat. Machine gun fire raked the rim of the ledge over which the men were pouring. Clutching their wounds, many fell back hundreds of feet into empty space. The lieutenant hailed them on with a .45 pistol. If he was going to attack head-on, thought Fred, he should be carrying something heavier, an M1-A, at least, rather than a puny sidearm. But Fred dashed forward to keep pace with the platoon leader who was leading the way toward a machine gun dugout. In the dim morning light, Fred could see it spitting deadly fire in all directions, its muzzle flashes emitting just as much sound as light. Then to his horror Fred saw that the machine gun was holding its aim on Lt. Ohashi. First its aim fell short. Its bullets kicked up dirt and rock, but the stream crept along the ground, stirring up debris, and stitched its way up to cut the lieutenant down. He crumbled and fell. Fred ran ahead, glanced at the lieutenant who was moaning and unleashed a grenade, then another to eliminate the nest.

Fred ran back to the lieutenant and knelt by him. He was holding his midriff where he had been blasted open.

"Help is on its way," Fred said, wondering how often he had repeated those words. "Just hold on, lieutenant."

"With this?" Lt. Ohashi said, bending his head to observe the wound and the blood spurting between his fingers. "I'll never make it. Must have hit an artery."

"Sure you will, lieutenant. Anybody who makes it through the Vosges makes it. You got to believe that."

"Take over, Sgt. Murano," the lieutenant gasped. "The 2nd platoon is yours. I knew I would be leaving it in good hands if anything happened to me."

Fred hesitated, wanting to help but not knowing what he could do, except screaming for the medic several times. He picked up his tommy gun and made ready to leave. He patted the lieutenant's shoulder.

"I've got a favor to ask," Lt. Ohashi said before Fred could move. "I don't know if I'm going to—"

"Shoot."

"A letter to my wife in my shirt pocket."

Fred reached inside his uniform and fished out a single, folded piece of paper.

"Finish writing it, will you?" the young officer said. "Tell her my very last thoughts were of her. Will you do that for me? She lives in Gary, Indiana. She'd want to hear it coming from a friend I trust."

"I will. You can count on me," Fred said. "But if I was your friend, why didn't you open up to me? You were quiet, most of the time."

"I don't know. A personal quirk, perhaps?" Lt. Ohashi groaned. He locked his hands tightly over his wound. "Can't get too close to your men, they said. You lose them...and you start taking it personally and blame yourself. Get too close...and you can't force them to fight. I was an enlisted man myself once, you know. You should have become commissioned, sergeant. You'd know what I mean." The lieutenant tried to smile but only managed to grimace in pain. He breathed heavily. "Just indulging in a last bit of condescension, Fred. You're helluva soldier and a damn fine poker player."

Fred stood up and got ready to leave. The lieutenant held up a bloody hand and stopped him. Fred knelt by him quizzically.

"Tell me, Fred," he said hoarsely. "The West Coast...why in the world do you want to return there?"

"Unfinished business, sir," Fred said.

The lieutenant nodded and arched his back in pain. "Now get going," he rasped.

Fred secured the letter in his pocket and watched as the young officer stretched his legs rigidly and closed his eyes. He patted him again on the shoulder, wishing he had spent more time getting to know him and, at the same time, glad that he hadn't. When he glanced back at the lieutenant, he saw his fallen friends, many of whom he would never see again. His eyes burned with the recollection. Leaving one of their own, all bloodied and alone, on the battlefield was always gut-wrenching. Hunched over he dashed through the crackling and sputtering gunfire to jump into the midst of the battle and lead his men.

Thirty minutes and the men of the 442nd broke the backbone of the Gothic Line. They streamed through the breach to try to tie up with the 100th Battalion and close the jaws of the pincer movement from the Ligurian Coast. They had achieved their objective and created a momentum. The deeper they penetrated into the mountains the stiffer the enemy opposition. But their onrush could not be stopped. Until they hit the Machine Gun Battalion Kesselring and its interlocking, deadly fire sighted in at high and low angles.

Momentarily staggered, the men clung to the ground. If anyone raised his head, he would have it raked off; if he stood, he would be cut in half. As familiar as the situation was to Fred, he found himself grow weak and stultified. Maybe it was a case of once too many or maybe taking the Jerries by surprise on Mt. Folgorito gave him a fleeting but false sense of invincibility, although he was much too realistic to believe he could escape the fatal bullet if it were meant for him. If only Sam and Mike were with him still as a team to enact the hop. They could have taken out one machine gun nest at a time, just waiting for that crucial pause that was characteristic of the MG-42. The Jerries still suffered from the habitual impulse to shoot at anything that moved. Now if it were a controlled movement as in the "Brahm's Hop" with... A couple of replacements? But, no. Sam and Jimmy were dead, Mike was badly wounded and out of the war for its duration. Fred could not count on anyone else to understand the coordination required. All at once the weariness he felt metamorphosed into a feeling of helplessness. He lay on the rock-strewn bed of dirt and closed his eyes tightly. He held them shut, frustration mounting. He abhorred the feeling. Anger rose in his belly like a volcano about to erupt.

Fred crawled fifty yards to the BAR man and instructed him to take on two of the machine guns dug into the side of the mountain and take the pressure off of him while he tried to get within range with his grenades and tommy gun. He slithered back to his original position and readied himself after passing along orders to the riflemen of his platoon to cover him. Then he began creeping toward the targets. Nothing fancy this time, he told himself. Unlike the battle in the Vosges Mountains with its undergrowth, fog and snow, he could clearly make out the position of the Jerries and see the machine gun and the helmet of the gunner. Have to meet them head-on, the hard way: he clenched his teeth and crawled closer. Bullets ricocheted off the rocks surrounding him. He lay still for a moment with the chatter of gunfire and the explosions of a mortar barrage filling the air. The usual roar and din of the battlefield triggered a creeping numbness. His mind wandered for an instant as though he were in a dream within a dream and had nothing to do except go back to sleep to dispel an ongoing nightmare. He shook his head to snap himself alert. Then he stood up and raced toward the first machine gun

The Last Fox

nest, his tommy gun blazing and a grenade held in his right hand.

He sensed more than saw the guns pointed in his direction as a figure on which to fix all gun sights. He ran hard, holding his breath and tightening his muscles in sheer concentration. He was about to fling the grenade, when he felt as if someone had dealt him a heavy blow to the stomach. The impact threw him back on the ground; he was stunned and mostly surprised. The hot pain spread in his midriff like a torch. He couldn't believe he had been hit. Not him, Fred Murano. Not with his lucky charm. All he was supposed to go home with was a few small scars in his cheek, ear and shoulder. He was still clutching the grenade, and he got to his feet and made ready to throw it. A burst from a machine gun cut across his thighs, and he fell to his knees. Again, in surprise. He flung the grenade, but it fell far short of its mark and exploded harmlessly. Another burst caught his outstretched arm, shattered it along with his hand and twisted him sideways as the arm flailed helplessly through the air. He ripped off another grenade with his left hand and staggered to his feet, lunging forward and flinging it with a sidearm pitch. It landed closer but didn't strike home. He sank to his knees again and caught a Schmeisser burst in the chest. He was slammed on his back and lay still in disbelief.

He was dimly aware of hundreds of feet pounding around him as the men were galvanized into action with cries of "Go For Broke!" They rushed the German positions, many falling under the withering hail of fire. But they persisted and knocked out the machine gun emplacements and kept moving to the next ridge of the mountain which was but one link in a chain of fortified mountains. But they had broken through. The Jerries either surrendered in droves or fled before the onslaught deeper into the Apennines.

Fred lay dazed. He knew he was badly wounded. The heat of

his body seemed to turn into a blazing fire where he had been hit, and the pain throughout his body, in his legs, stomach, chest and arm, was so intense that he thought his skull would split. All the splayed nerves that had lain dormant for so long screamed in unison. He clenched his teeth and shut his eyes tight. He willed himself to stay awake. If he was going to die, he wanted to be fully awake. Was that possible, he thought. But along with the faintness came the cold. The pain and fire gradually subsided. The numbness was not gentle but overpowering like the balm of death, the gripping hand of unconsciousness. He squeezed his eyes shut and snapped them open to chase away the darkness. He began to shiver and shake involuntarily as though he were lying on a block of ice that claimed all the heat of his body. He didn't know if he were dying or not. He would not die, he told himself as though from a distance. He could not die. There was too much to do with his life. He had to take care of Rhonda...see that the family was settled once the war was over. He had to complete his college education. There was much to do. He had a full life to live. He wanted to live to enjoy the freedom he had fought for so tenaciously.

Ah, but he felt so tired. The weariness that had dogged him since his baptism in hell at Monte Cassino turned into a poultice that drew off the poison of life and insisted on laying claim to his. His life, his dreams, his beliefs, his anger and outrage, his disgust, his hope for and condemnation of mankind, his insights and despair would all be drawn into oblivion. All he had to do was yield to the oppressive weight of the weariness, surrender to the imperative of death which so far had gone begging. Many had preceded him on the battlefield, and he had sent many to an unwanted end. Out of the surfeit of killing grew the weariness that had to be answered. But how? With his own life? He was a soldier, and he fought to survive in order to fight–another day, another battle. His body screamed to be free of life, and yet his spirit cried out for the freedom to live. He lay bleeding profusely, and a blackness took over his mind. His last thought was of the Indian head penny.

Fred awoke in a hospital bed in Livorno. When he first opened his eyes, he had no idea where he was or what had happened to him. Everything appeared blurred, and he was totally disoriented. He was dimly aware that a face was bending over him. A woman's face. Renee? Was it Renee? Or perhaps it was his mother. He tried to blink the blurriness away and dispel the fog that clouded his mind. As he awakened, be became increasingly aware of the wracking pain that shot through his body. Then he heard the din of the battlefield, the raging cries of combat, the moaning of the wounded and dying, and he knew that he had been shot up. The scene of the battle returned to him in full force, and he awakened and stared at the face above him. He tried to bring it into focus.

"You've been badly wounded, sergeant," a soft voice said. "It's a miracle you're still alive. When they brought you in, we weren't sure you'd make it."

Fred continued to blink hard, and gradually he could make out the features of the nurse's face hovering over him with concern knitting her brows. She held a bowl in her hands.

"You've been out of it for three days," she said. "It was touch and go there for a while."

"Luck...of the Irish," Fred said, when he could work up enough spittle to moisten his dry mouth. "And you've been looking after me all this time?"

"Sitting right here beside you, waiting for you to come to. You have enough morphine in you to knock out a regiment of men."

"I must have needed it."

"You were delirious. You were calling out names and cursing the war and what you called the 'pig pens'."

Fred could only wonder what he had said in his delirium or if he had made any sense. "You heard of them as relocation centers."

"Ah, yes, those nasty places. They shouldn't have happened."

The nurse's face came into focus. Fred could see she was a blonde with beautiful dark blue eyes, probably in her late twenties. He smiled weakly and noticed the bowl.

"My name is Brenda," the nurse said. "And who is Renee whose name you kept calling? A special girl friend?"

"Yes, she was special...(a pause and a hard swallow)...she really wasn't what you might call a regular girl friend. She was like a rare, innocent flower in the middle of..."

"You don't have to talk if you don't want to," Brenda said when Fred could not continue. "Here, have some good old fashion chicken broth. You'll need it to heal."

"I do have an appetite," Fred said and raised his head to receive the spoonful.

"You do?" Brenda said surprised and delighted. "I thought I was going to have to force it down you. I'd hate to do that to a wounded soldier."

"I promise to finish it all."

"You'll need every bit of strength you have to recover."

"With you beside me, Brenda, I know I'll make it." Fred was not trying to be brave. He just felt enormously lucky to be alive.

When he finished the bowl of soup, he sank back down into the pillow. In spite of the throbbing pain which seemed to cover his whole body, he fell asleep, concentrating on the warmth in his belly. It was almost as if he had downed a shot of smooth whiskey; the soft glow was a soothing balm in the center of a mass of pain.

When he awoke again, it was dark. He was not sure if he had slept through another day. He was groggy with sleep, but when his mind became sharper, the pain throughout his body seemed to leap alive, and he clenched his teeth to keep from crying out. As though she knew exactly what he needed, Brenda appeared by his side with a syringe and injected him with morphine. Soon a wave of somnambulance washed over his body and mind, and he drifted off to an ocean of peace, far away from the clamor and rage of the battlefield.

He lost track of time. The days seemed to be weeks or months. In fact, it was only the third day after he had come to, and Brenda, whom Fred regarded as an angel of mercy, stood by his bedside ready to change his bandages and feed him his meal. His ravenous appetite startled even him; his body seemed to be begging for sustenance to heal the shattered bone and tissue. Before feeding him, the nurse took his temperature, laid a cool hand across his forehead and nodded her approval when she read the thermometer.

"Good," she said and began feeding him. "No temperature. You're doing just fine, and you're going to be transferred to the general hospital in Naples. You've got a lot more surgery ahead of you, Sgt. Murano."

"You can call me Fred. I'm going to miss your gentle touch, Brenda."

"Just think positive. You're going to have a whole army of good-looking nurses hounding you in Naples. Something to dream about, eh, soldier?"

The next day he was loaded on to a ship in the Livorno harbor

291

along with many of the other wounded. In spite of the close quarters on board, the nurses bustled about efficiently. Fred was oblivious to their activity and the moans of the seriously injured. He slept most of the time and gritted his teeth with the onset of pain to stifle any sound coming from his lips. Sleeping and eating seemed to be the natural prescription he had set for himself to recover from his wounds. He knew his right arm and hand were badly torn up, but he could see nothing because of the bandages, and the pain in his chest was worst than in his legs, since it was triggered with each breath he took. Sleep was the key, and he took advantage of every shot of morphine to sink deeply into it.

The general hospital in Naples was filled with the wounded from the fighting going on in the northern part of the boot. He was far from the battlefields now, and to his constant amazement he was alive. No longer did he have to fight. The realization that he did not have to face the deadly enemy and engage in mortal combat brought with it a sense of relief, accomplishment and loss. He had done his duty, but it did not seem to be enough in the face of having lost so many of his friends–Sam and Jimmy. He knew he would eventually see Mike again and perhaps even team up with him. They had always been inseparable.

Arriving at the hospital in Naples, he was put into a bed next to a white GI who had lost a leg. Fred immediately recognized him. He was the noncom with the scar running down his cheek, the one who had slandered them in the bar in Naples. Fred did not think the GI recognized him, but he was wrong.

With one arm behind his head, the GI was pulling on a cigarette and blowing the smoke vigorously toward the ceiling. He turned toward Fred.

"You're that Nisei who slammed me down on the floor and nearly tore my fuckin' head off," he said.

"And you're Scarface," Fred said and smiled.

"Name's Ernie Storment. Used to be called Stud. Now I'm just a one-legged jackass. A fuckin' cripple. Also an all-around asshole. You should've killed me back then for bad-mouthing you Nisei. I heard a lot about your outfit since then and what you been through back home. Man, what a fuckin' raw deal. And you guys volunteering and racking up all those medals, turning out to be the best goddamn assault troops in the U.S. Army. Man, do I ever owe you an apology."

"Apology accepted. Sorry I roughed you up. Name's Fred Murano."

"Shit, man, you should've killed me. Me and my goddamn fat mouth," Storment said and seemed relieved by Fred's friendly smile. "Cigarette?" he said, popping out a Lucky.

"No, thanks," Fred said and waved his good hand. "I'd better give them up, because I got just so much lung left."

"Got the ever-loving shit shot out of you, huh?"

"You can say that," Fred said, wondering at the young GI's sense of realism.

"Fuck, man, I was point man going up this slope the engineers said was clean of mines, and BAM! Off goes this Shuh mine the fuckin' krauts made so it can't be detected and off goes my fuckin' leg."

"They'll make you a prosthesis, and you'll be good as new before you know it," Fred said.

"You sure?"

"Positive."

"Shit, they said it would take at least six months for the stump to heal and another two years before I can learn to walk regular. You know, and not give away the fact that I'm a one-legged, goddamn cripple."

"You'll be walking like everybody else in no time at all, and nobody will know the difference...as long as you keep your pants on." Fred smiled broadly and winked at the GI.

"Man, it's going to put a crimp in my love life, too," Storment laughed. "Who's going to want to fuck a cripple?"

"You might be surprised."

"You mean, it's a matter of me having enough moola to lay a broad?"

"It might be simpler than that," Fred said cryptically. "Find the right woman."

"You might be right, Fred," Stortment said pensively and blew a stream of smoke into the room. "You just might be right."

Fred lay back and stared at the ceiling. Seeing Storment and remembering how he nearly killed him for calling them "Japs" brought back memories of his friends. He could not get them out of his mind. They had been through everything together: baseball leagues, the evacuation, the stockyards and stinking horse stalls, the inland concentration camps, volunteering and training at Camp Shelby, the same baptism under fire at Monte Cassino in Italy. If his survival meant anything, it was to continue the fight that began in the battlefields of Italy and France. Carry on the tradition of the 442nd Regimental Combat Team whatever he did, wherever he went. In the name of what? The ideal that managed to survive everything. Freedom. And he survived to fight again.

Brenda, the nurse at the Livorno field hospital, was right. He was in for more surgery, much more. They cut away the bandages around his right arm and hand and removed them from his chest and legs. Luckily, the bones of his thighs were not shattered and remained intact, although they were chipped, and the bone fragments had to be removed. His sternum had to be pieced together again and a few useless ribs discarded. But the problem was with his right arm. The surgeons could do just so much for him. After the surgery, he was plunged into a new realm of pain, and morphine was his only hope for entering that vast ocean of peace that floated him on gentle lapping waves of ease. The process of numbing himself was total; it did not isolate itself to the mind as in combat only to find expression in the weakness of his legs. The stupor took over his entire being, numbing it in dead torpidity, and causing even his spirit to flee into some hidden corner of his soul while his body fought to heal itself.

As Fred lay languishing with his wounds, more wounded soldiers came pouring into the general hospital from Livorno. They were casualties of the battles fought in the Apennine Mountains where the Gothic Line was entrenched. Among them was a black who belonged to the all-black 92nd Division to which the 442nd had been attached after landing at Livorno from Marseille. He wound up in the bed to Fred's left, and introduced himself without hesitation as Jim Jones.

"Ya'll from the 442nd, right?" he queried.

"That's right, Jim," Fred said and gave him his name.

"Man, ah neba would of dreamt it, Fred, but ya'll shore do like to fight."

"Tell me about it. What happened after Mt. Folgorito fell?"

The large black man scratched his head swathed in bandages as though from habit and seemed to try to collect his thoughts.

"Why, ah believe ya guys smashed right through de mountains along de coast and took town afta town. Massa, Carrara, Aulla. Wasn't nothin' goin' to stand in yo' way. Ya'll took the naval base of La Spezia, an' in de four days of fightin' neutralized de reinforcements taken from Bologna. Dat's where ah got it. But we broke through. It's de end of de fuckin' krauts now."

"I'm glad to hear that," Fred said and sighed.

"Ya little guys shore do pack a pawful punch," the black said in admiration.

"We try," Fred said tersely.

It was the best news he could have heard. He could see his brothers-in-arms leaping over the mountain tops, crushing the opposition in the fortified towns and demolishing the western anchor of the Gothic Line while clearing the way into northern Italy. He could see them moving, forever moving ahead. Fred instinctively knew the war was about to end. The Jerries in Italy were finished. So were their brethren in Germany with the Allies pouring across the Rhine and the Russians pushing from eastern Europe. The realization that the war was soon to end in Europe brought about a rare, lighthearted moment...that passed all too quickly. Fred wanted to savor the realization, but the toll had been high, and he could not help but yield to a kind of sobriety that kept things in balance.

The doctors at the general hospital decided to keep Fred there as long as it was necessary to prepare him for the long arduous trip back to the States and admission to medical facilities where they could do more work on the bones of his arm and hand. His other wounds, especially in his legs, were doing fine, they told him, and they were especially pleased with the way his chest was healing. They complimented him on his attitude and asked him if he prayed a lot. Not particularly, he told them; he just had faith that he was going to knit well. He did not elaborate, that he willed himself from the very bottom of his inner being to be whole and healthy again. Much lay ahead of him, he felt, and he needed to be fit and strong, although, obviously, he would never again have full use of his right hand which he had not been able to examine because of the bandages. He had no idea what it might look like.

A few days before he was to leave Naples to go home, a

commotion arose in the hallway outside the ward. An insistent woman's voice rose above the others who were trying to dissuade her from entering.

"I must see," the desperate voice said. "I must see for myself. You know who I am. I have been here many times before."

The woman appeared in the room. Fred looked at her curiously at first. An Italian woman wandering around in the general hospital? Then he recognized her: Liza Bonachelli. Without hesitation he waved at her, although he had a sad duty to perform, and she came running joyously toward him, then stopped a short distance away when she was able to see who he was. She was suddenly downcast but walked slowly toward his bed. Fred had prepared a speech–for Jimmy–if he should have had the chance to go see her. That had been impossible, since he was still a stretcher case. Knowing that he could not venture out to visit her, he had intended to write her a letter from the States and send the money. Now he could in person. The fancy speech he had prepared drained out of him as he looked upon the beautiful, saddened features of a young woman who reminded him of his own Renee.

"Jimmy," she said plaintively. "Do you know what happened to Jimmy? Is he all right?" She stood by his bed, wringing her hands.

"Do you remember me?" Fred asked, stalling for time to let the lump in his throat settle.

"Yes, I do. You are Sgt. Murano, Jimmy's sergeant."

"You remember well, and it was such a long time ago or it seems like it."

"Yes, a long time ago. How is Jimmy? I've come here almost every day to check and see if he is not hurt. Where is Jimmy? I want so much to see him."

"Jimmy...," Fred said, remembering the last moments in the Vosges with his voice cracking. "Jimmy said...he loves you...loves you more than anything else in the world." He swallowed hard; he could not utter another word.

"He is coming back to Naples?" Liza said, hope rising in her voice.

Fred looked at her almost pleadingly as though begging her for a moment longer. The speech he had prepared for her was about Jimmy being a hero who did his duty to his country and to his brothers-in-arms, a man who was a good soldier and deeply in love with her. He wanted to tell her about the circumstances that had brought him from the concentration camps to Italy.

He merely said: "No, Liza. He's not...coming back. He was killed—"

Liza put her hands to her face, the horror of realization creeping into her eyes. The finality struck deeply. Her eyes said: My Jimmy!

"Oh, no," she cried. "Jimmy is dead!"

Fred wanted to take her sobbing form into his arms. Even if he were able to he would have felt just as helpless.

"He died...in France...in the Vosges Mountains. The last words on his lips...he told me...tell Liza I love her with all my heart and soul. He wanted to marry you and saved all his money." As hard a veteran as he was–or perhaps it was the war's fault, after all–he could not prevent the tears from welling in his eyes and coursing down his cheeks.

"I'll never see you again, Jimmy," Liza said and covered her whole face and bowed her head. "You are gone, gone forever. It is just as I saw in my dreams..."

"Under my bed, Liza," Fred said, wiping the tears away. "Get my bag out from under my bed, will you?"

The Last Fox

She stooped down and dragged out his duffle bag and lifted it onto the corner of the bed.

"Undo the cord," he said, blinking his eyes dry.

She did as she was told and spread open the mouth of the bag.

"On the bottom, there's a rolled up pair of socks. Dig it out."

She rummaged through the bag and came up with a tightly wadded up pair of socks and looked at Fred quizzically. Fred took the socks, squeezed them and gave them back.

"There's another pair in there."

She peered inside and dug out the other pair. Fred unraveled the rolled up socks and turned one upside down and shook it. Out tumbled a wad of money.

"Now there's a book in there called *German Classical Composers*. Get it for me, will you?"

She had no difficulty finding the book and handed it to him. He turned the book on edge, spine up, and jerked it up and down. Countless number of bills, lira, fell from its pages. He had converted all his winnings to Italian currency as soon as they touched Livorno.

"The money is all yours, Liza."

"All of this...for me? Jimmy made all this money?"

"Yes, he did. Jimmy wanted you to have it. It's for you and your family. He was always thinking of you and talking about you. You never left his mind."

"I have his letters, and I will keep them always. And I will say a special prayer for him."

"I know he'd like that, Liza," Fred said and smiled at her. He knew the two would have been happy together. If it weren't for the damn war...

"Your injuries, are they bad?" she asked.

"I'll be all right," Fred said. "I'll be going back to the United

299

States in a few days."

"Then I'll say a prayer for you, too, so that you will get well," she said. "I will never see any of you again, will I?"

"No, I'm afraid not. We'll be worlds apart."

Liza stuck the folded money down her blouse. She stepped over to the head of the bed and bent down to place a kiss lightly on Fred's cheek.

"Then it is goodbye." She backed away slowly, brushing the tears from her eyes, and turned to leave.

Fred waved his good hand and watched her departing figure. Silence filled the room, as if each injured man who witnessed the scene were trapped by their own thoughts about love, life and death. There was no glory on the battlefield, just honor and duty earned the hard way. Every death was, in fact, inglorious. Except perhaps Jimmy's. He had a woman to love him, even after death. Without the spirit of love, perhaps death on the battlegrounds of the world was the ugliest form of death of all.

If nothing else, war had turned Fred into a realist–the idealist was moribund like a flower going to seed–who was not afraid to look deeply into the raw, nightmarish makings of war and sanctioned killing. Sent into battle by policy and stratagem, Fred had been enforcing the ambitions harbored in the minds and hearts of men in inaccessible, distant and high places, couched in high-flown terms. The death of each soldier was death by policy. But wars have always been a part of historical reality. Ultimately, as a foot soldier, he had been fighting not so much for nationalistic goals, openly exploited, as for his own personal freedom...which by extension included the entire country. By fighting for freedom, he felt he was serving a higher master, not politicians or generals or an erudite abstraction. With Fred the fight was a personal one. Perhaps therein lay the seeds of his redemption, the seeds of the flower that died. Would it, in the end, take root, blossom and bear fruit?

By the time Fred was transported by ship across the Atlantic Ocean, the war in both Germany and Japan was over. There had been a short outburst of joy among the wounded, but it was short-lived and tempered by the reality of pain and in many cases living with the sobering prospects of being maimed for life. The killing machines of the battlefields were silent now, and the blood-stained ground itself would be covered with new, verdant growth that would hide the horrors of mortal combat between lone soldiers and great armies.

Fred wound up in Fitzsimmons General Hospital in Denver where they specialized in putting shattered bones together. He underwent numerous operations in which they wired and screwed together his forearm and hand over which they grafted skin taken from his thigh to form a glove. When they finally took the bandages off the reconstructed limb to show him their handiwork, he was horrified. The forearm was shriveled and bony as though transplanted from a long-dead corpse, and his hand resembled a mummified claw. He could hardly believe that it belonged to him. The fact the claw moved like a hand, responding to his own will, was even more repulsive. It was indeed a part of him. As he spent many long hours with the physical therapist, he came to accept the reality that the appendage was his for life and the doctors had done what they could to save it. The more he worked with the claw, learning to hold a fork, pencil, book, the more pride he began to take in it, and it came to represent not only a war wound but also something intangible–like the entire war and what it meant.

His other wounds were healing well, and he was even able to walk around the ward and visit other sections of the hospital where he found several wounded men from the 442nd. One was an Oregonian who had both feet almost shot off by an 88 while lying in a slit trench in Italy. He cheerfully offered his hand, saying that it was the hand shook by General Eisenhower himself. There was a radioman from Seattle who was attached to Headquarters Company and suffered a shattered shoulder, and a young man with the Cannon Company whose femur had been fragmented. A man from L Company whom Fred had not met before, although the two companies had fought together, was in for a blasted leg, the result of stepping on a mine in one of the last battles in Apennine Mountains. The Japanese community in Denver, ever mindful of the plight of the Nisei, would visit the hospital often and entertain the men and welcome them back home.

Fred had no idea what happened to his family after they left Tule Lake, not until the last letter from Margie caught up with him. The whole Murano family was still intact; Margie had manipulated the situation so that she and Arthur were able to remain in America along with their Issei parents. They returned to Portland, Oregon, the place of their origin, but had a hard time of it because of racial prejudice that was still very much alive on the West Coast, and they couldn't find housing or jobs. They doubled up with another Japanese family in a ramshackle house and worked at any odd, menial job they could find, such as pulling weeds from a white man's garden.

The last line of the letter hit Fred with all the impact of an errant projectile. It was inserted almost as an embarrassed afterthought. He lost his breath with the force of the shock. Rhonda had committed suicide in the state hospital by gnawing through her wrists and severing the arteries. Fred was tormented. If he could only have seen her and talked with her... He thought he could have brought her out of the dreadful prison she had locked herself in after the shock of being incarcerated. He had dreamt of the day when he would see her again. In spite of his wounds which drew the focus of all his energy to heal himself, he thought of his sister often and agonized over what he knew to be a strange, lonely existence of solitary madness and torture. Margie had mentioned the event in passing as if it were a dirty happenstance that was best forgotten. Fred knew the taboos of mental illness and suicide. It was not to be discussed. It was best swept under the carpet. And yet Fred was going to miss his sister, her sensitive charm and winsome ways. She had been the very epitome of feminine warmth and had possessed keen and fine sensibilities...destroyed, utterly destroyed by barbed wire fences. As he thought about her, he suffered an indescribable urge to ram his claw into the white man's face and demand if he had the intelligence to know what it represented. It was still a hand, it was pieced together, and it had originally clawed its way up a mountain. Now when he waved it, it would be a symbol of freedom and death.

Long days and nights followed, and gradually Fred emerged from a state of anguish, anger and outrage that he could not–dare not–give voice to, and he reconciled himself to the overwhelming sense of having lost Rhonda whom no one could have helped in the end, not even he who was her closest brother and confidante. Now in a grotesque sense, she was free, free of an egregious kind of torment imposed upon a human being by the age of wars...an age that was accompanied by the birth of raging demons encircling the globe, pitting man against himself.

Late summer eased into fall, and at long last Fred was discharged from Fitzsimmons General Hospital. He could not make the trip right then to see Lt. Taneo Ohashi's wife in Gary, Indiana, so he phoned her and told her about her husband and his last moments and promised to make the trip to see her when he could. He headed straight for Portland, Oregon to see his family and give them what back pay he had left, and enrolled at the University of Oregon to finish up his final year on the GI Bill. But not before looking up Mike Kojima, who had recovered from his wounds and was having a hard time making ends meet, since he could not find any job except as a gardener. The two men spent one glorious night of bingeing and celebrating their survival, and the occasion proved to be the only time Fred would be able to drink Mike, who was fond of his liquor, under the table. Fred made certain that even if everything else was forgotten that night, they would not forget each other's commitment to form a trading company in Portland to do business with Japan.

Moving to Eugene to attend college, he soon settled into a routine, supposedly a wreck of a man but very much intact and intent on getting his degree and enjoying the freedom he had earned. Or as he understood it, enjoying and nurturing the ideal of freedom that he had fought for, even though society was not ready to present it to him. Certainly, not on a silver platter. The world as it remained would probably sooner serve up his head on the platter and present it to him as a gift. But he had vowed in the battlefields and during his convalescence to fight racism wherever he found it, whenever he found it and give the next generation of youth a chance to find themselves in the grand enterprise of living a shared sense of commonality. Nothing was achieved without a fight.

The small tree-lined city of Eugene and its slow-paced life was the perfect setting for the compact campus of the University of Oregon. Fred did not have to own a car; he got around wherever he wanted by bicycle. Also, the distance between classrooms was short and made for a quick, easy hike. It took a while for Fred to get into the habit of studying, but by the end of the first term, he was just like any other student immersed in reading and cramming for exams. He did feel different, though. Much older–and perhaps wearier. During the colder months, he was able to wear gloves to hide the ugly claw, but when he took them off, he attracted curious stares from those whom he considered youngsters, although, in some cases, they were only a couple of years younger than he. He hoped they saw that he was home from a great war, that, like them, he was entering into a new world. But the claw came to symbolize something he was proud of, and he did not mind the stares or even the looks of disgust.

He shifted his major from History to Business Management with a minor in English. It seemed the sensible thing to do. Reading literature gave him the breadth and depth of under-standing that resonated with his experience. He tackled the business courses as a hard-headed realist. After all, business was going to be his bread-and-butter existence, and he intended to do well in it, making it a springboard to other enterprises growing out of the perspective of what he had learned from the war. But in literature, he began to find the seeds of renewal.

Chapter Fifteen

Outside the Haishan Chinese Restaurant in downtown Portland, it was dark. It was also raining, and the flickering, red neon sign of a cheap hotel winked its invitation through the downpour. The weather was as changeable as the mood of a nervous marmot, and the wind was now astir and brought the clouds from the west to advance eastward toward Mt. Hood hidden in darkness.

Hoary-headed with white, tufted eyebrows, Fred Murano sat with his elbows on the table, clasping a glass of beer in his bony claw. The old men of I Company, 442nd Regimental Combat Team, sat around the round table which held the scraps of food left over from the feast they had consumed. They had eaten eagerly, whether they had an appetite or not, to fulfill what they saw as one of the dictates of life. Eating to live was almost like a moral imperative. They had come to mourn the passing of Mike Kojima, and with that somber occasion embraced, they leaned back in their chairs, some now contented, a few tired but happy to have been able to get together for what might prove to be their last reunion. Now the after-dinner doldrums took effect...a blankness that sopped up conversation.

"Say," Fred said to break the silence, "wasn't that 1994 get-together in Bruyeres something?"

"Yeah," Herb Sakata, who stirred himself awake, agreed, "the fiftieth anniversary of the Allied liberation of Bruyeres...it was some doings, all right."

"You can say that again," Chik Tokuhara said, brushing back his white mane. "All those townspeople turning out, and all that good food, the band playing, singing and speeches. What a day to remember! Man, you'd think the people wouldn't have cared about us after half a century."

"And finding the old foxholes in the Vosges...gives you the willies," Herb said, hunched in his chair.

"Chicken skin, the buddhaheads call it," Chik said. "'I got chicken skin lookin' at da mountain', they said."

"The forest was just the same as it was fifty years ago," Fred said.

"Amazing that it could still be," Herb said, "after all this time."

"It's because the trees are full of shrapnel," Fred observed. "Can't harvest them."

"They should make a monument of the whole goddamn mountain," Chik said.

"The monument they did set up for us gave me what you call 'chicken skin'," Fred said, his throat tightening with emotion. "The people of Bruyeres are truly good people. They never forgot us. And there are thousands of us old farts of World War II around. Can you imagine naming a thoroughfare after the 442nd, besides setting up the monument and designating October 18 as 'Aloha Day' with the whole town decked out in the colors. Made me feel proud, so proud to belong to the 442nd. We were bound by honor and duty...

"Who can forget the media coverage and the U.S. Army Honor Guard that came all the way from Germany...all to welcome us back to their town? Remember what the monument said: 'To the men of the 442nd Regimental Combat Team, U.S. Army, who reaffirmed an historic truth here–that loyalty to one's country is not modified by racial origin...during the battle of Bruyeres broke the backbone of German defenses...' " Fred choked up and could not continue.

Herb wiped the tears from his eyes. "I never get tired of telling that story to my grandchildren...how we went in and saved that town and the Lost Battalion, too," he said and took a quick drink.

Fred swallowed hard and paused to compose himself. "Don't forget Biffontaine. The people there didn't forget, either. They have a monument to us tucked away in the woods. Our fight wasn't in vain, men. The men of the Lost Battalion will vouch for that."

"I'd like to believe that," Herb said soberly. "After what we sacrificed. But what about racism? It keeps spreading its tentacles. What the hell we fight for anyway? There's no end to it. It just won't die. It's like an infection."

"That's why I sponsored and financed the youth organization," Fred said. "It was a small start, but you have to begin somewhere...share your vision, what you've learned about the 'undercurrent of commonality'. That's what I call it. It's like the life-blood that ties us all together."

"With what in mind?" queried Herb. "We're all separate, like potatoes, carrots, onions, in a big pot of stew. It's a wonder we get along together at all."

"Now you're talking about what? A conventional view? A cultural jigsaw puzzle?" Fred said. "But what I'm talking about has nothing to do with one's cultural heritage. Don't get me wrong. Our cultural heritage is vital...to the soul of the community. But the individual is not going to find his soul as an American simply by seeking his cultural roots, though that could be a fine beginning. Most of all, he has to find himself. And he has to sink into his guts and find the undercurrent, the life-blood I'm talking about that feeds the soul of all Americans...from all walks of life, in the name of freedom and an ultimate sense of responsibility...to himself and to others."

"Man, you were always the one to put it together, Sarge," Chik said.

"Sounds risky," Herb insisted. "Wouldn't it be safer to stay in the pot of stew? Separate and unequal."

"Probably would be more comfortable," Fred said, "if you didn't want to think about the kind of person you want to be...to honor your birthright. To find your own worth. It's not easy. It's the hardest fight you can fight in this country."

"Is that what you fought for, Fred?" Herb asked.

"Yes, it is. Precisely," Fred said. "And that's what the monuments mean to me, and all the unit citations and medals pinned on our chests. It was a noble cause. The best of all causes. I hope it extends beyond our time."

"Didn't you say you commemorated the occasion after you got back?" Herb asked. "You did something, didn't you? Something special."

"I got rid of my Accord and went out and bought me a Cadillac, the only luxury I ever treated myself to."

"What for?" Chik said. "An Accord is a top of the line car."

"I had to have a big car suitable for the license plates: IAM 442."

"Isn't that showing off too much, though," Herb said.

"Allow me that one conceit, Herb," Fred said. "I know it may seem whimsical, but I want people to notice the plates and ask,

'What does that mean?' If they did I would proudly tell them what it meant to me personally."

"Has anyone ever asked you?" Chik asked. "Do they care?"

"A few people who heard of the 442nd came up to me and shook my hand."

"You're advertising yourself," Herb commented.

"Not at all," Fred insisted. "I'm proud of my record with the best fighting outfit in the history of the U.S. Army. The good people of Bruyeres made me finally see why I should be extremely proud. I could never could quite see what freedom looked like until they showed me. They set aside a special day for us, the day we *freed* them from the Nazis, and I wanted in some way to share that pride."

"It's still too much like beating your own drum," Chik said.

"...and tooting your own horn too loudly," Herb added. "None of us like to do that."

"It's about time one of us did," Fred said adamantly. "I want the whole world and a whole new generation to know about us and what we did."

"You mean, we're not just a bunch of Japs who were forced to prove our loyalty," Herb pursued.

"Exactly."

"...to a country that put us behind barbed wire fences with machine guns pointed at us," Chik said with a harsh twist.

"We made the supreme sacrifice, laid our lives on the line. Not to go on record that we are loyal Americans, which we always were...we know that...but to win our own freedom as any other freedom-loving American. Freedom from persecution and incarceration, freedom to..." Fred waved his claw, unable to continue. "Know of a better reason?"

"I never looked at it that way," Herb said. "It was just

something they made us do."

"I always knew you should've become an officer, Fred," Chik said.

"Wouldn't have sat well with me..would've been guilt-ridden and couldn't look you in the eye. Besides, it would have split Mike and me up. I stayed where I belonged and was needed."

"Now it's up to the younger generation," Herb said. "We're getting too old."

"Retirement not sitting well with you, Herb?" Fred asked, inexplicably glad to be able to change the subject. He was more or less whole but had survived when so many others hadn't. And Mike was gone.

"I used to play a lot of golf, but now, since my back is bothering me...sign of old age, I guess...I quit playing and just watch dumb TV. How's that for a life? Can you imagine, winding up watching The Boob Tube all day long? Gawd!"

"Hell, I play golf four times a week," Chik said, "and force myself to keep my interest up."

"Is that the only thing you can get up?" one of men shouted and laughed.

"Go to hell, Ben," Chik said. "I do just fine."

"Sure you do. Sure. Tell me more," the man called Ben said.

"Come on, now, Chik. Admit it," another man said. "It's all 'lookee, lookee, and no touchee', right? 'Fess up. You're through as the lady's man."

The laughter that erupted around the table lightened the general mood and prompted the men to order another round of drinks. They talked about the merits of having another reunion, some arguing that they were getting too old to travel and that their families always worried about them when they were out of town. Why not one last bash in Hawaii? Why not one in Japan? Why bother? They could always call each other and wouldn't have to see how old they were getting. It was downright disheartening to see old age set in. At least over the phone they could talk without revealing their condition.

The young waitress in the form-fitting, red and gold dress delivered their drinks. Chik smiled broadly at her as he had each time she passed by the table. The men took up their drinks, and several held their glasses up for no good reason except as a general toast.

Prompted by the gesture, Herb rose to his feet, somewhat bent, and raised his glass.

"I propose a toast to the rescue of the Lost Battalion," he said. "It was a battle to end all battles."

The men raised their glasses and said: "To I Company and the Lost Battalion."

"The battle will live forever in our memories," Fred said. "And so will our fallen comrades, especially Jimmy Hikida and Sam Hatayama. And here's to Mike Kojima."

They all made one final toast to the deceased.

"So many of us never came back," Herb said sadly, lowering his glass.

"So many of us never had a chance," said Chik. "Thanks to General Alvin Z. Bunting."

The men around the table gave a thumbs-down at the mentioning of the name.

"May his name go down in infamy," Herb said.

"Shit," Chik said and raised his glass higher, "may his ass be burning in hell."

The men of I Company drained their drinks and set their glasses down resolutely with a note of finality. Which was the cue for Fred to get up and make a short speech about the twilight years of their lives as veterans of the 442nd and the need to keep the torch of dedication alive and pass it on to the younger generation without letting the flame die out. The shades of idealism that he had carried with him into war such a long time ago had been over-whelmed by the dreadful shadows of what he had learned on the battlefields. But perhaps by fighting racism all his life, idealism had reseeded itself and found fertile ground that remained hidden somewhere in the recesses of a hard-bitten sense of reality. Therein lay the redemption he sought.

He made the men agree to tell their stories to their children and grandchildren, knowing that the reticent Nisei sometimes had to be prodded to speak out, particularly when it came to talking about themselves. Their story was a great one and should live on.

The party broke up shortly afterwards, and the old men went their separate ways. Fred drove a carload of passengers in his white Cadillac to the Portland International Airport and after dropping them off headed down the road to catch I-5 and return to his home in Eugene. The rain continued to fall heavily, and the tires of the Cadillac swished on the wet road with the whisper of urgency. He had no real reason to rush, since there was no one to go home to with his wife's passing, but he felt an indescribable urge to race down the highway to escape the morning's events. The trip usually took about two hours. He was sure he could cut thirty minutes off the time. The big car hummed and purred like a lunging predator as he kept pressing down on the pedal to pass the slower cars. Responding to his control, the powerful car moved in an out of the lanes with ease.

His mind wandered to the times when he used to take the Cadillac to eastern Oregon to open it up to 120 miles per hour and speed across the high desert country for the sheer joy of feeling the sense of freedom driving brought–with no particular destination in mind. For miles around there would be no other car except his white charger racing across the flat expanse, and sometimes he would wind up in some distant city like John Day, Baker or Burns, have dinner and then leisurely cruise back home. Driving the Cadillac took the place of golf and gambling which many of his friends were fond of, friends who could not understand his passion for driving at dangerous speeds in the wide open country at his age.

As he drove down I-5 with the windshield wipers slapping back and forth, he thought of the exhilaration of the open road and wished then that he was on one of the lonely stretches leading nowhere except to link with another road that took him to a faraway, new town. Seeing Mike Kojima finally laid to rest made him want to distance himself from an inescapable reality, stark and final in its harsh imprint. He struggled to prevent a form of hidden dread from taking over his mind but could not help his arms from becoming tense and his claw clutch the steering wheel ever more tightly. He sped down the freeway, pressing harder on the pedal.

Because of the constriction of dread he felt tightening his chest, he wanted to free himself of restraint and speed ahead as fast as the Cadillac could go. Perhaps he could outrace the grip of oppression and arrive home free at last to let out the howl of pain he felt. Mike! He wanted to scream out the name of his life-long friend and business partner, and ask him why death had to be so ignominious, why the body rotted and the spark of life became so feeble when in their youth they had endured the unendurable.

He wanted that freedom and invincibility back. He could not see himself in a nursing home quietly moldering away with the rest of the hapless and helpless souls that inhabited the sterile rooms and polished hallways, rocking back and forth in their wheelchairs to stay active, piecing together a jigsaw puzzle with geriatric patience, and learning how to weave and knit with fingers stiffened by arthritis. The image of himself, bent over and feeble, was intolerable. A nurse sweetly cajoling him to open his mouth wide for a spoonful of broth, mumbling endearments as she wiped the slaver off his chin with a piece of Kleenex, guiding the movement of his claw as he attempted to brush his dentures. He pressed harder on the pedal, and the Cadillac sailed down the road and wove its way among the cars that seemed to dodder along like slow-moving codgers ready to die on the spot.

He was speeding at more than 100 miles an hour on the rain-slick pavement. He shot past Albany like a bullet and pressed even harder on the pedal to outdistance the specter that was on his tail, a specter with a face that leered at him obscenely, grimacing and beckoning. He wanted to shout in his torment. Mike! Now he was truly alone. The stretch to the Coburg exit was the last long one, and after he passed Gateway he was practically home—home to the forested south hills.

An explosion suddenly jolted him out of his trance. A blow out! He instinctively stepped on the brakes but the vehicle swerved to the left and skidded off the road. He was thrown recklessly about like a rag doll as the car flipped over on its top, slid across the median and rolled over upright again at a tremendous speed and crashed head-on into an oncoming semi. The explosive rending of metal being smashed was like the mangling of armament when Sam killed the tank in the Vosges Mountains. Fred's realization of the collision and the sensation of pain coincided instantaneously.

The impact threw the steering column into Fred's chest. He nearly blacked out with the shock and gasped for breath and almost choked on the blood that spurted from his mouth. The smell of gasoline permeated the car. He was alert enough to work the door handle and was able to wrench himself away from the imbedded steering wheel and topple outside on the ground. He crawled weakly away. When he was about fifteen yards from the wreckage, the Cadillac exploded into flames with a roar and lit up the night scene.

He lay on the ground, his chest crushed, and breathed out blood. The driver of the trailer-truck was apparently unhurt, for he ran over to Fred with a blanket and covered him, then ran back to the cab. Fred was wide awake but stunned. He lay on the ground with the dampness seeping through his clothing. Minutes passed. They seemed interminable. He didn't know if he was dying or not and thought it odd, because he had heard that a person always knew when he was about to die. The injury was worse than the wounds he suffered during combat, and yet he had no fear, just as he had had no doubts he would survive his battlefield injuries. He was strangely lucid, as though the pain in his chest forced him to think clearly, and thought even if he were to die, it would be all right, because he would be finally free of any concern about rotting to death as Mike had. But as with his wounds he was confident he would survive, if only the medics would arrive on time. He wanted to cry out: "Medic!" He could only make a gurgling sound.

The big guns were roaring again, and the crackling of gunfire filled the air. Tree-bursts exploded all around him, and he found himself diving under a rock like a frightened ferret, fleeing the shrapnel sizzling in all directions. He could see the explosions now high up in the trees and spot the location of the enemy from the red-orange muzzle flashes in the descending darkness. The Screaming Meemies were shrieking and hissing derisively, and the 88's and 77's thundered their defiance. The ground exploded, and body parts were strewn all over the battlefield. Then there was complete silence. Someone had given the order to cease fire. Or was the war over?

He tried to reach into his pocket with his crippled hand. His arm was heavy and moving it required a tremendous effort. He gave up after a few minutes and lay still, blinking his eyes to stay awake, fighting both the pain and the cloud of oblivion that tried to crowd out his consciousness.

Soon he heard sirens wailing in the distance, sounding louder and louder as the ambulance approached the scene of the accident brightly lit by the fire consuming the Cadillac as though in a ritual of consecration. It slid to a stop beside him, its red lights flashing in alarm.

The paramedics dashed to his side while another wheeled a gurney to them. They threw back the blanket and mumbled to each other in hushed tones as they spread open his coat and shirt to examine his chest. One flashed a light into his eyes. Fred blinked them rapidly and moved his lips and tried to raise his hand.

"Hey, he's still alive!" the paramedic said.

"He's pointing at his pocket," another said and leaned over to listen to Fred whisper something into his ear. The paramedic reached into his right pocket and produced a coin. He held it up to Fred, and he nodded and extended his hand. The paramedic placed the worn penny in his hand, and Fred closed the claw as tightly as he could around it.

They soon had him loaded on the ambulance which crossed the median, sirens screaming, and headed back toward Eugene.

"Looks real bad," Fred heard one of the men say.

"Think he's going to make it?" another said.

"I doubt it," the first one said.

I'm going to make it, Fred shouted. But the words didn't

come out. He wondered why they had turned off the lights; he had his eyes wide open but could see nothing. Why did you turn off the lights, he asked. Again, he could not hear the words. Then he saw a different kind of light. It hung over him like a presence. An indescribable sense of peace washed over him. He closed his claw around the penny, and he knew everything was going to be all right.

He could still hear the siren wailing. The sound filled his mind, and he clung to it. It was his lifeline. It tapered to a whisper, and as the ambulance slowed to a stop, the wail vanished with a sigh.

Epilogue

Gallant are the thunderous sounds of war,
Timid is the soul before the onslaught of Death,
But great is the Honor of the soldier
Bound forever to Duty.

The wings of Victory beat the sky and the earth,
Freedom soars onward
To pave the way
For brave new hearts.

The song of Liberty won
Lies in the belly of Triumph,
To be sung when heroes fall
And then rise again.

–Sgt. Fred Murano

The Last Fox

Long and arduous lies the road to battle,
Short-lived is any promise of invincibility,
For death clamors with the voice of myriad guns,
And the resolute quail as the earth is shattered,
To open its wound for the valiant,
For them to seek shelter in the womb beyond reach.

–Cpl. Mike Kojima

Comrades plod in the
      stirred tracks of muddy roads,
They climb the steep slopes
      of uncertain and hidden fears,
Sneaking into the shadows of forests
      to cheat the eyes of death,
They wade into a field
      of woven streams of lashing fire,
To fall and die and vanish
      from the ungodly sight
Of men who move on
      to leave their own behind.

–Pvt. Jimmy Hikida

The Last Fox

Fighting side by side clawing with common valor,
The men embrace their battle-weary fears,

And crawl as one into the blind heart of dread,
Piercing the enemy's legions armed with angry Death,

Only to fall one after another in abysmal expectation,
Until a solitary figure staggers on alone,

Weeping tears of loss,

Seeking Victory
To replace the ashes of an unfinished end.

                                    −Pfc. Sam Hatayama

The Most Decorated Unit
in U.S. Military History

100th/442nd Regimental Combat Team

–1 Medal of Honor*
–7 Presidential Unit Citations
–9,486 Purple Hearts
–18,143 individual awards and decorations
–52 Distinguished Service Crosses
–1 Distinguished Service Medal
–560 Silver Stars
–28 Oak Leaf Clusters in lieu of second Silver Stars
–22 Legions of Merit
–4,000 Bronze Stars
–1,200 Oak Leaf Clusters representing second
 Bronze Stars
–15 Soldier's Medals
–12 French Croix de Guerre
–2 Palms representing second Croix de Guerre
 awards
–2 Italian crosses for military merit
–2 Italian medals for military valor

* UPDATE (June 21, 2000): 20 Medals of Honor
were awarded to the veterans of the 100th/442nd
RCT in a special White House ceremony.

Notes about the Author

The author is an ex-internee of the concentration camps. As a boy of nine he and his mother were evacuated from the West Coast and first entered the Tulare Assembly Center in central California. His father, a fisherman, had been arrested earlier by the FBI, because he had access to a fishing boat and was suspected of contacting nonexistent enemy submarines and warships off the coast.

With the whereabouts of his father unknown, Robert Kono and his mother were moved inland to more permanent camps called "relocation centers" in the middle of searingly hot deserts and frigid, windblown prairies.

Patriotism behind barbed wire kept burning alive. The inmates bought war bonds with the meager monthly allowance and the wages they earned in the sugar beet fields when outside labor recruiters flocked to the camps.

And the young men in the camps rallied when the call went forth for volunteers to join the fight against the Nazi menace that threatened the very fabric out of which they themselves had been cut. They were forged into a regiment that was so effective that the commanding generals vied for their dogged determination, for they never failed to take an objective.

The men of the 100th/442nd RCT were heroes to the young boy who saw the war as an enormous and confusing historical event which dehumanized him and his people. But the "Little Iron Men" rose as giants in the great battle and gave birth to a legacy that remained undiminished in his mind.

SUGGESTED READING

For readers interested in learning more about the fighting WWII Nisei GI's, the following list is provided.

1. *The Burma Rifles*, a novel, Frank Bonham, 1960
2. *Yankee Samurai*, Joseph Harrington, 1979
3. *Go For Broke*, Chester Tanaka, 1982
4. *Bridge of Love,* John Tsukano, 1985
5. *Unlikely Liberators,* Masayo Umezawa Duus, 1987
6. *I Can Never Forget*, Thelma Chang, 1991
7. *Honor by Fire*, Lyn Crost, 1994

The above list represents just a few of the many books available about the Nisei who flocked to the colors to fight in both Europe and the Pacific during WWII.

ORDERING INFORMATION

To order additional copies of *The Last Fox*, please contact Abe Publishing by mail, phone, fax or e-mail. When using the toll free number, please call between 9 a.m. and 5 p.m. PST. Fax and e-mail orders may be placed at any time.

Mail: Abe Publishing
P.O. Box 5226
Eugene, OR 97405

Phone: 800-535-5038 toll free
(Have Visa or MasterCard ready)

Fax: 541-485-3893

Email: abepublishing@hotmail.com

Add S/H: $4/one book, $6/two books
USPS Priority Mail: $5/one book, $8/two books
Int'l Shipping: $10/one book, $15/two books

All payments must be in U.S. funds. Sorry, no COD.
For pricing on larger quantities, please fax request.

The publisher invites you to look forward to more interesting titles that will challenge your imagination and speak with an authentic voice.

JAPANESE AMERICAN VETERANS ASSOCIATIONS

Japanese American War Veterans
http://ajawarvets.com

Japanese American Veterans Association (JAVA)
JAVA of Washington, DC
P.O. Box 391
Vienna, VA 22180
www.javadc.org   Email: admin@javadc.org

Go For Broke Education Foundation
P.O. Box 2590
Gardena, CA 90247

442nd Veterans Club
933 Wiliwili Street
Honolulu, HI 96826

Club 100 Veterans Club
520 Kamoku Street
Honolulu, HI 96826

100th/442nd RCT Website
www.katonk.com   Moderator: Michael Furukawa

442nd Veterans Archives & Learning Center
933 Wiliwili Street
Honolulu, HI 96826